The Future Play

Ida Heartthrobs Book Three

BETHANY MONACO SMITH

ISBN: 978-1-963450-19-4

For more information about this book, visit the author's website.
www.bethanymonacosmith.com

Editing by Lacey Braziel of On the Page Publishing
Cover Design by Bethany Monaco Smith
Formatting by Bethany Monaco Smith

About The Future Play

The Future Play is an angsty, emotional, new adult baseball romance featuring an extroverted event planner who is confident and sarcastic on the outside but insecure and lonely on the inside, and a sweet, introverted baseball player who uses cocky confidence as a mask. Their story is a slow burn told over two important time periods in their relationship (how they fall in love & what happens when life gets hard).

The Future Play is a complete standalone. Though it is part of the Ida Heartthrobs series, these books are only loosely interconnected and don't need to be read in a specific order. Jamie and Amanda are both side characters from the Friends Like This series. You don't need to have read either of those, but if you have read Friends Like This, please note The Future Play takes place over the same time as Broken Like This and then skips ahead to Heartbreak Like This. Keep reading for trigger warnings and a character list.

Are you ready to fall hard for Jamie and Amanda?

Meet the Characters

Because Amanda & Jamie are side characters from another series, there are a few side characters in this one. I did my best to introduce them clearly, but if you need clarification, you can jump back to this page at any time.

The baseball boy & the event queen:
Jamie Henderson
Amanda Hamilton

The "hive-mind" friend group:
Rae McKinley (eventually Cooper)
Aaron Cooper
Mackenzie Montoya
Hyla Montgomery
Sarah McKinley
Joel Wilkinson
Miles Hyun-Hansen

The other Ida Heartthrobs:
Trevor Matteny & Chelsea Winters
Jesse Wilkinson & Dani Malone

Amanda's family:
Pete- oldest brother
Josh- older brother

Jace- bestie/neighbor/surrogate sister
Libby & Bryce Hamilton- Mom & Dad

Jamie's family:
Marissa & Bill Henderson- Mom & Dad
Penny- little sister
Calvin- little brother
Mila- little sister

NY Metros:
(borrowed from author Jenni Bara)
Marc Demoda(#18)- Pitching coach & former pitcher
Corey Matthews(#4)- Starting pitcher
Ryan Daily(#45)- Starting pitcher
Declan Lowery(#33)- Third base
Beau Airington(#22)- Right field

Trigger Warnings

If you're looking for possible triggers in this book, this page is for you. If you're not, you can skip this page and dive into the story.

trigger warnings may contain plot spoilers

The female character in this book faces negative comments about her weight and fatphobia (in comments/ the press) and sometimes thinks negatively about her weight. She also struggles with rejection sensitivity and intrusive negative thoughts about herself. The male character in the book struggles with his mental health & occasionally partakes in underage drinking.

To all my beautiful bi babes...
I see you. No matter where you are or who you're with,
unapologetically take up space.

Prologue

Amanda

"WHY ISN'T HE ANSWERING?!" I am the perfectly broken picture of an ugly-crying train wreck as I throw my phone across the room. I swore I'd never be this girl. This pathetic mess of heartbreak. I'd never do it again. Then Jamie Henderson walked into my life, melted my walls, and made me believe I was worth something. Worth everything.

Mackenzie sweeps some hair from my face. "Maybe he had something with the team."

"No," I rasp. "The game was over hours ago. And even if he went out with the team, that's no excuse for him not answering."

I look around the room at my best friends. The women who chose me when I felt like I wasn't worth choosing. Mackenzie, Hyla, Rae, Sarah, and Chelsea. All five of them stopped what they were doing and surrounded me with love the second I needed them. Of course they're here. Ride or die. We always show up for each other.

But as much as I love them, they aren't the ones I need right now.

Everything is spiraling out of control, and it's supposed to be Jamie who's walking through this with me.

This can't be happening.

Not now. Not like this.

More tears stain my cheeks as my best friends move in closer, forming a circle of love around me.

"He promised he'd always show up when I needed him," I whisper, wrapping my arms around myself.

But that was before.

Before he achieved his dream. Before he was a major league baseball player.

He convinced me I was his dream too.

And maybe I was until he got what he really wanted.

Maybe I was an idiot to believe there was room for me and baseball in his life.

Maybe I was a desperate, pathetic girl for believing I meant *more* than the game he built his life around.

I know I'm desperate now because all I want to do is call him again. I want to believe I'm not in this alone.

"Oh, shit," Hyla mutters, blinking at her phone.

"What?" I ask, my chest tightening. Panic overtakes me. What if he was in a car accident? What if he's dead?

Oh God.

"Is he okay?" I cry.

"He's… okay."

Hyla glances at Chelsea, who looks at the screen and bites her lip.

"Just tell me!" I yell.

Slowly, Hyla crawls over to me, taking my hand as she flips her phone screen toward me.

My blood runs cold, and I'm hit with a new level of agony as my world crashes around me.

Part One

The Love Story Begins

1

Hot Mess Express

Amanda

EVERYONE OUT OF MY WAY. Hot mess express coming through.

The last thing I want is to be late today, but of course the weather is extra weathery as I make my way across campus, dodging ice patches and snow mounds.

I don't want to be late for a meeting with my potential new suitemates. We live in the same dorm and I've seen them around. They always seem friendly and kind. I need more of that in my life. I've exchanged a few texts with one of the girls—Rae. She and her friends are looking for a new suitemate because their current roommate is very introverted and managed to get a solo suite. Good for her because everyone should be able to have a space where they feel safe and comfortable. Good for me because that means I can get away from the roommate from hell, who constantly locks me out because she's always hooking up or having friends over and I'm not welcome. She's never even tried to be friends with me.

Whatever.

But these girls seem open and friendly, and I'm hopeful. I'm a social person. I love making friends, but unfortunately, I'm kind of shit at it. They never seem to stick or I end up with acquaintances who don't actually seem to like me that much. Am I the problem? The common denominator?

Nope. I have no mental energy for emotional baggage today, so let's pack that shit up and send it on a one-way trip to Antarctica.

I sigh in relief and pick up my pace when the dorm comes into view. I might actually be on time.

But the moment I think the words, the universe hears them, and it takes less than one second for me to realize what I just stepped on is ice and another second for me to end up on my ass.

I grumble as I carefully stand, trying to retain some dignity.

This is *not* a sign for how this meeting is going to go. It's just not.

Be positive.

I inhale deeply and exhale fully.

This is fine.

Until I take another step and almost fall on my ass again.

Motherfucker.

Another deep breath, then taking painfully slow penguin steps, I make my way back to the dorm. Once I'm inside, I haul ass up the stairs to their floor, not wanting to wait for the slow-ass elevator. I only calm my shit for two seconds when I get to their floor so I can check my phone. There's a message from Rae.

RAE

Door is unlocked so you can come on in 😊

Blowing out a breath, I get going again, not quite running, but definitely fast walking all the way to their room as I go over my checklist in my head.

I will be friendly but not over the top.

I will pay close attention to the vibes.

I won't act desperate.

I take a deep inhale as I get to the door.

I'll be myself.

I swing it open, starting with an apology the second I'm inside.

"Sorry I'm late!" I unzip my coat as I walk into the room. "That snow is terrible, and I almost fell on ice three times! I should've taken the tunnels."

Technically, SUNY Finger Lakes has underground tunnels, but not every building connects to them and sometimes they're more of a pain in the ass than they're worth, but given the actual pain in my ass right now... I should've used them today.

I look over at the three girls on the couch. Rae is the one with long-ish brown hair, then there's an adorable blonde who also looks like she could sucker punch you where it hurts, and a taller athletic built one with short, messy brown curls.

"Hey, no problem. Come sit. We have brownies," the blonde one says.

I drop my bag, toe off my shoes, and hurry around the couch to sit down because brownies? Yes, please. Especially with this God forsaken day.

Grabbing one of the brownies, I take a big bite. And *oh my god*. It's delicious. Possibly the best brownie I've ever eaten in my life—and I have high standards.

"This is so good. I'm seriously ready to pay you to let me live here."

Great job not sounding desperate.

Ugh.

But they all laugh.

"Well, before you get too excited, you should know our story," the one with the curly hair says.

My eyebrows shoot up, but really, I'm not that worried. The vibe here is low-key and upbeat. So I playfully ask, "Are you, like, murderers or in witness protection or something?"

"Not quite," Rae says with a sweet smile. "But we are best friends. Well, actually, let's go back a step. I'm Rae." She points to the blonde. "That's Sarah. And that's Mackie. Mackie and I have been friends since we were four. Sarah is my adoptive sister and my other half. And we're sort of a package deal because we come with three boys who live down the hall. We've all been best friends since we were kids, and we spend most of our time together. We're *a lot* and we know that. We want you to be prepared."

So far, I'm struggling to see the problem. Brownies, friendly girls, and maybe some cute boys? Sign me up.

"And are these boys hot?"

Again, they all laugh.

"Definitely," Mackie says, though that surprises me a little—or maybe my gaydar is broken—but I had her pinned as a lesbian. Maybe she's bi. Maybe I'm crazy. Whatever. Topic at hand.

"And are any of them taken?" I ask, mostly because I never want to make the mistake of playing with someone else's toys, but also because who knows? Maybe I'll magically meet my soulmate.

Mackie and Sarah both look at Rae.

"Thanks for that," she mutters.

"Ooh. I'm sensing drama."

"It's not that fun, but yeah. *Technically*, he's not taken, but if you want to live with me, I'd recommend you not go after Aaron," Rae says, and it's impossible not to notice the flash of pain in her eyes. It makes me want to hug her, but I'm not sure if she's a hugger, and even if she is, we've known each other for less than ten minutes.

"He's her person. Her best friend. Also her ex," Mackie says.

"And they're still madly in love," Sarah adds.

I nod because Rae seems to want to move on. "Aaron's off limits. The other two?"

"If you're in for a one-time hookup, there's Miles. Tall, swoopy dark hair. Joel is more of a short-term girlfriend kinda guy, but I doubt he's your type." I don't miss the way Sarah's voice catches on Joel's name. I definitely won't be messing around with him, either. "Don't worry, we've got more hot guys where they come from, too. Well, if you don't mind going back to Ida."

My eyes fly wide. "You're from Ida? No way! I'm from Woods Junction!"

My hometown of Woods Junction, New York is a fairly tiny town not far from the ᵗPennsylvania border. It's only about twenty minutes away from Ida. Now I'm meeting these girls here, three hours away, in Old Lake Town.

We all look around at each other. "I think it's fate," I whisper.

Seriously, doing a fantastic job of not coming off as desperate.

"As long as you don't mind our brand of crazy and trying to jump into a group of six best friends with a steep learning curve," Mackie says with a slightly devilish smile.

Okay, maybe I'm not being desperate.

I'm not, I tell myself.

I'm being me. So I continue that trend.

With a soft smile, I say the truth. "I'm outgoing, and I love being around people, but I had a hard time connecting with people in high school and was kind of a loner besides my best friend, Jace. She's two years older and has a complicated past with my brother, so I don't get to see her as much as I like. I've always wanted a big group of friends. Maybe I can co-opt yours."

Rae's smile grows. "I can't lie. It usually works out pretty well for us when we add a new friend. Been a while, but I think you might be a good fit."

I grab another brownie. "For these brownies, I'll contort myself into whatever shape I need to fit into. But this little friend group sounds amazing too."

"So what's your story?" Sarah asks. "How'd you end up at SUNY FL?"

"Oh, and what kind of horror story roommate situation are you trying to escape?" Mackie asks.

"My roommate horror story is a classic. She thinks the room belongs to her and her hookups and loves to lock me out."

"Ew," Sarah says.

"Yeah, I don't love it."

"Well, I promise I'm not like that," Mackie says. "You'll be rooming with me, and I'm usually the most laid-back of the bunch." She cups her hand around her mouth and loudly whispers, "The rest of them are very dramatic."

Rae reaches over and smacks her thigh as Mackie laughs.

"Oh, and by the way, my full name is Mackenzie. They just decided my name was Mackie when we were four, and it stuck. My mom always calls me by my full name. My dad and my girlfriend both call me Kenz."

"Girlfriend?" I ask.

"Yeah. I don't love labels, but I'm a lesbian. Even though it's not a big deal to me and shouldn't be a big deal, I usually throw that in early because—"

"Then the trash takes itself out?" I ask.

Mackie looks relieved. "Yes."

"Well, no worries here. I'm bi. And I get exactly what you mean. I finally taught myself to stop saying 'I hope that's not a problem' because fuck anyone who thinks it is."

"I'm here for that energy," Rae says.

"Same," Sarah says.

"So, Mackie-Mackenzie-Kenz, do you have a preference for what I call you?"

She shrugs. "I'll answer to just about anything."

I arch a brow. "So, what you're saying is I should come up with a ridiculous nickname for you and see if you'll answer to it?"

She laughs. "Sure. Why not?"

Her eyes dance with mischief. She seems to be the most playful of the three. They're all upbeat and fun, but it's obvious Rae wears her emotions on her sleeve. And there's something haunted in Sarah's eyes. Or maybe I'm reading too much into it. But I'm usually good at picking up on things like that.

"Well, I'll be working on nickname ideas over break."

"Hit me with your best shot," Mackie says with a wink.

Sarah laughs and shakes her head. "You two are definitely a good match."

"Fate," Rae whispers dramatically. And there's something in her voice that tells me she truly believes that. I'm cautiously optimistic that not only did I just find some new roommates for next semester but also some new friends.

WE'RE over an hour into a conversation about their wild friend group, how I ended up at SUNY FL, and what we're all studying, when the door to their room swings open and a band of boys walks in.

I'm pretty sure they said only three go here with them, but there's a fourth with them. I take a shot guessing which is which. Aaron is the easiest because of how he looks at Rae. Based on the physical descriptions they gave me, I figure out the other two fairly quickly as well. Then they introduce the fourth guy— Trevor—a friend from Ida, who then announces he brought a special present. And in walks Mackenzie's girlfriend, Hyla. It's a lot of people and big personalities, but I love being lost in it all.

As someone who often feels like I'm too big or too much, it's comforting being surrounded by people with similarly big energy.

Then Mackie and Hyla disappear to Mackie's room and Sarah and Rae suggest we make ourselves scarce.

We end up back in the boys' room, where there's barely enough seats for all of us.

"I think this calls for a weekend at the lake house," Joel says.

My eyes flit to Rae. "Lake house?"

"Yeah. Joel's dad has a lake house off campus. We hang out there on weekends sometimes. In case you were still wondering whether or not to be our roommate."

"I think that was already decided." I don't want them for their stuff. I want them for their friendship.

"How about a crash course in this crazy group of ours?" Sarah asks. "Up for a weekend of shenanigans?"

A weekend with all of them together in a house will either send me running in the opposite direction or indoctrinate me into this crazy hive mind. I really, *really* hope it's the latter. Only one way to find out.

I grin up at her. "Count me in."

I'VE OFFICIALLY BEEN INDUCTED into the hive mind.

The weekend at the lake house was a ridiculous amount of fun, and I was surprised to find myself bonding with not only the girls, but the guys too. They all seem funny and kind with varying levels of sarcastic streaks—which are important for me as someone who speaks fluent sass and snark.

I feel at home with this little group. They're my kind of chaos. Wild and sarcastic, but with a warmth beneath it all.

The only downside of the weekend was that I didn't get to bond with Mackenzie as much as I hoped, but I'm sure if I were in a long-distance relationship and finally got to see the person I love, I'd want to spend as much time as possible with them too.

Other than that, the girls have worked hard to include me as much as possible. They've already invited me to eat lunch with them and added me to their girl gang group chat. The girls even said that if I can deal with all their shenanigans, I could live at the lake house with them when they all move in their junior year, but I'm not going to hold my breath. I love that they want to include me and welcome me into the group, but I'm going to give it more than two days before I accept an invitation to live in the lake house with them in a year and a half. I want to make sure this sticks.

As we walk into our dorm, all laughing and chattering, disappointment washes over me. This weekend has been fun, but now I have to get back to reality. A roommate who wants nothing to do with me and treats me like an inconvenience. Who knows what will happen with this little group when the bubble of this weekend pops? I hope the friendship will stick. I hope living with them next semester will be great, but it's hard to trust it'll be as great as this weekend was. That they'll still seek me out in the next few weeks before I move in.

"I guess I better head to my room and see what hell awaits me." I put my playfully sarcastic mask on to hide the melancholy I'm feeling.

"We'll walk with you," Rae says.

I stop and blink at them a few times. "Are you sure?"

"Yeah, of course," Mackie says.

"That way we can make sure your roommate isn't mean to you. If she is, we'll fight her." Sarah smiles at me, eyes dancing.

I'm fine. This is fine.

Why is it that people being nice to me and actively choosing to support me makes me want to cry?

Probably a great question for a therapist.

Deep breath in. Push it all down.

"Sounds good."

I lead the way to my room, but when we get there, I'm unsurprised to find the door is locked. Not the handle lock that I have a key for, but the flip lock, so I can't get in.

"Seriously?" Rae asks. "This is what she does?"

"Yeah. Usually it's during the day, but there have been a few nights where I've slept in the study room downstairs."

"Fuck that," Sarah says, banging on the door.

"Go away! I'm busy," my lovely roommate calls.

"You know what? Screw this. Come back to our room," Mackie says.

"I—are you sure?"

"Soon it'll be your room too. And the couches are super comfy." Rae's smile makes me smile too.

"What about your roommate?"

"We've tried hard to include her, but she's overwhelmed, and we respect that. She prefers to be in the bedroom and have her space, so I try to give that to her. As long as you aren't in her space, she won't care," Mackie says. "Plus, I've been a shitty friend this weekend because I was a little obsessed with Hyla, and I'd love to spend some time with you. So, please?" She gives me big puppy dog eyes.

"Okay. Yeah. That sounds so much better than fighting with my roommate all night."

Rae throws her hand up victoriously. "Yes!"

With that, we all head back up to their room.

Once they've all unpacked and I've made a bed for myself on one of the couches, Mackie joins me on the other one with a blanket.

"Thanks for including me this weekend," I say quietly.

"Of course. You're one of us now."

All I can do is nod at that.

Mackie elbows me. "Assuming you want to be."

"I do. I'm just not used to it." Having people actively choose me isn't something I used to.

"Not used to people being friendly?" she asks.

I scrunch up my face, not sure of how to answer, which makes her brow furrow.

"Okay, who hurt you? Who made you feel like you don't deserve this kind of friendship?"

"My ex—" *Whoa*. Emotion bubbles in my chest and my eyes sting. *No*. Nope. Not going down that road. Not yet. Instead, I clear my throat and go for a slight twist of the truth. "My ex *best friend* cut me out and took our other two friends with her."

Mackie shifts closer and pulls the blanket over me too. "I'm so sorry. That's awful. Just know we're not like that. If anything, we hold on too tightly. I don't know if you noticed, but we're a little crazy."

I chuckle at that, feeling a little lighter. "I've noticed, but I think you're my kind of crazy."

"Good. Want to watch something?"

"*Gilmore Girls*?"

"You really are one of us."

Mackie puts it on, then we fall into an easy conversation. She tells me about her massive blended family and the bakery her mom owns, and I tell her about my two stinky brothers.

Rae comes out of the bathroom where she was showering and sees what we're watching.

"Ooh, *Gilmore Girls*. Perfect way to end the weekend. Sarah!" she calls.

Sarah strolls out and sees the TV too.

"Girl time?" Rae asks.

"Definitely."

"Sweet. I'll make popcorn." Rae goes to the kitchenette while Sarah joins us on the couch, cuddling up next to Mackie under the blanket.

Here I was thinking the bubble of the weekend would pop, but it's only getting bigger. It's a stupid analogy, but the point remains... they're not letting me go.

Rae plops down on the other side of me and sets the bowl of popcorn in my lap.

They're holding on to me. Choosing me. I try to tamp down my emotions at feeling so accepted. It's what I crave. Praise. Knowing I'm accepted or wanted. I need that from people, and even from those I love, I rarely get it. To have it now has me feeling all the things.

I'm not doing a good job hiding my feelings, though, because all it takes is one glance from Rae for her to ask if I'm okay.

"Yeah. Mostly. I don't know."

She elbows me gently. "If we're being too pushy about all this, you can tell us."

Her words only make my emotions swell more. It never crossed my mind that she'd think that—that their friendship was too much for me.

"No," I say quickly. "I love the way you've all included me. But it's hard to truly accept it. I'm scared of getting too used to it and then losing it one day."

"Why would you lose it?" Rae asks.

Mackie jumps in before I can. "Amanda had a bad experience

in the past. Her ex best friend ditched her and her other friends went along with it."

"Oh, Mands…" Rae throws her arms around me in a tight mama bear hug. "We already love you. And when we say we don't let go of people, we mean it. We fight. We call each other on our shit. We open our hearts and we work through the hard stuff. And we do all that because we know the power and importance of friendship. It hasn't been long, but that doesn't matter."

"She's right. People can fall in love in a day. Friendships can be formed just as quickly, and when you're willing to open up to each other and put in the work, those roots can grow deep quickly as well." Sarah reaches over and squeezes my arm.

"We're here for you, and that's not going to change." Mackie wraps her arm around my back. "Let us love you."

I take a steadying breath, sinking into the comfort of their friendship—the way they love. It's the way I've always tried to love people and how I've always tried to form friendships, but it never felt like I was enough for anyone—or maybe I was too much. I always blame myself. Always think I'm the problem.

Maybe I'm not the problem. Maybe I just hadn't found my people yet.

Rae rests her head on my shoulder. "It's okay if it takes a little while to sink in. Until then, we'll be watching *Gilmore Girls*, eating snacks, and showering you with love."

"All of that," Sarah says, reaching over to squeeze my hand.

"Told you," Mackie whispers, a sweet smirk on her face.

I let out a long breath and relax against the couch. "Thank you."

But their answering smiles tell me no thanks is needed.

We settle in, all nestled under the same blanket as we munch on popcorn, watch the show, and talk here and there. Again, I have to fight the urge to cry. After months of feeling out of place on campus and years of feeling like I don't fit at all, in a strange twist of fate and only a few days of my life, I think I've found my tribe.

2
Bring the Vibes

Jamie

"AND IDA'S star pitcher Jamie Henderson is the New York Metros first round draft pick!"

I throw my middle finger up at my best friend. "In case you were wondering, I haven't missed you."

Aaron Cooper laughs as he looks up from the computer he was sitting at. "I'm serious. That one came in at ninety miles per hour. We both know that's great for someone in their junior year."

"Yeah, except I'm old enough to be a senior." Thanks, Mom and Dad, for sending me to a hippie school with no actual grades for the first few years of my life. "Plus, it's a controlled environment here."

"Aw, is widdle Jamie afraid he can't make it to the big leagues?"

I smack Trevor Matteny in the stomach. "Fuck off."

"I'm just saying, of the two of us, I'm closer."

Trevor's playing at a D1 school, and might have a shot at the draft in a couple of years.

"Yeah, but I'm better," I fire back.

"There's the cocky, pain-in-the-ass kid I've helped train over the years." Aaron flashes me a shit-giving smirk, and I roll my eyes.

"I was never that cocky."

"No, you were a sweet little baby," Miles Hyun-Hansen says. He's the best catcher I've ever met, but decided not to keep playing baseball in college. Doesn't compute for me, but whatever.

"Funny, I remember little sixth grade you strutting around like you were the hottest shit in town," Joel Wilkinson says.

"For the record, I haven't missed *any* of you." Not true. Life has been boring while they've all been off at college. "And I'm sorry my parents spoiled me into believing that was true. It took three younger siblings to humble me. And, of course, the most humble pitcher in existence taking me under his wing and being my guiding light."

Aaron gives me a little shove. "Don't be a dick."

Despite being two grades ahead of me, Aaron's only a little over a year older than me, but we still have an older-brother and younger-brother dynamic mixed with mentorship and friendship.

And he did take me under his wing all those years ago, which was how our friendship grew. He's part of a bigger friend group that all welcomed little introverted me, who was never the best at making friends despite being friendly.

That cockiness was a show—to make myself feel more confident than I did. They all saw through that pretty quickly, even if they all tease me about it now.

The last few months with them off at college have been quiet and surprisingly lonely. I never connected with a lot of the guys on the team who are my age because I often played up, and once Aaron and his friend group accepted me, I stayed in my comfortable introvert bubble and didn't actively try to develop any other friendships—especially since some of the guys on the team are assholes and have been dicks to me in the past.

I have a few guys I'm friendly with, but we're not close like I am with these idiots.

"Remind me again why I invited all of you here?"

"Got me," Trev says. "Must've missed our pretty faces."

"Yes, I spent my nights dreaming of you," I say flatly.

"You could do a lot worse." Trevor grins at me.

"He could do a lot better too," Joel says under his breath.

Trevor playfully shoves him, and Miles sighs and rolls his eyes, the papa bear of their friend group pretending for a second that he's more mature than them.

"Are we going to stand around giving each other shit, or actually get back to pitching? Isn't that why we dragged ourselves out here?" Miles asks.

We're at a training facility about forty-five minutes outside of Ida because we're a bunch of baseball-obsessed idiots and what better way to spend the week before Christmas than doing baseball things? Since it's cold as tits outside, indoors is our only option.

I hate winter. I'd rather be on an actual mound. Nothing compares to being on the field with the dirt beneath your feet. Still, I'm thankful indoor facilities exist. Otherwise, I wouldn't have anything for months. No pitching. No baseball. And if there's no baseball, do I even exist?

Maybe my mom should've signed me up for drama camp during the off-season. Not that it matters, baseball always would've won out.

"Yeah. Let's get back to it. I need to work on upping my speed." There's only so much I can do here. A lot of it comes from my conditioning, so I need to work on a new plan for that.

I'm going to play in the majors. They might've been dicking around with me about being a number one draft pick, but I am going to hit the draft. Possibly out of high school. I don't know exactly what my path will be, but I'll never stop working to get where I want to be. If that means my life is eat, sleep, baseball, my family, and occasionally these idiots, then that's fine with me.

"Don't stress about the numbers. As much as you might think a controlled environment makes them higher, it's not what you're used to, so I'd argue that might not be the case. Focus on your mechanics. The tighter those are, the better your velocity is going to be. Let's rotate through your top five pitches and do a couple of each. I'll watch from here. Miles will watch from his end"—he looks over at Joel and Trevor who are still horsing around—"and those two knuckleheads will provide comic relief if you get stressed."

"Hey, I resent that," Trevor yells. "I give great advice."

"Mhm," Aaron says. "Such as?"

"Throw it straight. And fast."

I slow clap. "Wow. Thanks. With brilliant advice like that, how could I go wrong?"

"I know. I'm a baseball genius." Trevor does a pretend bow.

"Baseball idiot is more like it," Joel mutters. And they go back to dicking around again.

If my mind wasn't so twisted up stressing about the speed of my pitches and being ready for the season, I'd laugh. I might even join in. For a few minutes. The introvert in me can only handle that kind of shit for so long before I'm ready to retreat to my hole. Which is probably me watching a sci-fi movie in bed with a plate of nachos... assuming my younger siblings will leave me alone long enough for that.

Aaron puts his hands on my shoulders. "Relax. No one's handing out awards here today. Practice starts in a couple of months and you'll build on your conditioning routine. You can come here and throw every so often until the weather warms up to just cold and not frigid, but worrying about your game is the best way to throw off your game. Focus on what you know and work on having the best form possible. Let everything else go, or you'll lose why you love the game. Now, let's start with your two-seam fastball."

He steps back, tossing a ball up for me to catch.

All of that is why Aaron was a mentor on the team at a young age. He knows his stuff, but he's also great at getting to the root of someone's issues. If Aaron sees something off or has a suggestion of what to work on, I trust him. I almost want to push him to get out here and show me. But since he hurt his hand sometime about a year-and-a-half ago, he hasn't been able to pitch the same way, and he quit baseball because of it. It kills me because lately it seems like he's quitting on himself too, but there's only so much I can do.

"Okay," I say with a nod.

Joel walks over and plops my hat on my head.

"If you want to pitch well, you need to bring the vibes."

I shake my head, but can't stop my smile, because he's right. Putting myself in the right mental space is what I need.

I step onto the fake mound, then take a deep breath, trying to tune out the world. It's harder in here. On the field, I'm used to tuning out the noise around me and focusing only on what I see and feel. Still, I try to channel that feeling. Focus on my grip and my stance.

Slow down. Breathe.

This time when I throw, I put all my power into it and lean into the follow through.

"Ninety-three," Aaron says. "Go again."

Trevor puts a bucket of balls by my feet, and again, I smile. This is why I wanted them all here. They can dick around and goof off, but they also understand how important this is. And they understand *me*. They know why I hesitate or why I struggle because they've dealt with it too. It doesn't matter if it's pitching, hitting, or fielding, it's all in part a mental game. If that's off, everything else will be too. Being here with my friends reminds me why I love the game, which, in turn, reminds me what I'm fighting for.

The game I love, my place in the draft, a path to the majors, the future I want.

With my friends watching, I grab another ball, tune out everything else, and focus on the thing that matters most.

Baseball.

3

Baseball Boy

Amanda

I SLOWLY PUSH the back door of Joel Wilkinson's house open.

"Hello? I come bearing coffee," I call.

It's the first time I've ever been here, and Rae told me to just come in the back—no need to knock. I love how quickly this friend group has accepted me as one of them, but it's only been three weeks, which means my intrusive thoughts are still trying to convince me it's not serious, or they'll drop me when they get tired of me.

Why yes, I am aware that I'm the problem.

Or the mean thoughts in the back of my mind are.

"Did someone say coffee?"

A cute redheaded boy with bright blue eyes and a big smile appears from a doorway off the kitchen.

"You must be the new one," he continues. "I'm Jamie."

He takes the box with multiple trays of coffee and sets it on the counter.

"Thanks. It's nice to meet you. I'm Amanda."

His hot gaze trails over me for a second, then his smile widens.

"Well, if you bring coffee all the time, we're definitely keeping you."

He grabs one from the box, and I do my best to keep my smile up.

I always try to be thoughtful and go the extra mile, especially for people I care about, and the girls have already made me feel at home. More than that, they've made me feel wanted—chosen.

I hate the insecure side of me that reminds me those nice things also help make me indispensable. No one wants to get rid of the girl who brings the coffee or the donuts or the chocolate.

Jamie tilts his head slightly, watching me. "Sorry. I didn't mean—coffee is a bonus. You know you're stuck with them forever, right? They collect friends and make them part of the hive mind."

His cheeks tint pink, and I find myself smiling more naturally again, partly to put him at ease.

"It's fine. I—I'm..." *Pathetic.* Pathetic is the word I'm looking for.

"I don't know if you were thinking that. I just know what it's like to be taken advantage of by people for what you can give them. Not by this friend group. They aren't like that. I didn't want you to think I was doing that. Or would do that. Wow. I'm not starting off on the right foot."

At that, I laugh. "You're fine. Besides, what fun is it if things go perfectly smoothly? It's a better story when we're both stumbling over our words and acting like idiots."

"Ah, a story for the grandkids."

I slowly shake my head, some of the tension inside me uncoiling. "Where is—" I start at the same time he says, "What kind of coffee—"

We both laugh.

"Sorry. Ladies first."

I arch a brow. "I don't know how much of a lady I am. What were you going to say?"

I swear I see a hint of color in his cheeks again, but he just smiles and gestures to the box. "What kind of coffee did you want?"

"I'll take one of the sugar cookie lattes."

He pulls one out and hands it to me. "Okay, now it's your turn."

"Should we come up with some sort of system? Maybe cue cards for whose turn it is to talk?"

"Some kind of script would be really useful, so I don't say anything else dumb." He shoves his hands in his pockets, shifting from one foot to the other.

"No. I believe in us. We can do this." We lock eyes for a second, then I clear my throat. "So, where is everyone?"

"Downstairs arguing about whether to leave the table they always play cards on down there or bring it up here."

"Sounds productive."

"There's a reason I jumped at the opportunity to come up here when you came in."

"Aw, it wasn't just to meet little old me?"

"That sounded like I needed an excuse to force myself up here, didn't it? See, I really need a script."

"It's fine. It's like a bonding activity. Plus, with all the sarcastic responses to the dumb things we say, we're really getting to know our sarcasm compatibility, and I find that's incredibly important for a healthy friendship."

He laughs. "I suppose that's a good point."

My gaze snags on a pile of tablecloths on the counter. "So, if they're arguing, what can we do?"

He shakes his cup. "Drink coffee."

"I can drink coffee and get things done at the same time."

He arches a brow.

"I'm an event planner. And a smidge type A. Something always needs to be done, and I'm here to help do it."

"God, you sound like Thomas the Tank Engine. *Must be a really useful engine.*"

"Random reference."

"I have three much younger siblings. I know more about

Thomas, Daniel Tiger, and Bluey than I do about anything else pop culture related. Unless it involves baseball."

"Shocking. Another baseball boy." I grab the pile of tablecloths and head toward what appears to be the dining room. "Come on!"

After a beat, he follows me. "So, an event planner, huh? I thought Aaron said you'll be the girls' suitemate next semester."

"I will. But I'm not waiting until I have a degree to dive into doing what I love. Plus, event planning is hands on. The more jobs I do, the more I learn. I have my first solo job—other than stuff for my parents' friends—in a couple of weeks, and I'm treating it as the start of my business."

"That's awesome."

"Thank you. Now come on, baseball boy. Help me with these tablecloths."

I always feel more at ease when I'm doing something. Being busy keeps my brain focused and doesn't let me overthink. Jamie seems like a nice guy—not really surprising seeing as I don't think Rae and the girls would hang out with someone who was an asshole. Though the girls regularly like to pick on Rae for dating some douchey guy when she was really in love with Aaron. I can't imagine he was that douchey, though. Rae's a force to be reckoned with.

Speak of the devil. She blows into the room, coffee in hand.

"You are amazing. Thank you for bringing caffeine." She greets me with a kiss on the cheek, then looks at the tables. "What does your event planning eye say?"

"You guys do this every year. I'm sure you know what works."

Rae shakes her head. "It used to just be the six of us. It's slowly grown, but this year will be the biggest year. Give me all the suggestions."

Well, she asked. "Okay, well—actually, what can we move? Do we need to worry about Joel's parents?"

She snorts a laugh. "They're never around. Don't worry about that."

"Okay. Then I think we should move these two folding tables to the kitchen and make a buffet line with them and the kitchen counter. We can set up drinks in the dining room so people don't get caught up in the line for the buffet if they just want a drink." I peek over my shoulder. "And I think we should move the couches to the side in the living room so people can dance and move around more easily. If that sounds good to you."

"You are amazing! I'll go tell everyone else."

She flies out of the room, calling something to Joel.

"Wow," Jamie says. I almost forgot he was standing there. "You came up with all that in like thirty seconds?"

"I was thinking about it since I first walked in. My brain never shuts off."

"Well, I hope I get to attend an event you plan at some point. That was badass."

I smile, cheeks heating at the compliment. I'm not sure anyone has ever called my planning skills badass before, but then again, most of the things I've helped plan have been anniversary or retirement parties for people in their fifties and sixties.

"Maybe I'll have to come see you... baseball sometime?"

He laughs. "Pitch. I'm a pitcher."

"It's a deal then. If you sneak into one of my events, I'll sneak into one of your baseball games."

"Amanda!" Rae calls from the kitchen.

I turn to head for the kitchen, but Jamie calls after me. "I'm going to hold you to that."

I glance back over my shoulder. "Whatever you say, baseball boy."

"SO, WHAT'S THE PROTOCOL HERE?" I whisper to Sarah and Mackenzie. We're at the edge of the room, watching as Rae smiles and tries to pretend she's happy after having a fight with Aaron twenty minutes ago.

"Protocol?" Sarah asks.

"This is the first Aaron and Rae fight that I've been present for. How do we help? Go try to cheer her up? Remove her from the situation? Kick Aaron's ass?"

"He's kicking his own ass," Mackie says, nodding toward where Aaron is downing another shot. I cringe.

Aaron has been nothing but nice to me, but as someone already feeling deeply protective of my little girl tribe, I'm low-key pissed at him right now. Rae walked away in tears, and while Jamie and one of their other friends went after her, I want nothing more than to uplift her now.

"Rae's tricky," Sarah says. "She doesn't usually like to talk about it until she's ready. But she could use some cheering up. Come on."

We follow Sarah over to where Rae is standing as one of their friends tries to convince her to dance.

Sarah wraps her sister in a hug, then whispers, "Brownies and hot cocoa?"

"With caramel," Rae murmurs.

"I've got it."

I hurry into the kitchen and grab a plate, quickly filling it up with brownies. Then I find the salted caramel sauce and drizzle it over the top. Then I pour some hot cocoa into cups before digging around the kitchen like a rabid raccoon looking for a tray.

"Come on."

"I didn't mean to," Aaron slurs, and my anger at him fades. He's clearly heartbroken.

Joel and Miles help him up from the makeshift bar in the dining room and drag him toward the basement stairs. I focus on putting everything on the tray I found, trying not to stare at them.

When I turn around, I find Jamie staring at the stairway to the basement, arms crossed over his chest.

"You okay?" I ask.

He turns around, the surprise on his face quickly fading back to frustration.

"I hate seeing him do this. Getting drunk doesn't fix his problems. It only makes it worse. There are a lot of ways I've wanted to follow in Aaron's footsteps over the years, but I never want to be the person drinking to solve my problems."

I nod. "He probably needs extra support right now."

"Or a kick in the ass," he mutters. Then his eyes meet mine again. "Sorry."

"You don't have to apologize for having feelings. You're human. Not a robot."

"Thanks." He glances over my shoulder at the tray on the counter. "Go take care of Rae. She needs support too."

Then he turns and makes his way down the stairs.

After a second, I turn around too, and grab the tray to go find the girls, even though something inside me that I don't understand wants to follow Jamie and make sure he's okay.

4

The Event Queen

Amanda

"CHEERS TO THE BIRTHDAY GIRL!" Rae says happily, raising her glass of bubbly rosé and clinking it against mine.

My birthday was yesterday, and we had a little family party with my parents and Jace's family. They've been neighbors my whole life and are like our extended family.

Today, though, this is what I wanted. A low-key night with the girls who have become my closest friends. It's hard to believe it's barely been a month since I met them, but people say when it's right, you just know. And maybe they're referring to love, but platonic love is as—if not more—important.

I think I could probably live without romantic love if I had to, but now that I've had a taste of this camaraderie and support, I don't think I could go without it. Even with my former best friends, I never had a relationship like this. Unwavering love and friendship is what I've wanted for a long time, and it still feels a little surreal that I have it—but I'm forcing myself to quiet the mean voices in the back of my mind, and as Mackie suggested, let them love me.

After coming up with five ridiculous nicknames for Mackie— kitty boo boo, honey stuffins, Mack attack, smacky Mackie, and

MacWonderful—I gave up. With a straight face, Mackie let me repeatedly call her each one. I swear sometimes she's *too* easygoing. But I'm hopeful that'll make us good roommates. I'm fairly low maintenance when it comes to anything but my emotional needs, so it should be a good fit.

And she'll just have to live with me jumping on the hive mind train and calling her Mackie because trying to come up with over-the-top nicknames is exhausting.

"Thank you," I say, clinking each of their glasses. "I'm older, wiser, and obviously more beautiful."

"Obviously," Mackie agrees.

"We're all going to age like fine wines," Sarah says. "Because we'll be laughing the whole way."

"Oh my god, yes," I agree. "We have to be those crazy old ladies in the nursing home who are heckling the staff and playing card games all day."

"Sign me up," Rae says.

"Oh, and don't forget, eating sushi," Mackie says, popping the tops off the containers in front of us.

If I could eat only one food for the rest of my life, it would be sushi, no questions asked. These are all a bunch of specialty rolls from one of the local places, and my mouth is watering just looking at them.

Before I can dive in, my phone goes off. While I like to be present with the girls, I've been texting with Marissa, the woman in charge of the event I'm running next weekend.

"Sorry, is it okay if I check it? I just want to make sure I don't miss any important event-related stuff."

"Go for it," Mackie says.

I quickly check it, but it's only a text from the florist confirming the time for set up. I text back, then set my phone to the side again.

"Your event is in Ida, right?" Sarah asks.

"Yep. That massive Victorian home they recently renovated into event space."

"Did you want to come over to our place beforehand? We could do your hair and makeup," Sarah says.

I blink at her. Yeah, before dances my former friends and I used to do hair and makeup together like a lot of teen girls do, but there's something different about this. Something more.

"Uh, that'd be awesome. But I might be a little gross from setting up, so makeup might not be the best plan."

"Do you want to bring a bag to our house and shower there?" Rae asks. "Actually... do you need help setting anything up?"

"Oh, no. I'll be fine."

"Mm. Let's rephrase. Is anyone helping you set up?" Sarah asks, brow cocked like she already knows she's calling me on my bullshit.

"No," I say, trying to sound confident.

"How much do you have to do?" Mackie asks.

Everything.

"All the decor, oversee floral placements, make sure everything is ready for the caterers."

"That seems like a lot," Sarah says.

"It... is."

Rae bumps her knee against mine. We're sitting in a circle on my bedroom floor, all cross-legged, with the sushi like a holy platter in the middle.

"It's okay to ask for help. You're not being a burden. You're relying on your support system."

I stare at them for a second, then Sarah whispers, "Ask us."

Then they're all whisper-chanting it.

"Fine. Will you help me set up for my event next Friday? Please."

"That was physically painful for you, wasn't it?" Mackie asks.

"A little."

"Well, we'll just have to keep practicing it then. Like immersion therapy." Rae smirks at me. "But we'd be happy to help. We'll all be there whenever you need us."

"And when you're done, you're coming back to our place to shower, *and then* we'll do your hair and makeup," Sarah says.

"Okay."

Mackie knocks her knee against mine. "Once more with feeling."

"Okay. Thank you." I let out a long sigh. "I love you all. Now, can we eat? I'm starving."

"Whatever the birthday girl wants," Rae says.

But as I look around at them, I know I've already got everything I want.

I LOVE when an event comes together.

It might sound completely stupid that I've wanted to be an event planner my whole life, but for me, it makes sense. I love parties. I love creating an entire theme and decor. I love making people happy. Those are all things I get to do on a regular basis.

I probably don't need to go to college for it, but I don't just want to do this job, I want to excel at it, which means learning everything I can, whether in the classroom or in practice. Event planning isn't just one job. I'm part creator, part designer, part businesswoman, part counselor—helping people figure out what they actually want—and part travel agent. All while being the head bitch in charge. Event planning allows me to use every single one of my skills to perfectly organize chaos into something beautiful.

This is the first ever event I'm hosting for someone not connected to my parents. It's still not big. It's a small fundraiser with a silent auction, a couple of singers, and a few poets doing readings, all to help raise money for a new county arts center.

It's being hosted by one of the board members of the county arts council, though I've mostly spoken with his assistant and his wife—as he put it, he has no eye for planning, just goals he wants to achieve—and I'm the one working to make it all happen.

Watching it all happen.

Having the girls help me set up made everything go much more smoothly, and I hope if I need their help in the future, I'll be able to swallow my pride and fear of feeling like a burden and ask for it. We also had a fantastic time while they made me look polished and professional.

I'm not wearing any fancy clothes, just a pretty oversized light tan sweater with black leggings and high-quality black low-top sneakers. My hair is smooth and shiny, and the bottom strands have been curled. I feel like a badass boss, and it's a little strange to think that's exactly what I am. I curated this event.

I really need to choose a business name. The other day I made some social media accounts and started posting pictures of my process, but if I'm going to take this seriously, I need to figure out my branding and a website.

But that's future me's problem. Right now, all I need to do is make sure this event keeps running smoothly.

"Oh, Amanda!" I turn to face Marissa Henderson. She and her husband Bill have been great to work with through the event planning process.

"Is everything all right?"

She puts a hand on my arm. "It's excellent. I just wanted to thank you again. I keep getting compliments about how beautiful and well put together everything is. I just wanted to let you know that."

"Thank you. I really appreciate it."

She sighs dramatically. "I appreciate you. Bill is great about a lot of things, but planning any kind of event isn't one of them, and with four kids, I barely keep my head on straight most days. You made everything so much easier, and that alone will have me singing your praises to anyone and everyone."

My cheeks heat a little. "Thank you."

"Now, if only I could find my son."

My brow furrows. "I don't remember seeing any kids running around."

Because of the nature of the event, it was adults only. There will be another fundraiser in the summer that's more family-focused which is being set up by a different board member.

She laughs. "He's not much of a kid anymore." My eyes must widen, because Marissa laughs. "I'll take that as a compliment of how young I look."

"Definitely do," I say with a laugh.

A blast of cold hits my back as the front door swings open.

Marissa lets out a sigh. "There you are."

"Sorry I'm late."

A prick of awareness shoots through me, but it's not until I'm halfway through spinning around that I register whose voice it is.

Then I'm staring at him. Jamie. Jamie *Henderson*, apparently.

"Hey, Mom." He kisses his mother on the cheek, then his warm gaze sweeps over me.

"Well, well, if it isn't the event queen." Jamie smirks as he swaggers toward me, all fiery red hair, freckles, and aw-shucks smile. He's wearing a suit and looking... handsome. No. That's not the right word. He looks *dapper*. I don't know who even uses that word anymore, but it's the only one that seems right.

I suck in a breath and stop staring like an idiot since his mother is standing right there.

"Baseball boy. That's a great name, by the way. I might have to steal it. *Amanda Hamilton. Event Queen.* Or maybe queen of events? I'll have to play with it, but it could really help with my branding."

"Glad to be of service."

"You two know each other?" Marissa asks, pleasantly surprised.

"Yeah. Rae and the girls met her at school. Small world."

"It is a small world. That's wonderful. Their whole friend group is great."

"Yes. They are. Rae, Sarah, and Mackenzie actually helped me set things up today."

"Well, again, it all came together beautifully. Between that and you being a friend of the family, I'll be handing out your name as often as I can."

"Again, thank you."

"Of course. I need to go find Bill so we can keep playing host and hostess. Let me know if you need anything." She points at Jamie. "Don't cause any trouble."

He holds up his hands. "Hey, I'm the well-behaved one in the family." She narrows her eyes a little, then shakes her head as she walks away.

He leans in and whispers to me, "It's true. I swear."

"Mhm. I'll believe it when I see it."

He subtly winks at me, a playful smile on his face, and it's such a difference from the boy I met at Joel's house who stumbled over his words and seemed unsure of himself.

He looks around the place, taking it all in. "This is amazing."

"Thank you. Glad you think so. You know, when you said you wanted to see me in action, I didn't think that meant getting your mom to hire me to plan an event," I tease.

"Oh yeah. I was desperate before I even knew you. I heard all these rumblings about the event queen, and I had to see for myself. You should definitely steal that name, by the way. I have no doubt you'll rise to the top."

I look around the space. It's an old Victorian home that's been converted to serve as an event space. We're in the grand entryway, but there's a great room with a fireplace and a large dining room off this room, as well as a small access hallway to the kitchen.

"You think so?"

He follows my gaze, looking around the place and taking it all in. "You did all this yourself?"

"Well, there are caterers for the food, a florist did the flowers, and the girls helped me set up."

"But... *you* did this."

"I did. It was my vision, and I worked through every element to make sure it all came together perfectly," I say confidently. Because this is the one area of my life where I know exactly who I am and what I'm doing. The one place where the negative voices can't get to me—at least once an event is running. Imposter syndrome can yell at me as loud as it wants to until I'm in the middle of an event. Then I can't hear it over the sound of success.

"Then yes. I have no doubt you'll rise to the top. I've been to a lot of stuffy events and boring parties. This one has personality, but it's not over the top. That's hard to come by. Don't second-guess yourself."

I lift my chin. "Thank you."

Then, without a second thought, I pull my phone out and change the handle on my social media account.

The Event Queen.

Logo and branding ideas flow through my mind, and my stomach twists with excitement... and pride.

This is what I'm supposed to be doing, and it's time for me to invest in and shout from the rooftops about myself and my business.

Jamie

AMANDA HAMILTON IS a force of nature.

She glides around the party in a pair of black leggings, fancy black low-top sneakers, and a long sand-colored sweater, making sure everyone has everything they need and every second of the night is running seamlessly.

I've been to a decent number of parties like this over the years. My parents come from old money, and while fancy events aren't their preferred style most of the time, they'll go to ones for causes that matter to them.

This fundraiser party—gala, whatever it's called—is nothing

like the ones we've been to in the past. It's elegant, but it has personality. Which I'm sure is exactly what my parents wanted, but Amanda is the one who brought it all to life.

And I swear she never stops moving. When she's on, she's really on. It's a turn *on*. Except that I'm not going there. We can banter and flirt and have fun—that's obvious with the whole two conversations we've had—but I'm not going to risk the many friendships surrounding us by hooking up with her.

I'd rather have her as a friend than a hookup. She's brilliant and has a quippy, sarcastic side that's fun to be around. And that's just what I've gotten to see so far.

As the party winds down, I keep trying to catch Amanda, grab her a drink, or see if she needs anything, but she's always too fast for me. Though I do see her sneakily stretch her neck and her legs a few times.

I've played double headers and not been as exhausted as I am watching her tonight.

When all the guests have left, my parents go to praise the caterers—since they've been singing Amanda's praises all night—and I go find Amanda. She's slowly taking apart some floral arrangement.

"Hey."

She jumps a little and spins around. "Hi."

"Sorry. Didn't mean to scare you."

"It's fine. I was in the zone."

"You've been in the zone all night."

She laughs, her long hair swishing as she does. "I don't get to leave the zone until everything is done and put away, so—"

"Wait, you have to do all this yourself? I thought the girls—"

"They jumped in and offered to help me set everything up. I wasn't going to ask them to drag themselves back down here to work until midnight taking everything down. My brother said to call him if I need help loading my car."

"But—"

"Jamie, it's fine. The owners of the place live next door, and they said I could take all the time I needed, and just to text them when it needed to be locked up."

"You've been on your feet for hours, and now you're going to take down every single thing in this place by yourself?"

"Well, not the paintings. They came with the venue."

"That's it. I'm staying and helping."

"You don't have to do that."

"You're right. But I'm going to. You worked hard tonight while all I did was stand around. Helping you is the least I can do."

"This is just so you can hold it over my head until I come to one of your baseball games, isn't it?" She bites her lip as she smiles up at me.

"Obviously. You have to see me in my element to understand how amazing I truly am."

"And so humble."

"So..."

"Fine. Stay and help. But just know I'll work you to the bone."

I couldn't stop the dumbass smile on my face if I wanted to. "I wouldn't expect anything less."

"There they are," Mom says, walking over with my dad.

"Amanda, this really was a wonderful event. Thank you so much for all you've done."

"It was my pleasure, sir."

"Please, call me Bill. I never want to be in any kind of formal situation with people calling me sir."

I stifle a laugh at that, but my parents ignore me.

"I'll be passing your information along every chance I get. Do you have any business cards?"

"Not yet. But I do have a social media account and I'm working on a website. I'll send you an email when it's all finished," Amanda says without missing a beat.

"Perfect." Then Mom turns to me. "Jamie, ready to head home?"

"Actually, I'm going to stay and help Amanda clean up. I'll let you two deal with the rugrats—I mean my loving younger siblings."

Dad looks at Amanda. "Don't let him fool you. He's only offering to help so his siblings don't attack him the second he walks in the door."

Amanda tries and fails at hiding a laugh.

"Okay then, I guess we'll see you at home," Mom says. "Drive safe."

"I will. Night."

They walk out and I breathe out a sigh of relief. I love my parents, but they have the occasional tendency to be embarrassing —or totally roast me. It's all in good fun and mostly because I'm the oldest and the easy child compared to my three younger siblings.

As soon as the door is closed behind them, Amanda sighs too. Her posture changes, her whole body softening and slumping a little. Then she pulls out her phone.

"I need sushi."

I reach for my phone. "I can pay for it—"

"No. You're staying to help me. The least I can do is pay you in sushi. Anything you don't like?"

I shake my head. "I'm up for whatever."

"Sweet. A shit ton of sushi incoming." She taps a few more times on her phone screen, then sets her phone down on the nearby table. "Let's see if we can get all those twinkle lights down before it gets here."

She walks out of the room like a woman on a mission, and I follow after her, ready to be put to work.

"FINALLY," Amanda says, sitting down next to me on a

tablecloth on the floor, in the center of which is the mass quantity of sushi she ordered.

She hands me a bottle of fancy sparkling water, then pulls the lids off all the containers, doing a little happy dance as she fills up a plate.

Smiling, I grab a plate and add some pieces as well, watching her all the while. I've never seen someone so excited for sushi before.

She sighs happily once the full plate is sitting in front of her, then grabs a piece and takes a big bite, groaning with happiness. "Oh my god, yes." She finishes chewing, her eyes slipping closed like she's enjoying a lot more than food. "God, I'm a slut for a spicy crab roll."

I choke on the bite I took, my cheeks instantly burning red.

"What? Are you not used to *ladies* swearing?" she asks with a laugh.

I take a drink of water, then a deep breath in and out before answering. "No. I just wasn't expecting those exact words to come out of your mouth."

She shrugs. "No regrets. Spicy crab is the best. I would do many dirty things for one of these rolls."

She takes another bite, letting out a happy noise.

I have no idea what I was expecting from Amanda when I first saw her, but she's somehow exactly it and nothing like it all at once. She's fierce but playful, and there's a calm undercutting her wildness.

"So why event planning?"

"Why baseball?"

"Baseball chose me, and I couldn't resist the siren song of the field."

"Think you'll play pro?"

"I know I will. Just a matter of how and when."

"Confident."

"As are you. You know you're good at what you do. I know I'm a great pitcher. That alone won't get me there though. I'm dedicated and constantly pushing myself to be better. If that means making baseball my life until I get where I'm going, then I'm willing to do that."

She nods as she takes another bite. "Same." After she swallows, she continues. "I have a nonstop drive to learn and grow. And after tonight, I'm ready to fully commit to building a business. As for how I ended up in event planning, I guess that's also similar to you. I don't know if it chose me, but it's where I felt at home. I've always loved parties. I used to throw themed tea parties for all my stuffed animals and usually forced at least one of my brothers to participate. I was always on the planning committee for events in high school. Once an idea comes to me, I can see the whole thing laid out in my mind. It just makes sense to me. Plus, it's perfect for someone like me who always has a hundred tabs open in my brain."

She shrugs as she pops another piece of sushi into her mouth.

"Let me guess, you're the oldest child?"

She smirks at me, then slowly shakes her head. "Nope. I'm the youngest. And the only girl."

"Surprising."

"Why? Because I'm not a spoiled little princess?" Her eyes dance with mischief.

"That's not what I meant. Not all youngest kids are spoiled. My mom's the oldest in her family and she and my dad's older sister both have that oldest female child vibe where they're always thinking of what needs to be done, don't know how to slow down, try to do everything by themselves, and always feel like they need to take care of everyone else. You give off those vibes big time."

Her smile falters—just for second—like it did when I made that stupid joke about how we were keeping her because she brought coffee the day we met.

She grabs another piece of sushi, nibbling on it before she says anything else.

"It might be the curse of being the only girl in the family, but

I think it's more because my brothers sucked the will to live—or at least be present—out of my parents. Don't get me wrong, I can always seek my parents out and they'll be there for me, but a lot of the time, I was left to my own devices. Or I was told to ask my brothers, which usually ended up in me doing it myself anyway. Let's just say if anyone was going to get *Home Alone*'d in my family, it would be me. Not because I'm a little shit like Kevin McAllister, but because the squeaky wheel always got the grease in my house, and I never learned to squeak loud enough." She waves a hand like she's trying to clear away all the words she just said. "Anyway, that was deeper than it needed to be, so back to you. You have younger siblings?"

I stare at her for a beat. She wants to move on like she never said those words, but I heard every one of them. And I saw the hurt from them in her eyes. She tries to do everything because she never had anyone to help her. She doesn't want to bother anyone because she feels like that's what needing help is—demanding attention. It doesn't seem like anyone has ever looked at her and chosen her—until now. That blows my mind because she's a masterpiece. Talented, witty, kind, and just wants to help.

Fuck.

I need to get out of that mental space right now. Because who am I? Another person who wouldn't be able to choose her. Not the way she deserves to be chosen.

So I take a drink of my water and let her change the subject back to me.

"Yes. I have three much younger siblings. Penny is seven, Calvin is five-and-a-half, and Mila is three-and-a-half. Even though I'm used to the age difference, sometimes it still feels strange. Like I'm a mix of only child and older brother."

"How'd you end up with siblings so much younger than you?"

"My parents are trust fund kids who went right into working the type of high-stress corporate jobs that keeps their families' money strong. They barely paid any attention to me and almost got divorced before they realized how unhappy they were. They pivoted to careers they love, refocused on me and our family, and rekindled their love. Which led to my siblings. My parents are gross and can't ever keep their hands off each other."

She laughs. "I noticed that tonight. Your dad kept squeezing your mom's butt when they were dancing."

I groan, gagging. "Feel free to never tell me anything like that again."

"It's sweet. Wouldn't you want that? To still feel insanely in love with your partner after years together?"

I have to give her that. "Yeah, I guess I would."

"Of course, maybe you don't want to get married. Maybe it'll be all A-list parties and ball bunnies for you when you make it to the majors."

"Maybe one of those A-list parties will be planned by you. We'll see each other across a crowded room."

She laughs. "Another story for the grandkids, right?"

"Exactly." We eat in silence for a few minutes, but what she said before is eating away at me. "For the record, I do want that. Not the A-list parties. Love. It's just not something I'm focused on right now. Plus, I've seen enough relationships fall apart that it makes me wary."

"Your parents are still together. And clearly happy."

"They are. But I guess I mean more with my friends. Like everyone thought Sarah and Trevor would end up together. We were all shocked when it ended."

Amanda laughs and shakes her head. "As the newbie, that's so strange to me because I can't really picture them together. And maybe I'm reading into it, but I got the vibe that there's something between her and Joel."

"I have no idea. I've stopped trying to keep tabs on it. Then, of course, there's Aaron and Rae."

"Yeah, I feel like I'm learning something new about that every day. Seems like a bit of a dumpster fire."

My lips pull flat. "To say the least."

"You okay?"

My eyes flit to hers. "Yeah. Just frustrated with how Aaron has been acting."

"Well, from what I've learned from the girls, it wasn't just on him."

"No. It wasn't. But I hate seeing this downward spiral he's in."

"Have you talked to him since the Christmas party?"

"Yeah. I went over the next morning and pushed him... gave him a little shit. I don't know. It's how we've all always been with each other. I just want him to pull himself out of this space and fight."

"In my experience, you can't decide that for someone else. They have to decide that for themselves."

"Wow. That's very wise."

"Well, I am nineteen now." She playfully flips her hair.

"When was your birthday?"

"Last week. January sixth."

"Happy belated birthday. Now I really wish you would've let me pay for the sushi."

"You helping out is more than enough. Thank you." She looks around. "We should probably get back to it unless we want to be here all night." She carefully pushes herself off the floor, but I wait a moment, watching her.

Even though I shouldn't, all I can think is that I wouldn't mind staying here all night as long as I'm with her.

Thoughts like that are destined to get me in trouble.

"LOOK AT THAT. Completely finished, and it's not even midnight."

I shut Amanda's car door after loading the last box of stuff in the back.

"Only because you offered to help. I'd probably still be unstringing lights if you hadn't let me put you to work. So, thank you."

"I was happy to do it."

She stares at me for a second, then pushes onto her toes and wraps her arms around me in a hug. Everything about her is soft and warm—comforting.

I gently wrap my arms around her back. "Does this mean we're friends now?" I say the words, praying they don't come off like a douchey guy trying to friendzone a girl he's led on but isn't actually into. I genuinely like Amanda, and since romance isn't on my radar right now, I hope we'll be friends.

She laughs as she lands back on flat feet. "Yeah. I'd like that."

Our eyes meet, then we both laugh awkwardly.

"So, friends usually have each other's phone numbers, right?" I ask.

"They do."

Continuing our trend of being weird and awkward, we swap phones and add our numbers.

When we swap back, I keep my hand on hers for a moment. There's something about her that draws me in. It's something I've never experienced before, and I don't know what to do with it.

I know what I want to do, but that would lead to a messy can of worms being spilled everywhere, so I remind myself of the important word here. *Friends.*

"Well, I should probably get home and unload all my stuff."

"Do you need any help? I can follow you."

She laughs and shakes her head. "I'll be fine. I can do it myself."

"I know you can." Her eyes land on mine. "But that doesn't mean you should always have to."

"You're sweet." She stares at me for a beat. "That cocky, confident thing you put on, that's an act, right?"

That catches me off guard. It *is* an act. Other than the people who know me well, no one ever notices that.

I bite my lip and try to play it off. "What gave me away?"

She shrugs. "I'm good at reading people. And... I don't know. We don't know each other well, but I've only seen you slip into it around bigger groups. When it's just the two of us, you're quieter. Still playful, obviously still confident about baseball, but everything else falls away." She tilts her head as she looks at me. "Introvert?"

I laugh and run a hand through my hair. "Yeah. And you're right. That mask is one I slip on to help myself feel comfortable when I otherwise wouldn't. It's easy enough to do, but it's not the real me."

Her eyes flit to mine again. "I can see that. It's in your eyes. You're happier now. More peaceful." A mischievous smile dances on her lips. "Glad to know I make you feel that way."

Oh, it would be easy, so easy, to lean into that. To flirt with her. To test the tension sparking between us.

It would also get me in trouble.

"You're easy to talk to, be comfortable with. I appreciate you letting me see a little behind your mask tonight too."

"That's how friendships form, right?"

"Right."

She looks around the frosty night air. "Well, I should get going. Thank you for your help tonight. It means a lot."

"Take care of yourself. And if I don't see you before you go back to campus, have a safe trip."

"Thanks." With one last look, she walks around her car and pulls the driver's side door open. "Have a good night, baseball boy."

"Night, event queen."

The last thing I hear is her laugh as she climbs into the car. I step back onto the sidewalk and watch until she pulls away from the curb and makes it to the red light at the end of the street.

Hopefully tonight was the start of a solid friendship, even if the tension between us is going to make being friends with her more difficult than any other friendship I've ever had.

5
Valuable

Jamie

"OY, Commander, if we don't do something now, this ship is going down!"

"Roger that. Defensive measures!" Calvin runs over to me and pulls the cardboard lever next to me. Then he looks up at me. "Do that silly voice again."

"Oy, you better run down the floodgates and batten up your skivvies!"

Calvin doubles over laughing at my bastardized Scottish accent. Or is it Irish? Maybe Australian? I don't know. Baseball is my thing, not acting.

He straightens up suddenly when the massive box we're sitting in moves.

"We're under attack."

"Get behind me!"

I shove his little body behind mine, then stick my head out the cutout for the door, only to take a foam dart directly to the forehead.

"Gotcha," Penny says, pretending to holster her plastic gun.

Before I can pretend to be dead, Calvin jumps on my shoulders and sticks his head out the top hatch, hitting Penny square in the chest with a dart.

"Ugh! I hate you." Then she dramatically falls to the ground.

Cal looks down at little Mila, who looks back at him with big eyes.

"Mila, switch to our team."

She shrugs and climbs over me into the box. "Okay, we have to set course for a new galaxy," Cal says, despite the fact I'm his dead second-in-command hanging out of his ship. At least have the courtesy to put me out the airlock.

"No, we don't." And out of nowhere, Mila shoots Cal in the back with a dart. "Girls win."

Penny jumps off the floor and dances around.

"No fair! You cheated!"

"Mila never took an oath to you. She was still on my team."

Penny and Cal are only seventeen months apart in age, and they are almost always at each other's throats. Mila is usually neutral, unless Penny gets her hyped up on girl power. Then poor Cal doesn't stand a chance.

"You're a brat," Cal yells.

"Well, you're stinky!" Penny shouts.

As their older sibling, it's probably my job to intervene here, but I hate disciplining them. I like that they see me as their fun older brother and not a third parent. So instead, I let out a long groan, then slowly sit up, acting like a zombie... monster... thing.

Cal's eyes get huge. "Get in the ship! He's a zombie alien now!"

Sure, that's totally what I was going for.

"No," Penny says, coming to stand next to Cal. "He'll just follow us. We have to... Take. Him. Down."

She glances at Cal and Mila, then all three of them jump on me at once.

I put in some fake effort and thrash my arms, trying to escape. At least they're working together now.

Mom comes to the doorway and leans against it. "What's going on in here?"

I throw my hand out and let out a pathetic, "Help me."

"Hm," Mom says, watching my three younger siblings beat me up. Finally, she smiles. "Lunchtime!"

All three leap off me and run for the door.

"Finally," I sigh, then slowly get up, stretching my sore muscles as I walk toward the door.

"Don't even try to pretend you weren't enjoying that," Mom says, leading the way down the hall from the playroom to the kitchen.

My siblings are already sitting on stools at the kitchen island as Dad puts plates with chicken nuggets, ketchup, and fruit in front of them.

I sit down next to Cal, then Dad puts a plate of chicken nuggets in front of me.

My gaze drops to it. "Really? I'm seventeen, not seven."

Penny makes a derisive noise at that.

"That's why you get the special spicy sauce," Mom says, putting some sriracha mayo in front of me.

Dad looks at me with fake awe. "They grow up so fast."

"Just remember, the older I get, the older you get, old man."

"Old man? I'm still young and spry. Hip."

"Not making a case for yourself, honey," Mom says, sliding a salad in front of him.

Dad looks down at it and frowns. "I'll trade you for some nuggets."

I hold my hand out and wiggle it back and forth. "Not exactly an equal trade."

"Oh, sure. Now you want the nuggets."

I grab his bowl and my plate and walk around to the other side of the counter. After a few minutes, I sit back down and put a bowl in front of him and a matching one at my spot. Both are filled with salad then topped with chicken nuggets and ranch dressing.

"Fair compromise," Dad says.

"So, when are you planning to leave for Old Lake Town?" Mom asks.

I'm going up to SUNY FL for a long weekend to see Aaron *coach* his first game. After everything he's been through, he found his way back to baseball and out of the darkness. Amanda was right about that. He had to do it on his own. While I don't regret holding him accountable, I probably could've been more supportive. Which is why going up there today is also a surprise. We've talked plenty over the last couple of months, but it'll be good to see him in person.

"I'll probably pack and head out after this."

"And will Amanda be there?" Mom asks with zero subtlety.

I stop with my fork halfway to my mouth. "I'd assume so, since she goes there."

"Who's Amanda?" Penny asks.

"Just a friend."

"Mm. Friend," Dad says under his breath.

"What was that? I didn't quite hear you."

He picks up his iPad and looks at it like it's the most interesting thing in the world. "I just said 'hm.' There are all sorts of interesting things happening in the world right now."

"Smooth," Mom says.

"You brought it up."

"Is Amanda your girlfriend?" Penny asks.

"No. She's just a friend."

"Then why are you going to visit her?"

I sigh and set my fork in my bowl, turning to look over Calvin's head at Penny.

"I'm going to visit Aaron. Amanda goes to school at the same place. That's how I met her. She lives in the same place as Rae and the girls."

"Oh. I love Miss Rae. She's so much fun."

Rae worked as a nanny through high school and babysat for my siblings on occasion.

When no one says anything else, I take a bite of my food, hoping the conversation is over. I'm not that lucky.

"Can I see a picture of her?"

"Rae?"

"No. Amanda. Is she pretty?"

I feel the heat of my parents' stares on me as I lock eyes with my little sister once again.

"Yes. She's... pretty."

"Don't hurt yourself, son," Dad says.

Looking at the three sets of little eyes on me, I throw up a peace sign at my dad, then over my shoulder mutter, "Pretend my pointer is down."

Dad starts laughing so hard he almost chokes on his food.

"I have five children," my mother sighs.

"Seriously, you started this," I tell her.

"Can I see a picture, pleaseeeeee?" Penny whines.

"Fine," I sigh, pulling out my phone. I go to Amanda's social media and pull up a selfie of her smiling brightly, the sun behind her making her hair look redder, then hand my phone to Penny.

"Oh, wow. She's *really* pretty."

Yeah, she is. Only a moron would think she's not. She's gorgeous. But I sure as shit can't say that.

"And you think she's pretty," Penny says, handing my phone back. "I think you should date her."

Now Mom chokes and coughs on her sip of water.

"Serves you right," I hiss. Then I put my big brother voice back on and turn back to Penny. "I'm not going to date her."

"Why not? Oh. Does she not like you?"

I put a hand to my forehead. "She likes me fine. We just don't want to date. Contrary to what some people think, boys and girls can be just friends."

Penny's brow scrunches. "Well, I guess that's true. But you should still think about it. I think I'd like an older sister one day."

Again, I feel my parents' intense stares, but I make some kind of affirmative noise to Penny, then eat the rest of my salad as fast as I can.

If life were simpler, maybe there could be something between Amanda and me, but we both have separate focuses and goals, and we're determined to achieve them.

But as I load up my car and settle in for the drive, I can't deny that I'm excited to spend the weekend with her.

"SO, are you ready for your season to start?" Aaron asks as we lounge on the oversized couches in the lake house. My family has money, but I never realized Joel's family was loaded too. This place is huge and fancy. It has six bedrooms plus lake access. It's insane.

The game today was great. I got to see Aaron in action as a coach—not that I'd never seen it before. He's been working with me for years, but this was different. It was watching him in his element as a professional, and he kicked ass.

College starts a couple of weeks before we do, plus we're still on spring break, so I've got another seventeen days until my first game of the season.

"I'm ready. Not sure what to expect in terms of if anyone will be watching me."

"You know they will."

"Not big scouts. Not yet."

"There might be. Maybe not in person, but from a distance. Local media will be covering it for sure. Your name has gotten around, Jame. Even my coach knows. Don't underestimate the power in that."

"Do you think I'm good enough to make the draft out of high school?"

"Yeah. I do. You won't go as high as you would if you went to a D1 school first, though."

I nod slowly. It's a lot to think about, and there aren't a lot of guidebooks for stuff like this. Going from a high school athlete or even a college one into professional sports is a whirlwind. I have to think about agents even though I can't legally get advice from one until after I'm drafted. But I'm supposed to make those connections so I can have one I plan to work with when the time comes. It's confusing and stressful and not what I want to focus on.

"I just want to play the best baseball I can this year."

"That's all you have to do," Aaron reassures me. "You planning to do any camps this summer?"

"Not really. Coach mentioned some new one but couldn't tell me anything about it. I've done Cooperstown ones before, but I don't feel like there's that much new for me to learn. I need to hone my skills, not gain new ones. That's where you come in."

"Can you afford me? I don't know if you've heard, but I'm kind of a big deal coach now."

"Such a big deal. I'm truly honored and humbled to be in your presence."

He grins at me. "As you should be."

I lean back against the couch. "Think we'll still have this when I make it to the majors?"

"Of course. I'm going to be mooching off you for free baseball tickets. I'll crash on your couch and go to your games. Be your hype man."

I snort at that. "Yeah, right. I'd bet anything you and Rae will be married and popping out babies before I'm fully settled in the league."

His eyes meet mine.

"Yeah, I know you said it's a work in progress between you two, but the keyword there is *progress*. We all know you'll end up together."

"What about you and Amanda?" he asks.

"Not you too. My parents—and Penny—already bugged me about this earlier."

Again, I get that shit-eating grin.

"You know what I've learned over the years? If everyone else around you sees something, there might just be something there." Then he stands up and stretches, yawning for effect. "I'm gonna head up to bed. You coming?"

I stand too. "Nah. I'm going to grab something else to eat first. I'm starving. I'll be up after that."

"Sounds good."

He claps me on the shoulder and heads up the stairs as I go to the kitchen to find food.

And not think about Amanda. Not think about our playful flirtation or the way she always calls me baseball boy. Nope. I need to get Amanda out of my head.

"Oh, hi."

I spin around, the light from the refrigerator illuminating the kitchen.

That's a lot easier to do when she's not standing in front of me looking mesmerizing.

Amanda

I COULDN'T SLEEP. Not that it's a big surprise. My brain never stops. I'm always thinking of something I have to do. Something I can work on. An idea that will never turn into something. It's the curse of being a type A creative.

It takes melatonin, a sleep mask, noise canceling earbuds with calming music, and a blessing from the goddess of sleep for me to crash out. Once I do, I sleep like a rock, but until then, I'm wandering this giant fancy lake house in the middle of the night.

Or in this case, standing awkwardly at the edge of the kitchen —where I was hoping to find brownies—and staring at *him*.

Jamie Henderson. All devastating blue eyes, fiery red hair, and freckles scattered everywhere.

"Hey, Amanda," he chokes out, clearly as surprised as I am.

But the surprise fades in a second, and an easy smile lights up his face.

Or that's the light from the refrigerator.

I need to get a grip.

"Hey, Jamie."

He shuts the refrigerator door, then flicks on the light over the large kitchen island.

"I wasn't expecting anyone else to be up."

"Me either. But I couldn't sleep. Why are you digging through the fridge?"

He pats his stomach. "I'm a growing boy." He holds up a slice of cold pizza.

"Right."

I scoot around him, trying to act normal. But that's not so easy.

Since we first met at the Christmas party, there's been something in the air every time we're in the same space. Everything feels heightened. Electrically charged somehow. I hate it. I'm never tongue-tied around guys. Or girls. Or whoever I'm interested in. I don't care about anyone's gender or sexual identity, only that they're a decent human.

But right now, I can barely form a coherent sentence. I'm air headed and my insides feel a little too warm and gooey.

How many languages can I say *not an option* in? Unfortunately, not many. I learned American Sign Language years ago, and I've found it the most useful second language to know. I picked up a little Spanish because one of the cooks at the event company I used to work at is from Colombia and speaks it fluently. I figure if I'm going to work in event planning, the more languages I know, the better.

But something inside me doesn't want to believe Jamie isn't an option, no matter what language I say it in, and I've developed a ridiculous crush on him.

"What kept you up?" Jamie asks, and I almost jump out of my skin.

Another one of my shining personality traits. I get lost in my head a lot.

"My brain is always going and one thing led to another, and now... I need brownies."

He chuckles. "Rae makes the best brownies. I think there are some cheesecake ones in there."

I yank the door open and my mouth waters when I spot them.

As I pull the container out, my skin prickles. Jamie's body brushes mine as he reaches in and pulls the container of pizza out, already going for another slice.

I glance at him out of the corner of my eye and catch his smirk.

My hand stills on the container of brownies as Jamie's warmth fades away. Alone again, I lean a little farther into the refrigerator, suck in a deep breath, then turn around, summoning my bold side.

"Growing boy, huh?"

He grins at me from the kitchen island. "Yep."

"Well, I think I'm done growing, but you'll have to pry these brownies from my cold, dead hands."

He tilts his head. "Anyone who tries to control what you eat deserves what they get."

"Including having important body parts removed?" I purr.

He strides over to me, looking much older than he actually is. "Fair punishment. I'm serious, you know. You shouldn't ever have to make excuses for what you eat. Life's too short not to enjoy good food. I hate when I have to restrict myself or adhere to specific diets. I do it because being in good shape for the game is important to me, but if it wasn't for that, I'd eat pizza every day."

I blink at him, wishing I could find the right words or some sassy comeback, but I've always been aware that I'm not the skinny one. Well, not always. A doctor made a comment on it when I was ten, and it was the first time I thought there was something wrong with me. The doctor tried to suggest a diet, at which point my mother asked me to wait in the hall. I heard a few curse words before she stormed out. We never went back there again, but the damage was done. Especially because not too long after that, I started the hellscape that was middle school. Being the "chubby" girl wasn't fun.

Eventually, I learned to embrace my curves. I love my body. But the desire to meet that thin model-like appeal was conditioned into me. I have to actively fight against it. Some days that takes a lot of fucking energy.

"Thank you," I whisper.

He slowly shakes his head. "You're gorgeous. Don't ever doubt that."

Then he steps back and grabs two plates. He puts two pieces of pizza on his and two brownies on mine.

"Want to go sit on the back deck? It's a beautiful night."

"Sure. I'll grab some blankets."

Even though the cool night air would be welcome right now.

When we get out to the back deck, it's chillier than I was expecting, which must be why Jamie pulls me onto the padded outdoor loveseat with him and puts both blankets over us.

My arm grazes his, and I don't have to worry about being cold anymore.

Flames burn deep inside me, and for the first time, I wonder if this is a terrible idea.

But then he smiles at me, and it's so damn earnest, I can't help but smile back.

"So, how'd you end up here?" he asks between bites of pizza.

I pick at my brownie, savoring every tiny bite.

"I wanted to go to college somewhere in New York that was close-ish to home while still giving me space to explore. SUNY FL has an event management degree, which is better than a lot of places that just have hospitality with a minor in event planning or management. Plus, it's beautiful here."

"It definitely is." But his eyes are on me, not the dark lake in the distance.

"Tell me something about you. Something that doesn't have

to do with baseball," I say in an attempt to break the tension surrounding us.

"Not baseball? Sorry. Doesn't compute."

I bump my elbow against his. "Seriously. What do you do when you're not playing baseball?"

"Think about baseball?" His eyes dance and he takes another bite of his pizza. After he swallows, he continues. "Seriously, though, sometimes it feels like my life revolves around baseball. I'm not mad about that, but I don't have many other hobbies. Most of my free time is spent with this bunch of dorks." We both laugh at that. "And with my family."

"Tell me about them."

He shifts on the bench, tucking his legs up and turning so he can look at me. "Well, as you noticed at the event, my parents are disgustingly in love. They prioritize our family and are actively involved in all our lives. My younger siblings are endless chaos. Penny is just hitting the age of being fascinated by romance and love, but she's also really into everything 'girl power.' Her words, not mine. Basically, it's a lighter version of feminism."

"I like her already."

He stares at me for a second, like he's debating whether to say something. "I think she'd like you too." He clears his throat. "Uh, Calvin might as well have a stuffed tiger called Hobbes because he's that wild sometimes. Though he's also thoughtful and a bit of a science kid. Then Mila is precocious and hilarious and has everyone in the house wrapped around her little finger."

"They sound adorable."

He side-eyes me.

"They can be the tiniest terrors. Especially when they work together. But yeah, I love them. My family and baseball are pretty much my entire life."

"That's not a bad thing." It isn't. I'm not as tight with my family as he seems to be, but I love them. And event planning is a big piece of my life too. Granted, I also love volleyball and play in a rec league every summer. And now this friend group is a huge part of my life too.

"What about you? You told me you were the youngest and said you had older brothers. How many?"

"Two. Josh and Pete. Josh is two years older than me and the most obnoxious human in existence, and if we get along for more than a day at a time, hell might freeze over. Pete is four years older than me and more chill. I drove him crazy when we were little, but now we're pretty close."

"Thankfully, I think I'm old enough that I won't have to deal with any truly obnoxious stuff with my siblings. At least until they're teens, but hey, I won't be living at home by then."

"Are you sure? You never know. You might be in your parents' basement hosting some podcast about baseball stats while you wax poetic about your missed shot at the majors."

He puts a hand to his chest. "Ouch. That was just mean. Don't hit a man where it hurts."

"Baseball?"

"Exactly."

"What if I hit you *with* a baseball?"

"It would probably hurt less."

"Noted. Your preferred form of torture is having balls thrown at you."

He chokes on a laugh. "That sounds like the start of a dirty joke."

"I think once balls are involved, you're closer to finishing than starting."

"The event queen has a dirty mind."

I shrug. "I told you I grew up with older brothers. I learned a lot about sex before I probably should have."

He snorts at that. "I don't think there's a particular age for that, but some ways are probably better than others."

Something about the way he says that makes it sound like he knows from experience.

"How did you learn about S-E-X?"

He laughs. "Did my mom ever mention what she does for a living?"

I think back, then realize she never did. "I assumed she worked with your dad. Or stayed home with your siblings."

"Nope. She's a sex therapist."

My eyes fly wide.

"Yep. Which isn't a bad thing. I grew up in a very sex positive household, but I also learned a lot about sex at a pretty young age. Partially because I"—he makes a face—"accidentally walked in on my parents when I was eight or nine. My mom calmly asked if I needed anything and when I said I didn't, she asked me to go wait in my room until she came to talk to me. When she did, she sat me down and told me that sex is a natural part of life, that it's something private between two grown-ups who both agree that's what they want. Obviously, that was expanded on as I got older. There was never any shame placed on sex. My mom always talked about it in a positive way, though she encouraged me to wait until I could comfortably answer the questions 'what if the person you were with gave you an STI' and 'what if the person you were with ended up pregnant.' Then she focused on CHIP."

"California Highway Patrol?"

He shakes his head at my silly joke. "Consent. Honesty. Integrity. Protection."

"That's a good acronym."

"It is. Especially with consent coming first. My mom knows what men's sports can be like—the kinds of things it can breed and cover up. She wanted to make sure I knew the only thing I'm entitled to use to get off is my own hand."

A laugh erupts out of me, shaking my whole body. "Please tell me she used those words."

"Oh, she definitely did. But she's right. I mean, theoretically, sex toys could be involved too, but you know…"

"Wow. Well that's about a thousand times more than anything I ever got. My mom told me to always use a condom and to make sure I see it go on. Never trust a man to handle protection. Oh, and if anything *bad* ever happened to me, to tell her. I think that was when I was eleven. Maybe twelve. Not much to go on. Especially since I knew I was bi in middle school and no one ever gives any education about non-hetero sex or protection."

His brows lift a little and a soft smile appears on his face. "You're bi?"

"Yep," I say confidently. "My first and only relationship—if you could call it that—was with a girl. And I hooked up with both guys and girls in high school and college."

"Do you lean one way more than the other?"

"Nope. I'm right smack in the middle. Which is really fun actually." I give him a sly grin. "So many possibilities. Though I will say, so far, my sexual experiences have been better with women. I learned a hell of a lot more from a lesbian with a strap-on than I ever did from any of the guys I hooked up with."

Surprisingly he doesn't laugh or scowl at that. He nods in understanding.

"That makes sense. Women know where all the essential parts are and what feels good. Add the strap-on, and all they really have to do is master thrusting to have one up on pretty much any guy. That said, a lot of guys aren't interested in exploring. That was something else I was encouraged to do. Go slow. Explore. Learn. Don't jump into fucking just to have an orgasm—that one I'm paraphrasing."

"That's a good lesson." A gust of cold wind hits, making us both shiver. He pulls the blanket up farther and moves a little closer to me, his hand brushing my thigh as he does. For a moment, I can't move. I can't breathe. It's been a long time since I've been crushed out like this, and it's annoyingly inconvenient. I take a deep breath to clear my head, then try to continue the conversation. "How old were you when you first started exploring?"

What a great question to ask the guy I'm crushing on.

"Fifteen. But I was kinda hooked once I did. I didn't have"— he sighs heavily—"*vaginal intercourse* until like a year and a half after that. But once again, it became a preferred activity." His cheeks turn bright red.

Damn my stupid crush because he is seriously cute when he blushes and looks all earnest. I can't help but poke his cheek. "It's kind of adorable when you blush like that."

He lets out a long-suffering sigh. "I hear that way too often. I hate that I blush. I'm not uncomfortable with the topic or inexperienced, I just hate having any kind of intense attention on me. And if I do, I go from white as a sheet to as red as Clifford in under two seconds."

My brows dip in. "I'm not sure I'm comfortable with Clifford the Big Red Dog being a part of our sex conversation."

"Animated characters don't do it for you?"

"I don't know. I've watched some insanely hot anime porn."

His eyes widen a little and he shakes his head. "I swear, sometimes I truly don't expect the things that come out of your mouth."

"I thought you said you weren't innocent."

"I said I'm not inexperienced. And I'm not. I've watched porn —though I can't say I've watched any anime stuff—but most people don't casually say it."

I give a little shrug. "I'd rather let people see the real me and decide if they like it from the start."

He stares at me for a long moment. "I don't know how anyone could not."

"Well, I haven't had the best luck with friendships. At least not until the hive mind came along."

He chuckles at that. "They're definitely good at building strong friendships."

"How did you end up so close with everyone?"

"Aaron took me under his wing in middle school, and the rest of the guys he was friends with on the team—Joel, Miles, Trevor, their friend Nick, and even Joel's older brother Jesse—all made an effort to include me. And as that happened, I ended up hanging around them more and got to know the girls too. Plus, my family knows Rae's mom's family, so I grew up knowing the Abbotts and McKinleys from the periphery. But as I'm sure you've figured out by now, once this group claims you, you're theirs forever."

"I kind of love that." '

"So do I. They drive me nuts sometimes, but I love them all. And as an introvert, once I got out of elementary school, I struggled with making friends. It was easy to get absorbed in the group."

"Do you have any friends back home now?"

"Not in my grade really. I have a couple of guys on the baseball team who are cool, and I hang out with them at school, but the few I was friends with when I was young, I avoid as much as possible. Once they realized my family had money, they started taking advantage of that. I've always been friendly, but I didn't like how that felt. Outside of the team, I don't bother going out of my way to make new friends at this point. I'll go out with guys from the team sometimes, but never for long. I don't like spending too much time with random people. I'd rather be with *my* people."

"But you're here with me."

"I thought we agreed we're friends now. That means you are one of my people."

"I like the sound of that." I almost cringe at the words, but he smiles.

"So do I." There's a beat of silence before he continues. "You have any other close friends?"

"Not like this. My neighbor Jace back home is like a sister to me, but that's it. I used to have a friend group that I thought was great, but..."

"I get it. Looks like we both ended up where we were supposed to."

I lift my gaze to his. "Yeah. Guess so. I'm sorry you had people take advantage of you. No one deserves that."

He shrugs. "It is what it is. I get it. Some people grow up valuing things, not people."

"Be honest, if you're ranking things, baseball then people or people then baseball?" I tease.

He laughs. "Baseball is number one, of course."

"Somehow, I doubt that. You have too big of a heart. I bet you're a total softie older brother. You probably play games with them and read them bedtime stories."

"I'm that easy to read, huh?"

I shrug. "I don't know. You just stand out to me. It's easy to see your heart and your character."

He stares at me for a beat. "Thank you."

"So that means I'm right?"

He throws his head back. "I may have been playing a silly game with them before I left this morning. Yes, I read them bedtime stories regularly, especially to Mila. I even braid the girls' hair."

I blink at him, my heart melting a little at that. He's a good big brother. Pete might've learned that if our age difference had been bigger, but Josh? Never.

"They're lucky to have you."

"I'm lucky to have them. I'd give up baseball for my family in a heartbeat. I wouldn't like it, and I hope I never have to make a choice like that, but I would if I had to, and I'd never look back."

I slowly shake my head. "Screw anyone who ever tried to take advantage of you. I hope they get exactly what they deserve for not seeing how valuable you are."

Our eyes meet, tension growing between us.

"I hope you know how valuable you are too."

Again, he shifts closer, wrapping his arm around my back, and this time when I look up at him, I find those rich blue eyes staring back at me, gleaming with intensity.

Something stirs in my stomach.

What if I'm not the only one with a crush?

The reality is it probably doesn't matter. He's still in high school. I'm in college. We're three hours away from each other for most of the year, and when we're not, he'll be focused on baseball while I'll be focused on growing my business. Sounds like the worst way to start a relationship.

But here in this moment, alone in the dark with him, I let myself believe that's not true.

"Sometimes I feel like I'm too much for people," I admit.

"You're not too much. They just don't know how to be around someone who takes up space and opens their heart. And they're missing out. Because the way you care about the people around you is special."

My breath sticks in my throat, and I have to swallow hard before I can respond.

"How do you see right through me like that?"

He shrugs. "You saw through my mask too." And then his cheeks are smattered with red again.

I rub my thumb over the warm skin. Then there's another gust of wind, and I fully give in to the moment, leaning against Jamie and resting my head on his shoulder.

After a long moment of silence, I whisper, "Thank you. For letting me be one of your people. For the record, you're one of my people now too. I like spending time with you. You're easy to talk to—easy to be around."

Easy to fall for.

But I don't say that.

I barely let myself think it.

Whatever the connection sparking between us is, it can't go beyond this. It won't. Our lives are destined to move in different directions, no matter how undeniable the electric thrum beneath my skin is when he's touching me.

I can experience it, but I don't get to keep it.

I don't even know if he feels the same way or if I'm imagining it all.

But alone under this blanket on a chilly night, I absorb his warmth and let myself believe in the sweet little fantasy of Jamie and me being something more.

6
Unexpected Scars

Amanda

IT'S good to be home for the summer.

Or it would be if I didn't live with two stinky boys and my parents. Although technically it's just one stinky boy. Pete has his own place, yet he's always here.

When I walk into the kitchen, there are dishes everywhere, and Pete and Josh are dicking around.

Pete hits Josh with a spatula, and Josh playfully shoves him, only he does it a bit too hard, and Pete hits the kitchen table, sending orange juice spraying everywhere. Including onto my cute summer dress.

"Ugh. Really? Can you two ever behave?"

"Sorry, Mom," Josh says.

I give him the finger. "I'm not your mother. In case you forgot, I'm your *younger* sister. And somehow the most mature one here."

"Hey, I resent that," Pete says, walking over with paper towels to clean up the mess.

I snatch one from him and dab at my dress.

"Says the person who still comes over to his parents' house for every meal because he doesn't want to cook for himself."

72

"Mom likes it when I'm here."

I snort at that. "Uh huh."

"You're just jealous that she likes us better," Josh says.

He's teasing me. I know he's teasing me. He's my brother. That's what they do.

But the words cut like a knife. I know my parents love me, but those mean voices in the background love to ask if he's right.

"Don't be a dick," Pete says to him.

"Hey, I was defending you."

"And you don't have to be an ass to do it."

I put on my sassy, confident exterior. "I didn't realize Josh was capable of anything else."

He glares at me, then opens his mouth to say something, but I quickly hop over the sticky mess of orange juice on the floor and head for the back door.

"Have fun, boys. I'm meeting Rae and Jace for brunch in Binghamton. I'll see you later!"

Then I hurry out of the house before either of them can say another word.

I'm ready to go back to campus and live with my girls again.

I'M ALLOWING myself one full week of summer mode before I jump back into business mode.

I say that as I hurriedly type out a caption to the cute graphic I'm posting on my socials. Jace and Rae should be here any minute, but any extra minute is a minute to get things done.

Full week off my ass. I'd never give myself that kind of time unless I was horribly sick. Even then, I'd probably still be planning *something*. My brain never shuts up. I'm overflowing with ideas.

If someone could pay me to pitch event ideas to them and then put them on, it would be my dream job.

No sooner have I hit the bright blue button to post today's graphic when a text pops up on my screen.

From Jamie.

A little burst of excitement rushes through me.

We haven't seen each other since the weekend he came up for the baseball game, but we've texted—sometimes flirtatiously—since then. It's easy to be flirtatious with him. Easy to let my guard down, and that's not something I normally do. Especially not romantically. Though romantic might be a stretch. But there's definitely *something* between us.

BASEBALL BOY

Heard you're home for the summer. Thanks for the postcard.

> I thought people only send postcards when they travel.

BASEBALL BOY

Whatever. But seriously. You don't write. Call. Text. Send a carrier pigeon. It's like I don't matter to you at all.

> You think very highly of yourself to be worthy of the event queen's time.

BASEBALL BOY

Since I named you the event queen, I think I should jump to the top of your priority list. Don't worry. I know how you can make it up to me.

> Is it something dirty?

BASEBALL BOY

Would you like it or hate it if it was?

> Depends on what the dirty thing is. I've never tried anal, so that might be a dealbreaker.

BASEBALL BOY

Jesus Christ.

How red are your cheeks??

BASEBALL BOY

Not at all. You don't know me.

Mhm. So how dirty are we getting?

BASEBALL BOY

You? I don't know. I'll probably be plenty dirty
and sweaty tonight… I have a baseball game.
And since you owe me, I figured you might
want to come.

I get a stupid smile on my face at that. We've been joking about me going to see him pitch since we first met, but knowing he actually wants me to come makes me feel all gooey inside.

But before I can respond, my phone is yanked from my hand.

"No phones at brunch," Jace says sweetly. "Now where's the new bestie? I need to suss out the competition."

I snatch my phone back, then, resisting the urge to look at it or type a reply, I tuck it in my purse. "She should be here any minute. And there's no competition. You'll always be a sister to me."

She shakes her head. "That's just because you wanted me to marry your butt munch of a brother." She says it so smoothly, most people might not notice the hint of pain beneath it, but Jace and I have a similar shared pain. People who made us think they loved us but didn't choose us.

My ex did it to me. Josh did it to her. Dumbass. Especially because Jace is a total catch. She's sweet, smart, funny—not to mention gorgeous with her golden-brown hair and freckles.

"More like I wanted my brother to marry *you*. You were always way too good for him. I could never wish a lifetime of marriage to Josh on anyone I like."

She laughs at that, then grabs my hand. "Oh my god."

"What?" I look in the same direction and see Rae walking toward us.

Then Jace starts laughing, and the second Rae sees us, she stops and starts laughing too.

"Okay, what am I missing?"

Rae strolls over, her smile as bright and warm as the sun shining on us.

"I should've put this together," Rae says.

Jace turns to me. "You mentioned all the girls' names together, so it never registered for me, but it should have."

"What?" I ask.

"Okay, so you know how Sarah and Mackie love to pick on me about the"—she glances at Jace—"douchey guy I dated in high school to avoid my feelings for Aaron?"

"Yes. It's part of the friend group canon."

"I think I probably mentioned his first name—Davey—but not his last. Edwards."

I whip my head from Rae to Jace. My best friend and next-door neighbor. Jace *Edwards*. Then my head swivels back to Rae again. "Wait. Your douchey ex was Jace's cousin?"

Jace shrugs. "I love him, but... yeah. Unfortunately, sometimes he can be that way." She elbows me. "You know how that goes."

"Men," I huff, then shake my head, looking between them. "Were you two close at all? I guess we probably would've met if you were."

I breathe in deep and actively work to quiet the intrusive thoughts that Rae and Jace have some pre-formed bond or like each other better than they like me. It's a shitty thing to think. I hate that it even pops into my mind. But my insecurities always come to play, even when I didn't invite them.

Rae shakes her head. "I mean, we always got along and hung out at a couple of family gatherings, but we didn't really have a relationship of our own." Rae wraps her arm around my back. "I love that we have this little connection, though. Further proof that we were always supposed to meet."

And just like that, the intrusive thoughts slip away.

My friendships with Rae, Sarah, and Mackenzie—and the collective friendship we have together—have helped stop those ugly thoughts from rearing their heads so much. When you constantly have people building you up, it's harder for negative thoughts to tear you down. Their support has helped me feel stronger, and it's gotten easier for me to combat those thoughts too.

"Okay, she gets my stamp of approval," Jace says with a big smile. "Now can we please go inside? I'm starving."

"Yes, please."

AS WE'RE LEAVING the café after eating our weight in bagels, lox, stuffed French toast, and chicken and waffles, Rae loops her arm through mine.

"Are you doing anything tonight?"

"No. Why?"

"I was going to go to the high school baseball game tonight with Miles and Trevor. Want to come?"

I do my best to hide just how much that makes me smile. Jamie wanted me to see him pitch. "Yeah. Sounds good. Are you still friends with anyone on the team—besides Jamie?"

"Not really, but Aaron's helping the coach out. No matter how messy things are... I still want to support him."

I pull her a little tighter to me. "That's what makes you such an amazing friend. I'd love to go. Thanks for inviting me."

"Of course."

When we get to the parking garage, we all say our goodbyes, then split off to find our cars.

Once I'm sitting in the driver's seat, I pull my phone out and reread my conversation with Jamie from earlier. Then I send one last text back.

> Mm. Too bad I have plans tonight.

He doesn't need to know those plans are watching his baseball game with our friends. And hopefully hanging out with him after.

The voice in the back of my head reminds me that maybe I shouldn't.

But the connection between us is undeniable, and for a few months, we're both in the same place. Would it be the worst thing to have a little fun?

Jamie

SOMETIMES IT'S STILL strange being the number one starting pitcher on the team.

Since middle school, Aaron was always there. Even when he was struggling last season, he was considered the primary starter, even though I pitched more games. And with his injury, people had more questions about him than me. Sure, people paid attention to me, and to a degree, I've already made a name for myself— at least across the state—but this is the first year everyone's focus is on me. The time when everyone is realizing I don't just have a shot at the draft, but I'll be a strong contender. *No pressure.*

Aaron claps me on the shoulder and gives me a nod as I follow the guys out of the dugout to start the game. We're at home, which means we're on the field first. Some guys love hitting. That ain't me. I live for the feeling of the mound beneath my feet as I stare down a batter, ready to take control of the game and bring home the win.

Aaron holds the state record for most shutouts, but if I play right this season, I'm aiming for most wins. Arguably a harder stat to pull. Shutouts are rarer, which means you don't have to earn as many to hit that record. Pitching a shutout has never been my thing. Maybe I should care more, but I don't give a fuck if one hit slips by me. I care more if someone crosses the plate because of it —and when I'm pitching, they rarely do.

"Kick ass, Jame," my catcher, Z, says before heading to take his place.

"Thanks," I call.

Z is a year younger than me, but pretty good. He got some training in with Miles last year, which helped. Miles is so damn good it's hard to compare, but Z and I work well together. The team as a whole works well together. Unfortunately, that's where it ends for me.

Maybe I should make an effort to change that, but working well as a team is what matters. I know who my real friends are, and those are the relationships I'd rather focus on.

Miles said he and Trevor would be here tonight, so as I walk out to the mound, I glance over to the small set of bleachers next to the fence, and almost trip over my own damn feet when I see strawberry blonde hair glinting in the late afternoon sun.

I pause for half a second, just to make sure it's actually her.

Miss *mm, too bad I have plans* is sitting on the bleachers between Rae and Trevor, eyes locked on me. She arches a brow as she smirks at me, then flips a hand through her hair and looks away.

That's all it takes to remind me what I'm supposed to be doing.

Knowing that she's here kicks my adrenaline up a notch. Not my nerves. Fuck no. This is what I'm made to do, and I'm about to pitch the best game of my life to impress her.

Maybe I shouldn't want to show off for her when there's nothing going on between us, but I can't help it. Seeing her in action was mesmerizing, and I stupidly want her to watch me and feel the same way.

WE'RE ABOUT to start the top of the ninth, and I've been fighting with Coach all game to keep me in. He says I should rest my arm. He says we should let the other team have a break—since we're smoking them. Our best batters came to hit today, and I came to pitch. I've let two hits through, one of which was a home run, but I'm convinced that kid would've swung at any ball. He was fucking determined to break their no-run streak. It didn't happen until the seventh, but they haven't gotten another hit out of me yet.

I don't give a fuck if my arm is a little tired. I don't care that we're leading them seven to one. It's one more inning, and I've got three more strikeouts in me.

"C'mon, Coach. Please. Let me have this one."

"Why? It won't be a no-hitter or a shutout. What does it matter?"

I clear my throat and look at Aaron, who is staring back at me with one brow arched. I have no idea if he knows it's because Amanda is here. The connection between Amanda and me is something I haven't told anyone about—because they're a bunch of meddling meddlers who think finding your soulmate and getting married at nineteen is just what people do. *Small towns.* But Aaron is perceptive as fuck, so there's every chance he knows. He doesn't call me on it, though. Instead, he waits to see what I say to Coach.

"It proves my stamina. I'm still pitching well, and I can close out this game. It'll look good to anyone who's watching me and prove what I'm capable of."

Coach glances at Aaron, who shrugs.

"Fine. But if you injure yourself, it's on you. Got it?"

"Got it, Coach."

"All right. Get out there."

I tug my cap farther down and jog out to the mound. There

are a handful of cheers from the bleachers, but I don't look to see if Amanda is one of the ones cheering.

The only thing I need to do is close out this game. Earn the win all on my own. Yeah, yeah. Baseball is a team sport. But it starts with the pitching. Hitters aren't assigned a win or a loss at the end of the game. No infielders or outfielders have to worry if they get an extra L on their record. But pitchers do. We carry a certain responsibility for the game.

And tonight, I'm carrying us to the win.

I throw a couple of pitches with Z, then the first batter for the other team steps into the box.

Then I take a deep breath and do what I do best. My first pitch is a slider. And when the umpire calls it a strike, I smile to myself.

The thump of the ball hitting my glove sends a high through me, and I'm ready to go again. It's an easy one-two-three strikeout for this batter. Next guy up reaches for pieces of the first two pitches and fouls them off. I blatantly throw one a little high and outside, just to see if he'll reach for it. He does. If he's going to swing no matter what, I need to throw him one that'll make him miss.

So I rely on my old favorite. Two-seam fastball. And when the batter leans into the swing, I already know he's a second too late and swinging too high. When the ball lands in Z's glove, the batter walks away, muttering under his breath.

Another round of cheers come from the bleachers, but again, I focus on the plate.

Of course, it's my luck that the next batter up—the *last* batter up—is one of the best hitters on the team. He hasn't gotten anything tonight, so he's out for blood.

Z signals to me, and it's already what I was planning. There's nothing like a changeup to throw off a hungry batter.

And it does its job. It looks like a fastball coming out of my hand, but it's much slower, and when a batter is desperate for a hit, they won't be patient. They'll swing like it's a fastball and miss.

Strike one.

For the first time, I steal a glance over at the bleachers, just long enough to see Amanda's eyes locked on me.

Two more strikes.

The next pitch is a fastball that he hits but fouls off.

And that's the last ball he's touching. I'm determined now. Which means it's time to break out my specialty.

The two-seam fastball is one of my best pitches, but best isn't the same as a secret weapon. Aaron loved to throw a screwball to throw people off. Me? I mastered the cutter.

The cutter is similar to a fastball, but a little slower, and it curves the opposite direction as a two-seam. But coming out of my hand, he won't know that.

With one last nod to Z, I center myself, tune out the rest of the world, and throw.

"Strike."

Fuck. Yes.

Z and my teammates come to congratulate me, but my eyes are on the bleachers. Amanda is standing and cheering. When she sees me looking at her, she shrugs her shoulders while smiling, as if to say, *what's the big deal?*

I shake my head, and as I break free of my teammates, I snag a ball from Z and make my way to the fence.

Miles, Trevor, and Rae congratulate me on the game—though Rae's eyes quickly go to Aaron standing by the dugout. Amanda stands to the side, listening as they talk, but not saying anything.

Trying to be covert, I pull the marker I stashed in my pocket at the beginning of the inning and sign the ball I'm holding.

When Rae, Miles, and Trevor go to meet up with Aaron, Amanda lingers behind, that playful smirk creeping onto her face.

"Funny seeing you here. I thought you had plans tonight."

She shrugs. "I managed to make room in my schedule."

"And was it worth it?"

She tilts her head back and forth. "It was okay."

"Just okay?"

For a moment, there's a glimpse of sincerity on her face.

"You were amazing. I guess I get what all the hype is about now."

I clutch a hand to my chest. "Why are you always trying to hurt my feelings?"

"Someone has to keep your ego in check."

She's teasing me like we always do, but the tone of her voice makes me wonder just how much she sees.

And that's a road I don't want to go down... so I lean further into my cocky side and hold up the ball.

"Speaking of. This is for you. Might want to hold on to it. Who knows how much it'll be worth someday."

I toss it to her and she easily catches it, laughing as she looks at my signature.

"You really think a lot of yourself."

"What can I say? You showing up was an ego boost. Even if you did lie to me."

"It's not my fault you never asked what my plans were."

"And if I ask if you have plans after this?"

"I do." She leans in. "I'll be hanging out with the Ida Warriors star pitcher." She flips a hand through her hair. "Want me to get you an invite?"

She watches me as I drag my teeth over my bottom lip like I'm thinking about it. "You better."

"Henderson!" Coach yells.

"Gotta go. I'll see you in a few. Remember, hold on to that ball."

"WOW. THIS IS... MASSIVE."

Amanda blinks up at my house.

"It is, but with three younger siblings running around, it has a tendency to feel small. C'mon. This way."

I lead her around the side of the house, then key in the code on the gate that opens onto the wrap around deck. When we get around to the back of the house, I turn on the gas fire pit and flick the switch for the lantern lights.

"Hopefully, no one will bug us out here."

"Your parents don't seem that bad."

I give her a skeptical look. "Trust me. They're wild cards. Plus, if my younger siblings see you, they'll have a billion questions to ask. Especially Penny."

She sits down on an oversized outdoor loveseat, and I take a seat next to her.

"I wouldn't mind meeting them someday. If you were cool with it. Penny sounds fun."

"She is. Even if she knows exactly how to push my buttons. And I'm sure she'd love to meet you."

She tilts her head. "You know, that sounds like you're playing off the answer *she'd* love to meet me. But I said if you were cool with it."

"I'm cool with it."

Amanda slips her shoes off and extends her feet closer to the fire, wiggling her toes.

After the game, we went for dinner with Aaron, Rae, Miles, and Trevor, and I had to spend the whole night pretending Amanda wasn't across the table from me. Keeping myself from staring at her was a challenge. She draws me in. I've never felt like that before. This insatiable pull to be near her. Not to mention she's hot as fuck, sarcastic, and witty—which are also turn ons.

I want her. I want her when maybe I shouldn't. This can't go anywhere, can it? In three months, she's back at school. In a year... fuck, I don't know where I'll be. Aiming for a D1 college or headed for professional ball? I still don't know which path to take.

Sometimes I think I'm sure what would be better, then I wake up and think something else.

Amanda runs her finger down my arm, jolting me back to reality.

"Where'd you go?"

I look down at the flames. "In my own head. Introvert problems."

She laughs. "I don't know. I'm pretty extroverted, and I do that a lot too. I have a pretty entertaining internal monologue. Easy to get lost in."

"Why doesn't that surprise me?"

She shrugs, smiling brightly. Mischief dances in her eyes, and I want more. I want to know more.

"So, tell me something about you."

She gestures to herself. "What you see is what you get."

"That doesn't mean I've seen everything yet. What do you do for fun? What's a secret you don't tell many people? I don't know, I just want to know more."

I want to know everything.

Saying that feels dangerous though.

"Okay, for fun... Rae and I started doing kickboxing together in January and I love it. It's been great for my strength and stamina, but also my mental health. My favorite thing to do before I go to sleep is curl up under my blankets with a cup of tea and read. Total granny hobby, but the relaxed side of me is a bit of a granny."

"It's good to have balance."

"I'm striving for that. I tend to overwork myself and not slow down. Hanging out with the girls has helped with that. For how much they have going on, they're surprisingly good at balancing it all."

"So kickboxing, reading, reigning as the event queen. What else? Do you spend a lot of time with your family?"

"What those three things aren't enough? Actually, make it four. I also play volleyball. I played in high school and I do a rec league during the summers. I'm excited for it to start this year. As for my family... I don't know. We're close, and we do a couple of family trips each year, but with my oldest brother out of the house now, a lot of that stuff is few and far between. I know I can always rely on my parents, but we don't seek each other out to do stuff other than monthly family dinners."

There's something haunted in her eyes when she talks about her family. Even though it quickly fades, I want to know more.

"I hate seeing that look in your eyes."

"What look?"

"It's like a deep, permeating sadness. It never lasts long, but I get the sense it's always inside you."

She clears her throat. "That's very perceptive."

"That's the story of an introvert. We're always watching what's happening around us, even when we aren't saying anything."

"It makes me wonder what else you see." *So much.* But she continues before I can say anything. "I've had my heart broken, and it leaves unexpected scars."

I don't know who the fuck would ever break her heart, but they must be the biggest idiot on the planet. How could someone not know what they have when they have her? She's so honest. So genuine. And while all of her is gorgeous, her heart is fucking stunning.

"What about you, baseball boy?"

I stare at her for a beat longer, then let go of the rest of the questions I want to ask her.

There'll be time for those later.

Or there won't be, in which case, it'll be better that I didn't ask them.

"What about me?"

"What drives you?" She sighs heavily. "Let me guess. Baseball?"

I can't help but laugh. "I'm a simple man."

"Boy," she teases.

"I'll be eighteen in three weeks. *Man*."

"But baseball *boy* has a better ring to it."

"I'll always let you call me that, event queen."

She tilts her head. "I think I just like *queen*. Ooh, or you can call me *Your Majesty*."

I bite back the first thing that pops into my head.

Only in the bedroom.

Because fuck. I should not be thinking of Amanda like that. Except I couldn't stop myself if I wanted to. I'd rather beat off to thoughts of her for the rest of my life than ever look at porn again.

Amanda elbows me. "Come on. Tell *me* something. What's your secret? What don't you share with your family or the chaos of the hive mind?"

"Okay," I say slowly. I don't really talk about this with anyone. I probably should, but it's hard for me to not act totally confident about baseball. "I don't know what the hell I'm doing."

She turns on the loveseat so she's facing me, tucking her feet underneath her.

"What do you mean?"

"I have a lot of decisions to make about baseball over the next year, and it's scary as fuck. I have no idea where to start or how to handle it. I read blog posts and shit online, but it mostly confuses me more."

"What are you struggling with the most?"

"Whether to go to college or hope for—push toward—the draft."

"What do you want to do?"

"I'm not sure that matters."

Her brows pull in. "I think that's the only thing that matters."

"Not necessarily. It needs to be the best career decision for me."

"Do you truly believe—throw that cocky shit in the fire because I need the real Jamie to answer this. Do you believe you can make it to the majors either way?"

"Yes." Because no matter what path I take, I will learn and

grow and prove myself. I'm committed to this dream, and I'll see it through on any path.

"Then it's not really about a career decision. It's about what will make you happy. So take some time and figure out what you want. Only you can decide that."

I stare at her for a moment. "That's very wise."

"Obviously. I'm brilliant." She gives me her biggest smile.

"You're something." But brilliant doesn't begin to cover it. I let out a long breath. "Thanks for coming to watch me play tonight."

"Thanks for inviting me. I would've come either way, and I'm glad I did. Watching you play tonight was fun. Special. Your talent is clear, but it's the way your love of the game shines through that sets you apart. I've seen Joel play and Aaron coach, but this was different. You belong on the field."

"Thank you. That means a lot coming from you."

"Because I'm such a die-hard baseball fan?" she deadpans.

I shift closer, my gaze roaming over her gorgeous features. Her eyes are light brown with a shimmery bronze glint. Like everything else about her, they captivate me.

Her question, though playful, dances in my mind with varying answers. The bantery, flirtatious answer or the serious one.

When I look into her eyes, it's impossible to give her anything except total honesty.

"Because you're passionate. You work hard at what you do, and there's no doubt you'll achieve every goal you set, then raise the bar higher. That you see something similar in me means a lot."

Her eyes lock on mine, and slowly, she moves closer to me, like she's caught in my orbit and can't help but be pulled in.

When she speaks again, her voice is low. "You've only seen me at one event. I'm not sure that's enough to know—"

"It is. Take the compliment. I mean it. You know what I thought as I watched you flawlessly run that event?"

"Hm?"

"That you were mesmerizing. And you were. Brilliant and charming and one step ahead of every problem." She opens her mouth to say something, but I keep going. "But at the event isn't the only thing I'm talking about."

"What do you mean?"

"Tonight, at dinner, I noticed you tapping away on your phone, and when I caught a glimpse, I realized it was a lengthy to-do list. Then, I noticed you scribbling some design on a piece of paper you dug out of your purse. You're always thinking, always planning, but you're also paying attention. You were constantly glancing at Rae, making sure she was okay, making sure she didn't need you to jump in or change the subject, and I saw every time you reached for her hand or said something to make her laugh right when she needed it. I saw you reach for Trevor's hand when he was talking about a possible future in baseball and how sad he is that his dad is missing all of it. Yes, you're passionate about what you do, but you're also passionate about the people in your life. You care about them. And everything you do is done with intention. That's rare. I hope you see that." I lift my hand and tuck a few strands of hair behind her ear. "I hope you know how special you are."

Her chest rises and falls with heavy breaths as she stares at me.

"You noticed all that?" Her voice is soft and raw.

Her gaze connects with mine, and I'm moving closer without realizing.

"It's impossible not to notice you. You stand out, like a shining light in the darkness. Like a bold splash of color. My eyes are always drawn to you."

I comb my fingers through her hair as my eyes drop to her lips.

Her fingertips dance over my arm, lighting a fire beneath my skin. A fire that burns through my whole body, propelling me forward, until her breath is on my lips.

"Jamie..."

The desperation in her voice makes me lose all control, and I slant my mouth over hers, doing what I've wanted to do since that night we sat on the floor eating sushi.

Her lips move against mine, then her tongue drags over the seam, and I take the invitation.

And when her tongue touches mine? Holy fuck.

I've kissed a lot of girls. It's no secret I like to hook up.

But this?

No. This isn't kissing. This is cracking my ribcage open and exposing what's beating inside there.

And that's something I've never felt. Never done.

Her soft lips move against mine, her tongue playfully teasing me, and all I can think is that I want more. So much more.

More of her. More of us.

Except. Fuck me. There isn't any us. There can't *be* any us.

What the fuck am I doing?

I can't give her what she deserves. I can't give her all of me.

Which means I shouldn't be doing this.

Amanda

JAMIE'S satiny lips violently tear from mine.

When I lift my eyes to meet his, the cozy warmth I was surrounded in shatters and falls away. Coldness seeps in, and before he can say I word, I jolt backward.

He extends a hand toward me. "I'm sorry."

And even though I told myself I knew nothing could happen. Even though I was ready to just have fun... those words break something inside me.

"I shouldn't have..." He opens and closes his mouth a few times, searching for something to say, but it's pointless. "You're incredible," he stammers. "But baseball has to be my focus right now. I don't have anything else to give."

I nod as I stand and smooth out my clothes, holding my head high and keeping my face a stoic mask to hide the pain shooting through me, aiming straight for my heart. I don't know when I got so caught up in him, but it was a mistake. Fuck crushes. Fuck people who make you think they want you, then change their minds. Fuck love. I'll stick to hook ups. That's what I should've done this whole time. The second I felt anything for Jamie, I should've put distance between us. That's on me.

"I'm sorry. I shouldn't have done that."

Kissing me when he knew he wouldn't choose me is on him.

I glance down at him one last time. "No. You shouldn't have."

Then I walk away, keeping my shaky legs strong.

"Amanda," he calls after me, but I don't look back.

He may not have been trying to hurt me, but I got the message loud and clear. There's chemistry between us, but chemistry is nothing compared to love. His first love will always be baseball, and there's no chance I'd ever compete with that.

I'M exhausted when I get home. Thanks to the makeup wipes I keep in my purse, I don't look like a raccoon anymore, but my eyes are still red and puffy. I hate that I cried over him. That I gave him that power.

It takes me a minute to climb out of the car. I just want to magically teleport to my bed where I can wallow for the night, then get up in the morning, put my big girl panties on, and move forward.

None of the friend group needs to know about this. Even though it's unlike me to keep things from the girls, I kept my crush on Jamie a secret because that whole group likes to meddle —not that I can say anything, I meddle for them too—and I didn't want to deal with that.

It's for the better now. We can move on. I can play the friendly part when I have to with Jamie. Otherwise, I don't plan to talk to him anymore.

When I get in the house, the first thing I hear is my brothers talking.

Ugh. The last thing I want is to deal with other humans right now.

"That's what you get for being a dick, Joshy," Pete says, laughing as Josh swears at him.

They're splayed out on the living room couches playing video games.

"Hey, Mands," Pete says, but when he looks up at me, his brow furrows. "Are you okay?"

Josh looks up too, and it's a fifty-fifty chance on whether he says something that makes me want to punch him or if he threatens to beat someone up for me.

And I can't handle either one, so I turn around and walk out the back door, down the steps, across the lawn to Jace's house, then climb onto the doors of the storm cellar like I've done hundreds of times, and knock on Jace's window.

The latch unclicks, and that's all the invitation I need to open it and climb through.

I shut it behind me, then slip off my shoes and climb into bed next to Jace.

"What happened?" she whispers.

"Remind me to stop catching feelings for people who don't actually want me."

Jace rolls over and wipes a tear off my cheek.

"If they don't choose you, they don't deserve you."

She squeezes my hand then rolls onto her back again. I repeat those words over and over as I stare at the ceiling, trying to reinforce my self-worth. But as I drift off to sleep, it's the thrumming ache of rejection that surrounds me.

7
Stupid Boy

Jamie

THERE'S an endless barrage of sounds around me as I stare out into my backyard. People are talking, glasses are clinking, my siblings are shrieking down by the swing set, and people are walking back and forth all around me.

It's my birthday party, and yet I'm the least festive one here.

Of course, big gatherings plus being an introvert aren't the best combination, but these are all people I like. And I'm having fun. I am. But the problem is I'm painfully aware of who's not here.

It's been almost a month since that night sitting just a few feet away on this deck with Amanda. Since I realized I had feelings for her and blew my chances with her all in one fell swoop.

I thought I had to stop things because I couldn't have it all. When I leaned in to kiss her, I didn't realize how deep my feelings ran. Then our lips met and everything snapped into focus. I thought it was just a crush—an infatuation that would fade in time. I thought she felt the same. But I was wrong on all counts. I had feelings for her. I *have* feelings for her. Worse, it seems like she had feelings for me, and I hurt her. Right after I thought I couldn't imagine how anyone could ever let her go, I did exactly that, and the gut-wrenching heartbreak in her eyes is something that will haunt me forever.

I spent the next week trying to come to terms with that, while kicking myself for crossing that line. For screwing things up. In the weeks since, I haven't stopped thinking about it—or her. All I want is to fix things with her, but I'm not sure what fixing it would mean. Even if I did, it doesn't matter because she refuses to answer any of my texts. I haven't even bothered trying to call because if she hasn't responded to any of my apologies over text, she isn't going to answer her phone for me.

"Hey." I almost jump when Aaron claps me on the shoulder. He hands me a soda as he points at me. "Are you having fun?"

"Yeah."

He laughs. "Wow. That was convincing."

"Fuck off."

"You're so nice to me. Now, come on. Tell me what's wrong."

"I'm an idiot."

"Sure. But why this time?"

"Have I mentioned you're going to be a great guidance counselor one day?" I deadpan.

That's what Aaron is studying now, and he's enjoying himself. It's a perfect fit for him. He's great with people. He's kind, and he's a good listener. Of course, with his friends, he's also a shit-giving pain in the ass.

"What a shining vote of confidence."

I roll my eyes, then look back out over the side of the deck.

Aaron grabs me by the arm and drags me away from everyone. "Seriously. What's up? Are you bummed about turning eighteen? Usually people are pumped about that."

"No. I mean, it doesn't really matter to me. I've felt like an adult for a while now." That's the fun of committing your life to making it in professional sports, always hanging out with people who are older than you, and having three young siblings. You grow up faster when you're surrounded by responsibility.

"Then what's going on? I know big parties are hard for you sometimes, but you don't usually look like this."

"Like what?"

"Like you want to punch something. Or cry. Or both."

I blow out a breath. "I'm not that dramatic. I just... messed up. And I'm kicking my own ass about it now."

His brow furrows. "Something with baseball?" Of course that's exactly what he'd think. It's what anyone would think. That's what I get for making baseball most of my personality.

"No. With Amanda."

I meet his gaze, watching as his eyebrows go up. "Amanda, huh?"

"Look, before you jump into meddling mode—"

"I'm not going to jump into meddling mode. That's reserved for the rest of the friend group. Or if you're being an absolute idiot and need a kick in the ass."

I rub my hand over my face. "I might."

"What happened?"

I tell him, and the way he winces as I finish talking, confirms what I already knew. No Reddit post needed here, folks. I am the asshole.

"What do I do now?"

"That depends on what you want to happen—why you're upset. If you're upset you hurt a friend by crossing the line, time and space are probably going to be key in salvaging that."

"And if I hurt my own feelings too?"

He sighs. "What do you want from her, Jame?"

Everything.

Fuck. That's what I think every time I ask myself that question.

"I want what I can't have."

He narrows his eyes. "You want her *because* you can't have her or you realized what you wanted too late?"

I look down, kicking at a small rock on the edge of the deck. "The second one."

"So, what was all that shit a few weeks ago?"

Right. The weekend after what happened with Amanda, the guys and I were going out to the Baseball Hall of Fame in Cooperstown, and as we do, we were giving each other shit. Aaron asked me something about Amanda and I made some dumb joke about going home with blue balls every time I was around her—not totally untrue because everything about her is a turn on—after I doubled down on the *I can't have a relationship because of baseball* thing.

Aaron told me not to sideline the rest of my life for baseball, and that's part of what made me text Amanda my fourth apology —and also sent me spinning over the fact that maybe I *can* have what I want. That I can have more than baseball. I've spent the past three weeks turning that over and over, feeling like a dick, wondering if there's even a sliver of hope, and living with the ache of missing Amanda.

"Me being a dumbass."

"Clearly."

"Again I ask, what do you want from her?"

"I want to be with her," I mumble.

"You're going to need to sound a hell of lot more certain than that if you talk to her."

"I want to be with her... but is that crazy? We're apart most of the year. Who knows where baseball will take me this time next year? How can I get wrapped up in a relationship that's destined to be difficult from the start?"

Aaron stares at me for a moment, then folds his arms over his chest. "Did baseball come easily to you? Did you immediately know you wanted to be a pitcher? Were you automatically the best?"

"Of course not. You know that."

"And yet you're one of the top high school pitchers, not just in New York, and you have a strong chance at being drafted next year. How did you get from there to here?"

"I worked my ass off."

"And was it worth it?"

"Obviously, it was worth it."

His arms drop to his sides. "Just like anything worth having is."

Damn.

That was a perfect four-seam fastball right in the middle of my zone and I totally fucking missed it. Hell, I didn't even swing.

"If you want to be with her, you have to fight for that. You can build a relationship over distance—in a lot of different situations—every single day. But you have to want to. And all those people out there who say relationships mess with your head? Fuck that. Not good relationships. Not healthy ones. And if you build it right, that's what you'll have. You'll have something—someone—that bolsters you as you step on the mound each time. But you have to decide whether that's what you want, and if you're willing to put the work in to have it."

"It's annoying that you're always right. How do you do that?"

He grins at me. "Easy. By fucking up and learning along the way." He smacks my shoulder. "Come on. Let's go take your mind off it. I can rally everyone for a wiffle ball game."

"Yeah. Okay. That sounds fun. Thanks. I'm going to run inside for a second, but I'll meet you out back."

"Sounds good."

He heads for the deck stairs, while I open the sliding door, walk inside, and take the stairs down to the lower level.

When I get to the bar area downstairs where there's another refrigerator, I pull it open and smile to myself.

I look around, then quickly pull one of the cupcakes off the stacked trays in the fridge, and lick some of the icing off as I close the door.

"You're not supposed to eat those until later."

I clutch a hand to my rapidly beating heart as Penny stands there, arms crossed.

"Give me a heart attack, kid. Jeez."

"You're breaking the rules."

"It's my birthday. I can do what I want." She stares at me. "And if I give you half, you'll have no reason to tell anyone."

She stares at me for another beat, then breaks into a wide smile as she holds out her hand. "Your secret is safe with me."

I hand her half the cupcake. "Pleasure doing business with you."

We walk over to the nearby couch and sit down, both licking at the frosting on our cupcakes.

"So, why are you sneaking cupcakes?"

I shrug. "I was feeling sad and wanted something to make me feel better."

"Mm. Yeah. Cupcakes are good at that. But why are you sad? It's your birthday. Did someone steal one of your presents?"

I chuckle at that. "No. I made a mistake."

"What kind of mistake?"

"I hurt Amanda's feelings."

Penny's brow furrows. "Well then, you should feel bad."

"Yeah. The thing is, I *really* hurt her feelings, and she doesn't want to talk to me anymore."

"Oh."

"Yeah."

"Did you apologize?"

"I tried, but she won't answer me."

"Why did you fight?"

I run my free hand through my hair, then take another bite of my cupcake. "That's complicated, but—"

"Did she want to date you?"

I frown at that. How is she so perceptive?

"Maybe. The thing is, I did something I shouldn't have—"

"Did you kiss someone else?" she asks, horrified at the thought.

"No, but... it doesn't really matter. What matters is that I want to date her, but now she won't talk to me."

"Hm."

She takes another bite of her cupcake, and I do the same. We eat in silence until we're both finished, then she brushes the crumbs from her hands, dabs her mouth with a napkin, and stares me down.

"You need to grovel."

I choke on a laugh. "What? Where did you learn that word?"

"I overheard my teacher talking to one of the other teachers during lunch. Her boyfriend did something really bad, and she said if he was going to get her back, he'd have to grovel. So I think you should probably do that."

Damn. I'm starting to think everyone else in this family—or my life—is smarter than me.

"Any suggestions on how to do that?"

She shrugs. "I don't know. But *not* flowers. My teacher threw those in the garbage and then grumbled something about how he didn't even show up in person."

Wow. I'm a little worried about her teacher right now. Maybe I should mention something to Mom about getting the teacher some chocolate from Penny. Seems like she needs it.

Which brings me back to Amanda.

I need to apologize to her in person. The question is, how do I do that when she refuses to see me?

"Can I go back and play now?"

"Yeah. Thanks for the advice." I hold my hand up for a high five and she smacks it.

"Any time."

Then she runs out the back door, leaving me to figure out what the hell I'm doing.

Out back, I see Aaron and Joel setting up the bases.

Nothing like baseball—or wiffle ball—to help me figure it out.

I run upstairs to change into some more comfortable clothes, and as I'm walking through the kitchen on the way back to the deck, something on the bulletin board catches my eye.

An event invitation for this Thursday, and at the bottom is Amanda's name and a logo with the words *Event Queen.*

We connected while deconstructing an event together. If we're in that small of a space, she can't avoid me all night. I can apologize in person. Then I'll help her take everything down, buy her more sushi, and apologize some more. Looks like I better find a good suit for Thursday night.

Amanda

I LOVE BEING in the middle of an event. My brain settles in the chaos, picking apart every little thing that needs to be done and handling it. I go into a weird kind of autopilot and just do all the things. It makes me feel powerful and makes time pass in a second. Yeah, I'll crash tonight like I always do after an event, but hey, at least there was room in the budget to hire setup and take down for this one so I can just focus on running it.

When I got the call about the event from a friend of Marissa's, I was instantly on guard, wondering if Jamie had something to do with it—since it happened less than twenty-four hours after that night on his deck. It quickly became clear it had nothing to do with him, though, and I've been grateful ever since. This has given me something to focus on for the last month that doesn't have to do with baseball or a stupid boy who plays it.

That's what I changed his name to in my phone. *Stupid boy*.

Something kept me from blocking him, even though by his third apology attempt I wanted to.

Who apologizes over text?

People who don't mean it.

I tend to think I'm the problem a lot. I blame myself when I shouldn't and think there's something wrong with me.

Slowly, over the last few months, I've gotten better about not doing that. Having a big supportive friend group helps, but I also have a fuck around and find out button, and when someone pushes it, I go into angry, cut-a-bitch mode. My glare could kill you from across the room, so watch out. Most of the time it's for my friends, but when someone really hurts me, that hardened version of me takes over to protect myself.

It's not that I carry myself angrily, but when the person who hurt me comes around, my walls go up. As much for their protection as mine.

A quick check-in with the caterers tells me everything is going well there, so I head out to the main event area to check in with the host. This is the launch party for a small, female-owned legal practice, and I'm honored to be a part of it. They were trying to plan the party themselves before they threw up the white flag and called me. Apparently, Marissa had been recommending me for months. I should send her a thank you note, since I don't think they're here tonight.

But when I spin around, I second-guess that and everything else. Because staring at me from across the room, looking stupidly hot in a suit, is Jamie Henderson.

I close my eyes, take a breath, and steel myself. Walls in place.

He can't hurt me. I don't know why he's here, and I don't care. I have a job to do, and that's more important than a stupid boy.

THE ONLY THING I hate about event planning is having to squeeze in time to eat. If I don't eat regular meals, I turn into a raging monster until the inevitable blood sugar crash that leaves me shaking and nauseous. Unfortunately, power bars taste like dirt and leave me feeling hungry thirty minutes later, so I usually end up hiding in the kitchen and stuffing my face during a lull in the event.

Super sexy, but it's better than me losing my shit or fainting because my blood sugar is dropping to the bad place.

One of the catering crew sets a bottle of water in front of me and gives me an understanding smile.

"Thanks," I murmur as I reach for it, then glug down half at once.

The event wraps up in a little under an hour, so this is the last lull.

Once I've finished eating and drinking, I take a few deep breaths, use the nearby bathroom, and touch up my makeup, but when I walk out of the bathroom, I collide with a hard body, and when hands land on my arm, I don't have to look to know who it is.

I jump back, shield firmly in place, and glare up at Jamie. "What are you doing here?"

I get his charming boyish grin in return. "I was invited."

"Your parents were invited." I know because I checked the list, so I could prepare myself if his name was on it.

"Well, I borrowed their invitation and came in their place. Penny had a dance recital tonight, so they couldn't make it."

"That's nice for Penny. I'm sure she'd rather you were there too."

I go to move past him, but he shifts slightly so he's in my path again.

"Actually, she wanted me to be here."

I snort at that. "Really?"

"She wants me to make up with you."

"Uh huh. Look, I need to get back—"

"She does. Because she knows how much it means to me. How much you mean to me."

"Well, I'm glad your sister knows. Does she also know you're a liar? Because how you acted doesn't say I mean anything to you."

"I'm sorry."

"Sorry for kissing me? Or sorry for leading me on and making me feel like you wanted me when you didn't?"

"Both."

"Great. We're done now. Bye."

I shove past him, but he grabs my arm and spins me back around.

"I'm sorry I hurt you. I didn't mean to lead you on. I'm sorry for kissing you the way I did—without thinking it through first. Without realizing how much you mean to me."

I bite back a bitter laugh as I clench my hand into a fist. "So now that you don't have me anymore, you suddenly realize how much you want me? You know Passenger wrote a pretty great song about that. I'm pretty sure they still play it on the radio about a billion times a day. *Let Her Go.* Give it a listen, cry your feelings out, then move on. Because we're done."

"You don't understand." He shoves his hand through his hair. "Fuck. I thought we were having fun. Until I kissed you, and realized the feelings I have for you could never just be about fun. So I stopped it because I didn't want to lead you on. Baseball has been my focus for most of my life. I didn't think it was fair to you to offer any part of me if I couldn't give you all of me. I thought it had to be either or."

"And you chose baseball."

"Yes, but... baseball is a part of me. But every day I go without talking to you, I realize how much you became a part of my life. How much I looked forward to every conversation with you. Every glance from you. Every touch." He takes my hand, and for some stupid reason, I let him. "I thought I had to choose, but I realized I don't want to. I can't promise you it'll be easy, but I want to try. Let me take you on a date. Please."

I stare at him for a moment, then yank my hand away. "So, let me get this straight. You had to kiss me to figure out you wanted me. Then you had to miss me to realize you wanted to date me enough to make room for me in your life. Now you're crashing the event where I'm *working*, begging me to go out on a date with you because *now* you know what you want?"

"And to apologize," he says quickly.

"I don't need your apologies. You cannot just come here in the middle of an event that I'm running and bring in all this personal shit. How would you feel if I stormed the mound in the middle of a game? Would that be okay?"

He looks down. "No."

"You're damn right it wouldn't. You had a month where you could've come to see me in person, but all you did was *text* me. Not even a phone call. So forgive me if your apology doesn't come off as sincere."

"But it is. I know I made a mistake. I know doing this would be complicated, but I'm in. I'll do whatever I have to do. Please, give me a chance to fix this. To show you how much you mean to me."

I slowly shake my head, channeling every bit of strength I have to keep from crying. "I did this once. I fell for someone who could never quite choose me. Not the way they were supposed to. I believed all the pretty words she told me, and I ended up with a shattered heart because of it. You can say you're sorry a hundred more times, and that's not going to make me believe it. Your words don't mean anything to me anymore. If you want me to believe you're interested in me, you're going to have to prove it with your actions." He opens his mouth, but I straighten up, hardening my expression. "But it won't be tonight. It won't be here. I have a job to do, and you need to leave."

Then, like I did a month ago, I walk away with my head held high, because I am done with stupid people playing stupid games. I'm better than that. I deserve more than that, and I'm not sacrificing my self-worth for some pretty words. If his heart is hurting and he wants me that badly, he can man up and prove it.

8

I'm the Asshole

Jamie

I GROAN as I roll over in bed, my head pounding with a hangover level of headache despite not having a drop to drink.

Last night did not go well.

I'm a fucking idiot. Again.

Why did I think I could waltz into that event like Prince Charming and Amanda would just fall all over me? I can't waltz. And Prince Charming is way smoother than I'll ever be.

Which is obvious by how hard she shut me down.

She was right. I should've called her over the last month. I should've made a real effort to apologize. And I shouldn't have tried to do it at her work.

I can't even imagine how I'd feel if someone ever did as she pointed out and marched up to the mound in the middle of a game to apologize to me. I'd lose the respect of the team and my coaches.

Add that to the list of things I'm going to apologize for.

Things I'm going to show her I'm sorry for.

Because I'm not giving up.

No matter how it might look, I'm sure about my feelings for

her. It's not that it took me kissing her to realize how much she means to me. I already valued her as a person and as a friend. I felt a connection to her. I stupidly thought maybe we could take advantage of that friendship and enjoy each other in a different way, but when we kissed, I realized that *connection* is because of feelings that have taken root somewhere deep inside me.

Either way, I should've talked to her before I kissed her, but that desperation for her is what pulled me in. Spending a month without her name lighting up my phone, without seeing her in the bleachers at any of my games, or without seeing her mischievous smile, has been hell.

She has so much vibrance inside her, and I hate myself for taking away even a piece of it.

It's also clear that connection between us wasn't just my feelings for her, but also her feelings for me.

Feelings I disrespected, which hurt her. I'm not going to be dramatic and say I broke her heart, but I definitely broke something special between us and maybe put the tiniest crack in her heart.

All of it has to be fixed. All of it has to be healed.

And it will be.

As soon as I figure out where to start.

If our conversation last night was any indication, this won't be easy—or quick. Not that it should be.

Last night wasn't groveling. It was the desperate apology of a boy.

I'm going to man up and tackle this like an adult. If I want a real relationship to grow between us, I've got to plant seeds and water them—not a sex joke.

Amanda deserves to be shown not just how sorry I am or how much I want her, but how special she is.

She's amazing, and any guy—any person—would be lucky to have her. I have the whole damn world to compete with. Luckily, competition motivates me. Not as much making things right—better—with Amanda does.

Now I have to figure out how.

And I think I know the perfect person to ask.

"OUCH." I rub the back of my head where Trevor smacked me.

He sits back down in his chair across the table from me, arms folded over his chest. "You're lucky that's all I did. After everything you just told me, you're lucky I don't kick your ass for hurting Amanda. She's awesome. You were a dick."

Something like a growl rumbles in the back of my throat.

Wow. It's safe to say my feelings for Amanda are on a whole new level. I've never felt possessive over anyone before. Never wanted to claim them as mine. Suddenly I understand how Aaron is with Rae in a way I never have before.

"I know I was a dick. That's why I'm here. I need your help."

While Aaron might love Rae and has done a lot of things that make her—as she says—*swoon*, they're a mess, so I don't fully trust his judgment on this one. But Trevor dated Sarah for like three years in high school. Even though they broke up, it's not because he did anything wrong, it was because as they got older, they realized it wasn't the right fit. While they were together, though, I remember Trevor always going above and beyond to do things for her and setting the example of what a good boyfriend should be.

I've decided that's how I'm going to treat this. Like Amanda is my girlfriend. Call it manifestation or setting up the right play, but it's what I'm doing.

She deserves to be treated like the queen she is, and unless she looks me in the eyes and says no, I'm going to be the one to do it.

"I'm not going to talk to her for you," Trevor says, looking out the large picture window next to us. We're at a sandwich shop in downtown Ida—The Pit—which is owned by one of our friend's family. "This isn't seventh grade, and also I don't think you deserve to be defended."

"Thanks for kicking me while I'm down, but I'm not asking you to talk to her. I need help with ideas. She said she's not going to believe any apology I make—"

"Fair."

"But that I need to show her. And I want to. I'm just stuck on where to start."

He grumbles. "Fine. But just for that, you're buying me dessert too."

"Whatever you want. Just help me. I'll get on my knees and beg."

He arches a brow, a smirk breaking through his grumpy expression. "No offense, but you're not the kind of redhead I want on their knees in front of me."

I squint at him. "You don't have a thing for Amanda, do you?"

"No, jackass. And that's not the kind of red hair I'm picturing." He looks lost in thought for a moment before he snaps out of it. "But yeah. Fine. I'll help you. Where do you want to start?"

"I don't know. That's why I'm asking you for help. There's no hope for me if I can't get her to let me in. But I don't know where to start."

"You need to reconnect with her."

"Obviously. But how do I do that if she won't talk to me or do anything besides glare at me from across the room? Help me. Teach me. Explain it to me like I'm stupid."

The derisive look he gives me tells me there's no *like* about it.

I'm a fucking idiot.

Like I don't already know that.

"If you want her to open up, you need to meet her where she is."

"Literally?" I ask, and he looks like he might strangle me.

"Find what's important to her and figure out how to... I don't know. Get involved? Give that special thing to her—not a metaphor for your dick, by the way. I can't do all the work for you."

"Okay. I get it. I'm thinking I should ease into it. Maybe thaw things between us first before I try to talk to her again. So I want to start with something where she doesn't have to see me, but will know I'm thinking about her." He opens his mouth, but I cut him off. "Not flowers. Penny nixed those. They're too impersonal, apparently."

"Okay..."

"I like the general idea though. I was thinking coffee, but unless I know where she's going to be, I can't just have someone randomly deliver her a coffee."

Trevor tilts his head back and forth. "She does love coffee. And she's a sucker for a latte, which means she'll be going to a coffee shop. You just need to figure out her favorite place. Lucky for you, she posts a bunch on her Instagram."

I wince. "Yeah. Uh, she might've unfriended me and removed me as a follower on all social media. I requested again, but she hasn't approved it."

Trev stares at me for a moment, then sighs and grabs his phone. After tapping the screen a few times, he holds it out to me. But just as I'm about to grab it, he lifts his hand. "Don't make me regret helping you with this. Fix things with her. And so help me God, if you hurt her, it won't just be me kicking your ass. I'll get all the guys to help—actually, scratch that, I'll get all the girls to help. You know how ferally protective they are of each other."

"Noted," I say, taking the phone. "I'm not going to fuck it up."

Again.

Amanda

BEWITCHED Books and Coffee might be my favorite place in the world.

It's a tiny little shop just outside of town in Woods Junction.

They have a fun selection of books in the romance and fantasy genres, including a lot of indie authors. I came to a signing here last year and met two amazing local authors, who I've since read the entire backlists of and am trying not to stalk too hard on social media.

But the best part is that they make delicious lattes. The coffee part of the shop isn't the main selling point, so most people just looking for a good cup don't come here. They hit one of the chain places or stop into—the also fabulous—Mixed Brews in nearby Lacy Creek. One of my favorite things to do is wander the aisles here while I sip on an iced pistachio shortbread latte with pistachio cold cream. It's the best.

Last night was a fiasco. Not the event—that went amazing, and I had several people ask for my information—but Jamie.

Who in their right mind thinks it's okay to bring personal drama to where someone is working? Ugh.

Boys.

Men.

Who needs them?

Although, that's when someone inevitably says they should just be a lesbian, and since the first person to break my heart was female, I can confidently say that doesn't solve problems.

What does solve problems? Books and coffee. Works every time.

Jace holds the door open for me as we walk into Bewitched. I've barred her from mentioning anything relating to Jamie, so we can be centered here in the holy ground.

Jace orders her drink, then I order mine, but as I give the woman working at the counter my name, her eyebrows go up.

"You come in here a lot, right?"

My cheeks heat a little. "Yes."

"Well, we appreciate that. It seems like someone else knows too. At least, if you're Amanda Hamilton."

"That's me," I say in confusion.

"Perfect. Your drink is already paid for."

I squint and look at Jace, who shrugs.

"There's a tab open here for you... it's enough to get a nice drink every day for at least a month," the woman behind the counter says, looking at the screen.

"Does it say who it's from?" I ask.

"I don't have a name here—not a real one."

"What does it say?"

"Baseball boy..."

Damn him.

This is my safe space. This is...

What is this?

"Okay, thank you," I say, then let Jace pull me away from the counter.

Stupid Jamie Henderson, crashing my sacred space to give me one of my favorite things. Everyone who knows me knows how much I love coffee. You have to really pay attention to know where I like to get it from though.

But the thing is, I don't remember ever mentioning this place. Maybe he assumed?

"So... baseball boy, huh?"

"Shut up. We agreed. No talking about *him.*"

"But you're thinking about him."

"I never said I couldn't do that." It wasn't my plan, but he interrupted my plans to stew in my anger by doing something one could consider sweet.

That I want to consider sweet.

It's not quite an apology. But it's better than anything else he's done in the last month.

We grab our lattes when they're ready, and make our way around the store, checking what's new and seeing if there are any new signed copies.

When I see a particularly cute display of blind date with a book options, I snap a picture, getting a piece of my coffee cup in the shot too. It's not until I've uploaded it to my social media that

I realize I've done that same thing in this shop many times. But when I go to my follower requests, Jamie is still in there. Which means... he found someone else and went through my account on their phone? Because even though I've been planning to bring the girls here for a girls' day coffee and shopping adventure, I haven't told them how often I come here. The only way he could've gotten the information was to find it himself.

And that changes something inside me. I look down at the coffee in my hand.

I asked him to show me.

One little thing like this doesn't fix anything. It doesn't make it better. It doesn't mean he'll follow through. But it melts away a tiny piece of my anger, and that's something.

THOUGH A PART of me wanted to go get my prepaid coffee all weekend long, I didn't want to take advantage. What Jamie did was meaningful, but if some paid-for coffee is all there is, that feeling would fade. By Monday, though, I gave in and went again. When I did, not only was my coffee paid for, but so was one of their homemade brownies with a handwritten note from Jamie.

He drove all the way there to leave me a note.

I've been trying not to overthink what it means—that he'd leave me a note rather than just come see me when he's already in Woods Junction. He doesn't know where I live, but he could've easily gotten my address from one of the girls.

But the note was cute and sweet.

I know this brownie might not be quite as good as Rae's, but any brownie is a good one, right? When you're savoring every chocolatey bite, I want you to

*know that how you feel when you eat a brownie is how
I feel when I'm with you. Comfortable, safe, like
nothing else is wrong in the world.*
  —Jamie

Another bit of my anger melted away when I read that. When I went in again on Thursday, there was another surprise. This one was a specially requested blind date with a book. One with a baseball playing hero who screws up with the girl he cares about and has to grovel.

I smiled like an idiot when I saw that description.

Anger is harder to hold on to when someone shows their heart.

I knew Jamie had a kind one. It still doesn't change what happened, but I'm slowly starting to believe he's genuinely sorry. I'm willing to listen to him apologize this time if he wants to try again.

When I got in my car and unwrapped the book, I found that it was not only a specially picked blind date with a book, but that it was a new one from Jade Jackson, one of the local authors I met, and it was personalized and signed for me.

This morning when I went in, there was another handwritten note to go with my coffee—and a breakfast sandwich.

Good luck today.
  —Jamie

Which is why I'm standing here, maybe stupidly, looking around the giant gymnasium for Jamie.

Today is one of the tournaments for my three-on-three volleyball rec league. If that's what the *good luck* note was for this morning, then maybe...

I shake my head at myself. I need to stay focused so we can

kick ass.

If he comes, he comes.

It's no big deal.

At least that's what I keep telling myself because the last thing I want to do is get my hopes up, just to have them crushed again.

I LOVE the action and fast pace of volleyball. I always have. I'll get lost in my head if I have to stand around for too long. I'll never forget playing goalie in soccer and being endlessly bored or getting stuck in the outfield in softball. If I got to hit and run the bases the whole time, I might've enjoyed it more.

I loved basketball, but at barely five-foot-four, it wasn't the right fit for me. I'm still a little short for volleyball, but on my high school team, I mostly played special defense or libero. With three-on-three, the positions are a bit different, but defense is still my focus, and I'm frequently the first person the ball comes in contact with.

Being out on the court always gives me a bit of peace in the same way planning an event does. It's clear I thrive in chaos. I'm sure a therapist would love to dissect why, but that's a Pandora's box I'm not planning on opening.

"You're kicking ass today, Mands," Rae says, handing me a water while I wait for the next match to start. She and Mackie have been here all day long supporting me.

Only two matches left in the tournament. If we win our next one, then we get to play in the final too. I like the girls I'm playing with this year. We're not destined to be lifelong besties, but we get along and all have the same passion for volleyball, while still enjoying the fun of it being a rec league.

"Thanks," I say to Rae after a glug of water.

Mackie looks around the room, eyes alight with mischief.

"See something you like?" I tease.

She looks back at me, eyes dancing. "Lots of things. So many short shorts."

"Oh boy. Do I need to take you and shove you in a cold shower?" Rae teases.

"Rude. But... maybe? Nah. I'm enjoying myself too much. Which is nice. After everything." Mackie's relationship with Hyla fell apart, and it killed me to see her suffer because I know that pain. But I also recognize that it's different because I think they both still love each other, even if I don't fully understand Hyla's side of the story. I don't dislike her, but it's hard to trust someone who you can tell is hiding something—or who hurts one of your best friends.

I glance around the gym too, mostly checking on the match still going to see who we'll play, but also to see if I find any cute butts in short shorts.

Out of the corner of my eye, I swear I see that familiar fiery red hair, but when I turn all the way, I don't see Jamie.

At this point, I'm just gaslighting myself into imagining he's here.

Even though I hate myself for wishing he would've come. It's unrealistic that anyone wants to give up their Saturday and sit in a hot gym all day. I'm grateful Rae and Mackie are here. Sarah came for the morning, but then she had to work. Jace is out of town with her college bestie, or else they probably both would've come. Pete stopped by for a bit too. No surprise that Josh and my parents weren't here. My mom will absentmindedly tell me congratulations when I get home later.

It's no big deal.

I don't do this to have people come watch me. It's something special I do for myself. But having people I care about choose to come and watch me play—when they're excited—it means a lot.

The other match ends, and as the announcer calls for us to get set up, Rae and Mackie give me big hugs, then go to find seats again.

I watch them as they go, grateful they chose to be here, and trying not to think about the fact that if I hadn't met them six months ago, I might've been alone here all day.

But as the words roll through my mind, my gaze lifts, and I blink, then blink again, certain my eyes are lying to me.

There, sitting casually in the bleachers and eating popcorn, is Jamie.

He came.

When my gaze connects with him, he winks at me, then goes back to eating his popcorn.

My heart pounds, and I'm trying to stay calm because, again, this doesn't mean anything. Not yet. It's a start, but... fuck.

Nope. I need to stay focused.

But the fact that he's here, watching me, is impossible to shake. I want him to watch. I want to put on a show for him. Because even though I wish it wouldn't, Jamie being here means a lot to my stupid, traitorous heart.

WE WON the whole damn tournament.

As the two other girls on my team this year surround me in hugs—which makes me feel even shorter than I am—my eyes drift back to the bleachers where Jamie was.

He's standing now, cheering and clapping.

One of my teammates goes to hug her parents, and the other picks up the little boy toddling toward her before her husband walks over and wraps them both in a hug.

It's beautiful. But the loneliness seeps in again. I'm so thankful for the people who were here to cheer me on today. But this high at the end... it's hard not having someone rush to the floor and sweep me into their arms. I know many people value me. I'm important and special to them—and that feels good. But just once, I'd like to be someone's everything.

I blink back the tears prickling in my eyes as Rae and Mackie run over to me.

"You were amazing!" Mackie throws an arm around my neck, and Rae does the same.

"Thank you." I wrap an arm around each of them, feeling that gratitude again that I found them—my tribe—and they accepted me so willingly.

"I'm such a buzzkill, but I have to run so I can get home to shower before I have to babysit tonight." Rae gives me a big hug and a kiss on the cheek. "I love you. You were amazing. Girls' night and sushi to celebrate this week!"

"Yes, ma'am. Love you too. Drive safe."

She waves as she walks away, then Mackie slings her arm over my shoulder. "So, what do you think? Should we go out on the town? Fake IDs? Find a college party?" She waggles her eyebrows at me, even though I know Mackie would much rather be home watching a movie.

I'm about to say that, when I track Jamie walking toward us.

The heat of Mackie's gaze lands on me.

"Jamie came to watch you?"

"Guess so," I croak.

She spins me to face her. "What haven't you told us?"

I give an innocent shrug.

"Uh huh. I totally believe you," she says flatly.

"Your perceptiveness is annoying."

"Tell me something I haven't heard before." She pokes my cheek. "Oh, you totally have a crush on him."

"I don't—it's complicated..." I sigh. "Don't mention it to anyone. Please?"

She mimes zipping her lips. "I'll take it to the grave, babe."

"Hey, Amanda. Macks," Jamie says as he gets to us.

"Hey, Jame. I was just heading out."

Mackie slips her arm off my shoulder, but I grab her hand, flaring my eyes at her.

"You—"

"Gotta run. I have to... meet Miles. Yeah."

"Mackie," I hiss.

She kisses my cheek. "Love you. Bye!"

In true Mackie fashion, she smacks my ass as she turns to walk away, trouble in her eyes.

I watch her go, knowing I'm now alone with Jamie. And the scarier part is that I might want to be. Why did she leave me? I need a chaperone, so I don't do something dumb and get my heart crushed all over again.

Slowly, I spin around and plaster on a smile. Not too big of one because we haven't talked yet, despite how much I appreciated all the little things he did for me over the past week.

"Hi. Thanks for coming."

He stares at me for a moment, then steps in, resting his hand on my arm as he kisses my cheek. "You were amazing. Congratulations."

"Thanks." My stupid voice comes out all breathy, and *ugh*. For half a second, I thought *he takes my breath away.*

I need to get my head back in the game and not let my heart rule here. He did nice things, but that doesn't magically fix things between us, and I need to remember that or I'll end up with a more bruised heart than before.

"I might have to start calling you the volleyball queen."

"I'm not *that* amazing. It's just a rec league."

He shakes his head. "In your second match, you did some crazy combination of spin, lunge, and dive, then twisted and bumped the ball perfectly to your teammate. I wish I'd taken a video of it."

"I—wait. Second match? How long have you been here?"

"Well, I had to take Cal to soccer practice this morning, so I didn't get here until a little while after the start of the second match."

"So you were here for the whole thing?"

He shrugs, shoving his hands into his pockets. "Pretty much. I wanted to see you. And... I know how it felt when you came to my game. I guess I was hoping I could make you feel the same way." He looks around before meeting my eyes again. "So, any plans right now?"

"Nope. I was just going to shower and head home."

"Any chance you'd let me take you out for ice cream to celebrate?"

Even though part of me wants to channel that anger to protect myself, it's pretty well dead at this point. This is an easy first step. Ice cream to break the ice.

"Sure. That would be nice. I'll just go shower quick, then we can go."

"I'll be here." His warm smile does something to me, and as I walk away, I can't ignore the rush of excitement that runs through me.

I hate that I still want him. Especially since I still don't fully trust him or his intentions. But I guess there's only one way to find out.

Hopefully ice cream will help me cool off, otherwise I might make some bad decisions that my heart will hate me for later.

Jamie

I SUCCESSFULLY GOT Amanda to get ice cream with me. Now I just need to not fuck anything up tonight. It's not a date, but it's a start, and I'll take it.

"So..." Amanda drawls as we wait for our ice cream to be ready. "How much have you been stalking me?"

"I don't know what you're talking about," I say smoothly.

"Mhm. So you just happened to want to get ice cream at my favorite ice cream shop?"

"It was close."

"We passed three others on the way. You knew about my tournament. And you knew my favorite coffee place."

"I may have called in a favor. I'll leave any names out of it for their protection."

She squints at me. "I know it wasn't one of the girls. We can't keep secrets from each other—other than emotional turmoil—to save our lives." She stares at me for a beat. "But it doesn't really matter. I appreciate the coffee and the notes." Her eyes drift up to the sign at the top of the building. "And this."

"You were right last week. It was wrong of me to crash the event you were working." I rub the back of my neck. "Sometimes I'm a dumbass."

She looks at me, eyes dancing, and I brace myself for a sassy remark, but the window slides open again and the girl sets out our ice creams.

We take our bowls and head for a picnic table, where I choose to sit next to her instead of across from her. Pulling a paper from my back pocket, I set it on the table between us.

"You were right about a lot of things. I wrote a whole apology letter, just to get my thoughts out the way I wanted to. You can read it if you want, but I'm going to say a lot of it now. If you'll let me."

She gives me a small smile. "I guess I could practice my listening skills."

"Okay. The first thing I need you to know is that I value you and your... friendship. Friendship doesn't feel like the right word because sometimes we felt like more than that. But from the moment we met, I've enjoyed talking with you and being around you, and that only grew the more we got to know each other. There's always been a connection between us, and when I kissed you that night, it was because I couldn't hold back anymore. That pull to you was too strong. I can't say I fully regret it. That kiss lives rent free in my mind."

She laughs a little and some of the tightness in my shoulders eases.

"But I shouldn't have done it like that," I continue. "I should've talked to you first about what I felt *and* what you felt.

That kiss changed things though. It didn't make me realize how much you meant to me, but how deep my feelings were—are—for you. It scared the shit out of me because I knew we couldn't just have fun. So I stopped things. I know it seems like I was choosing baseball, but I truly didn't think I could have both. In my own stupid way, I thought I was protecting you from me. The reason I didn't try to apologize in person was—at first—because I convinced myself I couldn't have both things. Then I was coming to terms with the fact that maybe I could. Once I realized and understood that, I had to face how I handled things and figure out where to go. Storming the event wasn't my best plan, but I'm an idiot hung up on a girl I really like, and I did a dumb thing. I'm sure I missed some other things I fucked up on, but I am truly sorry for hurting you and the many ways I handled this situation wrong. I'm hoping you can forgive me and maybe we could try to move forward. Because my feelings haven't changed, and I really want to give this—us—a shot."

She swirls her tongue around her spoon, licking at the ice cream like she's done the entire time I've been talking.

My stomach is in knots as I wait for her answer, but she hasn't punched me or bitched me out yet, so I'll take it.

"Thank you." Her voice is soft and filled with vulnerability. "For apologizing, and for... hearing me. Sometimes it seems like I'm drowned out by white noise."

I slide a little closer, resting my hand on her arm.

"I always see you. Always hear you. If you're anywhere near me, I can't help but pay attention. I'm sorry I didn't do a good job of that the night we kissed."

She watches me for a moment, then nods and goes back to eating her ice cream. I do the same, even though I really want to say something else. Apologize again. I want to fix this.

But pushing someone when they're already on the edge doesn't help. I know that. So I shove another spoonful of ice cream into my mouth to keep myself quiet, but out of the corner of my eye, I watch her. She has three scoops. One cookie dough.

One cookies and cream. One brownie batter. Sounds like a good combination, but I've always been more into fruity things, so I went with my old faithful—cherry vanilla.

"Happy birthday, by the way," Amanda says, out of nowhere.

I drop my spoon into my dish and turn to look at her. She does the same, though she keeps eating her ice cream as she does.

"Thank you."

"Did you have a good party? I'm—" She clams up, rolling her lips together. After another bite of ice cream, she starts again. "I was going to apologize for not being there, but—"

I rest my hand on her arm, giving it a little squeeze. "You don't need to be sorry for that. I got what I deserved."

"Maybe. But... I don't know." She sighs.

"It was a good party. Could've been better if I hadn't messed things up with an amazing girl, but there was good food, a wiffle ball game, and my favorite cupcakes."

"What kind?"

"Vanilla with raspberry filling. I'm a sucker for a cake with fruit in the middle."

"Hey, Jamie."

"Hi, Jamie."

Two girls slowly walk by our table, arms linked as they laugh together. I've hooked up with one before, and the other hit on me in the past.

I barely give them a glance and an up nod so they'll keep walking, but Amanda looks at them, then quickly looks away. She tries to pull away from my touch, but I move closer. She is the only thing that matters to me tonight.

"Does that happen a lot?" she asks, somewhere between amused and annoyed.

"Uh, sometimes..." My cheeks flame red, giving me away.

She lifts her arm, and I finally move my hand, letting her brush her thumb over my cheek.

"Why are your cheeks so red? We've talked about sex before. And two girls saying hello to you makes you blush?"

"I don't like that kind of attention on me. Plus, it's not easy for me to just talk to people."

She quirks a brow. "Didn't you say you liked to hook up a lot?" Wow, I wish I wouldn't have told her *that*. "How did you do that if you're not comfortable talking to random people?"

I sigh and ruffle a hand through my hair, then take a bite of my ice cream. "This is going to sound so dickish, but usually they came to me."

Some of her playfulness drops at that.

"Got it. And are you still—never mind."

"Hooking up? You can ask me."

"No. It's none of my business."

I tilt my head, unable to stop the stupid smile growing on my face. "Do you not want me to hook up with anyone else?"

Please say yes. That means I still have a shot.

She stares at me for a long beat, then goes back to eating her ice cream before she finally answers me. "It wouldn't be the best way to win me over."

Her voice has that same guardedness to it she's had ever since we kissed.

She's not ready for me to be playful yet. She needs my sincerity.

I rest my hand on her thigh, drawing all her attention to me. She needs to hear these words and know they're the absolute truth. "I'm not hooking up or trying to hook up with anyone else. Partly because that would be a really shitty thing to do. But mostly because you're the only one I want."

She swallows hard, staring at me like she's trying to see my soul through my eyes. Who knows? Maybe she can. Maybe that's her superpower. All I know is she's my kryptonite. When I'm around her, I'm weak.

"Why me?" Her voice is hushed and raw.

"What do you mean?"

"Why me? Why do you want me?"

The vulnerability in her voice mixed with the pain in her eyes absolutely guts me. I hate every person who has ever made her question her worth. And I know I'm one of them. Which is all the more reason I need to fix this now. I need to show her how much she means to me.

I take her bowl of ice cream and set it on the table. I don't want anything between us while I say this.

Our knees brush as I shift closer, then gently run my fingers through her hair.

"You're asking that like it's a choice. From the moment I met you, I've been pulled to you, and the more I get to know you, the more captivated I am. You have a hold on me that I wouldn't lift even if I could. In only knowing each other a short time, you saw the mask I put on, and you've never judged me for who I am underneath it. You are a mesmerizing force of nature, and to be in your path means to be overtaken by the beautiful storm you are. There's never been a choice, Amanda. From the moment you walked into my life, there's only been you. And I hope, in time, you'll believe me when I say that's all I want. I want to be yours. The person you rely on and let take care of you and protect you and your big, beautiful heart. It's never been a choice, but even if it was, I'd choose you a thousand times. And I'll do whatever it takes to earn your forgiveness and trust."

She stares at me for a long moment. An arduous, painful moment. I'm sweating, wondering if I took it too far or not far enough—if she's about to reject me.

"Okay," she breathes.

"Okay…?"

She laughs a little. "I forgive you. And I'd like to rebuild that trust between us, then see what happens."

"Does that mean you're saying yes to a date?"

She grabs another spoonful of ice cream, swirling her tongue along the edge of it.

"I'm saying you have to keep showing. You said all the pretty words. Now it's time to prove you mean them, baseball boy."

Then she does the last thing I'm expecting and presses a kiss to my cheek.

I reach over and rest my hand on her thigh, and we continue eating in a comfortable silence.

I have every intention of proving how true my words are. No. Intention is the wrong word. This isn't about intention. It's about action. I know what the stakes are here. It's the championship game. Every single action makes a difference. Which means doing it all right because every move I make is a play for the future I want us to have.

9
Someone's Dream

Amanda

JAMIE HAS CONTINUED to do what I asked. Only he's not just showing me how he feels, he's showing up.

In the two weeks since our ice cream reconciliation, he's come to both of my Wednesday volleyball rec games. We hung out at a bonfire at Joel's. We've also texted every day. Half the time they're not about anything at all, but he texts me when he thinks of me, and I've started doing the same when I think of him. It's sweet. It's just freaking sweet. And I've never had that before. Not someone trying to hook up or get in my pants. Not someone who wants me only when it's convenient for them. Someone who cares, who wants to know me, who wants to build something.

Every time I start to internally question things, he keeps showing me that. He met me at Bewitched for coffee and let me talk his ear off about books. But I also learned that he likes sci-fi books, and I'm on a mission to find a good one that blends sci-fi and romance, so maybe we could read it together.

Because as much as I need him to prove he's serious and rebuild some of the trust between us, I don't want that to be one-sided. Putting even a little bit of my heart out there is still hard for me, but I have feelings for him, and if he feels the same way for me, I owe it to myself not to say no just because I'm afraid of getting hurt again. As much as some part of me wants to stay angry, I believe Jamie didn't intend to hurt me, and while intentions only mean so much, they do mean something. So I'm giving him this chance—and giving myself a chance too.

Which is why I'm sitting here now, embracing one of the biggest pieces of him. Not only have I gone to see a few of his baseball camp scrimmages, here I am at the Binghamton Knights' stadium watching a game with him.

When he texted me earlier today and asked if I wanted to come with him, I was hesitant for a second, but I want to get to know him better, and seeing him play and watching him watch a game are two different vibes.

"Want anything to eat?" he asks.

"A hot dog?"

"Coming up."

He signals to one of the people walking around selling food and orders a hot dog for me and nachos for him.

He groans happily as he takes a bite of his nachos, and I can't stop my laugh.

"Good?"

"Mhm. You know how you said you... *love* spicy crab sushi? That's how I feel about nachos."

"You'd do dirty things for them?"

"One hundred percent. Of course, it's better if they're loaded nachos. Like melted cheese, taco meat or maybe some chicken, guac, salsa, or maybe some pico de gallo, sour cream, and then top it all off with cheese sauce."

"Sounds deadly."

"Oh, no doubt. But they're my favorite food."

"Good to know."

He takes another bite and makes a throaty noise that doesn't at all make my body flush.

I take a bite of my hot dog, then out of the corner of my eye notice that I'm not the only one who noticed Jamie's love of nachos. Or maybe it's just Jamie.

Jealousy flares in my stomach.

I want to grab him and yell 'mine!' at the top of my lungs. Except he's not mine. Is he?

Instead, I clear my throat and lightly elbow him. "You've got a fan club."

He looks up from his nachos. "Huh?"

I nod in their direction. "Those girls keep looking over at you and giggling to themselves."

He doesn't look. Instead, he turns his head and openly checks me out. "Funny. I didn't notice. In fact, my eyes have only been on one person all night."

There's a loud crack of a bat and then cheers, and Jamie whips his head back toward the field.

"And baseball," I tease.

He almost smiles, but then his face falls and his shoulders slump as he turns back to look at me. "Should I not have invited you here?"

I was kidding when I said that. Of course he's going to watch the game. Initially I felt a bit prickly about baseball, but what was he supposed to do? Choose me after one kiss when he's been working toward a career in baseball for most of his life? That's crazy. And when I really thought about it, I wasn't mad about him choosing baseball. I was mad he couldn't even conceive the possibility of being with me and playing baseball, yet he kissed me, knowing that.

If anything, I recognize that if I'm going to be with him, I need to embrace how big a part of his life baseball is and will continue to be.

I rest my hand on his arm, and he tracks the movement with his eyes.

"I'm glad you invited me here. It's fun watching you play, but it's also cool to see how you watch a game. This is important to you, which means... it's important to me too."

His gaze lifts to mine, eyes wide. "Really?"

"Yes."

His smile is so bright it radiates around me, filling me with his warmth.

"I'm glad you're here."

"Me too."

He wraps his arm around my back, gently rubbing his thumb over my upper arm as we eat our snacks and watch the game.

The rest of the game goes fast as the Knights make quick work of the visiting team, and as we stroll out of the stadium, Jamie takes my hand. It's so easy to lean back into this feeling. Part of me wonders if I'm letting him back in too easily, but I think a month of silence and waiting for an apology was enough distance. I'm not rushing into anything. There's still trust to be rebuilt, but I want to rebuild it.

"So, I have a question for you," Jamie says when we get to his car.

"What's up?"

"Any chance you'd like to spend the day with my mom, me, and my younger siblings tomorrow? I've been meaning to ask you for a few days, but I keep chickening out. My dad will be out of town, so we wanted to do something fun with the kids. We're going to have lunch and go mini golfing. If you're interested."

I bite back my smile. "Why were you afraid to ask me?"

"It feels like a big deal. Meeting my family."

"I already know your mom."

"I know, but my siblings—especially Penny—will be excited, and they have lots of energy and big personalities."

"Jamie, do you want me to come?"

"Yes."

"Then I'll be there."

"Yeah?"

I press onto my toes and kiss his cheek. "Yes."

He wraps his arms around me, and though it takes me a

second to quiet the voices telling me not to give in, I drown them out and hug him back.

It might be a little messy, but I like the path we're on, and I'm cautiously excited to see where it will lead.

I'M WAITING in the entryway of Mixed Brews, a large coffee in hand. Mixed Brews is in the neighboring town of Lacy Creek, and it's technically two businesses in one. On one side is a coffee shop and on the other is a brewpub. The brewpub is where I'm having lunch with Jamie and his family today, but I got here early so I could grab a coffee because... coffee.

I also snagged a copy of local author Zoey Holloway's latest book. Before they go live in the big stores, she usually will put a few copies at local indie stores. Since she's from Lacy Creek and knows the owner of Mixed Brews, they have a stand of her books there, and I was excited to find this one.

"Cal, wait for us," Marissa calls as the door swings open right in my face and a little boy comes tearing through.

I quickly side step into his path. "Whoa, buddy. Slow down."

Marissa and a young girl step through the door.

"Thank you so much." She laughs a little when she realizes it's me. "Hi."

"Hi. I got here early." I wiggle the coffee in my hand.

"Well, I'm glad."

She looks down at Cal, who bounces in place. Seems every bit like the chaos Jamie described him as.

Speaking of Jamie... he strolls up to the door, then ducks as he walks through with a little girl—Mila, I'm assuming—on his shoulders.

"Cal, you can't run away like—" He stops short as his eyes land on me. "Hi."

The other little girl—Penny—looks up at Jamie then back at

me. "Wait. Are you Amanda?" She turns to Jamie and whispers, "*The* Amanda?"

Jamie's cheeks instantly go pink, but he smiles and nods. "Yes. *The* Amanda." But his voice says something else. Not *the*. *My*. Like he sees me as his.

As much as my brain yells at me to keep my guard up, my heart is all melty and gooey. Part of me is still wary. But with each passing day, the wall around my heart crumbles a little more.

"You have to have lunch with us!" Penny exclaims.

I squat down so I'm at her eye-level. "I am going to have lunch with you. And how would you feel about me coming mini golfing with you too? We could team up."

She bounces up and down. "Yes, please!"

"Can we eat? I'm starving," Cal whines.

"Only if you can walk to the table like a well-behaved child might," Marissa says.

Cal pouts. "That's no fun."

Mila takes his hand. "I'm hungwy too."

It's adorable how Cal softens with Mila's hand in his. It reminds me of how Pete's demeanor changes between Josh and me.

"Ready for chaos?" Jamie's warm breath tickles my ear as his hand lands on my back.

I glance up at him. "I'm sure I can handle it."

We end up in a half-circle booth, Jamie on one side of me and Penny on the other, then Mila, Cal, and Marissa.

A waitress comes to get our drinks, and I order a raspberry lemonade, which means Penny and Mila do the same. They're adorable, especially as Penny giddily asks me what I'm going to have to eat. It's clear she's already a fan of mine. I'll have to ask Jamie why that is later.

"What are you having?" Jamie asks, inching closer.

"Mm. I'm thinking I'll start with a salad, then probably have a hot honey fried chicken sandwich."

"Sounds delicious," Jamie rumbles in my ear.

"Let me guess, you're getting loaded nachos?"

His eyes shimmer with trouble. "You were paying attention."

"Yes, I was. I don't want this to be one-sided."

Jamie opens his mouth to say something, but before he can, Marissa says, "I'll order a couple of appetizers for the table. Any requests?"

I look over at her, but then freeze in horror at the waitress walking toward our table. Not the same waitress who took our drink order.

Not here. Not now.

But it has to be her. The dark brown bob, long, leggy build, and dangly earrings. Maci. My ex.

"I need to go to the bathroom," I say quickly, shoving at Jamie so he'll let me out of the booth.

"But the waitress—"

"Can you order for me? Hot honey chicken sandwich with special fries, and a salad with Thousand Island dressing." He looks at me in confusion, so I do my best to school my features, then say, "Please?"

"Okay." He glances at me, then in the direction of the waitress, but lets me out.

I hurry toward the bathroom, hoping she didn't see me. Not that it matters if she's our waitress for the whole lunch. What am I going to do? Hide under the table every time she comes over?

In the bathroom, I splash some water on my face, chastising myself for my ridiculousness. I'm reacting to this like I've been triggered, and that's completely insane. It's not like it was an abusive relationship. I need to get over this. It's been almost three years. We were in the same school for another two years after it happened. It shouldn't be affecting me this much to see her now.

Fuck.

How do I play this? Ignore her? Pretend I don't recognize her? Be sickeningly sweet, while giving her my *yes-I'm-judging-you* face? That'll have to do.

One more deep breath, and I walk out of the bathroom, but as soon as I do, I'm not alone.

Jamie pushes himself off the wall he was leaning against and walks over to me, concern all over his face. "Are you okay?"

Crap. Now I feel like even more of an idiot.

"I'm... fine."

"No offense, but you don't seem fine."

"It's ah... the waitress is my ex."

"Oh."

"I haven't seen her since high school ended, and it's just... weird."

He steps in closer, sliding his hand into mine. "Just weird? Because when you were yelling at me at the event, it sounded like she hurt you. I don't want to push you, but I want to understand."

I sigh and roll my eyes. "It's hard to keep my guard up when you're being sweet."

"Good. Because I want you to let it down. Let me in. Let me be the one to protect your heart."

"That's a lot to ask," I whisper.

"Then take it one thing at a time. I promise to keep showing you the truth of my feelings."

"Fine," I sigh. "I guess if you're determined to date me, you should know my baggage."

"It's the only way I can help you carry it."

I stare at him for a long beat. It's hard to let the most vulnerable part of me out, but he's working hard to show me I can trust him. More than that, I feel safe with him. And I'm doing my best not to let my brain overthink or undermine that.

"Okay. Maci, my ex, was my best friend from early elementary school until the beginning of eleventh grade."

"How long were you two together?"

"Theoretically, a little over a year, but we were never official. If you ever see me giving Hyla my *yes-I'm-judging-you* face, that's why. Sometimes I see similarities there that make me extra protective of Mackie."

"Why is it I know exactly what face you mean?"

I shove his shoulder. "Stay on topic. Unless you don't want to know the story."

"Tell me."

"We met in elementary school and formed a little group with two other friends. There was always a little something extra between the two of us, though. It wasn't until the summer before tenth grade that things shifted. We were having a sleepover and joking about something, and she said she wanted to know what kissing a girl would be like. I already knew I was bi and had for a while, but hadn't actively come out to anyone besides my family and Jace. So, I told her. She asked if I'd be willing to kiss her, and I will never forget how exciting that thought was. I'd never kissed another girl before. Only boys. So, we did. We ended up under my covers all night touching each other while we kissed. She didn't want to tell anyone, but she wanted to do it again, so every week we had a sleepover. Every week we kissed and touched each other. Until sleepovers lasted all weekend and we were at each other's houses after school every day."

"Wow. I'm guessing things were complicated if you aren't sure whether to consider it a real relationship."

"You could say that. It was about six months in that we agreed it was a relationship, and after some talking, we agreed I could tell my parents. It made sleepovers a little more supervised, but I felt so free. We could be a couple. Except at school. Or her house. She was afraid of how her parents would act or how our friends would handle it, so she wanted to wait. It was a secret, but I was her secret and she was mine. At the end of the school year, she agreed we'd tell everyone when we went back in September. We spent all summer together. We did *everything* sexually speaking. And we were in love."

I let out a bitter laugh and shake my head—at the pain that

still simmers inside me because of it, or my own stupidity, I don't know.

"*I* was in love with *her*. That desperate, longing kind of love. I was so excited for school to start, but once it did, she got quiet and distant, then refused to speak to me. When I showed up at her house, she told me I needed to get over my feelings. The quarterback of the football team asked her out, and she was going to date him. She said everything with us was an experiment, and she didn't want to be with a girl. I tried to call her out, but she walked away and had her mother ask me to leave and not come back. She stopped speaking to me and so did our other two friends. Nothing makes you question your worth or your sanity like someone convincing you they love you, then telling you it was all in your head."

"Jesus. That's fucked up." He stares at me for a moment, then steps forward and cups my cheek. "You deserve so much better than that. And she is insane for letting you go. Clearly, she didn't know what she had, or she never would have. You're magic and light and kindness personified. I'm sorry she hurt you, and I'm sorry *I* hurt you. I swear to you, I will never take a second of you, your time, or your beautiful heart for granted."

"Jamie." His name is a hushed whisper as it slips from my lips.

Then gently, so gently, his lips brush over mine. A whisper of a kiss that both lights me on fire and makes me want to collapse into him. To give in and let him have me. Let him take care of me in the way I've craved for so long.

"Let's go show her what she's missing out on," he says, breath tickling my lips as he rests his head against mine.

"What?" Something about him being so close and the tone of his voice has me feeling a little loopy.

"We're going to go back out there. You're going to sit up tall and let me show her what she's missing." He brushes some hair off my shoulder, his fingertips grazing my neck. "With every little touch, she's going to know you're mine, and you found someone who values you. Because I do, Amanda. I see your worth and I'm grateful you're even bothering to talk to me. And until you unequivocally tell me no, I'm going to consider you mine. Mine to take care of. Mine to protect." He trails his fingers over my collarbone. "Mine to adore." He leans in, lips hovering over my neck. "Because you deserve to be adored." Then he firmly presses his lips against my neck, and I have to bite my lip to keep from moaning.

My hands slide into his hair, not sure if I want to lift his head or keep him there.

Slowly, his lips pull from my skin, and he whispers in my ear, "I've got you."

It's impossible to argue with that, so I let him take my hand and lead me back to the table.

"Sorry about that." I slide into the booth, and Jamie takes his spot next to me, wrapping his arm around my back.

"Is everything okay?" Marissa asks, eyes going from me to Jamie.

"Yes, I..."

"The waitress is Amanda's ex, and she didn't treat Amanda well," Jamie says in a low voice to his mom.

"Oh. Would you like me to see if I can get a different waitress?"

"No," I say quickly. "It's fine. She deserves to be able to make money at her workplace. I need to get over it."

Marissa reaches across the table and pats my hand.

"That's kind of you."

I shrug, but my shoulders instantly drop as Jamie slides closer. I glance toward the bar and see Maci walking toward us with our appetizers.

"Just so we're clear," Jamie murmurs in my ear, "everything I'm about to do are just some of the things I've been dreaming of doing with you." A chill rolls down my spine. "But tell me if anything is too much."

He rubs his hand down my back, then twirls some of my hair around one of his fingers as he leans in and kisses my jaw.

Now I want to leave this table for very different reasons.

It's easy to pretend to be lost in the little touches Jamie gives me. If anything, keeping my demeanor PG in front of his siblings is harder.

I want to grab him and kiss him like a maniac.

It's safe to say I've fully moved on from what happened. Even though there are moments when my brain tries to convince me he's playing a game or will hurt me, his actions speak louder. That's why I asked him to prove it, and he's doing that more than I could've imagined.

"Okay, here are your appetize—Amanda."

Maci almost drops one of the appetizer platters, but corrects herself in time to set it gently on the table.

Jamie leans in closer, continuing to twirl my hair around his finger as he kisses my cheek.

"Hi, Maci."

Jamie's hand drops from my hair and he grabs a plate. "What can I get you, babe?"

I run my hand down his arm. "A little of everything."

I look away from Maci, and for once, I don't feel small and weak. I'm calm and confident.

Maci doesn't say anything else to me, she just says to let her know if we need anything, then walks away.

My shoulders soften as she goes, and I lean against Jamie. "Thank you."

"My pleasure." He flashes me his most charming smile, then wraps his arm around my back.

Penny stares hard at us for a moment, then breaks into a smile and claps her hands. "Yes! I'm going to have a big sister one day."

I slowly turn to look at Jamie, whose face is unsurprisingly bright red.

"Long story," he whispers.

"I can't wait to hear it."

And maybe stupidly, my heart takes off running with Penny's words, and some small part of me hopes she'll be right.

TODAY HAS BEEN MORE fun than I imagined it would be.

The rest of lunch went smoothly, and though there was a hint of awkwardness each time Maci came to the table, I kept a relaxed smile on my face and let Jamie fawn over me. That felt good for an entirely different reason.

It's never easy to run into an ex, and running into someone who hurt me so badly could've ruined my day, but Jamie eclipsed all those feelings, and instead, we created some beautiful memories today.

After lunch, we went mini golfing, and Penny and I teamed up against Cal and Jamie. And we kicked their butts. Penny had fun rubbing that in Calvin's face, but Jamie told me next time *we'll* have to team up. I was planning to head home after that, but Penny talked me into joining them for dinner and a fire.

It ended up being a really fun night, and as I stand by my car outside Jamie's house, I feel markedly different from the last time I was here.

Jamie leans in close, pressing me against the side of my car. His gaze flits to my lips, and my heartbeat ticks up. Instead of kissing me, he dips his head and brushes his lips over my jaw, making me squirm in the best way.

All the blood in my body rushes south, and for the first time, I let myself imagine what it would be like to do a lot more than kiss him.

"Jamie." My breathy voice surprises me, and it must pull him back to the moment too, because he leans back, standing up straight as he pants.

"Sorry. I—"

"Don't be." I reach for his hand, my eyes catching on the bulge in his pants.

I hope he thinks of me if he...

Oh my god. I can't believe I'm actually thinking that.

"Any chance you'd be willing to let me take you on a date next weekend?"

"I have a family thing... but I was wondering if you'd like to come?" My voice squeaks a little on the last word.

A soft smile appears, and he runs his fingers through my hair.

"You want me to come? What kind of *thing* is it?"

"There's a block party in my neighborhood, and we usually have some fun with that earlier in the day, then have a cookout with Jace's family in the late afternoon. It would be nice to have you there for the cookout."

"Then I'll be there."

A rush of excitement whirls through me. "Good."

He leans in again and kisses my cheek. "I'll be thinking of you until then. And I'll be there on Wednesday to watch you play volleyball."

I rest my hand on his chest and look into those captivating blue eyes.

"I can't wait."

He reaches down and pulls on my door handle, guiding me against him for a second so he can pull the door open.

"Drive safe."

"Thanks. Have a good night, baseball boy."

His eyes light up at that. "You too."

He shuts the door and watches as I back out, waving as I pull onto the road.

My heart pounds as I drive away. I'm in so much trouble—at way too much of a risk of getting my heart crushed. But I don't care. I'm falling for him. And I'm trusting him to keep me from slamming into the ground.

Jamie

I'VE GOT THIS.

Penny gave me a pep talk before I left the house. Taking relationship advice from my seven-year-old sister might be a new low, but she's smart and perceptive and has the candidness that only a child can.

All my introvert senses are tingling as I climb out of my car and make my way down Amanda's driveway. *I'm doing this for her,* I remind myself. And that's all it takes. I want to be here for her.

She's waiting to say yes to a date with me. This is all part of me proving myself worthy. I'm showing up for her. Her ex didn't put her first. Sure, her family knew, but that was because she pushed for it to happen. I want the world to know she's mine—even if it's not official yet.

It will be. Because I don't give up on the things I want.

If I'm sure of two things in my life, it's that I will make it to the majors and I'll get Amanda to say yes to a date with me. From there, it'll be a new battle of proving myself, but if I lay the groundwork now, that'll make it easier.

When I step into the beautifully set up entertaining area of the backyard with trellises, vines, and natural wildflowers, everyone turns to look at me.

And there go my cheeks.

Off to a great start.

Amanda pushes out of her chair, eyes big, and when those stunning whiskey eyes meet mine, I see overwhelming joy.

That alone is worth how uncomfortable I feel right now.

"Jamie, hi."

"Ah, is this your *friend*?" a woman I'm assuming is her mother asks.

"Yep," she squeaks. "Mom, this is Jamie."

"Jamie Henderson," I say, walking over and offering my hand. "It's nice to meet you, Mrs. Hamilton. Thank you for having me."

"It's nice to meet you too. And call me Libby, please." She looks at Amanda. "Is he your *boy*friend?"

"Yes," I say at the same time Amanda says, "No."

A girl with dark blonde hair, who I'm assuming is Jace, snickers at that.

"You better not be stalking my sister or trying to convince her to join a cult," a guy with auburn hair and the same sarcastic tone as Amanda says.

"Eh, as long as it's not one of the ones with murder-suicide pacts..." A different guy, this one with light brown hair, says.

"Let me guess, you're Josh," I say flatly. He arches a brow and looks like he might say something snarky, but I turn back to the other guy. "And you're Pete."

"That's me."

"Oh, right," Amanda says, stepping over to me. "Uh, that's Jace." She points to the girl. "That's my dad, Bryce." She points him both out, and then nods to the other two adults. "And those are Jace's parents. Jace's friend Sienna, her brother Miguel, and their dad will be here later too."

"Cool. It's nice to meet you all."

There's a chorus of agreement, but one voice cuts through it all.

"So, I'm confused. Are you dating or not?" Jace asks dramatically.

Amanda shoots her a death glare.

"Well, it's not official. I'm still working on getting her to say yes to a date. I kind of screwed that up originally, but I have every intention of making her my girlfriend."

"Cool. Break her heart, I break your pitching hand." Pete smacks me on the shoulder as he walks toward the table where food is set up.

My eyes fly wide, and he grins at me over his shoulder. "Yeah. I figured out who you are, *baseball boy*."

"You're dead to me," Amanda calls.

"Wow, and here I was expecting a sweet little family get together."

Amanda snorts. "You picked the wrong house."

"Not a chance." Finally, I wrap my arms around her, and I

love the way she melts into the hug and buries her face in my chest. "Hi."

"Hi," she whispers, looking up at me. "I'm glad you're here."

I press a quick kiss to her forehead. "So am I."

I let her go, then she pulls me over to a plastic loveseat, and we sit down.

"So, Jamie, you're a pitcher?" Amanda's dad asks.

"Guilty."

"Are you any good?" Josh asks.

Amanda glares at him, but I just wrap an arm around my girl.

My girl. God, I hope she will be.

I never would've expected that someone would completely throw me off my game—throw some of the importance of my game out the window—but Amanda did. And I'm happy to get lost falling down the rabbit hole, as long as I'm falling with her.

"He's amazing," Amanda says, jutting her chin out. "He's going to play in the majors." She says it so confidently, like it couldn't be anything other than the truth. And while I believe in myself and I have a lot of other people who do too, her believing it means something more.

"Really?" her dad asks.

"Yeah. I mean, there's nothing official at this point. I've got almost another full year until I'm eligible for the draft, but that's what I'm working toward—and have been working toward for a long time. My coach is confident I can get there, and I am too."

"Any idea which team you'll play for?"

"Whoever will take me," I say with a laugh. "But I'd love to play for the Metros if I get the chance. They were one of the main teams we all watched and rooted for growing up. It would be amazing to play for them one day."

Amanda squeezes my hand. "Then you will." When I turn and meet her gaze, she smiles at me, then leans in and lowers her voice. "Since you always get what you want, right?"

I slip my hand out of hers and squeeze her thigh, giving her my cockiest smile in response.

"So, how did you two meet?" Amanda's mom asks.

"Jamie is a friend of Rae and everyone from college. We met at their Christmas party."

"But we got to know each other when I showed up to an event my parents were hosting and she was there running it." I rest my arm over Amanda's shoulders, brushing my thumb over her upper arm. "I pretty much fell for her right there, watching her in action."

Amanda's gaze darts to me in surprise. Maybe it wasn't overt, but the feelings took root that night. She captivated me, and she's been on my mind ever since.

"She is incredible. We're proud of all she's accomplished building her own business at such a young age."

Amanda softens, her eyes growing big. "Thanks, Mom."

Her mom leans over from her chair and kisses Amanda on the cheek. "You know we're proud of you."

But something in Amanda's eyes tells me she doesn't inherently know that—and even if she does, she needs to hear those words and receive that praise, but she usually doesn't.

Yet another thing I want to make sure I do for her.

She deserves to be told and shown how amazing she is, and I'll do it like it's my damn job.

"WANT A TOUR OF THE HOUSE?" Amanda asks as we walk across the driveway, carrying some plates inside.

"And get to see where the event queen grew up? I'd love to."

So far, Amanda's family barbeque has been fun and low-key. I've gotten a little grilling, mostly at the hands of Jace and Pete with a few snarky barbs from Josh, who I admittedly don't like. He doesn't seem to like me either, but I don't give a fuck. If he treats my girl badly, I won't mince words. Her family seems nice overall, but what Amanda told me all those months ago about her parents being too burned out from her brothers to give her much attention definitely tracks. It's clear they love and support her, but I don't think they *see* her. They don't see what she needs from them—especially not emotionally. Amanda doesn't like to tell people what she needs. But as her family, they should know her well enough to see through that.

I can't change how everyone else sees her, but I can show her how I see her.

We set the plates in the sink. Then Amanda takes my hand, looking adorably nervous.

"It's this way."

But the second we start down the hall, Pete steps in our path.

"Hey, Jamie, can I borrow you for a second?"

Amanda crosses her arms over her chest. "What are you doing?"

"I just need his help with something."

"Find Josh."

"We all know he's useless." Pete winks at her and she sighs heavily.

"It's fine. I'm happy to *help*." We both know that's not what this is, but that's fine. If I can survive pitching a state championship game in front of hundreds of people or getting reamed by my coach for something dumb, I can handle a few minutes of being grilled by Pete.

Amanda spins around and looks up at me. "You don't have to."

"I know. I'll be fine. I'll meet you upstairs after?"

She nods. "Second door on the left."

"Got it."

I give her arm a squeeze, then with a menacing look at Pete, she heads for the stairs.

He watches to make sure she's gone, then nods toward the kitchen behind me.

"Let's sit."

"Sure." I walk back to the kitchen and take a seat at the island. He doesn't. He stands on the other side and stares down at me.

"So... you and Amanda."

"Yes. Working on it, at least."

"Interesting."

"Look, if you have concerns or questions, go ahead. Hit me with them. I'll answer whatever you ask."

He leans over the counter on his hands, staring at me. "Okay then. Are you the reason my sister came home in tears a couple of months ago?"

As much as I intended to stay cool through this, I have a terrible poker face, and those words catch me off guard. *She was crying?* I knew I hurt her, but not that badly.

"If it was the middle of May, then probably. I didn't..." I clear my throat. "I didn't know about the crying though."

"Of course you didn't. She doesn't show people her most vulnerable side. Especially when she's been hurt."

She shows me. But I can see where she wouldn't have that night.

"What I want to know," he continues, "is what you did, and why I should trust that you won't hurt her again."

"She didn't tell you?"

"No. She came home, took one look at me and Josh playing video games, then went and crawled through Jace's window."

"Well, if she didn't tell you, I'm not going to betray her trust by explaining. That's her decision. What I can tell you was that I didn't mean to hurt her. I thought I was protecting her—protecting us both—but I wasn't. And once I realized that, I had some things to come to terms with before I could talk it through with her. Then I tried, messed up again, she let me have it, and since then, I've been doing everything I can to show her how much she means to me. I'm not perfect, but I see her, and no one is angrier at me than I am for hurting her in the first place." I stand up from the stool. "Now, if you don't mind, I need to go talk to her. As much as I appreciate you standing up for her, you're not the one I need to talk to about this. She is."

He stares at me for a moment, then gives an approving nod. "Go ahead."

I don't need his fucking permission, which is why I'm already moving down the hallway before he's finished speaking.

I hate knowing I hurt her—that I made her cry.

When I get to Amanda's room, I pause in the doorway, watching her as she scribbles a note on a piece of paper and pins it to the bulletin board above her desk. I swear, her mind never stops moving.

I shouldn't be surprised that her room has an entire aesthetic vibe that I see and immediately associate with her. Light purples and pinks melt together with creamy tans, but not in a way that seems girlish. Pillows and wall hangings with quotes dot the space. Everything is low-key, but perfectly placed.

There's a cozy chair by a bookshelf in the corner, and there are tons of pillows and a fluffy throw blanket on her bed.

It's the picture of refined comfort.

"This room is perfectly you."

She turns around with a smile. "Thank you. Event planning isn't quite interior design, but they flex a lot of the same muscles. It helps that I know what I like." She puts a hand on her hip and stares at me, smile growing. "I think you'd look pretty good in here too."

"Yeah?" I cross the room to her and wrap my arms around her.

"Mhm."

I love the feeling of her arms wrapped around me as she rests her body against mine.

I run my fingers through her hair, and she looks up at me. "Are you okay?"

I put my hands on her shoulders and look into her eyes. "Did I make you cry?"

Her lips pull flat. "What did Pete say?"

"It doesn't matter. Did I?"

She pushes out of my arms and shrugs while shaking her head. "I—it wasn't you—I got my hopes up, and..."

Not letting her get away with that answer, I cup her face in my hands. "Tell me the truth."

"Yes, I cried that night. But I shouldn't have given you that power so easily."

"No. I shouldn't have taken anything about you or our friendship—what it was growing into—for granted. I'm sorry my carelessness hurt you."

Tears well in her eyes, but she blinks them away. "I'm not good at this."

"At what?"

"Being vulnerable. Letting someone else see my hurt."

"I see it whether you let me or not. I always see you."

"Jamie..."

I sweep my thumb under her eye and wipe away a tear, then lean down, resting my forehead against hers.

"I'm sorry I hurt you, but I promise to keep working to fix that hurt and to protect your heart in the future. And I'll do my best to show that with my actions."

She stares at me silently for a moment, those caramel eyes gazing intently into mine.

"Thank you for being here," she whispers.

"Thank you for letting me in."

This time, she pulls me into a hug, holding me tightly. I gently kiss her head and something inside me cracks open.

I didn't know I wanted this, but now that I have it, I don't think I could ever go without it. I couldn't go without her.

"Are we okay?" I ask.

She smiles up at me. "We are. And we have been." She rests one hand over my heart, and it's almost too much.

It's not even that no one else has ever made me feel like this, it's that I never conceptualized what this would be like. It was impossible to imagine because I couldn't have imagined her.

"Has your room always been like this?"

She laughs and steps back. "Definitely not. It's always been an extension of me, and that has changed over time. I think the first design of my room was mostly rainbows and unicorns. That was in elementary school. Then there was the middle school makeover, which featured a lot of teal for some reason, and aggressive patterns that felt more *adult*. Then there was the early high school makeover. My mom didn't let me paint my room black, so I hung black blankets on the walls. It looked like a witch's den. It was the tipping point to finding what I like though. It morphed into black and tan and then black and white with pops of neon color—especially pink—to what it is now. I think this is most reflective of me. It has the vibrance I crave, then some of those dark hues from my witchy era. Along with the quotes on the wall, most of which are feminist or empowering in some way. Everything is more toned down now. I'd like to believe I'm the same way. Maybe not toned down, but refined."

"It definitely is. It's all blended together seamlessly and totally fits the vibe I get from you." I look around. "Except maybe those."

She turns and looks at her bookcase. "Ah, yes. My bears."

I follow her over to the bookshelf. On one shelf sits a row of bears with shirts from various places. One is a Winnie the Pooh from Disney World. The rest all have names of places on them.

"Souvenirs?"

"Not exactly. Souvenirs are things you collect from anywhere you go. These are meaningful. I only get bears from places I really loved visiting or that hold special meaning to me."

"Is that why there's one from SUNY FL?"

"Yeah. I didn't buy it until the end of the year. That's when it became special. Because I knew the friendships I made there would last forever." She elbows me lightly. "I'll have to add one for whatever team you get drafted to."

"To go with this?" I pick up the baseball I signed for her. "You kept it?"

She shrugs, that deep vulnerability shimmering in her eyes. "I was hurt, but I didn't hate you. My feelings for you didn't disappear, so I kept it. Probably would've kept it either way, since it's going to be worth *so* much money one day."

I set the ball back down. "Don't ruin it by joking around."

"Maybe a part of me didn't want to give up." We stare at each other for a moment, the weight of it all settling between us. "So, uh, you really think you'll play for the Metros?"

I take half a step back, letting the tension dissipate. "I don't know. I hope so. Plus, I like the idea of being somewhat close to Ida."

"There are other teams in the Northeast. Like maybe the Revs?"

I tilt my head and she smiles. "How did you know I like the Revs?"

It's not exactly a secret, but the Revs and the Metros are rivals, and if I had to pick, my loyalties would lie with the Metros every time. But I have to admit, the Revs are a damn good team.

"One of their games was on last weekend at Mixed Brews. You kept looking out of the corner of your eye, and I saw you restrain your excitement when Kyle Bosco hit a home run."

Damn. I'm not the only one who's been paying attention.

"I'd be an idiot to turn down the Revs—or literally any chance at playing professionally. If I get to play for the Metros, that's the dream, but I'll be happy anywhere I make it."

She shifts closer, trailing her fingers down my arm. "Well, wherever you end up, I'll be there to watch you play."

My already soft heart melts at that. Her words show me she's not giving up on this... whatever's growing between us. She sees the potential there too. A future. For so long, when I imagined making it to the majors, it always felt a little lonely. Sure, I'd have my family and friends to celebrate with me, but the idea of having someone who's by my side through it all? It's almost too much to hope for, but I won't stop hoping, because Amanda deserves to be someone's hope. Someone's dream. Someone's wish. There's no doubt anymore, she's mine.

10
Choose You

Jamie

"HENDERSON! Get your head in the game!"

Signing up to be part of the first year of a baseball camp run by my coach has been one of the best and worst decisions I've ever made.

Best because it's focused on honing our skills, and with Aaron helping out with coaching, I'm seeing all the little areas I still need to work on.

Worst because my coach knows me too well and doesn't let me slack off in the slightest, even if my slacking is better than some guys' A game.

I'm not slacking today, but I'm preoccupied. I'm officially the guy letting a girl distract me from my game, but it's not because of a fight—at least I don't think so. It's because she hasn't responded to a text from me in almost twenty-four hours. And while I'm not a needy SOB, that's unlike her. I'm not stupid enough to think she's ghosting me when her last text to me was the heart-eyes emoji and the words *goodnight, baseball boy.*

I'm more worried something's wrong, and she wouldn't tell me because she doesn't want to bother me. I wish she'd realize she's never bothering me. She's not a problem. I don't understand why no one else in her life has ever made her feel like she's the best fucking thing in the world, but I'm going to keep telling her that and treating her that way.

She left for vacation with her family this morning, so she might be busy, but if anything, I would've expected her to text me on the car ride. Maybe I *am* a needy SOB.

"Sorry, Coach," I say as I run off the field. One more hour and I can check my phone and try to figure out what's going on.

"You stressed about draft stuff again?" Aaron asks, walking over to me.

I did as Amanda suggested that night on my back deck and started thinking about what I want. That's not just a short-term question, but a long-term one as well. So, I talked about it with Aaron, who offered to reach out and try to get some advice from current major or minor league players.

"Not specifically," I say casually. It's always in the back of my mind, but definitely not the forefront right now. I'm hesitant to mention Amanda to him because I know how this friend group can be. Meddling and pushy. Trevor can at least keep his mouth shut. I want to have a chance to let things with Amanda grow before adding in all that chaos.

"You're being cagey."

"Just worried about a friend."

He squints at me for a long moment. All my friends are his friends, so he must know I'm talking out of my ass. That's confirmed when he arches a brow then breaks into a grin.

"Ah, this friend wouldn't happen to have long strawberry blonde hair and a hurt-my-friends-and-die attitude, would she?"

My cheeks give me away. I couldn't lie if I wanted to all because of them and my stupid pasty white skin.

"Maybe."

"What's wrong?"

"Eh, we text a lot. She hasn't responded in the last day or so and we left things on a good note, so I'm worried. She tends not to let people in. But she's on vacation, so I might be overthinking it."

He frowns. "She didn't go."

My stomach drops. "What? Why not?"

He gives a little shake of his head and pulls out his phone. "She's sick, I guess. I don't know exactly. The girls mentioned it in our group chat this morning."

Of course not the group chat I'm in.

"Here." He holds up his phone, and I read through a few of the messages.

RAE

Sarah, how's Mands?

SARAH

I don't know. She wouldn't open her bedroom door because she didn't want to give me her germs. There was plenty of easy to eat food in the fridge, and I left a bunch of Gatorade and crackers there. She said it's a nasty stomach bug. I'm guessing so since it's been almost two full days of her not being able to eat much.

MACKIE

That sucks. Do you think she needs anything else?

SARAH

IDK. Her parents are out of town, but she said Pete is checking in on her before and after work.

MACKIE

We should make a schedule to check in with her.

RAE

I'll figure something out in a bit.

"Tell them no one needs to stop by tonight."

Aaron gives me his biggest know-it-all smile. "Will do."

Two full days? And she didn't even mention it to me yesterday?

She has to learn she is not a burden, and she deserves to be taken care of.

Now I just need to get through an hour of training camp so I can show her.

AMANDA'S HOUSE is dark when I get there around five. It's not that late, but it feels like it is when I walk inside.

"Amanda?" I call as I walk through the kitchen. Nothing.

I stop to grab some Gatorade, water, and crackers, then head upstairs. But when I get to her room, it's empty. There's a bucket by the side of her bed and half-empty bottles on her nightstand.

"Amanda?" I call again, something sinking in my gut.

When I turn around, I see the bathroom light streaming from under the partially closed door.

I cross the hallway and shove it open, my heart leaping into my throat when I see her lying on the floor.

I drop to my knees next to her and sweep some hair off her face. She looks up at me, tired and confused.

"Baby, how long have you been here?"

She tries to shrug, but can't. Her lips are chapped and peeling, she's sweaty, and her forehead is hot.

"Okay, we're going to the hospital."

Her face crinkles up, and she shakes as she cries. Or tries to. No tears come out.

I sit down on the floor, then carefully pull her toward me, easing her upright and resting her against me.

"What are..." She coughs and clears her throat. I reach for the bottle of water on the floor and hand it to her. She only takes a few sips before setting it down again. "What are you doing here?"

"You weren't answering my texts, then I found out you were sick. I came over to check on you."

"I'm sorry," she says weakly. "I didn't want you to worry. Or feel responsible. You should go so you don't get sick too. Then your siblings—"

"Don't worry about all that. My parents are no strangers to dealing with horrific viruses in our house. That said, this seems like norovirus, and we had that in the spring. Usually the immunity lasts for a bit, but even if it doesn't... I don't care."

"Are you sure?"

"Yes, I'm sure. There is nowhere else I'd be right now. You need someone to take care of you, and I want to be that person. I'll always take care of you. Always show up when you need me."

She sniffs again and leans against my chest.

"When was the last time Pete was here?"

"This morning. He's working late tonight."

"Okay, I'll text him and tell him not to come. We're going to the hospital, then we're going to come back here and binge watch movies until you fall asleep."

"I don't know if I can move," she whimpers.

"I've got you. Just hold on to this"—I hand her the water bottle—"and tell me where your purse is."

"Coat rack. Back door."

I shift her in my arms, then slowly, carefully, get to my feet.

"Jamie—"

"Shh. Let me take care of you."

"But I'm too—"

"If you say something about being too heavy to carry, I'm going to put you in time out."

She's quiet for a second, then she whispers, "Not spank me?"

A laugh slips out. "Good to know you're still in there."

She buries her head in my chest and groans. "Barely."

"Don't worry. I've got you. I'll be your sexy nurse and have you feeling better in no time."

"Thank you."

"You don't need to thank me. Just let me take care of you."

She looks up at me with shimmering eyes, and it hits me how truly gone for her I am. I would drop everything to be here for her. Even baseball. That's a sobering and surprisingly not terrifying thought. It feels right. Like I'm exactly where I'm supposed to be.

"AM I DEAD?" Amanda groans.

I rub my thumb over her cheek. "No. If anything, you're finally getting some of your spark back."

"I don't feel very sparkly. More like glowy in the way someone describes a pregnant woman whose skin is shimmery with sweat from puking all morning."

She grimaces at her own words.

"Hey, you haven't had any, uh, *explosive* events since we got here."

"Yeah. I finally don't feel like I'm going to puke every thirty seconds. And everything hurts a little less."

"Because you're hopped up on painkillers. And lots of fluids."

She winces as she looks at the needle in her arm. Apparently, my girl is not a fan of needles.

"I just want to go home. I feel gross and I'd at least rather be gross there."

I flick the IV bag. "Almost empty."

"That it is," the doctor says, walking into the room. "You're looking better. How do you feel?"

"Ugh. But not like I'm going to keel over and die."

"I'll take the improvement."

"I'm still a little nauseous, though. I'm afraid I'm going to go home and end up back in the same place."

"Well, lucky for you, the nurse is on her way in with a shot of an antiemetic. That should get you through. Try to get some food down when you get home and stay as hydrated as you can."

"I'll make sure she does."

"All right. The nurse will be in with the shot and discharge paperwork. Take care."

"Thank you," Amanda musters weakly.

I run my fingers through her messy hair.

"I hate that you have to see me like this."

"You're beautiful."

She opens her mouth to say something, but the nurse walks in before she can.

"Okay, I hear someone is ready to be set free. You just need a little something special to get you through."

Amanda whimpers at the needle the nurse holds up.

"The good news is you don't have to look at it going in."

"What do you mean?"

"This one goes in your butt cheek."

I stifle a laugh as Amanda squeaks, "In my butt?"

"Come on, baby. You'll be fine. Just flip over and stick your butt out."

She hits me with that death glare, so I drop a kiss on her forehead.

"I hate you," she grumbles.

"Nah. You could never *hate* me. Come on. Roll over. I'll hold your hand."

She slowly rolls onto her stomach, and the nurse pulls the tie on her gown.

Amanda buries her head in the pillow. "This is mortifying."

"I don't know. You've got a cute butt."

The nurse snickers, and Amanda whips her head to look at me, but when she sees my eyes locked on her, she softens.

"Perfect," the nurse says.

"Ow!" Amanda whines.

"It'll burn for a second, but I promise it'll help. You can roll back over now. I'm going to get this IV out, then you can get dressed." The nurse looks at me. "If you want, you can go grab the car, then pull up to the entrance."

I look at Amanda, uncertain. "Are you going to be okay getting dressed?"

"I'll be fine."

"Okay." I lean down and kiss her forehead again. "I'll see you soon."

She grabs my hand as I pull away, the touch sending sparks through me. Her eyes glisten with tears, and it breaks me.

I wrap her in a hug. "It'll only be a few minutes, then you've got me all night."

She nods and wipes her eyes, and reluctantly, I walk out of her room.

The whole walk to the car, I'm twisted up. I don't think I'm just trying to date her anymore. I think I'm falling for her. I *have* fallen. I told her I'm going to consider her mine, but even that isn't strong enough to explain what she means to me. All too quickly, she's become a massive part of my life, and that's how I want it to be.

As grateful as I am that she's letting me take care of her, I'm also pissed no one else is around. How long would she have laid on that bathroom floor before Pete found her? I know the girls were going to check in too, but it drives me insane that she's so afraid of bothering someone to let anyone take care of her. And I'm a little pissed that her parents would go on vacation while she's obviously really sick.

She said they had it planned for a long time, but that's no excuse. I can't imagine my parents doing that with any of us. My mom still brings me Gatorade in a kiddie straw cup when I'm sick and makes sure I have everything I need.

I wish Amanda wasn't so used to being an afterthought. That's something I need to change.

When I pull up to the entrance, they haven't wheeled her out yet, so I grab my phone and type out a text.

> Hey, Coach. Sorry, but I won't be at training camp tomorrow. I've been at the hospital with a friend tonight, and they still need someone with them while they recover. If everything goes okay, I'll be back on Friday.

Out of the corner of my eye, I see them wheeling Amanda out the door. I shut my screen off without sending the message, then hop out of the car.

"Can you get up okay?" the guy pushing the wheelchair asks.

"I've got her." I swing the door open, then wrap my arm around Amanda's back and help her into the passenger seat.

Once I'm back in the driver's seat again, I grab my phone and send the message.

"Everything okay?" she asks.

"Yeah. I was just letting my coach know I won't be there tomorrow."

"What—Jamie... you have to go."

"No. I don't. I told you I'm going to take care of you, and I meant it."

Her eyes fill with tears. "You're choosing me over baseball?"

The surprise in her eyes breaks me a little. "Yes." I press a kiss to her cheek. "Now, let's get you home."

The heat of her gaze stays on me as I pull out of the parking lot.

I will do everything in my power to prove to her that she deserves to be chosen, and even if no one else does, I'll choose her every time.

Amanda

JAMIE UNDERSTOOD THE ASSIGNMENT. Maybe better than I did. Because when I told him to prove how he felt—that he truly wanted me—I meant for him to show up. To make an effort to spend time with me, and he's done that. I was expecting him to ask me out on that date again when he came to my house for the barbeque, but he's taken it all slowly. He's done exactly what I've asked. He's shown up for me.

Now he's doing something I never expected. He's choosing me over baseball. And that warms something in the cold, dead romantic part of my heart.

I'm still not sure where the change came from, but it's hard to care with his arm wrapped around me as he helps me up the stairs to my bedroom.

For once in my life, I don't feel uncomfortable with someone other than my parents caring for me. The truth is, I really wanted my mom when I was lying on the bathroom floor.

I almost called and asked her to come home. I know she would have. But they planned that vacation over a year ago. Even if I couldn't go, they deserved to. Sure, a part of me still hoped my mom would choose to stay with me, make sure I was okay, and go later. But I said over and over that I'd be fine, and I wasn't going to take it back at the last minute.

So I suffered alone. Pete was helpful, but I could tell he was tired. He works for Rae's dad doing something... techy. I don't know. He's passionate about it, though, and has been putting in extra hours lately.

I appreciated Sarah stopping by, but she works as a nursing assistant at an OBGYN. The last thing I wanted was for her to get sick.

And just maybe letting someone else take care of me is a form of being vulnerable that's hard for me. But it came easier than expected with Jamie.

"Here we are." He swings my bedroom door open, and I wrinkle my nose at the smell. I'm not sure if it's me or the room or both, but everything smells gross. I feel gross.

"Ugh."

"Are you okay? Need the bathroom?"

He's so cute with his caretaking. I'm guessing at least some of it is learned from having young siblings, but I get the sense it's also in his nature.

"No. Well, actually, yes. I want to take a shower."

He pulls his arm from my back and takes me in. "Do you need any help?"

"No. I'll be fine." But as I say it, the world spins and I have to grip the doorway.

"Uh huh. I don't think so. If you have to hold the door frame to stay upright, there's no way I'm letting you anywhere slippery, unsupervised."

"You just want to see me naked," I tease.

"Obviously." He steps in closer, brushing his thumb over my cheek. "Let me help you."

"Fine. I might need your help to change the sheets afterward too."

"Whatever you need." He wraps his arm around my waist again and guides me toward the bathroom.

When we get there, he leans me against the wall, then gets towels from the cabinet.

I make an attempt at getting undressed, but I almost lose my balance several times.

"Need some help?" Jamie asks with a roguish smile.

"Are you that desperate to see me naked? Or did you just want to cop a feel?"

"Why can't it be both?" He moves closer, the warmth of his body surrounding me. "No. The truth is, I don't want to risk you falling. You might break a leg. Or a hip. Then we'd have to go to the hospital again. There'd be more needles. And I wouldn't even get to see you naked."

"Good to know where your priorities are."

"You're my priority." He says it so simply and smoothly, like it's nothing. But those words are everything. They mirror the intimacy of this moment.

I bite my lip as I nod, and slowly, he reaches for my shirt.

His fingers trail my navel as he pushes my shirt up, then carefully pulls it over my head. He ends up with his face right in front of my naked boobs—because no one wants to wear a bra when they're hurling their guts out. I'm sure they're a sweaty mess of gross, but Jamie doesn't seem to care. He chokes on a breath, then stands up straight.

"Okay there?" I ask.

"Fine. Just..." He clears his throat. "Don't hold it against me if you *see* anything. I'm staring at the girl of my dreams, and she's so damn stunning I can barely keep it together."

My body flushes at the compliment.

I try not to spend too much time thinking about my body. I buy clothes I look good in and don't pay attention to the size. But sometimes those societal standards of beauty creep in. The same ones I learned from diet commercials growing up. The things that told me I'm not good enough as I am. That there's something wrong with my body.

I make it a point to call myself beautiful, and say nice things about myself in those moments.

I've never felt self-conscious hooking up with someone because they wouldn't have wanted to hook up with me in the first place if they didn't find me somewhat attractive. Plus, it's low stakes.

But with Jamie? I'm weirdly glad him seeing me naked is happening like this. I didn't have time to feel nervous about my body before he complimented it. And even though I shouldn't need that affirmation, I want it. Everyone wants their partner to find them attractive—to enjoy their body. And even though he's not technically my *partner* yet, he's become my person. And that might mean more.

"Wait till you see the whole thing," I tease in as sultry a voice as I can manage when I'm still way too close to falling over.

His fingers dance along the waistband of my sweats. "Just know, the next time you're naked in front of me, I'm going to touch you everywhere and enjoy every moment of your beautiful body writhing under my touch."

I suck in a sharp breath as he pulls my pants down.

"Don't make promises you won't keep."

"Oh, I'll keep every delicious word." He sighs as he steps back and looks at me, eyes tracing the length of my body. "You are stunning. So utterly beautiful it's hard to breathe."

"That's probably just because all your blood is rushing south," I say, eyes drifting to the obvious bulge in his gym shorts.

He cups my cheek and meets my eyes. "Take the compliment. Now, do you have a stool or something you can sit on in the shower?"

"Hall closet. There's one from after my dad had his knee replaced."

He nods, then goes to get it.

Once I'm set up, the shower is easy enough. I do all the washing and Jamie uses the detachable shower head to help me rinse off.

It might've felt more sensual if I wasn't so exhausted. Between the ER visit and the shower, it's almost ten at night. I'm surprisingly hungry and utterly exhausted.

Jamie pulls the stool from the shower as I wrap a towel around myself.

"Sit."

Then he grabs another towel and carefully wraps it around my hair, gently drying the strands. When my hair is damp instead of dripping wet, he pulls the towel away, then grabs my hairbrush.

I almost protest, but he whispers, "Trust me."

He slowly moves the brush through my hair, stopping and working out each knot before continuing on. This... this is the sensual moment. One I might beg him to repeat one day when we get to shower together.

With tenderness and care, he runs the brush through over and over until it glides smoothly, making sure not to pull on a single strand.

"There's a leave-in on the sink that helps with frizziness. If you want to put some in."

"Sure. Just tell me how much."

"Just a penny sized amount and rub it between your hands, then work it in."

He looks up and his eyes meet mine in the mirror. He squints a little, then smiles and turns around. "Are you enjoying this?"

"Maybe."

"Good."

He works his hands through my hair methodically, getting every single strand, and when he's finished, he runs the brush through a few more times.

I'm not sure I've ever let someone take care of me like this. Let my guard down so completely. I asked Jamie to prove it. But I gave myself an assignment too. To work on opening up to him and being vulnerable in a way I haven't allowed myself to be with another person—not romantically, at least—in a long time.

I've never been more vulnerable than I have been over the last few hours, but this is different. I'm openly choosing that vulnerability, and to my surprise, it feels good. It feels right. And I'm really happy Jamie is the one I'm doing it with.

I'M A MESS. Not a hot mess express.

Like a train wreck. Everything's a mess and a couple of things are on fire.

I sniff back tears as I pull the blankets up farther. After my shower, I sat in my desk chair and got dressed while Jamie put fresh sheets on my bed. Then I ate a couple of bowls of mashed potatoes, some saltines, a bowl of vanilla coconut ice cream, and drank a bottle of Gatorade. My stomach feels better, but I'm still tired, achy, and emotional. I always feel this way when I'm sick.

"Hey, what's wrong?" Jamie asks the second he walks back into the room.

I wave my hand in front of me. "Nothing. It's stupid. I always get weepy when I'm sick."

He sits down next to me, resting his hand on the back of my neck, then running it down my back.

"What's making you cry right now?"

"You're... here."

He nods exaggeratedly. "I know. I'm pretty terrible company."

At least that gets a laugh out of me. Then I clutch my stomach. The muscles are sore from all the puking.

"No. I mean... you're here. You came to take care of me. You made me a priority."

"And someday, you're going to stop being surprised by that."

I rest my head on his shoulder, savoring the comfort he gives as tears roll down my cheeks.

"Sometimes I wonder if I push people away too much and they assume I don't want them around, so they don't go out of their way for me. Other times, I think I'm too clingy. I didn't want to get anyone else sick—"

"But you deserve to be taken care of. Listen, as nice as your folks seem, it's not okay that a vacation and their sick daughter were equal choices. You should've been the priority. I'm sorry you weren't. For the record, the girls were going to make a schedule to come check on you. They knew exactly why you didn't want them here, and they didn't give a shit. I just told Aaron to tell them not to come because selfishly, I wanted to be the one to take care of you. And don't you dare ask why."

I bite my lip to keep myself from saying something I'll regret. Something that I'm not even sure I fully feel yet, but keeps dancing in my brain regardless. *Love*. It's just because I'm an emotional mess.

I force out a breath and snuggle into his side. "Thank you. I'm glad you're here."

"Good. Now, you're going to relax and watch *One Tree Hill* while I run my fingers through your hair until you fall asleep. And when you wake up in the morning, I promise you're going to feel a lot better."

He kisses my head, and any arguments die. I'm exhausted, and for once, it feels nice to let someone take care of me because they want to, not because they have to. Not because I'm a burden. Jamie wants me. He wants to care for me. And that thought alone is enough to soothe my frayed edges, allowing me to relax a little more until I drift off to sleep.

JAMIE WAS RIGHT. I'm feeling a lot better today. Still tired and sore, but I've been able to eat and drink okay. Mostly easy to eat foods, but it's better than before. We even went for a walk around the block.

Now we're relaxing in my bed. I'm not really ready to sleep yet, but I'm too tired to do anything else. And like last night, my emotions are haywire, but this time, I don't think it's from sickness. I like Jamie being here, and I'm worried I've gotten too used to it. He has to go back to training camp tomorrow—I want him to—but now that I've slept in his arms, it's going to be hard not to have that all the time.

Jamie runs his fingers through my hair. I'm lying down, facing away from him, even though the 2005 version of *Pride and Prejudice* is playing in the background.

"What's wrong, baby?"

I sniff and quickly wipe my eyes, but I'm sure I'm not hiding anything.

He rubs one hand down my back, then goes back to playing with my hair.

"Are you feeling sick again?"

I shake my head, then notice the slight tug on my hair when I do. It takes me a second to realize he's braiding my hair.

"It's sweet that you learned to braid hair for your sisters."

"I actually like it. After a while, it becomes mindless. Almost like a fidget toy. But with your soft hair, I never want to stop touching it. I could play with it all day."

Ah, stupid tears.

I sniff again, and he lightly tugs on my hair.

"What's wrong?"

"This. I'm… getting too used to it."

"Good," he whispers.

I roll over to face him. "What changed?"

"What do you mean?"

"You said you couldn't give me anything because of your commitment to baseball. Now you're choosing me over baseball. What changed?"

"I understood what I had to lose." He brushes his thumb slowly across my cheek. "I thought baseball had to come first because outside of my family and friends, no one had ever compared to baseball. But all it took was one day of not talking to you to realize how deeply I feel for you. It took longer to deal with that fact and convince myself I could have both things. Once I did, there wasn't a choice. Wanting you isn't a choice. Caring for you isn't a choice. You're everything, and you deserve the world, so I'm going to give it to you. If that means baseball has to be an occasional sacrifice, then it will be. I hear that's what good relationships are. Compromise and sacrifice when needed. You've had too many people not choose you, but I have, and I'll continue to do that as long as you let me."

Fuck.

I'm so screwed.

I'm falling for him, and that terrifies me because it won't be easy. Distance will be a big part of our future, and as a clingy, sometimes emotionally needy person, that's going to be hard for me. But like he just said, it's not a choice. I want him the way he wants me. Nothing has ever been more terrifying, but it's never been more exciting either.

"Yes," I say suddenly.

"What?"

"Yes. I'll go on a date with you."

His smile lights up the room. "It's cute that you think we haven't been dating for the last few weeks. But I do have a special date I want to take you on. Once you're better, I'll officially ask you the way you deserve to be asked."

"Jamie," I whisper, cupping his cheek. Then I press my fingers into his skin and pull him to my lips.

His breath hitches, then he wraps his arm around me, fingers curling into my hair as he deepens the kiss. His tongue twists with mine and every thought drifts away. Every fear. There's nothing but the two of us. And unlike the last time, there's no hesitancy, no holding back. Every swipe of his tongue is more powerful than the last. I claw my fingers through his hair, pressing against him.

He breaks the kiss long enough to look at me, then dives forward, claiming me all over again. It's so easy to get lost in the connection between us, the tension swirling around us, the heat growing more intense with every second.

We untangle slowly, and as he pulls away, he brushes his nose against mine, then he shifts so he's lying next to me and wraps his arms around me.

There's a comfortable silence as we hold each other. And then, letting myself be vulnerable one more time, I say, "Jamie?"

"Yeah?"

"After training camp tomorrow, would you come over? Stay the night again?"

He buries his face in my neck. "I'd love to."

With those words, another cracked piece of my heart heals a little.

11
Our Future

Amanda

"SO, are you guys excited to go to Charleston later this week?"

We're having a girls' night at Rae and Sarah's house. Our first one since I was horribly sick a little over a week ago. Though they were all ready to storm my house, I told them I was okay. I just didn't mention that Jamie was the reason for that. They know he stopped by, but not that he spent days taking care of me. I'm pretty sure Aaron knows a bit more, but if he does, he hasn't told the girls.

It's not that I'm trying to keep secrets, but there's something about what Jamie and I are doing that's sacred. It's ours. And I'll happily gush to the girls when I'm ready, but for now, I'm happy that it's just for us.

"I'm ready for the beach," Sarah says. "And a vacation."

"Same," Mackie says.

"I am trying not to get my hopes up, but... I don't know. It's mine and Aaron's special spot. Maybe we'll find the magic we need to finally fix things."

I grab her hand and squeeze it tightly. "I hope you do. Macks, what about you and Hyla?"

I may not love how Hyla treated her, and it's hard to trust

Hyla's intentions, but I know Mackie still loves her, and I never want to see one of my friends hurting.

Mackie shrugs, but she can't hide the pain in her eyes. "I guess I'll see when we get there." She waves a hand in dismissal. "Anyway, what are you going to do while we're gone?"

"Enjoy the peace," I say playfully.

"Ugh, rude," Rae says. "You know your life would be boring without us."

And empty. But I don't say that.

"Less drama at least."

Rae sticks her tongue out at me.

"Well, I still think you should come with us. You can be Mackie's plus one to the wedding. Or just lounge on the beach," Sarah says.

"That does sound good, but I'd feel like an... I don't even know what number wheel. Odd man out."

Which isn't really the truth. The truth is Jamie isn't going to the wedding either. It's some friends of the friend group. Hyla and Trevor's besties, I guess, but Jamie wasn't close with them. And the idea of having Jamie all to myself for a whole week— especially since baseball camp will be done—sounds even better than lounging on the beach.

"Well, you never would be, but I understand not wanting to tag along to the wedding. Either way, if you change your mind, you're always welcome," Mackie says.

"I appreciate it. I expect lots of pictures and updates."

"Yes, ma'am," Rae says.

"Yeah, gotta keep you updated on Rae and Aaron's drama," Sarah teases.

"And on that note, I need brownies."

"Oh, yes, please."

We all climb off Rae's bed, but as we go to walk downstairs, my phone goes off.

I walk slowly so I can quickly check it, since I'm totally hung up on a certain boy.

BASEBALL BOY

How's your night going?

Good. Hanging out with the girls.

BASEBALL BOY

Damn. Does that mean I can't sneak in your window tonight?

Though he hasn't done that, he did spend every night my parents were on vacation at my house and snuck me into his house a few times so we could sleep in the same bed.

That and I'm not letting you risk falling off a ladder and breaking your neck.

BASEBALL BOY

Aw, you care about me.

Maybe 😏

BASEBALL BOY

Can I see you tomorrow?

Definitely.

BASEBALL BOY

I'll text you in the morning. Have a good night, gorgeous.

You too, baseball boy.

I tuck my phone away, then quickly school my features before following the girls into the kitchen.

Ugh, I'm a total swooning mess over him, but my heart is so happy it's hard to care.

COFFEE IS my favorite part of the morning. Jamie is still insistent on paying for my coffee even though things are good between us, so I started putting a few dollars in the tip jar every time.

Walking up the stairs and into Bewitched, I'm energized by my need for caffeine. Although I'm not sure if it's actually the caffeine I'm hooked on or the comforting feeling I get from a cup of coffee.

When I pull the door open, I almost do a double take. Everything is even prettier than normal. There are twinkle lights all over, giving the whole place a cozy glow. It also smells deliciously of chocolate, and when I get to the counter and am about to order my usual, I notice a sign that says their drink of the day is my favorite seasonal beverage—one they usually have around Valentine's Day—chocolate lava cake latte.

The woman behind the counter smiles at me like she knows exactly what I was going to order.

Once my drink is ready, I make my way over to the seating area, only to stop in my tracks when I find all the tables covered in bouquets of pink and coral roses and rose petals spread all over the floor and chairs.

"Would you believe the lady at the flower shop said this might be too much?"

I spin around and see Jamie standing there holding another bouquet. This one is bigger and has baby's breath in it.

"What does the event queen think?" He steps closer. "Too much?"

I pretend to think about it. "Well, that depends. You have to know your audience. What does the lucky girl this is for think?"

He wraps his arm around me and looks into my eyes. I love the height difference between us. Seven inches. So I always have to look up a little, he always has to look down a little, which means there's nothing to distract us, we're focused wholly on each other.

"I don't know. What *does* the lucky girl think?"

"It's perfect."

"Good." He brushes his lips over mine. "So, will you finally let me take you on a fancy date and spoil you?"

My cheeks heat and excitement whirls through me. "Yes. I'd love that."

He sets the bouquet on one of the nearby tables and sweeps me into his arms for a kiss.

It's swoony and romantic, like I'm living in a '90's rom-com.

I rest my hand on his cheek and get lost in the feeling that I'm his. That I'm wanted. That all this is for me. I'm always the one planning life's special moments. It means a lot to have a special moment planned for me.

Laughing, I break our kiss. "You know, if you ever propose to me, you're really going to have to kick it up a notch. You're setting the bar high asking me on a date."

"Not just any date. *The* date." He sighs happily. "I'm excited to spoil you. You have to promise no complaints. No saying you don't need or deserve things. You're going to let me give you everything."

"Everything?" I whisper, a little too sensually for this tiny bookshop.

His gaze intensifies, his smile morphing into a devastating smolder.

"You'll have to wait and see."

And just like that, I'm on fire for him.

"How's this weekend sound? Friday night? Everyone will be in Charleston, and we can enjoy ourselves while they're away."

"Sounds perfect to me." I look around the shop. "You did all of this to ask me out?"

He shrugs. "You deserve the best. And what's better than mood lighting and a billion flowers?"

I look down at the drink in my hand. "And my favorite drink? How did you know?"

"You post a lot more than you realize on your social media."

"You're such a stalker."

"Hasn't led me wrong yet."

"Mhm. We'll just see how this date goes."

"Trust me, you're going to love it."

I lean back a little so I can look up into his eyes. "How long have you been planning this date?"

He gives a little shrug. "Since the beginning or middle-ish of June."

"Before the infamous event showdown?"

"That makes it sound a lot cooler than it was. Even though you were a total badass yelling at me like that. It was hot."

"Jamie."

"Yeah. Before that."

I set my coffee down on the table and throw my arms around him. "I can't believe you've been planning it for almost two months."

"When I want something, I'll do anything to get it. And there's nothing I want more than us."

I hold him tighter, fingers curling into his hair.

That L-word rings in my mind again, but I tamp it down. It's too much. It's too soon.

But.

But my heart says.

It's there, whether I'm ready to accept it or not.

And if our date is anything like he says it's going to be, I might not have a choice.

Jamie

FINALLY.

Two months of planning. Six months of wanting her. Almost nine months of knowing her. It's all been building since the moment I laid eyes on her in Joel's kitchen. My world changed that day in the best possible way.

Hopefully, tonight will be the night she officially becomes my girl. And I'll be her man.

For most of my life, my dream has been baseball, and if you'd asked me a year ago, I would've said nothing would change that. Romance and love are for the future. But now I understand we don't get a choice on that. When the right person comes along, you fight with everything you have to make it work.

I'm not naive. We're young. There are going to be multiple challenges in our future. But I don't quit. When I'm committed to something, I see it through, and I don't half-ass it. I give my absolute all. Will there be a balance in figuring out how to do that with both baseball and the girl I... am falling for? Fuck. I don't think it's falling. I might actually be in love with her. Which sounds crazy since this is our first official date, even though we've had plenty of lunch dates, coffee dates, and I've spent multiple nights at her house, holding her while she sleeps and feeling like the luckiest man alive.

Okay, yes. Fuck it. I'm in love with her.

Am I going to say that tonight? Probably not. I'm not a lunatic.

I've just caught the same bug a bunch of my friends have— love. Love when you're least expecting it.

I wasn't expecting it to find me at eighteen, but I'm not risking losing it by worrying about my age or her age or any of the rest of it. We'll figure it out. If we really want to, we can.

Okay, maybe I'm a little naive.

But I'm not giving up.

I'll fight with everything I have to be the man she deserves and make her happy. And that starts tonight.

Again, fuck it. It started months ago, and that further proves I'm an idiot, but I'm *her* idiot as long as she'll have me.

I'M hopeful that Amanda's entire family won't be there when I knock on the front door. I want to pick her up and revel in the moment, not be on the receiving end of inquisitive or downright menacing looks. Especially when I asked her to pack a bag.

Maybe I'm overshooting with my hopes, but I'd rather want it and get shot down than not take the risk at all. I want to enjoy a weekend alone with her.

I haven't heard much from everyone down in Charleston, other than a text that Aaron and Rae finally got back together. It's about time. They've both grown a lot in the last year, and I have a feeling nothing will hold them back this time.

I'm grateful that them being in Charleston and focusing on all the romantic things down there means they aren't paying attention to us. We've made it seem like we're just friends.

Which we are.

But we're more than that too.

And hopefully, today, we become an official couple.

I swing my car door open and grab the bouquet I brought—not just flowers, but wrapped heart-shaped cake pops too—and head for Amanda's front porch.

When I knock on the door, it swings open immediately, and my breath sticks in my lungs. Holy shit, she's gorgeous. She's wearing a spaghetti-strap dress that cinches above her waist, perfectly showing her cleavage, then the fabric flows down to just above her knee. It's light pink at the top but uses a floral pattern to fade into almost all maroon at the bottom.

Her hair looks even silkier than normal and is styled with some gentle curls over the bottom half.

She's so stunning it's hard to breathe.

"Hi." God, I'm an idiot.

She laughs a little, smiling sheepishly. "Hi to you too."

I look beyond her. "Anyone else around?"

"Nope. They went out for the day. I told them I had plans with the girls—they don't need to know the girls are in Charleston."

"Sneaky." I can't stop staring at her, taking in every inch of her perfect body. The open toe booties she's wearing show off her toned legs, and everything about her look ties together seamlessly. "I swear I was going to be a lot smoother than this, but I can't help it. You're stunning."

Her cheeks flush, and she reaches for my hand. "Thank you. You look incredibly handsome."

I feel like nothing compared to her. I'm wearing fitted light gray dress pants with a light brown belt and matching loafers, and a cream-colored button down—with the top unbuttoned and the sleeves rolled halfway up my forearms. I managed to somewhat tame my hair, but all of that pales in comparison to Amanda. She's steal-the-show gorgeous, and at every stop on our date tonight, I know she'll turn heads.

"These are for you." I extend the bouquet for her and she takes it, smelling the flowers and pulling out one of the cake pops.

"Thank you."

"Do you have everything?"

Her eyes meet mine, dancing with mischief. "I think so." She grabs a clutch off the table by the door, and when I see a larger bag sitting on the floor, I reach in and grab it.

"Good. Then let's go."

I hold out my arm to her, and she slips her arm around my elbow.

This is it.

After all these months, I'm finally getting my date with Amanda. Now I need to make sure I get every moment of tonight right.

"SUSHI, HUH?"

I shut the car off and turn to Amanda, who is smiling as she looks at the building in front of us.

"I will never forget how you looked at that sushi when I helped you the night after the event. I knew if I was ever lucky enough to take you on a date, this is where I would take you. Or somewhere with great sushi. My mom recommended this place."

She looks away from the building slowly, meeting my gaze. "Why did you stay that night?"

"You needed help. And… I wanted to get to know you. From the moment we met, I felt that spark between us."

"Me too. I might've developed a little crush on you after that night."

I reach over and run my thumb over her cheek. "I'm still sorry for not taking your feelings into consideration the night I kissed you. You deserve to be chosen." I lean in and kiss the corner of her mouth. "To be treated exactly like the queen you are. I screwed up before, but I'm not going to do that again. I will do anything— everything—to be worthy of you and your heart."

"I know. You keep showing me. With every tiny thoughtful gesture, I know you see me. I hope you know I see you too." She brushes the back of her hand over the side of my face. "I see behind the mask."

"You always have." I let out a shaky breath, then force the words out all at once. "Amanda, will you be my girlfriend?"

Her eyes fly wide, surprise dancing in them. Her lips curve up into a massive smile, then she grabs my shirt, dragging me to her. "Yes. I would love to be your girlfriend." Her lips brush mine, then she pulls back with a devastatingly sexy smirk. "But it's cute that you think you haven't been my boyfriend for the last few weeks."

Fuck yes. I love that she thinks that. That she knew all along how much she means to me. Still, I run my hand up the side of her neck and look into her eyes.

"It hasn't been official though. And I want it to be. I don't ever want you to question where you stand with me. You're mine. The world should know that."

Again, she grazes her lips over mine, but it's not enough for me. I curl my fingers around the side of her neck, holding her in place as I deepen the kiss. She needs to know how serious I am.

Now that I have her, I'm not letting her go. I won't give up or walk away.

She moves a little closer, her hand resting on my chest, then her breath hitches, and she pulls back.

"I don't want to get too caught up here."

I trail my lips over her jaw. "You're right. We should save that for later."

She shivers in response, and I can't help but smile to myself.

"Sushi?" I ask, leaning back and flinging my door open.

She blinks a couple of times and fumbles for the handle of her door. "Yes, please."

Amanda

I AM A PERFECTLY SPOILED PRINCESS, and for once, I'm allowing myself to revel in every second of it.

Our sushi dinner was the best I've ever eaten in my life. Don't get me wrong, it was expensive, but I might have to splurge on that a couple of times a year. It was fantastic.

Now we're at some trendy dessert bar that smells like chocolate, vanilla, and heaven.

"So, I have an idea of what you might want, but take a look at the menu, and we'll see if I'm right."

I arch a brow at his cocky smile. "You know, as much as you like to use that cocky, confident exterior as a mask, you also have a cocky side. Though I'm starting to wonder if it only comes out for me."

He leans in, breath tickling my ear as he speaks. "You're always saying dirty things to me."

I give a playful shrug. "I think you've just got sex on your mind."

"I've got you on my mind."

"We could skip dessert," I tease, setting my menu down.

"Not a chance. My girl deserves the best, and that's exactly what you're going to get."

I'm trying to trust that he's right about that. He's shown me a lot over the last couple of months, and even though I said yes to him tonight—and I'm excited about that—I'm still nervous. I go back to school in two weeks. What happens then?

I don't want to think about it.

"I like when you call me your girl."

"Want to know a secret?"

"Tell me."

"I've been calling you that in my mind for months now."

"Manifesting?"

He tilts his head back and forth. "More like knowing what I want. I decided to consider you my girl and treat you like my girl, and I hoped that would help show you how much you mean to me."

"I appreciate that. I hope you know me saying yes—to this date or being your girlfriend—wasn't only about how you took care of me when I was sick. I appreciate that, but it was just a part of the bigger picture. You showed me you're paying attention—to me, to my words, and most importantly, to what I don't say. I've never had that before. Not like this. I hope I'm able to give you the same thing."

He cups my face, brushing his thumb over my bottom lip. "You do. From that night at the event, you've always seen right through me."

I tilt my head, begging him to kiss me again.

"Ready to order?"

Jamie and I break apart at the sound of the server's voice.

"Yep," Jamie clears his throat and glances at me. "Can I order for you?"

"Only if I can order for you."

He smiles at that. "Go ahead then."

I look at the server. "A vanilla raspberry cake."

Jamie's smile gets even bigger. "And... the chocolate lava cake?" He raises his brows in question, and I nod.

"Yes. The chocolate lava cake. Thank you."

"Phew. Got it right. So did you. How'd you know?"

"It was similar to the cake you said had at your birthday and you always love fruity things. And frosting." I give a little shrug, and his eyes dance like he's thrilled I've noticed those little things, but he shouldn't be surprised. I notice them for the same reason he does. "And how did you know I'd want a chocolate lava cake?"

Mine was a harder guess since there were several things on the menu I would've really enjoyed.

"Because your favorite seasonal latte is the chocolate lava cake. And when I asked you why, you told me it's because it's like drinking brownie batter. I figured a lava cake gives the same vibes. Plus, I know how you feel about brownies."

"You're always paying attention."

"Baby, it's impossible to keep my eyes off you."

And, ugh. *Swoon.*

I'm so head over heels for this boy, it's ridiculous.

Every time I look at him, my heart races and my body flushes as I think about what might happen next.

JAMIE HOLDS me close as we walk down the street toward his car. When we get there, he presses me against the passenger side door for a long kiss.

"Don't take this the wrong way," he breathes against my lips. "But I got a hotel room for tonight." He clears his throat and leans back. "Actually, it's for the whole weekend. Not for sex—I mean, obviously, I want you. But we don't *have* to. If all we do is snuggle, I'll be happy to have you in my arms."

I press my finger to his lips to shut him up. "I want to snuggle with you." Then I lean in, face just inches from his. "And I want to do so much more." I lightly press my lips to his, then give his bottom lip a quick bite.

He jolts back, gasping. "Okay, good. Let's go."

A laugh bubbles out of me as he grabs my hand and opens my door for me, his cheeks blazing red the whole time.

I'm ready to have some fun.

"HERE WE ARE." Jamie swings open the hotel room door and flicks on the light.

It's not just a hotel room, though. It's a whole ass suite.

"Jamie... this is huge. You didn't have to do all this."

He sets our bags down and wraps his arms around me. "I wanted to. You deserve all the best things. I just want you to know how much you mean to me. I messed up before and—"

"And I forgave you. We've moved forward, and it's important to me that you know none of that happened because of things you gave me or money you spent. It wasn't that you paid for my coffee, but that you knew where I liked to get it and how frequently I went there. All the little things you did that showed me how much you care for me are what mattered." I rest my hand on his chest. "You told me once that people tried to take advantage of you because of your family's wealth. I need you to know I will never do that. I'll never take advantage of you. I'll never take you for granted. You're what I want. Even if that scares me because all I see is a countdown until we'll be apart."

"Do you want this to work?"

"Of course I do."

"Then we'll make it work."

My chest still aches thinking about not having this every day. We waited so long to have it, and I'm a little obsessed now. Every second I spend with him makes me want more. Makes me want to hold on a little tighter.

"But I'm going to miss you. Like heartachingly badly."

He bites his bottom lip. "Well, as happy as I am to know I've wormed my way in there, we'll find ways to make it easier. I'll come visit. We'll text all the time like we do now. We'll talk on the phone. It might take some adjustments, but we'll figure it out. As long as we both want to."

"I want to. You have no idea how badly I want this, Jamie."

"I do, because I want this too. I want you. I need you." He hesitates for a second, breathing heavily. Then his blue eyes bore into mine, staring into the depths of my soul. "I love you, Amanda."

Oh my god.

He said... he just said...

Tears well in my eyes.

"I wasn't going to say it tonight. Maybe I shouldn't have. You don't have to say it back—"

I leap into his arms, wrapping my arms and legs around him and kissing him with every bit of the love inside me.

He stumbles back a step before he rights himself and kisses me back, one hand tangling in my hair.

I rip my lips from his, staring into the ocean blue eyes of the man who started stealing my heart the moment I met him.

"I love you too."

His chest rises and falls with heavy breaths, then his lips are on mine again, tongues twisting as our souls tangle together. I'm on fire for him in every way.

"I love you," he mutters against my lips, his hands roaming over my skin, every touch branding me as his.

I lean into him, pressing my body flush to his and feeling a certain hard muscle straining for release. I want more. I want all of him. Slowly, I reach for his belt, and his hands still on my back.

Then his fingers are moving again, fumbling with my zipper as I untuck his shirt. We messily try to get our clothes off without breaking our kiss. I never want him to stop kissing me or touching me. I'm desperate for more and ready to rip my dress off my body to have it. He shrugs his shirt off as I undo the button on his pants. Finally, I get to touch every muscle, every inch of skin I can find.

When my dress finally melts into a pile at my feet, his fingertips dance up my back, and I shudder with desire.

He takes half a step back, his hot gaze trailing down my body.

A blush creeps up, heating every inch of my skin. He's seen me naked before, but that was different.

"Like what you see?"

"You're perfect."

I want to shy away from the praise, but he grabs my chin between his thumb and forefinger.

"Don't do that. Don't try to play it off. Own it. You are beautiful, sexy, absolutely breathtaking. You're gorgeous. Don't doubt that for a second."

"You... look good... too," I choke out. Because my eyes have dropped to *that* muscle, and okay... I've read a lot of romance books and the guys always have giant peens that the girl is afraid of. Usually I roll my eyes at that because it's a little silly. And while I don't think Jamie could split me in half or anything, he is *big*. Deliciously big.

"See something you like?"

My confident side comes roaring back as I reach for him. "I feel something I like too."

"Fuck, Amanda."

He wraps his hand around the side of his neck and stares into my eyes. "Tell me what you want."

"You." I run my finger down his chest. "Every inch."

I've spent weeks—okay, *months*—dreaming of this. But I didn't dream it would happen like this. After creating a beautiful relationship. After a confession of love.

I need him now.

"I'm yours," I whisper.

He walks me backward toward the bed.

"I think we've covered the rest of the acronym, but there's one part we haven't talked about. *Protection*."

"I'm on birth control, so that covers the pregnancy side of things. I was tested at my gynecology appointment last month. All good. You?"

"I got tested at my annual in June. I haven't been with anyone else since... we started getting to know each other."

"Really?"

"You're the only one I wanted, even when I was too big of an idiot to see that or understand what it meant."

"Well then, if you're okay with it, we can just rely on my birth control."

"No condoms?"

"No."

"Why does this feel like another act of trust?"

I swallow and meet his gaze. "Because it is. I've never let any guy go without a condom before."

"I've never gone bare with anyone before."

"Good," I breathe. "Then I'll be the only one you've ever felt like this."

"Does that turn you on?"

"Ye-es," I hiss as his lips roll over my neck.

"Mm. Good. I can't wait to feel you pulse around my cock."

"I'm ready," I say breathlessly.

"No, you're not. Not yet. I haven't seen you come nearly enough times yet."

With one last kiss, he helps me onto the bed, settling me right in the center. Then he takes his time, kissing down my chest, teasing my nipples, grazing his lips down my navel as my core heats.

I'm already fisting the sheets and he hasn't even touched me down there yet.

"Is my girl ready for me?" he rumbles, and fuck, he's never looked sexier. Confident. In control.

I brush my fingers over his cheek. "You're not blushing."

The smile he gives me is almost feral. "Because I'm comfortable with you. I want to make sure you get everything you need. And... I like talking dirty. It's fun, and it keeps me in the moment. I've never gotten the chance to use it much, but I'd like to have some fun with it now if you'll let me."

"Yes." I quickly nod. It's hot as fuck.

"Good," he breathes. "But you haven't answered me yet. Is my girl ready for me?"

"Yes. Please."

He glances up at me as he kisses lower. Lower. "Such a good girl, using your manners."

I whimper, that slight praise making me even hotter. I need him to touch me. Fingers, tongue, I don't care. I need *something*.

Then finally, there's the softest brush of his fingers against my opening. He glides them up, smiling as he watches me.

"You like it when I call you my good girl?"

"Yes. I love it. I'll be perfect for you."

"I have no doubt." He shifts down farther, spreading my legs wider. "Good girls show me how much they like what I'm doing. I need to hear you scream and cry out. Otherwise, I won't know you're enjoying it. Can you do that?"

"Yes."

"Good girl."

Those words are a hit of straight dopamine.

But they're nothing compared to how I feel when his tongue swirls around my clit.

My ass launches off the bed, but he grabs my thighs, holding me tight to him.

"Yes, more," I whine, letting him know what I want—how good this is.

One hand slips off my thigh, then one finger swirls around my opening, and with his mouth on my clit and one finger pushing inside me, I'm lost in ecstasy.

I stop thinking—stop worrying—and completely let go.

Words and noises burst out of me, but I don't know what they are—other than words of affirmation. Begging for more.

My body flushes and tingles.

No one has ever gotten me so close, so fast.

But no one else has ever made me feel like Jamie, and that matters.

God, it matters so damn much.

He's perfect. We're perfect.

"Jamie, Jamie... yes. I—ah." I cry out, pulling my legs up to give him more access. Then I glance down at him, and it's all over. "I'm coming... oh my god. Yes. Yes. Jamie."

My body convulses as my orgasm rips through me. Jamie doesn't stop, he works me until I'm shuddering from how over-sensitive my clit is, but rather than stop, he simply lifts his lips and replaces them with his fingers.

Slowly, he shifts so he's lying next to me, lazily kissing my neck as he continues to stroke my sensitive clit.

"That's one," he rumbles, voice dripping with sex.

I reach for his cock, but he stops my hand. "Not yet. It's still your turn. I got to feel it. Now I want to watch you fall apart for me. Can you come again for me? Can I watch your beautiful body as you shatter?"

"Yes. Please." I'm a desperate, sloppy mess, and I love it. I love feeling free, owning my sexuality, and feeling so rooted in my body.

He flicks his thumb over my clit. "How can I get you there?"

"Fuck me with your fingers while you play with my clit."

"Mm." He nips at my neck. "My girl knows what she likes."

Two fingers press against my entrance, and I grind into the touch.

"Please, can I have what I want?"

A feral grin crosses his lips. "I can just imagine you on your knees, begging for my cock. But not yet."

He shoves his fingers inside me, and my eyes roll back.

Some people love oral—don't get me wrong, I enjoy that too

—but when it comes to foreplay, there's nothing I love more than this. The inner and outer stimulation playing together, especially when Jamie slightly curls his fingers and they hit the perfect spot.

Fuck.

I don't know what kind of noises I'm making anymore, and I don't care.

I'm dropped into my body, focused on every tiny sensation as I let him own me. I've never felt more aware, more turned on.

My fingers curl into his hair as my head drops back. I'm free to just be and revel in my pleasure.

I didn't think it could happen again so quickly, but there's power in letting go. My orgasm crashes through me as I cry out, pulsing around his fingers. It lasts longer than any orgasm I've ever had, and when I'm finished, my eyes open just enough to see his hooded eyes locked on me as he stares at me in awe.

"Holy fuck," he groans. "I almost came watching you. I've never seen someone come like that before—be so lost in it." He groans again, and kisses me. "I need more."

I force my limp body to move as I sit up.

"No. You need someone to take care of you."

Jamie

AMANDA IS a beautiful mess of knotted hair and smudged makeup as she settles between my legs.

"Do you want to take control or let me have it?" she asks.

Fuck.

I love the idea of being in control of her—of seeing exactly how much she can take—but not yet.

"Show me what you can do, baby."

"Yes, sir."

Oh, shit.

My cock leaks at her words, and she takes that opportunity to swirl her tongue around the tip.

"Don't feel like you have to take all of me," I quickly add. I don't have some giant monster dick, but it is big. Bigger than any of the guys I know—because let's face it, you see shit in locker rooms. And I never want to hurt the person I'm with.

She looks up at me from under her lashes, then takes me as deep as she can, hand wrapping around the base as my tip hits the back of her throat. There's a little gag, and she pulls back, then does it again.

"Amanda..."

She moves fast, sucking hard and taking me deep.

I shouldn't be surprised she's as fiery in the bedroom as she is in every other way.

The problem is, she's too good. My eyes grow heavy and my balls tighten.

Grabbing her hair, I hold her in place for a second, then pull her off.

She looks at me in surprise.

"That's not where I want to come."

Her jaw goes slack, and she slips her hand between her legs, rubbing her clit.

I watch for a second, then grab her and pin her beneath me.

"What do you like?"

"Usually a bit of everything, but I really, really like to be *fucked*. Hard. Feel free to be a little rough. Slap my ass, pull my hair, give me a hand necklace if you want..."

I drop my lips to hers. "I will fuck you till you're screaming my name and can't move, but I'll also stop the second you tell me to."

She runs her thumb over my cheek. "I appreciate that, but there's nothing I want more than this. I want to feel you."

I slip my fingers between her legs again and gently push two inside her.

"I need to make sure you're ready."

She nods, and that hazy look filters over her again.

I fuck her with two fingers, then add a third, almost getting lost in how much she enjoys it. When she's nice and relaxed, I pull my fingers out and line my cock up at her entrance.

"Ready?"

"Please," she whimpers.

I push inside her slowly, but halfway in, she gets frustrated and uses her feet to shove at my ass.

"Just do it."

I stare at her for a second, then let that primal part of me take over. One I don't tap into often, but that makes me want to growl and roar and prove this woman is mine. No one else will ever know her body like me. No one else will ever make her come the way I do.

I thrust in as deep as I can, watching her face. There's a flicker of pain, but it's washed away by pleasure.

"Good?"

"So good," she murmurs.

"It's about to get even better."

I grab one of her thighs and shove it up, then wrap my other hand in her hair, using them both as leverage as I fuck her like an animal.

She bucks and writhes beneath me, moaning as she urges me on, begging me for more.

"Harder, Jamie. Please, please..."

I let go of her thigh and wrap my hand around her neck. "Look at how perfectly you take my cock. You're doing amazing, baby. No one has ever made me feel this good."

"I'll do anything you want," she whines.

"Rub your clit. I want to see how hard you can come."

"Yes, sir."

I thrust harder, driving into her so hard I'm worried that I might hurt her, but she takes it all and begs for more.

"I'm so close," she whispers.

I've been fighting off my orgasm since I watched her touch herself while taking my cock. I've never seen something so hot in all my life. Amanda splayed out beneath me, writing under my touch is the most delicious fantasy come to life.

"Jamie... Jamie..."

She screams as she shatters around me in long, hard pulses.

"Fuck... fuck... Amanda." My words turn to groans as I spill inside her, her perfect pussy drawing out my orgasm longer than ever before.

We collapse in a tangled, sweaty heap, kissing furiously, like somehow all that only took the edge off.

"Okay?" I ask, tracing the red spots on her neck.

"I'm perfect. Well, close."

I laugh a little. "What could make it better?"

"Room service and round two."

"You're perfect," I mumble as I reach for the phone.

"*We* are," she whispers.

And fuck room service. The vulnerability and happiness on her face has me ready to go again right now.

THERE'S nothing like the feeling of Amanda's naked body curled around mine. Her leg is thrown over my legs, and her head rests on my shoulder. Her fingers are curled into my hair, and I can feel her breath on my cheek.

It's a perfect moment. We've had so many imperfect ones along the way, but I'm grateful for all of them because they got us here. I never could've imagined the way I'd fall for her. It changed everything, but I also think it's made me better.

"I could stay like this forever," she whispers, face buried in my neck.

I stroke my hand down her arm. "So could I."

"I'm going to be needy and annoying when we're apart. I hope you're ready for that."

"I'll take whatever you give me. And there's nothing needy or annoying about missing your person." I pull her tight to me. "I'm going to miss this. Holding you in my arms is my favorite thing."

"Please don't make me cry," she says with a laugh.

"I'm not trying to." I sweep my thumb across her cheek and lean back a little so I can see her face. "I hate that being loved and wanted makes you this emotional. You deserve to be cherished, and I hate every person who has ever made you feel anything less than that."

She gives a tiny shrug. "It wouldn't be as special if everyone did it. It means more because it's you. Because you chose me when you didn't have to."

"You're mine, babe. I think you always have been. We just had to find each other. I know being apart is going to suck, but I need you to promise me you won't hide your emotions from me. Call me anytime. I might not always be able to answer, but I'll call you back the second I can. I'll talk you through your fears, your pain... your orgasms."

She laughs at that, then kisses my neck.

"Seriously, I promised you I will always show up when you need me, and that won't change just because we're in different places. I'm not going to lie and say I assume it'll be easy. I know it won't be. I'm sure there will be growing pains and uncomfortable moments, but I'm committed to figuring this out with you. You're the one I want. The only one I want. I'm not willing to give up on this. My answer will always be that until you look me in the eyes and tell me we're done, I'm all in."

"I'm all in too. Just know I'm going to be an emotional mess. I'm kind of attached to you now."

I pinch her side. "Literally."

She laughs and buries her face in my shoulder again.

Wrapping my arms around her, I roll her over and lie on top of her, staring into her rich, warm eyes.

"I don't care if you're emotional. All I care is that you give those emotions to me. They're mine to help calm and carry."

"You're too good for me," she whispers, eyes turning glassy.

"No. We're perfect for each other. And when we're apart, we're going to remember all the reasons why. Because even from a distance, we'll still see each other in a way no one else ever has. When you're missing me, text me. And I'll do the same. I'll visit you as often as I can. At least once a month."

"You're willing to do that?"

"Yes. I am. And one of these days, you're going to stop questioning that and automatically trust how much I care for you." I kiss across her collarbone. "How badly I want you." My lips trail up her neck. "How deeply I need you." I pull back and look into her eyes. "How much I love you."

"I love you. Thank you for being willing to go slow. To work on this—on us. The foundation of trust we built will help us grow from here. And I want to grow with you. I want everything with you."

"I want everything with you too. And I know we can have it. All the hard work we've put in so far will make navigating the distance easier, and that distance will be good practice for when I make it to professional ball and am on the road a lot."

"Have you decided what to do about the draft?"

I swallow hard and nod. "I haven't told anyone. I don't really want to tell anyone besides you. Not yet. But I want to go for the draft at the end of senior year."

"Ten months," she whispers.

"Yep."

"I'll be by your side every step of the way. If we're doing this, all the vulnerability and openness has to go both ways, so let me in. Tell me when you're scared. Let me comfort you when you're frustrated or anxious. I'm on your team, and whenever they call your name, or however the draft works—I guess I better brush up on that—I'll be the one there beaming with pride. Wherever you end up, I'll be there too."

"Even if it's not with the Metros?"

"Wherever it is, we'll figure it out. We'll make it work."

"Are you sure?"

"That's what it means to love someone. To choose them. Wouldn't you do the same for me?"

"Of course I would."

"Then don't question it. I see my future, and there's no doubt you're a big part of it."

"I see our future too. And it's going to be beautiful. Because we've chosen each other, and as long as we're willing to put in the work, we can have it all. We *will* have it all. I want everything with you for as long as you'll let me have you."

"Jamie..." she breathes.

"You're mine, Amanda, and I'm yours. All yours. Always yours."

"Mine."

"I promise."

We crash together, tongues tangling as we lose ourselves in the depth of the connection between us and the love blossoming beneath it all.

The truth is, I don't know what's going to happen or exactly what my future will look like, but I know Amanda will be by my side for every moment of it.

Part Two

One Year & Nine Months Later

12
Don't Hate Me

Amanda

"HOLYFUCKINGGO," I angrily sing at the person driving the car in front of me.

The last thing I need is to be late right now. I'm already in a time crunch setting up this event. Whose bright idea was it to coordinate an event literally two days after moving home from my junior year of college?

Oh, right. Me. I'm usually the problem.

"Come on!" I shout at my windshield, as if that will somehow make the timid driver in front of me turn faster. "You have the right of way. Gooooo."

Fucking finally. And... yep. Now the light's red.

It's fine. I'm fine.

Deep breaths.

Go through the list again.

My business has grown since I started it two years ago. I've planned events in Old Lake Town when I'm there during the school year, and I consistently run events during winter and summer breaks back home, but this is the biggest one I've done so far.

I've planned weddings, retirement and anniversary celebrations, surprise parties, work events, business launches, and more, but this is different. Today is different. It's an entire charity gala planned and overseen by only me.

Yes, the local rich ladies' club—not their actual name, but that's what they are, people with more money than sense trying to do something mildly helpful for the world—had input about how they wanted it all to go, but the actual coordination and hiring of caterers and delivery of everything has been on me.

And I fucking love it. I love being in control and helping shape what could be a simple event into something perfect.

Except right now. When I'm five minutes late and sitting at the world's longest red light.

When I finally get a green arrow, I gun it onto the street where the large entertainment venue is, my blood pressure only dropping when I finally pull into the parking lot.

As expected, all four of my free labor volunteers are standing there waiting for me.

Sure, they're my friends. And my older brother. But it doesn't matter. I don't ever want to waste anyone's time or inconvenience them. They're doing something nice for me by helping set this all up. The least I can do is show up on time.

I wasn't expecting to have to stop at the florist on the way, but she had a question about one of the displays and needed me to look at it.

It's fine, I tell myself as I get out of my car and grab my purse and the box from my front seat. But it doesn't feel fine. It feels like I'm being disrespectful and unprofessional. That's not who I want to be. It's especially not who I want some of the most important people in my life to see me as.

"Hey, sorry, I'm late."

I come to a stop in front of Rae, Hyla, Jacie, and Pete.

"It's fine," Rae says, her smile warm and comforting as always. "We all just got here too."

"I know, but I don't want to waste your time." I move past them and up the stairs toward the building. It's one of those big ones that's all glass, metal, and concrete and looks too modern for the open fields around it. But the price was right, and the inside is gorgeous.

"You're not wasting our time," Hyla says, pulling her long blonde hair up into a ponytail.

"But you're doing me a huge favor, and you especially won't be home much starting soon." Hyla recently finished training as a flight attendant and will be traveling with a baseball team.

Hyla wraps her arm around me. "So what better way to spend it than with one of my best friends?" She pops a kiss on the side of my head, then rings the bell for the security guard before I can.

Of the mistakes I've made in my life, not trusting Hyla when we first knew each other is one of the greatest. Though we've had a strong relationship for years now, I let my baggage with my ex cloud my judgment at first, and I didn't see how deeply Hyla was hurting. She's been through more than anyone should have to in life, and once I realized that, I saw how much support and love she needed and was determined to help give it to her. She's always the first to give all that love right back and show up when anyone needs her. I'm lucky to have her, and I'm painfully aware of that since we almost lost her five months ago. She's doing much better now, and I'm proud of her, but it makes me want to cling on a little tighter, and always know for sure she's okay.

"Seriously, stop stressing, Mands. You know we love you. We're happy to help," Jace says.

"Do you want me to start grabbing stuff from your car?" Pete asks as the security guard opens the door.

"Can you drive it around to the front?" Balancing the box, I fish around for my keys before Hyla steps up, pulls them from my purse, and tosses them to Pete.

"Thanks," I sigh.

Rae lifts the box from my arm. "We're happy to help. Stop stressing. Or at least stop stressing about us. By the way, Aaron said he's sorry he couldn't come help, but he had plans with the guys."

I swear something dances in her eyes when she says that, but it's probably just the mention of her husband. Their wedding is one of my favorite events I've done. It was in a beautiful barn on her grandparents' property, and she and Aaron had so many fun ideas.

I will never stop being grateful that she, Sarah, and Mackenzie needed a suitemate halfway through freshman year of college, and I was indoctrinated into the greatest friend group in existence.

When I finally step into the air-conditioned space, I let out a sigh of relief. Then I look around, taking in the large open room with beautiful oak flooring, the bar along the windows at the back of the building, and the terrace beyond. My creativity sparks as I see my vision for the place come to life. There's a lot to do, but with hard work, we can handle it in three hours. Then I'll be going to the nearby gym to shower, before coming back here to meet with the caterers and get changed into my dress for the evening.

My adrenaline and focus kick in, working together to put me into directorial mode. I know exactly what needs to be done, who needs to do it, and how it should all flow when it's finished.

Rae bumps her hip against mine. "Ready?"

"Let's do it."

THREE HOURS WENT by in a blink, but other than some tiny touches, it looks incredible. Before I head to the nearby gym to shower, I need to turn on all the diffusers. I chose a mix of vanilla, lavender, and citrus oils, which should blend together nicely. Everything looks immaculate and exquisite without being too stuffy. It's a perfect combination of classy and warm, which will hopefully also be the combination that makes people want to pull out their checkbooks.

The rich ladies' club is hosting this event to help fund a

new hospital wing. Something good to come out of all their money. Why they can't just put up the money themselves is beyond me, but hey, I'm making a pretty penny for organizing this too. Some of which I'll use to tip the caterers and staff extra as well.

I'm certain they got my name from Marissa, who happily throws it out there as often as she can. She also tells them I'm her daughter-in-law, which is sweet, even if it's not true. It didn't take long for her to solidify her spot as a second mom in my life, and sometimes, I feel closer to her than my actual mom. For smaller events, she sometimes brings Penny and Mila to help set up because they love being involved—Penny likes to boss everyone around and Mila likes to make things pretty.

The hot afternoon May sun beats down on me as we walk out of the venue. It's going to be a double body wash shower. I'm like the Grinch at this point. *Stink, stank, stunk.*

"Thank you all so much for helping. I literally couldn't have done this without you. I'll buy you all coffee and cookies. I promise."

"No bribes needed," Hyla says, giving me a hug. "But I'll always take a coffee date."

"Agreed," Rae says. "It looks absolutely stunning in there. Be proud of that."

"Thank you."

"No problem." She gives me a big hug, then she and Hyla wave as they head for their cars.

"Need anything else?" Pete asks, his curly auburn hair glinting in the sunlight. Josh is the only one of us three who didn't get some piece of the redhead gene.

"Nope. I think I'm good. Just need to shower and get back here to meet the caterers."

Jacie pulls me into a hug. "I love you. Tonight is going to knock their socks off." She lets me go. "Then you'll be the talk of the town. When you get famous, remember the little people."

I roll my eyes at that. "Yes, when they give me the key to city hall or whatever the hell it is, I'll be sure to thank the wonder that is Jacie Edwards in my speech."

She winks at me. "I can't wait."

"Okay, if you two are done, I'm starving. Jace, want food?"

She shrugs as she looks at Pete. "If you're buying."

He pins her with a look, and I stifle a laugh.

"What? I'm barely a year out of college. I'm so poor. I have a roommate. And all I eat is ramen and instant potatoes. Please? I'm starved."

"You make almost as much as I do," Pete sighs.

Despite the way Jacie is trying to play my brother, she works at a business consulting firm—where Miles also interns—and she's not hurting for money.

"Fine. I'll pay this time. Text us and let us know how it went," Jace says to me. "Love you."

"Yeah, love you, sis."

"Love you guys too."

I watch them for half a second as they walk to their cars, bantering as they go, and for a moment, I almost question if there's something going on between them. Then I remember what the hell I'm supposed to be doing and haul ass to my car.

"AMANDA, we can't thank you enough. Everything about tonight is stunning," the rich lady in charge says.

"Thank you. It was my pleasure."

"Well, we'll be certain to sing your praises."

"I appreciate that."

She squeezes my hand, then walks away, though she's caught almost instantly by her husband, who pulls her onto the floor for a dance.

As usual, I'm standing off to the side, watching. It's my job to do that, of course. But it's not against event planner rules to dance. In fact, a few of the ladies have already tried to set me up with their sons or grandsons. One was thirty-five. Don't get me wrong, he was hot as fuck, but I'm twenty-one. I might enjoy reading age-gap romances, but I don't want to live one. Not that I'm on the market anyway.

My eyes drift to the dance floor again, and for half a second, loneliness creeps in, but just as quickly, I push it away and focus on my next task. There's still plenty to do to make tonight spectacular.

Jamie

"THE QUESTION for tonight is will Jamie Henderson make it through this final inning with a no-hitter?"

I smile as I take the field. I never get tired of hearing Trevor announcing while I'm playing. Unless he's giving me shit, but he tries to leave that to the other announcer. Not that there's been much to say so far this season. I've been killing it, and so has the team.

It's my second season with the Binghamton Knights. After I was drafted to the New York Metros, I ended up here with their AAA affiliate. They were originally going to send me to either their high A or AA team, but they sent me here first to get in some practice time with the team and see what I was capable of. I ended up staying. My path wasn't common, but I've proved myself every step of the way.

Last year was part showing off my abilities and a lot of adjusting to the schedule of minor league baseball. Though I got called up for three Metros games, I only pitched in two. This year, my goal is to show my growth, and if I'm lucky, get a call up for more Metros games, and prove I'm solid enough for the majors. If I set myself up right, my hope is to start next season playing for the Metros.

If I keep playing like this, they'd be crazy not to, but it'll depend on what happens with the upcoming draft.

Either way, my focus has to be on right now, and *right now*, I'm in the top of the ninth looking at a no-hitter if I close this inning out strong.

Trevor rattles off some of my stats and a story he loves to tell about the combined no-hitter Aaron and I pitched together back in high school.

I dig in and focus on the ball in my hand and getting it straight to my catcher's glove.

The wind teases my skin as the crowd cheers behind me.

That sweeping feeling of gratitude washes over me.

There's not much in life I love more than this.

"NICE WIN, man. You were on fire tonight. Strikeout, strikeout, strikeout, baby. That's how we do it at the Knights," my teammate Archie says, smacking my butt as he walks by.

I laugh and shake my head. "It was a team game."

"Dude, take the credit where it's due. You kicked ass tonight. The rest of us didn't have anything to do while you were on the field," our first baseman says.

"Thanks, man."

"So what are we thinking? Drinks to celebrate? I know plenty of people who won't card the badass starting pitcher of the Binghamton Knights," my catcher, Keltie, says.

I finish buttoning up my shirt, then pull my already-tied tie over my head. "Sorry, boys. I've got somewhere to be."

"Lame!" one of the guys shouts.

"Seriously, you're going to blow us off?" Keltie nags.

"Not blowing you off. I never said yes. I've got somewhere better to be. And no offense to any of you, but someone much hotter to be with."

"I do take offense to that. Direct offense!" Archie yells.

"Ask me if I care," I call over my shoulder as I walk out of the locker room.

I almost run into Jesse Wilkinson as I go.

"Tell me I don't have to do any press." In addition to being another former Ida kid and Joel's brother, he's the media and marketing manager for the Knights.

"Why? Got somewhere to be?"

"Probably a hot date," Trev says, strolling up behind him. "Great game, man."

"Thanks."

"He's right," Jesse says. "Fantastic game. And no. No press right now, but I have an interview scheduled for you next week. The details are in your email."

"Yes, sir."

He sighs dramatically. "What have I told you about not calling me sir?"

"Only your girl gets to call you that."

Trevor chokes on a laugh.

"Exactly."

Well, can't say I don't get that feeling.

"Then I'm free to go, right?"

"Please. You're insufferable." Jesse deadpans.

"Baseball players. So self-centered, am I right?" Trevor says, barely keeping a straight face.

"Fuck you both very much. Goodnight."

Then I haul ass out to my car. There's somewhere more important I need to be.

A VALET TAKES my keys when I pull up in front of the event center. Everything about tonight is similar to charity events I've been to for the Metros organization, but this isn't about publicity or showing up for my team.

Not my baseball team, at least.

When I walk inside, I'm almost instantly handed a glass of champagne.

Aaron said letting my scruff grow in would age me a little, and it definitely has. Less baby face means less being carded. I'm barely twenty, but I could pass for closer to thirty, especially if I harden my gaze a little. At an event like this, no one cares anyway.

I sip on the champagne as my eyes sweep the room, and it only takes seconds for me to find her. Her strawberry blonde hair is pulled into a simple low ponytail and a slinky black dress holds tight to her curves. Curves I want to trace with my lips, my tongue.

Don't pop a semi now. That wouldn't be a good look.

Amanda stands off to the side, watching like a wallflower, though she's anything but. She hasn't spotted me yet, so I move around the side of the dance floor until I'm walking toward her perfect ass and exposed back.

I walk slowly up to her, then lean down, letting my breath tickle her ear. "Has anyone told you how stunning you look tonight?"

She spins around and arches a brow. "Not yet."

I take half a step back and let my eyes trail over her. "You are deliciously perfect. Utterly breathtaking."

Two weighted breaths pass as we stare at each other, then I grab her hand and drag her down a nearby hallway for employees only.

The second we're alone in the dimly lit space, I press her against the wall, boxing her in.

"What are you doing here?"

"Should I be somewhere else?"

I lean down and graze my lips over her neck, skimming my hand up her thigh.

"No," she breathes. "I just—didn't think—" she stammers as I pull the skin of her neck into my mouth. "Jamie..."

I lift my lips and brush my nose against hers. "I needed to see you."

Our lips collide in a frantic kiss, and she rakes her fingers through my red hair, pulling me closer. Slowly, I slip my fingers across her thigh, letting them trail up the inside, until they brush her underwear.

She gasps and leans her head back. "We can't do that."

"Mm, but do you know how badly I want to?" Again, I brush my lips over her neck and she tilts her head, giving me more. "I want to push my fingers inside you and graze my thumb over your clit until you're pulsing around me and coating my fingers. Then I'd thrust my cock inside you as hard and fast as I could until you were a screaming, panting mess and your pussy was painted with my cum."

She lets out a shuddery breath.

"But I guess you're right. We can't do that here."

"You're right. We can't." She forces a breath and meets my gaze, eyes twinkling. "Especially since I've got a boyfriend at home, and he's been a *very good boy*." She tugs on my tie with each word.

I can't stop myself. I dive forward and capture her lips again, this time sinking my teeth into her bottom lip before I pull away.

"Well then. I guess you should get back out there."

She stands tall, straightens out her dress, then quickly checks her makeup on her phone camera.

"I should."

"I'll be watching." Then I smack her ass and watch her go.

She gives me the sultriest little look over her shoulder, then disappears around a corner.

Once she's gone, I lean against the wall and let out a sigh, slowly counting backward from twenty, trying to calm myself down. Then I adjust my pants and head back out to the event area. It's going to be a long night.

IT WAS DEFINITELY A LONG NIGHT, and Amanda is exhausted and resting in the front seat as I drive.

It's not until we're almost there that she squints and looks around. "Where are we going?"

I just squeeze her thigh and smile.

Usually, we stay in the guest house on my parents' property, which is where I've been living for almost a year.

But tonight that changes. Hopefully, my girl doesn't kill me.

"Jamie!"

"Trust me?"

Her eyes narrow, and she sighs, resting her hand over mine. "Always."

The way she looks at me says more than her words do. Of course she trusts me. I earned it. All the time spent building our foundation before we officially started dating, and the twenty-one months since, I've shown her over and over again.

Our first few months together were a learning curve in trust and jealousy, but with nightly phone calls, regular visits, and me constantly pushing her to share her thoughts and emotions, we got through it all.

She's been my greatest supporter, cheering me on at every possible game and soothing me if I lose. Walking through every step of my baseball career has been better with her there. I wouldn't be the man I am without her, and in my quest to give her everything, I'm surprising her and hoping she won't be pissed.

The building I pull up in front of is newly renovated and looks modern on the outside, but the apartments inside are in a range of styles.

"Jamie, what is this?"

Again, I just smile, then hop out of the car and go around to her door. I extend my hand to help her out, then grab the bags she'll need right away and sling them over my shoulder before leading her inside.

I wave to the security attendant, then head for the elevators as Amanda's head swivels around, taking everything in.

"I don't understand. Are we seeing an apartment this late at night?"

"Maybe."

Seeing is a loose definition. She will be *seeing* it.

We get off on the third floor and I head for the apartment—number seventeen.

Amanda trails a step behind me, still tired and confused.

I unlock the door, but before I open it, I turn to her. "Please don't hate me."

Then I swing the door open and step inside, holding the door and revealing the beautiful two-bedroom apartment. It's not huge, but it's more than big enough for the two of us. It's a semi-rustic style with some farmhouse vibes. Lots of wood tones and wide plank floors.

Originally, I'd been looking for places for Amanda and me to see together, but when my realtor told me this one would be snatched up quickly, I applied the day I saw it, because the moment I walked in, the place screamed *Amanda*.

There's a small area to take off shoes and coats and a little closet by the door, then it opens into the living room, kitchen, and dining area. They're all moderate sized, nothing massive, but plenty functional. Down a hall at the edge of the kitchen is a full bath and the guest bedroom—which will be for Amanda's office—then the master bed and bath. Again, nothing huge, but it's all her style. And hopefully decorated to her taste since it's mostly her stuff.

"Jamie, what—what—"

Tears fill her eyes, and I brace myself. She might yell at me or she might be happy. It's hard to know for sure.

She looks at the furniture in the living room—one of the few things I bought new with the help of my mom, Penny, and Jace.

"This is beautiful," she breathes.

I let out a sigh of relief and wrap my arms around her. "Good. Because it's all ours."

She lets out a laugh of disbelief. "When did you do this?"

I shrug. "Eh, I signed the lease last week. I explained the situation, and they'll add your name whenever we stop by the security office for your key card to enter the building."

"But the furniture..."

"Yeah, uh, maybe we should go on a little tour."

"Okay," she murmurs, letting me lead her down the hall where I already have some pictures hanging up.

First, I stop at the office and swing the door open.

"Oh my god. This is... perfect." Her desk, her bookshelves, her giant beanbag chair, and a shelf of plants are perfectly positioned throughout the room along with twinkle lights strung around the top.

I owe Dani, Chelsea, and Mackie so many flowers. Or coffees. Chocolate. Something.

Dani is Jesse's girlfriend and an interior designer, and after showing her the pictures of Amanda's bedroom, she styled it all perfectly. She was here today doing that while the guys moved everything in.

I had lunch delivered and sent Aaron money for coffee, but nothing feels like enough. We have the greatest friends in the world.

"Oh my gosh. This is... perfect. I can't wait to work in here." Then she turns and runs to the room at the end of the hall and swings the door open. Her happy squeal has me dashing after her.

Again, Dani nailed it. She took the vibes of Amanda's room and added some muted blues as well. She also added twinkle lights in here. All of Amanda's wall hangings are blended with a few of my baseball ones. Somehow Dani made it all look seamless.

Amanda spins around and dashes over, leaping into my arms.

"This is amazing."

The kiss she gives me proves how amazing she thinks it is.

"So it's okay I surprised you?"

She cups my face, looking into my eyes. "As always, you see me. I had no idea my dream apartment existed until we walked in here. I always assumed any apartment would be bland or boring, but this... it's all the things I love. And you took all the stress off me by having—well, I'm assuming you had our friends move all this in. I thought there was something mischievous in Rae's eyes when she said Aaron was busy with the guys."

I laugh as I set her down. "Yes. The guys moved things, Dani took the pictures of your room and created this—"

"Oh my gosh, that explains the random questions about bedroom design she was asking in the group chat."

"She's good. Plus, Mackie and Chelsea were here helping to set up and organize everything."

She slowly shakes her head. "Between setting up and helping move things, that accounts for pretty much all of our friends. They're amazing." She loops her arms around my neck and leans into me. "So are you."

Then her hot lips are on mine, kissing me roughly, but before I can deepen the kiss, she pulls back. "I barely even looked at the kitchen!" She dashes out of the room, and I watch her go, so in love with every wild bit of her.

After a moment, I follow her and find her bouncing around, opening all the cupboards and doing little happy dances at each thing she finds.

"New pots and pans?"

"A gift from my parents."

She spins around and runs over to me, throwing her arms around me again. "Our own place. I can't believe we have our own apartment!" She sighs happily. "I can't believe you did all this. I love you."

I run my hand up the side of her neck and look into her eyes. "I love you too. I'm so excited to live here with you."

Slanting my mouth over hers, I pull her close, curling my fingers in her hair as we kiss. And even though I thought she'd be too tired, she fumbles with the button of my pants, then skims her hand over my crotch.

It's a frantic race to shed our clothes. I grab her hand, ready to drag her to the bedroom and christen it, but my girl has other ideas. She yanks me back and pulls me to the floor with her.

"Right here in the middle of the kitchen?" I ask with a laugh.

"I can't wait. I need you inside me right now."

Probably, but she also likes doing it in as many different places as she can. We've fucked in almost every inch of the guest house.

I lean against the kitchen island, and she climbs onto my lap, kissing me as she slides down my length.

She doesn't waste a second before riding me fast and hard. My girl is as desperate for me as I am for her. I palm her perfect ass and buck into her, matching every one of her thrusts.

This is the fastest way for either of us to get off, and tonight is no different.

In moments, we're both moaning, crying out, coming apart at the seams.

She collapses against me while I'm still pulsing inside her.

I wrap my arms around her, panting heavily. "Welcome home, baby."

She lifts her head off my shoulder, that stunning smile dancing on her lips. "Welcome home, baseball boy."

I rest my head against the cabinet as she buries her face in my neck again.

It's been a long time coming to get here, but I love where we are now.

13
Baseball Boyfriend

I WILL ALWAYS hate travel weeks.

Jamie comes home tonight, but being apart for the last week has sucked. I've had events, volleyball, and my friends to keep me entertained, but I always miss him. Especially at night. The bed always feels lonely. If there was any sort of consistency in our lives, I might consider getting a pet, but that's a long way away.

> Less than twelve hours!

BASEBALL BOYFRIEND

Counting down the seconds. Love you, baby.
Good luck today!

> Lol. Pretty sure I'm the one who should be saying that. Pitch awesome.

BASEBALL BOYFRIEND

You have a half-day tournament, so good luck, kick ass, and I can't wait to hear all about it.

> Back at you. Love you. See you soon! If you need a pick-me-up, text me any time and I'll sneak into the bathroom and send you a shot of my tits.

BASEBALL BOYFRIEND

> As badly as I want to see that, there are too many prying eyes around. I'll have to settle for the live show tonight.

> I'll be waiting.

He sends a kissing face emoji, and I finally tuck my phone in my bag.

"How's Jamie?" Chelsea sings from her spot next to me on the bleachers.

Chelsea Winters is one of my best friends in the universe. Which is saying something since I have a whole tribe of them now. We met at the beginning of fall semester when she started working with Rae and then dating Trevor. She easily became a part of our friend group, and we've formed a strong bond. We both love volleyball, so we teamed up for the rec league this year along with Dani.

We named our team the Ida Heartthrobs after the town that none of us are from but bonded us anyway, and the fact that we're hot as fuck badass babes.

One of the douchey guys from another team tried to mansplain how "heartthrob" is only supposed to be used for men. He was on the receiving end of three withering glares and a speech about feminism.

Secretly, our team name is also a little nod to our guys, since they are three hotties from Ida, who everyone always wanted, but they only have eyes for us.

I've gotten a lot better about not questioning that. I've had to. Of course, in almost two years, Jamie has shown me over and over again how much he wants me and how deeply I can trust him. With him on the road and even at the minor league level having ball bunnies around, my trust in him has been put to the test, but I don't even question it now. Jamie has shown his loyalty and put my heart at ease. He comes home as quickly as he can and is always ready to worship me. I do everything I can to make him feel the same way.

Our relationship is far from perfect, but it's beautiful, hard-won, and something we both continue to work on and fight for every day. If I could describe *my* perfect relationship, that's exactly what it would be. Even in our rough moments, he always makes me feel seen and understood. He is my safe place and my home, and I'm grateful for how hard we've worked to be here now.

I elbow Chelsea. "He's fine. How's Trevor?"

"A sweet little grumpy bear like usual," Chelsea says.

Dani laughs at that. "He's so soft for you. It's adorable. You know he's going to be here with a jug of water, cheering you on, scowling at all the guys—especially the ones we have to play against—and making sure you're hydrated."

"And Jesse will be right next to him," Chelsea throws back. "Probably with ice cream."

"Honestly, I wouldn't be surprised if he convinces Garrett to bring the truck down."

One of Jesse's best friends owns an ice cream place, and would probably happily sell ice cream to all us sweaty and overheated players.

I smile along with the girls, but that pang of sadness hits me. I wish Jamie could be here too. I love when he's cheering me on, but this is a part of life—a part of his career. One that I'll probably never get used to, but I'm okay with that if it means I still miss him. I'd rather feel those achy pains in my heart than not care when he's gone.

"You two ready?" Dani asks.

Chelsea and I stand up, and follow her onto the floor as the announcer calls out, "And in our first matchup, the Ida Heart-throbs versus the Good Old Boys."

Chelsea, Dani, and I look at each other and snicker.

Time to hand the douchey boys their asses.

"YES, I can add those flowers to the list, but it will increase the price of the bouquets."

The bride I'm on the phone with sighs heavily then says she'll confirm with her mother, who is paying for the wedding.

"Okay. Have her call me directly if she has any questions. Anything else?"

When she says no, I happily end the call and put away my phone.

I have a love-hate relationship with planning weddings. Some couples are incredible to work with and have fun ideas and input. We work together to make the day their dream, no matter the budget. It all started with Aaron and Rae. I planned their wedding in four months, and it was amazing. It'll go down as one of my favorite events ever planned, and that's only partly because I love them so much. I've done a handful since then, and they're always either awesome or terrible, nothing in between.

This one has been terrible, bridging on migraine territory every time I have to solve a disagreement between the bride and her *mother*. The groom is as useful as a dull nail, and usually looks like he'd rather be watching paint dry than having a conversation about the wedding. The bride and her mother are either crying happily in agreement—rare—or they're yelling at each other while the mother threatens to not pay, and the bride threatens to uninvite her from the wedding. Somehow, I've become the family therapist. I'm not sure who I feel worse for.

Besides myself.

Whatever. I keep business hours. In theory. So the work phone is going off—because I do not give clients my actual number anymore after one called me at three in the morning. Any other chaos will have to wait until morning.

I made food earlier, so all I have to do is warm it up when Jamie gets home.

I take a peek at the clock—almost nine—then change into my silky pajama set and climb into bed for a little nap. Jamie should be home around eleven, so this will give me time to warm dinner up, so it's ready when he gets in.

I'm so ready for him to have a day off and be home for the whole week.

After setting my timer for an hour, I turn the noise machine on and settle in.

When I wake up, there will be an hour or less until I'm finally in Jamie's arms again. That achy feeling hits again, but I revel in it. It's a sign of our love, and I'm always happy to honor that.

Jamie

WE GOT OUR ASSES KICKED. Not that I'm surprised. It was drizzly. It was the last game of a road trip, and everyone was exhausted and ready to be home. I gave up more hits than I wanted and two runs, but the reliever they put in gave up five more runs. We ended with a seven to two loss.

It hurts, but with the season we've had, it's not a huge deal. It's all part of the game.

I'm still going to beat myself up a bit because that's what I do. I always want to grow and get better and slumpy games like this throw me off, but my coaches were quick to remind us we still dominated this series.

None of it matters right now though, because all I want to do is get home to my girl. We're back earlier than we thought we'd be, and I always love that because it's a little extra surprise for her.

The apartment is quiet when I walk in, though some lights are on.

I find Amanda in the bedroom, asleep on top of the covers, and the timer on her phone about to go off.

I stare down at her, splayed out beautifully. She's so peaceful like this.

She's mine.

My cock thickens as I stare at her, then I flick her timer off and carefully crawl onto the bed, ready to give her a much better wake-up call than her alarm.

Carefully, I pull down her silky little sleep shorts, spreading her legs and putting her slick pussy on full display.

I wonder if she's dreaming of me. If she's been desperate for me. How many times she touched herself this week while missing me.

Settling between her legs, I lap my tongue up her center, enjoying her sweet and tangy taste, then work my way up and swirl my tongue over her clit.

She moans in her sleep, and my cock leaks in my pants.

Gripping her thighs, I lick her clit again, then suck it into my mouth.

She inhales sharply, and I glance up, watching as she stirs. Blinking a couple of times, she looks down at me, her eyes going wide. Joy fills her face, but it's quickly replaced by pleasure. She fists my hair and rolls her hips, riding my face.

Yes, baby. Take what you need from me.

I love waking her up like this. There's an extra high when she's sleepy and relaxed and she's malleable under my touch. All it takes is the swirl of my finger around her opening and her body seizes, pulsing in long contractions as she whimpers and whines.

My cock is painfully hard as it pushes against my fly, but I don't care. All I care about is her.

"Jamie…" She wiggles her hips and pulls away from my touch. "How long was I asleep?"

She fumbles for her phone as I sit up and crawl over to her.

"You're home early," she says happily, sweeping her hand over my face as I lie down next to her.

"Yep. I missed you so much I made the bus driver speed."

She laughs and kisses me. "I missed you too. That was quite the way to wake me up."

I give her my best charming smile. "Did my girl like that?"

"So much." She pulls me to her lips again. "God, I missed you." Another kiss. "I love you." One more kiss. "I'm so excited to have a whole week with you and watch you kick ass at home."

I trail my finger over the low-cut V of her tank top. "How was your day? How was the tournament?"

She gets a catlike smile. "We won."

"Of course you did. You're amazing." A flicker of pain shoots through me. Leaving her is hard every time, and I hate it more when I miss things like that. "I wish I could've seen it."

"Trevor recorded a bunch of it. He and Jesse were commentating through the whole final match."

I roll my eyes. "Of course they were."

"How was the game?"

"We lost. 7-2."

"I'm sorry, babe." She kisses my neck.

"It's okay. Part of life. I gave up two runs early on and our team wasn't hitting well. Then the reliever gave up five."

"Five? And you have to take the loss for that? I hate baseball statistics," she seethes. It's so cute how invested in all things baseball she's become. She and Rae have bonded over that. If we weren't an antiquated society and allowed women to play professional baseball too, Rae would've been the one who wanted to go pro.

Trailing my fingers through her hair, I look into her eyes. "It's okay. I'm just happy to be home."

"I'm happy you're home. And I know exactly how to cheer you up."

I arch my brow. "Oh really?"

"Yes." She grazes her lips over my jaw. "You need to fuck my mouth."

My cock, which had died down to a semi, comes roaring back to life.

"Oh, really?"

"Mhm. Stand up."

I do as she says, and pull my shirt off as I go, breathing a sigh of relief when the button down hits the floor. Tugging my T-shirt off next, I move to drop my pants.

When I look down at my girl, she's lying in the center of the bed, her head tipped back over the edge, mouth open for me.

Ah, fuck.

She's right. She knows exactly what will cheer me up.

Turns out Amanda loves to be out of control in the bedroom—some of the time at least. Sometimes she owns me and rides me until we're both shaking messes. Others she pins me down and blows me, not letting me have an ounce of control. But then there's the side of her that's most open and vulnerable, and she loves to be fucked, spanked, choked, have her hair pulled, and choke on my cock.

I'm happy to oblige.

Her hand wraps around the base of my cock, then I grab one of her tits and hold her as I sink into the wet heat of her mouth.

The groan I let out is unholy, and a shiver runs through me.

As much as I'd love to stand here and own her mouth like this for as long as possible, watching her eyes water as she gags, I can't hold out. Being apart for days at a time means sometimes our reunion sex is short-lived—at least the first round. But as I come down her throat to the sound of her choking and sputtering on my cum, it's hard to care.

I rub her cheeks as I pull away, then grab her water bottle while she sits up.

"Okay?"

She grins up at me. "I'm perfect."

Sighing, I look around. I hate being away, but there's nothing like coming home.

"So am I."

WE'RE CUDDLED on the couch eating quiche and hash browns while we talk about everything that happened during our week apart. I relay all the nonsense the guys on the team got up to. She asks me if one particular teammate cheated on his wife *again*. He did. Like he always does. It's disgusting, but from what the other guys on the team told me, she knows and she cheats on him too. It's a super toxic relationship, and it only makes me more grateful for what I have.

I can't imagine being with anyone else besides Amanda. I can't imagine ever wanting to. She's it for me. I think about proposing sometimes, but I want to wait until I'm finally playing for a major league team—the Metros, assuming they don't trade me. Planning a wedding while adjusting to an entirely different place and life doesn't sound fun.

I do everything in my power to make sure Amanda knows how much I love her, though she doesn't seem in a rush for a ring, either, despite plenty of our friends heading in that direction.

"That was delicious. Thank you for cooking."

"I'm happy to, but I'm going to beg you for homemade chicken wings this week. You make the best ones."

"We can do it tomorrow? Maybe invite some of our friends over?"

She tilts her head back and forth. "Maybe. It might mess with my plans to keep you naked all day, though."

"Even while I'm making the wings? A little pain with pleasure is fine, but I don't want to risk bodily harm."

"I guess I'll just have to take advantage of you now." She climbs onto my lap and grinds over my crotch.

"Mands," I groan.

She pulls her shirt off, letting her tits fly free right in my face. I suck one into my mouth and tease it with my lips and teeth. She hisses in response, combing her fingers through my hair.

"Where do you want me to fuck you?"

"Right here. Doggy style."

She moves to climb off me, but I grab her ass, holding her still, then I slip my hand under her shorts, rubbing the skin for a moment before I spank her.

She whimpers, and her head drops to my shoulder.

"Get naked and get ready for me." I pull the hair tie from her hair and twirl one of the stands around my finger. "And I need this wrapped around my hand."

"Yes, sir."

"Mm, you're making me leak, baby. Need to be inside you and remind you who you belong to."

I move to stand, but when I'm halfway off the couch, my phone rings.

Glancing down, I groan—in annoyance this time.

"Who is it?"

"Dave."

Amanda scrambles off the couch and reaches for her clothes. "If he's calling you this late, you should probably answer."

I nod, quickly buttoning my pants as if my agent can see me.

A whoosh of fear rolls through me. A late call like this could mean a trade. I'm hoping the Metros wouldn't do that. I know the coaching staff there—particularly the pitching coach—like me a lot, but this is a business too.

I grab the phone and answer, putting it on speaker. If it's any kind of bad news, I want Amanda to hear it too so I don't have to tell her.

"Hi, Dave."

"Jamie. Don't worry. Nothing scary. I'm calling with some good news, actually."

Amanda slips her shirt back on and pulls her shorts up, then sits down on my lap.

"We're listening," I say.

He laughs a little. "Hi, Amanda."

"Hi, Dave."

"What's going on?" I ask.

"You're being called up."

My eyes flare. I've been hoping for it. "How long? A game? Two?"

Dave chuckles. "No, Jamie. You're being called up. Trade deal just went through and they let go of one of their pitchers in the deal."

"Without a replacement?" Jamie chokes out.

"You're the replacement. They're betting on you."

My heart hammers in my chest. It's actually happening. After all these years. All this work.

"Baby," Amanda whispers, tears in her eyes. "You did it."

"Congratulations, Jamie," Dave says.

"What—what... now?"

"They need you here tomorrow. There's paperwork to sign—since technically they're buying out your minor league contract and you'll be getting at or slightly above the base required salary for a major league player."

I blink a few times, trying to wrap my mind around that number. It's like twenty times what I'm making now.

"Then they want you to meet the team, particularly the pitching staff and other pitchers, and then you and I have some things to discuss. We already have an apartment lined up to show you. It's in a great neighborhood."

My mind spins with all the information.

"I know this is a lot, but for now, take a deep breath and enjoy this. You've earned it."

"Thanks, Dave."

"We'll talk tomorrow. Have a good night."

"Night," I mumble, everything setting in at once.

The call ends, and Amanda grabs my arms.

"Jamie?"

Emotion swells and my throat tightens. "I did it."

She leaps into my arms. "Hell yes, you did. I'm so proud of you. Looks like we're going to New York City."

I start laughing despite the tears streaming down my face.

Amanda cradles my face in her hands. "Dave was right. You earned this. You earned every second. You get to live your dream. My heart feels like it's flying out of my chest. I'm so insanely proud of you. I love you."

She kisses me, and I fall into it. I wouldn't be who I am or where I am without her. Achieving my dream is the ultimate fantasy, but doing it with her by my side is everything.

There are a million things to do. So much to plan. So much that's going to change.

But I don't care. I can't care. We'll figure it out.

Because it's finally happening.

I'm officially a New York Metro.

Life Changing

Jamie

EVERY SO OFTEN YOU'RE aware of a life-changing moment when it's happening, and when I step onto the field at the Metros stadium with my hand wrapped around Amanda's, I know this is one I'll remember forever. It's the start of a new journey, one that's destined to affect every part of my life.

It's been a whirlwind twenty-four hours. Not even. It's been just over twelve. After the phone call last night, we went over to Aaron and Rae's apartment because I had to tell Aaron in person. Plus, I wanted his advice, and I figured Amanda would want to talk to Rae too. I'm so thankful for Amanda. She's endlessly supportive, but I know this is a shift in her life too.

We crashed for a few hours, got up early, packed some things, went to my parents' house to tell them and my siblings the good news, then drove here. It's barely lunchtime, but it's already been an insanely long day. I'm running on adrenaline and excitement right now, but once we're out of the stadium, I know I'm going to crash.

"What do you think?" Marc Demoda asks. He's the pitching coach for the Metros and used to be one of their pitchers. He was the first person I met from the team. Aaron reached out to him on my behalf, and he came to see me play long before any other scouts did. He and Aaron got to know each other and bonded over hand injuries that took them out of the game.

Though I've met most of the team in passing, and had conversations and at least slightly gotten to know others, Marc is my main point of contact here.

"It's just like I remember it." For Aaron's bachelor party back in October, I called in a favor with Marc and organized a game with some of the Metros players going up against our friends from high school right here at the stadium. Yes, I have every intention of reminding all the Metros guys we beat them—at least I will if they give me shit.

"Ready for it to be your home?"

"Hell yes."

"Photographer's here," Dave calls from near the dugout.

Marc waves him over and Dave joins us.

"These are just some publicity shots, so we'll get a few of you on the mound, and Amanda, if you're open to it, we'd like to get a few of both of you."

"Sure," she says with a smile. Then wiggles her brows at me and gives me a little push. "Go flex some muscles."

A woman with a clipboard walks onto the field, followed by another younger woman.

The woman with a clipboard approaches, and her energy tells me she's probably someone in charge of PR. "Actually, let's get a few of you both first, then Amanda can get started on her tour of the stadium." She gestures to the younger woman behind her, who smiles at Amanda.

I grab Amanda's hand and lead her out to the mound. All the while, the camera snaps behind us. They take a few cutesy shots of us standing together on the mound, then Amanda turns to me and looks up into my eyes, a troublemaking smile on her face.

"You're totally imagining fucking me here, aren't you?" she whispers.

My cheeks heat and my eyes flare. It doesn't matter how long it's been. Sometimes, the things that come out of her mouth still surprise me.

"Baby, you're killing me."

"Because you're thinking about it now, right?"

I wrap my hand around the side of her neck and lean in to kiss her.

"Hey! We aren't paying for a couple's shoot!" Dave calls.

Amanda laughs and steps back.

"You just like causing trouble."

She slowly shakes her head. "Nope. I like seeing you smile. And you have been, but not like that. I can see the way your mind is whirring. Stop. Let it go. Take all this in." She quickly kisses my cheek. "This is your dream. Revel in it."

Then she squeezes my hand and scampers off the mound toward the woman waiting to give her a tour.

Marc's eyes flit from her to me, and he shakes his head with a smile.

A glove and a ball are dropped at my feet, and we get back the photoshoot.

I'VE SIGNED SO much paperwork today my fingers hurt.

Not really. My hands are conditioned as fuck. Is hand porn a thing?

Wait, did they do that on *Friends*?

Whatever. Clearly, my sanity is slipping. It's four in the afternoon and we have one more thing to do after this before we can head back to the hotel. I'm wavering between pumped and absolutely exhausted.

As I slide the last paper across my agent's desk, his phone goes off.

"Yeah? Perfect. Send her in."

My brows dart up. The only *her* I care about is sitting right next to me.

"What's up?" I ask.

Dave smiles. "You were called up at the perfect time to land a great publicity opportunity. A sports reporter was pitching an idea of doing a profile piece on what life is like for a new player to the major league. One of the youngest pitchers the Metros have drafted in a while and a superstar who rose from a fifth-round pick to AAA in a matter of weeks is an even better selling point."

The office door swings open, and Dave stands.

"Emily, come on in."

I stand as well and take in the thin woman with short dark hair tucked up in a ponytail.

"Jamie, this is Emily Thomas. Emily, this is Jamie, and his girl-friend, Amanda."

"Nice to meet you both," Emily says, projecting an air of confidence.

I glance at Amanda out of the corner of my eye. Thankfully, she keeps her *yes-I'm-judging-you* face to herself. Not that she typically does it in a bad way. It's all about getting a read on people and deciding whether she thinks they're decent humans.

"You too," I say.

"Yes. Definitely," Amanda says, sitting back down. She has a soft smile on her face, so I guess that means Emily passed the vibe check.

"So what does a profile piece entail?" I ask. I've never done more than interviews with bloggers or local press, or an occasional podcast. All less than an hour of talking and I'm done. I've had media training. Though I give Jesse a lot of shit, he knows his stuff, and he trained us all well. "It's different from an interview, I'm assuming."

"Yes. An interview will be part of it, and it's what I'll use to tie the whole piece together, but it won't be one interview, it'll be many. Lots of informal ones with you, those closest to you, and ideally, some people from the team. I'll be at some games you pitch, both at home and traveling. It'll also involve me following you around, seeing what your daily life is like, what I find in the moments when you're not talking."

My eyes go to my agent. "No offense, but that sounds like everything I was trained not to do with the media."

Dave nods. "We will have final approval of the profile. Ideally, it's meant to paint you in an interesting and positive light."

"And how long will you be following me?"

"Most of the rest of the season. The plan would be for it to come out around the playoffs. And don't worry, I won't be popping up everywhere in your life. It'll more be for certain games or team events. Interviews will be scheduled. I'll never just show up at your door."

"And any other press will know she's a reporter, right?" I ask Dave. "Because that's how rumors start."

I rest my hand on Amanda's thigh, looking over at her.

"We will make it clear that's the case, and Emily can post about it on her social media."

"Besides, that really shouldn't be a concern," Amanda says. "A meeting looks different from something untoward. She's a professional, so that won't be a problem."

Emily clears her throat. "Thank you. Some women might... assume the worst."

Amanda flashes her a smile. "You're clearly a badass if you're rising in the sports industry. Especially since that's always harder as a woman. You shouldn't ever have to worry about someone assuming the worst."

"Thank you. So much better than needing to pull up my social media and prove I'm a lesbian and in a relationship."

Amanda rests her hand on mine. "Are you okay with this? It's your call."

I glance at my agent. His smile says it's my call, but his eyes tell me my decision better be yes.

"I'm okay with it as long as I have the freedom to set some boundaries. I'm a private, introverted person, so a lot of attention is a struggle for me. I know that's already increasing now, which is all the more reason I want to control it where I can."

Emily nods. "I'll always respect that. All I ask is that you respect my time in return. If we've planned to meet, I expect you to be on time and focused, not late, drinking, or being combative."

"I can do that."

"Okay, then. Dave has the contract, but you should read through it as well." She looks at Dave. "Have it back to me by Friday, so it'll be ready for his first game?"

"Will do. Thank you, Emily."

With a nod, she walks out, and I want to sag in my chair. Now the exhaustion is kicking in. Though it's an honor to have someone wanting to do a profile on me, the thought of having to be on more than I already will be is a touch overwhelming.

Amanda slips her hand into mine, and a bit of peace flows through me. I'm so grateful she's here with me. It makes handling all the changes and chaos easier.

With the contract sent to my email, we head for our last stop of the day.

"SO AS YOU CAN SEE, this is a great neighborhood. The building has lots of amenities. It's very safe, and the apartment is surprisingly spacious."

It's also dark, extremely modern, far from the stadium, and doesn't feel like home the way our apartment in Ida does.

I kept the lease for that because I want Amanda to be able to live there whenever she's in town and for us to live there together in the off-season. She'll be heading into her senior year of college in a few months, then after that, we should finally have less distance in our lives. I can't expect her to travel with me to every game, but hopefully she'll travel to some at least. Then we'll live here during the season. Maybe not *here*.

"It's nice, but..." I trail off, glancing at Amanda, who couldn't hide the look on her face if she tried, which is why she's staring out the window. "Not exactly our style."

"You know, it's not as easy to find exactly what you want here like it is in a small town. This is a month-to-month lease for a good price. Give it a try. If you hate it, at least you'll have somewhere to live that's not a hotel while you find somewhere else. I think you'll really end up liking this neighborhood, though."

I glance over at Amanda again and sigh. "Okay. That's fine."

"Perfect," Dave says. "I'll have the paperwork drawn up. It should be move-in ready by this weekend."

"Sounds good. Thanks for all your help." I extend my hand to Dave, and he shakes it.

"No problem. I'm going to go downstairs and speak with the property manager. Come down when you're ready."

I nod, and he walks out.

Slowly, I make my way over to Amanda and wrap my arms around her from behind, leaning into her and inhaling her scent.

"What do you think?" I ask, even though I know the answer.

"I hate it," she says with a laugh, spinning in my arms. "But we'll figure it out. We'll find ways to make it ours. And if we don't... this is a big city."

"I'm so glad you're here."

She wraps her arms tightly around me. "There's nowhere else I'd be. You told me once that you didn't see your future, you saw *our* future. I'll walk through it by your side."

Gently, I press my lips against hers, getting lost in the comfort and safety that wraps around me. My mind is still blown in the best way. I expected times of going back and forth between AAA and the majors, but this is it. All in. I know I've earned it, but it's still insane. My skin prickles with awareness that this is a moment my life is changing forever.

All but this. I rub my hands up and down Amanda's back.

This is the one thing I know will never change. I'll always have her. We'll always have each other, and we'll find our way through whatever comes next together.

Amanda

IN ANOTHER LIFE, I could've been a city girl.

I love my small towns. I love my small-town friend group, but holy shit. Less than twenty-four hours in and the sheer volume of places to go and things to do is filling my explorative, foodie, extroverted cup.

Jamie is at the stadium for some of the day, so I'm off to meet up with a friend, because I happen to have one—and only one— in the city.

Mark Abbott is a quarterback for the New York Bandits, the best team in New York, and a rising star throughout the country. He's also Rae, Sarah, and Dani's cousin. He sees all of us in the friend group as additional family members, and treats all the girls like extra sisters to protect.

He greets me with a hug when I get to the table at a cute little bistro.

"Thanks for being my lunch buddy today. This place looks amazing."

"I'm happy to have some company besides sweaty meathead football players."

I laugh at that, perusing my menu. "I'm surprised you're here and not in Ida."

Mark got caught in a whirlwind romance back in February while on vacation. In a hilarious twist of fate, she lives in Ida. Since it's his off-season, he's been spending a lot of time there.

"I had a few meetings, plus I need more clothes. I was doing laundry twice a week."

"Aw, that's adorable. You're so in looove," I sing.

He rolls his eyes. "Okay, maybe I'll take the sweaty meatheads."

"Please, I'm infinitely better company and I smell good."

"Well, I'm not going to smell you because you're like a little sister to me, and also, I don't want to get punched by Jamie, so I'll have to take your word for it. How's he doing?"

"Good. A little overwhelmed. It's a lot for his sweet introvert soul, but he's also extremely excited."

"I remember that feeling, and I'm not an introvert."

Being an extrovert runs in the Abbott genetics.

"How are you doing with it?" he asks.

"I'm fine."

"Nope. Way too quick an answer."

Sighing, I set my menu down. "I'm good. This isn't my thing. I'm here to support Jamie."

"We both know that's not true. Your life is going to change now. To some degree, you'll be in the public eye. And even if you weren't, it's still a change of location and lifestyle."

"Admittedly, I don't love the location—well, not the apartment they found for us. It's horrible, but I didn't want to push it. Jamie needs somewhere to settle, even if it's temporary. I can survive hating it for a couple of months, then we can look for somewhere new during the off-season."

"Just remember, you still matter. You know, Frannie and I have spent a lot of time talking about what this upcoming season will look like. She's going to try to be at home games when she can and spend weekends here, but she's not giving up her job or the rest of her life just to be here. It'll suck, but we both know it's the right call. I know you and Jamie have been together longer, but you still need to make a plan and talk about how all this is going to work. If you don't, you're going to be the one who ends up struggling."

Well, damn. He didn't have to punch me right in the gut.

"I know. But it's different. You're already established in your career. Jamie is just starting. I want to support him in every possible way. It'll be a lot to manage, but I'll figure it out."

"Just remember, you still matter. Don't get so caught up in being there for him that you forget to do things for yourself."

"I appreciate that. And I've still got plenty of things happening. I'm in the midst of planning a wedding that's happening in July and another event back home as well."

"That's right. I forgot you're the event queen. Now that you're down here, would you mind if I gave your name to someone?"

"Not at all. I can plan events from a distance and as long as I don't double book myself, I can make sure I'm where I need to be."

"Cool." He grabs his phone and types out a text. "One of my teammates and his wife are putting on an event but their planner delivered her baby really early, so she's taking time off to be at the NICU with the baby. They need someone to step in."

"I'm happy to jump in and roll with the plans already formed."

Then my stomach leaps with excitement. I shouldn't get ahead of myself. But running an event for an NFL player? That could be huge for me. If Jamie is going to be here for almost half the year, my business will be partially based here.

I make a mental note to update my website and make sure my social media aesthetic looks perfect.

There's definitely going to be a learning curve for Jamie and me through all this, but if anyone can handle it, it's me. Turning chaos into something beautiful is what I do. There's no reason I can't do that in my own life.

LUNCH WITH MARK WAS FUN, but some of his words were

a stark reminder of the changes Jamie and I will be facing in the coming months.

I'm headstrong and determined, even on a bad day, so I've been plowing through most of the changes so far with a plucky good attitude and bad bitch energy.

Leaving lunch today was a slap in the face of what I can expect, though, as paps waited outside the restaurant and snapped picture after picture while yelling questions at Mark and asking me who I was.

It shook me a little at first, but then I turned my withering glare on them and felt a little better.

Now I'm navigating the subway, trying to get back to our hotel. I've checked the stops three times, so I'm reasonably confident, but I still feel very much the small-town girl in the big city.

My phone rings as I wait for the train to pull up, and I smile when I see my favorite name on the screen. *Baseball boyfriend.*

"Hey, babe."

"Mands—where are—"

"What? I can't hear you."

"When—back—"

A train pulls to a stop, and I press the phone harder to my ear. "I don't know if you can hear me, but I'm about to hop on the subway. I should be back to the hotel soon, and we can talk then. I love you!"

Then I hang up and scurry into the car.

Definitely a learning curve for this stuff, but I'm confident I can figure it out and be a pro at all this in no time.

WHEN I WALK into the hotel room, Jamie is on his phone and pacing.

"She's back, gotta go."

He hangs up and walks over to me, concern and frustration on his face.

"Where have you been?"

"I went to lunch with Mark. I told you this morning that I was going to. Then I explored the area for a bit. I was getting on the subway when you called. What's wrong?"

He sighs and runs a hand through his hair, then unlocks his phone.

"This."

He turns the screen toward me, and it's filled with articles about Mark... and me.

"Jesus." I grab the phone from him and read through the headlines.

Some call me a mystery woman. Some imply that I'm a home-wrecker. One somehow knows who I am and questions if Mark is planning a wedding.

Jamie looks over the edge of his phone and clicks on one specifically that identifies me as his girlfriend and has way too many details about me. It also questions whether Mark and I happen to be friends since we both have ties to Ida or if we're having an affair.

I'm about to turn the screen off, when I catch a glimpse of the first comment. Unable to stop myself, I scroll down to the comment section, my throat tightening as I read through them.

Like he'd cheat with someone who looks like her.

He could do a lot better.

No guy wants a fat cow like that.

Fat slut is probably playing them both.

I wonder if she jiggles while they fuck.

Tears fill my eyes and Jamie is instantly next to me.

"What?"

I try to turn the phone screen off, but he snatches it out of my hand, reading through the comments.

I sniff back my tears. People are mean. They're assholes who sit behind keyboards and insult others to make themselves feel better. I shouldn't let their words bother me. I know who I am.

It shouldn't hurt.

But it fucking does. Because some of the deepest wounds— the ones I've worked hardest on and try to bury deep inside me— involve my weight.

The people who matter love me exactly as I am, but that doesn't make it easier to be the source of such unnecessary vitriol.

"I just need a minute."

I hurry over to the bathroom, ignoring as Jamie calls after me.

The bathroom isn't very big, so I have nowhere to go. I sink to the floor, leaning against the bathtub, and pull my knees up to my chest. Everything hurts, and all I want to do is break. I'm trying and failing to hold it together, so I stop fighting the tears.

I feel awful. And was Jamie being accusatory when I first walked in? Is this what I have to look forward to anytime Jamie and I do anything? There's a lot I can manage, but I don't know how to manage this.

Normally, this is when I'd find myself surrounded by the girls in a cocoon of love, but I don't have that here. I miss them. I miss my perfect dream apartment. I miss home.

Jamie knocks on the door. "Mands..." He tries the handle, and when it opens, he walks in, pausing when he sees me.

I try to wipe my tears, but more come.

He sits down next to me and wraps his arm around me, fingers curling through my hair.

"Are you mad at me?" I sniff.

"No. I'm mad at all those fuckers who wrote those things about you."

"But *were* you mad at me? Because it seemed like you were when I came in."

"I was mad at the situation and mad that my agent was yelling at me like it was all my fault, not the paparazzi's."

"I'm sorry."

"Don't you dare apologize." He sighs and rests his head against mine. "We've got a learning curve to figure out, but we can do that together."

"I'm not going to make you look bad, am I?"

"No. All it'll take is one post on social media to clear it all up. Even if we didn't, it wouldn't make a difference. It's okay. But you're not okay. And that pisses me off because I don't want anyone hurting you."

I wipe at my eyes. "I need to grow some thicker skin."

"No. I like your beautiful heart just the way it is. I like all of you the way you are. People are awful and cruel, and I'm sorry you were on the receiving end of it, but that's a reflection of them, not you. From the moment I first saw you, no one else has ever compared. You are stunning. A goddess. A queen. My queen. I hate that those words hit somewhere deep down and make you think they're true because they're not. If you could see yourself through my eyes..." He sighs, but it's not a tired sigh this time. It's like he's in awe of me. He tilts my chin so I'm looking at him. "You would never doubt your beauty, inside or out. I love you."

"I love you too. I'm sorr—"

"Nope. You have nothing to be sorry for."

"But I'm supposed to be supporting you."

"We're supposed to be a team. I'm sorry I was snappy with you when you walked in. I was stressed. But it's going to be okay. I'll call Dave back later."

"And tell him what? What should we do?"

"We either ignore it and give them nothing, or—if you think you'll spend more time with Mark—we make a quick social media post about it or ask him to. It establishes what your friendship is. And mine too. I'm glad he'll be in the city some of the time when I am. It's not the same road, but he's walked a similar one and I could use his advice."

"Is it a total copout to ask him to post something?"

"No. Dave even said it would make more sense. He was yelling at me because we didn't get our stories straight this time."

"I didn't think about this side of things," I whisper, feeling pathetic.

"Neither did I. But we'll figure it out. Even if we make mistakes along the way, we both have good hearts and good intentions. That's all that matters." He wipes the tears off my cheeks. "Now, I need you to promise me something."

"What?"

"That you won't read any more comments."

I bite my lip. That's going to be hard. The curious and people pleasing pieces of me will always want to know, even if I shouldn't.

"I'll do my best."

He narrows his eyes but lets it go.

We sit in silence for a moment. I still feel like shit, but it's not quite as bad with him next to me.

"How was your day?" I'm desperate for a subject change, and I'm hoping maybe he'll have something positive to tell me.

"It was good. The apartment is ours, so we can start moving things in this weekend. Dave recommended renting furniture, and I agree that sounds easier."

I nod. "That makes sense." Plus, I don't want to move my shit into an apartment I hate that I'm determined to be out of by the end of the season.

"We can start with the basics, then make a list of specific things. Oh, and I officially picked my number today."

The tinge of excitement in his voice perks me up. In the past, he never cared much about his numbers, and took whatever he was assigned.

"What did you pick? Did you stick with six like high school? Or keep thirteen from the Knights?"

"Neither. I picked twenty-six. Do you know why?"

I shake my head, and he smiles, eyes shining. "Because December twenty-sixth was the day my life changed forever." He caresses his thumb over my hand as I stare at him wide-eyed. "The day I met you."

"Jamie..."

"Now I'll always have the most important piece of my life with me."

More tears well in my eyes, but at least these are happy ones. I squeeze his hand, and he squeezes mine back.

"I also found out when my first game pitching will be."

I grab his arm in excitement. "When?"

"Next week. Tuesday. In L.A. Will you come? The Metros allow wives or girlfriends to travel with us. We'd have our own room, and—"

I lean in and kiss him. "You don't have to convince me. I'm not missing your official Metros debut."

He lets out a shaky breath. "Good. Because I couldn't do this without you."

I gently run my thumb over his cheek. "How long will we be there?"

"Monday through Thursday. We should be able to do a little sightseeing on the days I'm not starting."

"Sounds perfect," I say, even as I realize I'll have to miss volleyball next week. I'll probably go back this week and pack some things for both of us. There's no way we brought enough with us. After that, I'll make a schedule of where I'll be when, and I'll have to check my important dates with the team's travel dates.

For a second, I wonder if I should quit my rec league, but I don't want to do that. I love playing with Chelsea and Dani, and with this being our last year of college and full-time careers starting soon, I don't know if we'll play next year or not. I don't want to miss out on this. I'll also need to factor in the wedding and other events I'm planning.

Jamie rubs his thumb over my hand, drawing my attention back to him.

"Thank you for being here with me. I could probably do it alone, but everything is easier with you here."

"There's nowhere else I'd be," I say, and despite all the conflicting feelings I have right now, it's the absolute truth.

He pulls me into his arms, and I melt against him. My safe place. My person. Even though the familiar sense of peace and home washes over me when I'm in his arms, for the first time, I'm questioning how I'm going to handle all this.

15
Magical

Amanda

"I'M SO EXCITED!" Rae does a little happy dance as we walk toward our seats.

It's in the reserved section for family, though it's not with the WAGs this time, which I'm grateful for. They haven't been mean to me, but outside of a couple of the people I'd already met—or the wives of a couple of the players I'd met in the past—most didn't go out of their way to get to know me. Which is fine.

I have my tribe, even if they aren't always here.

Jamie's parents surprised us by flying out with the kids to see Jamie pitch his first game—which he won. He said he savored the boos from all the L.A. fans, and I believe it because that cocky smile was firmly in place all night. And it might have been a bit of a turn-on.

Which means I might have blown him in the hotel room before we met his family for dinner.

I'm a slut for seeing my man happy and confident. The only thing that turns me on more is when he's all innocent and blushing. Hot as fuck.

Today is Jamie's first home game pitching, and Rae and

Aaron came down for it, along with Trevor and Chelsea. I love having part of my tribe by my side for the game.

I started paying closer attention and learned more about baseball because of Jamie, but I fell in love with it because of my friends, before Jamie and I were ever together. Some of my favorite college memories are nights shivering under a blanket together at the college games.

Aaron and Trevor are both looking around the stadium in awe. They both got to play here for Aaron's bachelor party, but for two guys who have battled injuries and lost the ability to play like they once could, seeing their friend living the dream hits different. They're proud and excited, even if it hurts a little.

Rae elbows me when we sit down. "You're beaming, proud girlfriend. I love seeing it."

"Me too," Chels says.

The girls have been my rock, as usual, while dealing with this transition. They video call me when I'm not here and make it a point to find me and spend time with me when I'm back home. And when they found out about that article and all those comments, they were ready to go *No Body, No Crime* on the people who said that stuff. I love them for it, and Goddess knows I'd do the same for them.

I should probably take a harder look at why that protectiveness and ferocity doesn't translate to my own life, but the easier thing to do is plow on and ignore it.

"I can't help it. He always looks hot when he's pitching, but sitting in a sea of people who are all staring at him and knowing he's *mine* does things to me."

Rae and Chelsea look at their guys and smile the same way. No matter what they're doing, when you love your partner, seeing them do something they love and succeed makes you happy too.

The guys line up outside the dugout, as the singer prepares for the National Anthem. Jamie's eyes sweep the section, and I feel the heat of his gaze the second it lands on me.

I give him my sultriest smile, and a tiny wave before he looks away, and I swear I see the faintest hint of color on his cheeks.

Through all the chaos of the last couple of weeks, these are the moments that make it worth it.

I think I'm going to enjoy being an MLB girlfriend.

Jamie

"YOU LOSING YOUR SPARK ALREADY, kid? One win and you have to fight for the next one?"

"What can I say? I feed on the tears of the losing team's fans. There are fewer of them here." I spin to face Declan Lowery, the third baseman and a shit-giving grump most of the time. "I think you're still mad about the first time I pitched in this stadium and struck you out."

There's a chorus of "oohs" from around the dugout.

Yeah, I'm never going to let anyone we played against for Aaron's bachelor party forget that a bunch of ragtag small-town kids beat their asses. Plus, I know he's trying to get under my skin.

Yeah, my first game was a clear victory for the Metros. I only had a handful of hits and only let one run through over the course of eight innings. I was pissed when they pulled me, but these days, complete games are a thing of the past. I was lucky I got any of those on the Knights. They're strict about it at the collegiate level too, and it makes me that much more grateful I didn't go for college ball. This is where I'm supposed to be.

Today's game has been more of a pitcher's duel. Again, I've only let one run through, but the team has also only scored one.

"Maybe one of you should get out there and hit the damn ball," Marc Demoda says. As pitching coaches go, he's been great. Not that I have a ton of experience. No one compares to working with Aaron, but Marc comes close. I think it helps that he's still close to the game. He isn't a decade removed from pitching. He still remembers what it's like. "Stop psyching your pitcher out or you'll screw us all over."

"Yeah, behave, Dec," Ryan Daily, one of the other starting pitchers says.

Declan just rolls his eyes.

"Maybe you should all shut up and pay attention," Marc says.

I smile to myself. Close games like this are stressful, but they're also more rewarding.

"Might pull you after the next one," Marc says to me.

"After the sixth? Really?"

"You want the win?"

"Obviously."

"Then trust me. We'll see how you do next inning. If it's easy, we'll keep you in."

"So bring my A game. Got it."

Marc nods approvingly, and when I have a second of quiet to breathe, I let out a shaky breath as I stare out at the packed stadium.

It's a lot to adjust to, but I'm loving every second, even if sometimes I need to take a breath, ground myself, and remember why I'm here, how hard I've worked, and how important it is to enjoy having what I've worked so long for.

"HERE'S to win number two for the Metros' star pitcher!" Aaron says, raising a glass.

Everyone else here is already twenty-one, but being the Metros' newest pitcher comes with a fun perk of not being carded.

The game continued as a pitcher's duel. I stayed in through the seventh, then they had one of the relievers come in. The other team wasn't as smart. They let their pitcher go an inning too long, and we scored three more runs between the sixth and the eighth.

We ended the game four to one, and I walked away with my second win of my major league career. Not that I'm counting.

We all clink our glasses together, but I shake my head. "Not star. Not yet. I haven't earned that."

"But you will," Trevor says. "And it's an honor to watch while you do it. Proud of you, man."

"Thanks. I appreciate you all being here."

"I think that deserves one more toast," Rae says. "To friendship."

Again, we all clink our glasses, but as we do, Amanda's phone rings.

She digs it out of her bag and puts it to her ear while apologizing. "Amanda Hamilton."

I watch raptly as she switches into business mode. It's ridiculously hot.

"Yes. I'd love to. Tuesday morning—yes. I can do that. Are you sure you don't need to see—oh. Well, that sounds great. I'll see you then. Take care. Bye." She stares down at her phone with wide eyes. "Wow."

"What?"

She turns to me, eyes alight with excitement. "When I had lunch with Mark, he mentioned one of his teammates needed help with some event coming up that the previous planner had to back out of for health reasons. He didn't mention it was for Wendell and Alannah Pierce."

My eyes fly wide. Wendell is one of Mark's teammates, and one of the first people to sign with the Bandits when the team started twelve years ago. It's widely reported this season will be his last. His wife is a former model, and they had some epic love story years ago. Unlike a lot of people in those positions, they still seem really happy and they do a lot of good.

"I need more context," Rae says. Unsurprising. Rae is a baseball girl through and through.

"It doesn't really matter except that the foundation the gala is for is *their* foundation. The one they started in honor of their daughter when she came out as trans. It helps support trans youth and young adults, particularly the most at risk who may not have safe environments or home lives." Amanda sucks in a deep breath. "So, no pressure," she squeaks.

I wrap my arm around her and kiss the side of her head. "I'm so proud of you. You're going to rock it."

She lets out a shaky breath. "I hope so. Oh my gosh! I hoped I'd find a couple of events to work on down here, but I wasn't expecting it to be *this*."

I grab my glass again and lift it. "To living our dreams."

Amanda smiles up at me as everyone else toasts to that. Instead of tapping our glasses together, she leans up and kisses me.

A lot of good things are happening right now—the building blocks of our future in many ways—but none of it means as much as having her by my side through it all.

I DON'T LOVE this apartment. It's never felt like home. It feels a little too sterile. Like a vacation rental. A place you stay temporarily, but never get cozy in.

Tonight, though, at least there's enough space for Trevor and Chelsea and Aaron and Rae to stay the night and not have to shell out for a decent hotel here in the city.

Them being here tonight means a lot to me. They're part of why I'm here right now—especially Aaron. If I'm ever lucky enough to win any kind of award someday, I'll be thanking him. Seeing the pride in his eyes tonight was indescribable. I'm living a dream we all had at one point, and so far, I'm kicking ass at it.

Just like my girl is kicking ass at her dreams. The event she's taking over is an entire charity gala. That's huge. Especially because it's not a small-town rich ladies' gala, but a massive New York City gala with a lot of super rich folks attending. This could change everything for her.

"I'm proud of you," I whisper as she crawls into bed. Sound carries like crazy in this apartment, and it drives me nuts, especially with people here.

She shrugs. "I got lucky."

"You worked hard. You *have* worked hard for years. And it shows."

She climbs on top of me and runs her hands down my chest. "So have you. *And it shows.*"

Her lips brush mine, and I have to fight back the instinctive moan. Wrapping my arm around her waist, I flip her over.

"Can you be quiet?" I whisper against her lips.

I swear we can hear if someone is talking quietly two rooms over. So with Trevor and Chelsea in the guest room across the hall and Rae and Aaron on the sleeper sofa in the living room, we have to be *very* quiet.

Slipping her underwear off, I push one finger inside her. She bites her lip as she arches beneath me.

"I don't know," she breathes. "Can you?"

Then she leans up and sucks on my neck just below my ear—the spot that makes me crazy.

"Only one way to find out."

Stripping my shirt off, I lean back and shove my boxers down, then pull her barely-there underwear off. She shimmies out of her shirt, as I grab her hips, then thrust into her *hard*.

She slaps a hand over her mouth trying to cover her yelp.

I silently laugh, but she gets me back by reaching for my balls and gently massaging them. I barely contain my throaty moan, then relent.

"Okay. I'll be gentle."

Holding her tightly, I pull out and thrust in again, but not nearly as hard this time. With our bodies flush, the intensity is still there. Then she smiles up at me. It takes a second to figure out why. She does some sort of witchcraft and tightens the muscles of her vaginal wall.

My eyes roll back at how good it feels. She must like it too because a haze settles in her eyes.

We continue like that, small, perfectly positioned thrusts and the tense and release of her pelvic floor muscles.

It shouldn't feel this fucking good, but it does, and we're both barely keeping it together. We're drenched in sweat, slick bodies gliding together as we get close to the edge and fall away again.

My orgasm hits out of nowhere, and my whole body locks up. It's all I can do to keep from screaming her name, but I can't hold back my repressed grunts.

I stay inside her, angling my hips and continuing the shallow thrusts as I work her clit with my thumb until she's falling apart under me, face twisted in ecstasy as her mouth falls open with silent screams. She milks my sensitive cock, almost making me come again.

She sighs contentedly as I flop down next to her.

"I need another shower," I whisper.

She laughs, still quietly, but louder than a whisper. "That was so much hotter than I thought it would be. I think we edged ourselves."

"Just a bit. I didn't know your—"

"Pussy is magical?" she asks with a sweet smile.

"Oh, I knew that," I sigh, kissing her neck. "Love you, baby."

"Love you too. I know I need to get up and clean up, but I don't want to. Just... hold me for a few minutes?"

"I'll hold you all night."

Wrapping my arms around her, I tug her close, burying my face in her hair.

How did I get this lucky?

Not only have I made it to the majors, but I have an incredible woman next to me who is living her own dream.

It's only been a couple of weeks, but I think this is a sign that we're going to good places.

16
Growing Pains

Amanda

"MAYBE YOU JUST SHOULDN'T COME TO the wedding!"

I rub my temple as the bridezilla from hell screams at her mother yet again.

"You're lucky to even *have* this wedding, missy. After all the grief you put me through."

I wonder if there's a way to screen for people like this in the future. They're paying me a good amount, but I'm not sure it's worth it.

"What if we did a classy, biodegradable confetti? Then you won't have to worry about glittery plastic or spending extra money on rose petals."

Yes, this is what their fight is over. The confetti guests will be given to throw at the bride and groom. I'm proud of myself for keeping my face neutral when *I* would like to be throwing things at *them* right now. Ugh.

They look at each other tentatively and smile. Then they collapse into a dramatic hug saying how much they love each other and shifting gears to another wedding topic—how ugly the bride's sister will look in her dress.

This is my personal hell.

Thankfully, with that last crisis averted, our meeting ends, but no sooner am I out the door of the café when my phone rings.

Cursing to myself, I dig through my bag and fish out my work phone. "Hello, this is Amanda."

"Amanda, hi. It's Alannah."

"Hi, Alannah. What can I help you with?"

"I wanted to talk about the flower colors and then the lighting. I'm standing in the middle of the space now, and everything is so harsh. We want something that's soft, warm... inviting."

"We can make that work. We don't have to use all of their lights. Light strands can give great warmth and ambience without being aggressive."

"Hm. Do you think we could get some strands of colored lights in addition to some white ones? Pink and blue for the trans flag?"

"I'll start looking as soon as I'm home and can get on the computer. Now, what did you need to discuss about the flowers?"

She launches into a conversation about displays, colors, and making sure nothing is too gaudy as I walk back to my car.

The second I hang up the phone, I pull out my notebook and scribble down everything we talked about so I don't forget anything. In the midst of it all, my regular phone alarm goes off, reminding me I'm meeting the girls for lunch.

Shit. That meeting this morning took longer than I planned for. I quickly look up some of the lights Alannah mentioned and send them to her so she can get an idea, then let her know I'll email her more details later.

When I open my calendar to add a reminder for myself, I cringe. A mixture of blocked out colors stare back at me. Jamie's travel schedule, the schedule of when I'm traveling with him, my scheduled events, everything I need to do for those events, plus small snippets of time blocked out for family and friends.

It's Wednesday now, and I'm in Ida for the rest of this week. Jamie will be back tomorrow night, so after the wedding on Saturday, I'll head back down to the city. On Tuesday, we leave to go to

Arizona, and I'll be working other than at Jamie's games. I still try to go, even when he's not pitching. Then I'll be back to Ida for the last volleyball tournament that Saturday. Thankfully, I won't be missing anything next week since our last Wednesday game is tonight. Then on that Sunday, I'll head back to New York City to do all the final preparation for the gala the following Saturday night.

Inconveniently, Jamie will also be pitching that day, but their game is late afternoon, so he should still be able to go to the event, and I know several of the Metros are on the invite list.

My head is spinning with how chaotic the next two weeks will be, but it'll be worth it. Well, I don't know about this wedding, but I'm honored to be a part of the gala, and the planner who did most of the planning for the event was fantastic. She kept detailed notes and information, so there wasn't much I had to do besides some final things and little changes. The only hiccup was finding another set up and tear down crew because the others had only been in contact with the other event planner and had booked another event that night when they hadn't heard from her, but I got it taken care of.

Because I'm a badass.

I lean back against my car seat and close my eyes, reveling in that feeling for a moment.

But then my phone goes off in my hand and I let out a whimper. This bad bitch is exhausted.

When I look at the screen again, I find info from the contact form on my website. It's someone looking to book a consult sometime in the next two weeks. I let out an unhinged laugh, then email her back that it'll have to be the first week in August instead.

I let out a breath, shoulders still a little tense, but when no other notifications come through, I put my work phone away, then grab my regular phone and snap a selfie.

[picture message]

> My day is crazy, and I'm afraid if I put my phone down, I won't pick it up again, so I wanted to wish you good luck now. Miss you.

A second later, I get a text back.

BASEBALL BOYFRIEND

[picture message]

Heaven help me. He's wearing a backward ball cap and he's shirtless with sweat glistening on his chest.

BASEBALL BOYFRIEND

Busy day here too.

> Is that picture trying to threaten me with a good time?

BASEBALL BOYFRIEND

Maybe. I think I'd like to threaten you over the phone tonight. Sound good?

> Sounds perfect. Talk later. Love you!

BASEBALL BOYFRIEND

Love you too, babe. Keep kicking ass.

With a sigh of relief, I set my phone to the side, then I remember that I'm about to be late for lunch with the girls and haul ass out of my parking spot.

"I LOVE ICE CREAM," I sigh happily as I sit down at the table with Chelsea and Dani. We're at Dani's friend's ice cream shop, enjoying some delicious homemade ice cream after kicking ass at our volleyball game. The physical outlet was definitely needed after all the mental gymnastics and planning I've been doing.

"Same," Chelsea and Dani agree.

"Thanks for working with me about the volleyball stuff. I'm sure it would've been easier to replace me."

Dani's brow furrows. "We weren't going to replace you. If anything, we would've just quit. We're a team. We go down together."

Chelsea sets her spoon down and looks at me. "Yeah. You're not replaceable. We love doing this *with* you."

"Thanks." As usual, I suck at taking compliments, even if I did need to hear that. The stupid, insecure part of me is afraid my friendships will fracture or fade since I'm not around as regularly, but the girls have only held on tighter.

"Are you doing okay?" Dani asks.

"Yeah. It's just been... crazy. I think I might even be happy when it's time to go back to school. My schedule will probably be less chaotic. But I love that I get to be here for nights like this and for the tournament next Saturday."

"Make sure you're still taking care of yourself."

What is that?

But I nod, then lift my spoon. "Ice cream is a great first step."

I know I'm running myself a little ragged, but it's worth it to build my business, spend time with the people who matter, and support Jamie. Once these events are done, it'll slow down—at least a little. It's temporary, and that's why I can push myself.

Plus, the rest of the night will be all relaxing, snacking, and enjoying some downtime.

No working.

No working.

None at all.

Unless I have a really great idea.

I HAD a great idea about how to organize the lights and flowers for the gala, so I spent the last hour doing a quick mockup so I could send it to Alannah.

As I plop on the couch, turn the TV on, and find Jamie's game, I cringe realizing I missed the first inning—and the score is already one-one in the second. I cross my fingers and throw up a prayer to the goddess of sports—that's totally a thing, right?—and hope the team can turn it around because my man needs a win.

Jamie

I WANT to throw my glove into my cubby and scream as we walk into the visitor's clubhouse, dejected after a bruising loss.

A loss that I helped us earn. Sure, our reliever gave up three runs in four innings, but I gave up four runs in five. *Fuck my life.* It's my third loss of the season. My third loss in a row. And the worst part is, other than a couple of games, mine have consistently been the ones we've lost. I thought I was starting out strong, but it's looking more and more like overconfidence.

At least that's what every fucking article says about me. All those shitty analysts, most of whom have never played the fucking game. Why don't they give it a try before they crucify the rest of us?

I'm exhausted and pissed, and I want nothing more than to go home to Amanda's arms, but we're on the road and she's not here. Which shouldn't piss me off, but it does. I know she's had a lot going on lately, but she *could* have scheduled things differently and come on this trip, and when I'm feeling fucking awful like this, I hate that she's not.

"Let it go, Jame," our right fielder Beau Airington says. He's a typical fun-loving playboy, who even after a loss like this isn't grumpy like the rest of us.

It's easy for him to say that. He's not the pitcher. He's not the one the win or loss sits on.

When a player gets a hit that turns the team around, he's praised, but he doesn't get a W next to his name. And if one botches a play, he'll be the talk of all those sports shows, but there won't be an L next to his name. The pitcher carries greater responsibility, and I'm failing the team.

I can't remember the last time I had three consecutive losses. A team I was on? Sure. But me? Nope. The Metros put their faith in me, and after two decent games, I'm letting them down.

"Seriously, don't take it so hard. You're still finding your groove," Ryan says. "Look around the league, and you'll find you're not even close to being in the bottom half when it comes to stats. You're doing well for a rookie."

I'm not doing well for me, though, and that pisses me off.

"Come on, shower and we'll take you out for dinner, maybe some drinks, and get your mind off it," Beau says.

"I appreciate it, but I've got a meeting to get to, and I'm exhausted. I just want to get back to my room as soon as possible, order room service, and pass out."

Beau claps me on the shoulder. "Let us know if you change your mind."

I give them a nod, then head for the showers. I want this fucking day to be over with.

I don't know why Emily needed to travel with the team or interview me here. I'm trying to be nice to her because she's doing her job, and I know this is what I signed on for, but I'm in a shitty mood and don't particularly want to talk about baseball or my life. No part of me is ever going to like exposing the inner parts of myself to the world. It's not who I am. The only person who gets those pieces of me is Amanda.

And she's not here.

Emily and I meet at the hotel bar, and I do my best to keep a smile on, be as friendly as I can manage, and give her more than three-word answers. But when she says that's good for the evening, I practically jump out of my chair—or I would if I had any energy—and head for the elevators.

By the time I make it back to my room, I have a text from Amanda telling me she loves me and to call her when I'm ready. But when I open the door, cold loneliness washes over me along with bitter anger.

I'm not sure who or what I'm mad at, but all I want to do is sleep it off.

I strip out of my suit, then flop onto the bed and reluctantly pull out my phone and call Amanda.

"Hey, baby," she answers, her voice soft and dulcet.

"Hi."

"I'm sorry about the game. Do you want to talk about it?"

"Enh."

"Or we could switch to a video call. I can show you my boobs. They usually cheer you up."

In some ways that's tempting, but looking at what I can't have when I really want it sounds like cruel punishment, which is why I didn't video call her in the first place. I didn't want to see her face and miss her more. That thought makes me feel guilty, which adds to my cranky mood.

"I appreciate that," I force out. "But I can barely keep my eyes open. I think I need to crash."

There's a long pause. Something about that probably hurt her feelings, but I can't think about that right now.

"Whatever you need." Her voice is still soft, but it's resigned now. "If you want to talk tonight or tomorrow before you leave, I'm here. I can't wait to see you on Saturday night. I love you."

I can hear the uncertainty in her voice when she says it, and it makes me feel like a jackass. She's worried I won't say it back. I don't know how she could ever think that after almost two years together. But saying the words that resonate from deep in my soul is the least I can do.

"I love you too. I'll text you before I get on the plane tomorrow."

"Okay. Goodnight."

"Night."

I hang up the phone and stare at the ceiling for a moment. Glancing over at the hotel phone, I consider calling for a meal, but I have no appetite. Instead, I set my alarm, flick off the light, then roll over and pray sleep will take me.

Tomorrow is another day, and I need to get up, work harder, and figure out my shit before I cost myself my spot on the team. They could decide I'm not worth it any time. I could get sent back to the minors. Or traded. Fuck. I've got to get my head together before I lose the dream I've worked so hard for.

Amanda

I'M WEARING my comfortable and sexy silk pajamas as I wait for Jamie.

I went straight from the wedding to driving down here. Every time I make the drive, I remember how much I loathe driving in the city, and I'm starting to wonder if it would be possible to afford a car service to drive me back and forth—some of the time, at least. Today it would've been amazing, since I was exhausted.

I took a quick nap on the couch as soon as I got back here, then took a bath and ordered some takeout. It got here ten minutes ago, and I'm keeping it warm in the oven, since Jamie should be home from the game any minute.

At least he's not pitching today, so I'm hoping he'll be in a better mood. It was hard not being able to comfort him, and even harder that he wouldn't let me in. When he faced losses in high school or with the Knights, usually we talked for an hour, had some kind of phone sex, and he felt a lot better. Me not physically being there wasn't as painful as it seemed to be on Wednesday.

It made me feel crappy, especially since I'd had a good—if chaotic—day. I never mentioned that we won our volleyball match or the breakthrough I had in the final layout for the gala. It seemed wrong to talk about my success when he's struggling. Which is also weird for me because I like sharing everything with him. I've gotten used to that.

I try to ignore the prick at my heart when I think that.

This is temporary. Growing pains.

The door swings open, and Jamie walks in. When he sees me and a relieved smile appears on his face, my worries melt away.

I hop off the kitchen stool and walk over to him. He drops his bags and pulls me into a bear hug, holding me close and burying his face in my neck.

"How was the game?"

"We won. Probably because I wasn't pitching."

He moves to pull away, but I hold him tighter. "Don't do that. You're an amazing pitcher, and you're great at proving yourself. It might not happen all in your first month, and that's okay. You've got what it takes to meet this dream and soar higher, to even bigger ones."

He sighs, leaning into me more, fingers curling in my hair. "I missed you."

"I missed you too."

We stand like that for a moment, in a cozy cocoon of our love. This is the love that we've walked through distance and separation for. One that grounds and heals us both.

"Will you try to be at every game I pitch? I'm just... better with you there. And even when I'm not, I need you after. Please."

I run my fingers through his hair, trying to tamp down the slight frustration I feel. I appreciate that he wants me there. I'm his partner. But I can't drop every single thing in my life to serve him, and for a good chunk of our relationship, I sacrifice significantly more of myself than he has to. I sacrifice having him there to support me and cheer me on. Sacrificing the things that I love, that make me who I am, isn't something I'm willing to do—not anymore than I already have.

But... there's probably a better way I can balance my schedule. And with volleyball almost finished, there's no reason I can't try to be at every game he pitches—at least until I go back to school in a little over a month.

"I'll do everything I can to be there."

"Thank you." He pulls away with a soft kiss to my head.

"There's Italian takeout in the oven."

"Perfect. I'll just go change into something more comfortable."

"And hopefully more revealing," I tease. He chuckles and goes to walk away, but I grab his hand. "I love you."

He turns back and kisses me. "I love you too. God, I'm so much better when I'm with you."

He squeezes my hand and heads for the bedroom, and as happy as I am to be back in his arms, I'm worried about the weight he's putting on me, and what'll happen when I can't be there for him.

Growing pains, I remind myself again, but it doesn't stop that needling little worry in my heart.

17
Cry It Out

Jamie

I WATCH from the kitchen island as Amanda flits around the apartment, stuffing things in bags and occasionally stopping to furiously type something on her phone. I'd offer to help, but I've learned by now I would only distract her from her thoughts. The chaos is all part of her preparation.

Like a pregame ritual.

Maybe I need something like that to help me get my game back on track.

We lost the last game I pitched, though at least for that one, I didn't take the L. I let three runs through in the first six innings, but the other team let four through, so we were still on track for the win when I left the game. The problem is, the other team's reliever only let one more run through, while ours let three through. While he took the loss, in my mind, it was still on both of us because we both let equal numbers of runs through. And frankly, I should be improving my game from here, not getting stagnant.

I'm pitching again tonight, and my stress levels are higher than they should be. It's getting in my head, and I know that's making it worse. Part of me wants to call Aaron and beg him to come down here—to help me out. He always helped me through my funks in the past. But that's not his place anymore. The amount of laughter and eye rolls I'd probably get at bringing in my high school mentor to help me would be ridiculous.

But Aaron is good at finding and fixing problems, and I haven't developed enough of a relationship with the other pitchers to ask them—or even our pitching staff. Yay, introvert problems. Something I need to get over if I'm going to succeed.

Fuck it. I'll go in a little early today, talk with Marc, maybe see what options I have.

Amanda whizzes by and over to the giant blue-black refrigerator. She frowns every time she sees it. I know she's not happy here. Yet another place I'm failing. I don't have enough bandwidth to manage it all, though. Some things have to give, and the apartment can be solved in the off-season. My game has to come first right now so my off-season isn't permanent.

Amanda sets a thing of bagels on the counter, then grabs a knife.

I instantly hop off my stool and round the counter to her, grabbing the knife before she can cut one of her fingers off.

"I'll do that."

"I can cut a bagel."

"You sound like you're hyped up on drugs right now, and you're practically shaking. I'll do it. Let me help you."

She sighs and leans against the counter, nodding. "I'm sorry. I'm... today is a lot. Like a lot, a lot. I'm excited, but I'm nervous. I've never hosted anything this massive before, and I want to get it right. Not just because it's great for my business, but it's an important cause."

I finish slicing the bagel and pop it in the toaster, then put my hands on her shoulders. "It's going to be amazing. You work insanely hard to make every event as perfect as it can be, and you are one of the most capable people I've ever met when it comes to rolling with the punches and solving problems on the fly. You're brilliant." I kiss her cheek. "Beautiful." I kiss her other cheek.

"And deeply passionate." I press a soft kiss to her lips. "It's all going to be amazing, and I can't wait to see it."

"You said you think you might be an hour late?"

"Hopefully less. As soon as the game is done, I'll be hauling ass to get there. It's not too far from the stadium, so it should be quick."

Much quicker than getting from our apartment to the stadium, which takes forever. There was twice the mileage between our apartment and the Knights stadium, but it took half as long to get home. I am not used to city life.

"Can I tell you a secret?"

I wrap my arms around her back. "Always."

"I love when you walk into an event, and I can feel you watching me from across the room. It's an extra boost of confidence."

"Mm. If that's the case, I'll be your stalker all night."

"I like the sound of that."

The bagel pops up from the toaster, and though she reaches for it, I grab it first. "Go sit. I know how you like your bagels."

Again, she melts a little and heads for one of the stools.

"How are you feeling about the game today? I'm sorry I can't be there." Her voice is a little tight when she says it, but I don't know why. I know today is important to her, and while I wish she could be both places, that would be next to impossible. Plus, it's not like I won't see her after the game.

"Trying not to get too in my head, but it's probably a losing battle. I need to find something to get me out of this funk."

I slide the plate across the counter to her, and she catches my hand, resting hers on top of it. "I don't think it's as much of a funk as you think it is."

"I've seen guys who are better than me bounce between the minors and pro ball for months at a time—"

"Yeah, but your contract was taken over. It wasn't a random call up in a pinch. This is different."

"I could still get sent back."

She slowly shakes her head. "I somehow doubt they would've gone through all this effort just to do that. Have some grace for yourself."

Coming from the one person who might be harder on herself than I am on myself.

"I just don't want to lose what I've worked for. I don't want to be the butt of the joke. The guy who couldn't hack it in the majors." I meet her eyes, trying to lighten the mood. "And end up podcasting from my parents' basement."

She smiles softly, but there's an edge of sympathy there that I hate.

"That was never your fate. Let yourself adjust. By the way, have you eaten breakfast? You seem like you've been eating less lately, and I'm not sure I can keep living with you if you start meticulously counting calories."

"Thanks. Glad to know what your deal breaker is."

She gives me a sweet smile. "Food is one of the best parts of life. I won't apologize for that."

"And you never have to," I remind her. I hate that she ever feels poorly about her body. "Don't worry. I had a protein shake earlier and I'll grab something else in a bit."

She eyes me with that mama bear concern, but lets it go. "Okay."

I turn back to the fridge and get her a glass of orange juice.

She smiles up at me when I slide it in front of her, and for a moment, I feel a shred of peace and normalcy. This is how things used to be. It's how I want them to be again. I just need to get my head out of my ass and get through this rough transition.

MY STOMACH BURNS as I walk toward Marc's office. I'm not great at asking for help, or even admitting I need it. I never realized how easy Aaron made things on me by always noticing there was a problem and calling me on it.

When I get to Marc's door, I hear laughter from within, and I second-guess knocking. But the door is cracked, and Corey Matthews, who is lounging in a chair by the desk spots me instantly.

"Hey, rookie. Need something?"

"Uh, I can... come back."

My stupid cheeks burn, but Marc appears at the door with a look of mild concern on his face.

"Everything okay?"

"Yeah, I just wanted to talk with you about—do you think there's anything I can be doing differently? Working on?" I've never had to ask that question. Aaron always said I was great at taking direction, but he also gave me direction constantly.

I suddenly feel very coddled.

Marc gestures for me to come into his office, then gives Corey a look like *get out*, but he doesn't move. The privileges of being the pitching coach's chosen family. But then that makes me think of the vibe between Aaron and me, and it gives me a shred of hope that maybe this is the right call.

I need to get over myself and admit I need help if I want to fix things.

"I don't feel like I'm hitting my stride the way I want to, and I'm curious if you've seen anything I can work on."

Marc looks at me. "I've made a few little notes, but you're still new. Still settling in. We've played against some hard teams with great hitters. I don't think there's anything you're doing wrong. We can make some tweaks to what you're working on, but you know how much of this game is mental, and all the training in the world won't help with that. If you think that's a part of it, consider going to see the sports psychologist for the team."

I blow out a long breath. Psychologist? I guess it's an option, but I've always been able to get myself through these things before.

"What did you used to do?" Corey asks.

"What do you mean?"

"If you had rough patches or losing streaks, what did you do?"

"Usually, I'd get together with my friends—the guys I came up with, especially Aaron—and play. We'd have fun, and they'd help me out. But I've also never had a losing streak like this before."

Corey sighs and mutters something under his breath. "Look, I think you're doing fine for a rookie. Plus, you don't need to worry about being the star while they still have me."

"You can get out of my office any time," Marc says to him. Then he looks at me. "Take it one game at a time. Let's see how you do today, okay?"

I give a quick nod. "Yeah. Thanks."

His words run through my mind as I walk out of the room.

"Seriously, get out of my office," Marc says to Corey as I walk down the hall.

It makes me smile. I miss my friends. I've gotten good at burying that feeling deep down and leaning into the introvert side of me, but I was lucky to play AAA close to home and have them close. They're all pains in my ass, but I miss having them right there. Though I consider texting Aaron and asking if he'll come down for a game—come see if he notices any issues—I don't do it.

This is mine to fix, and I need to get used to that.

One game at a time, so let's try to make this one a good one.

I WANT to throw something other than a baseball right now.

I started the game out strong. Only a couple of hits over the first two innings. Then a run got through in the third, and another in the fourth. Now we have a runner on third, two outs, and a full count. I'm dangerously close to walking this batter because of how badly I'm pitching. My first two throws were strikes, but after that I couldn't throw anything but perfect pitches to foul off or horrifically bad balls. I almost hit the guy with the last one.

Marc stands in front of me, staring at me after giving me a speech to get me out of my head.

"You want to stay? Or do you want me to pull you?"

I swallow and take a deep breath. We're still up by one. I only need one more strike.

"No. I can handle it."

He nods. "I know you can. Close it out."

He smacks me on the shoulder and jogs back to the dugout.

After a moment, I get ready and throw the next pitch. Another. Fucking. Foul.

Breathe.

I force myself not to look over at the family area since Amanda won't be there.

It's okay. I've got this.

My catcher signals for the throw, and I prep my favorite pitch. Two-seam fastball. It's perfectly thrown, and for a second, relief floods me as I watch it fly toward the plate.

Then it connects with the bat to a deafening crack, and I watch as it soars over my head and over the back fence for a home run, taking the score from us leading 3-2 to them leading 4-3.

"YOU'VE GOTTA LET IT GO," Beau says. "We won the game."

"No thanks to me."

Our reliever came in and closed that shit out strong. We won 7-4. But not because of anything I did. And because I didn't go back in for the sixth after things turned around and we started getting our bats going, the reliever was credited with the save. Not much stings more than that. I'd rather lose and know the loss was shared than feel like I was the worst member of my team for the night.

"All right. You want to stay and work on some stuff? You said that's what you did with your friends, right? If you want to stick around, I'll try to help," Corey says, though he sounds like it's physically painful for him to offer.

"It's not a bad idea, but don't overwork your arm," Marc says.

"Anybody else? Daily?" Corey asks.

Ryan looks at him. "Can't. Beau and I are headed to the gala." He looks at me. "Shouldn't you be too?"

I glance at the clock. "We got done a little early. I should have forty-five minutes or an hour if I push it to work on stuff."

"All right, I'll meet you out there," Corey says.

A couple of other guys volunteer to stay, and I let myself have a spark of hope that maybe this will help.

Amanda

"IT IS an honor to have you all here tonight supporting us and the incredible trans community." I clap loudly as Alannah speaks. "We also want to say thank you to all the staff here tonight, to Paige, who did so much leg work to make this possible, and Amanda for stepping in and making sure everything about tonight has been flawless." She meets my eyes and raises her glass. I raise mine in response, and as she finishes speaking, pride rushes through me.

Tonight has been amazing so far, and it's an honor to be a part of it.

As everyone gets back to what they were doing, I glance around the floor, a quick flash of excitement rolling through me when I see Beau and Ryan from the Metros. I look around, more specific this time, but don't see Jamie.

I make my way over to where Ryan is with his wife, Bridget.

"Amanda, this is absolutely beautiful." She looks up at Ryan. "Can we go back in time and have her plan our wedding?"

Ryan just laughs, then leans in to kiss my cheek.

"Hey, Jamie's running a few minutes late, but he should be here soon."

"Thanks."

Alannah gets my attention, and I hurry across the room to see what she needs, hoping Jamie will be here by the time I'm done.

MY STOMACH TWISTS. It's been an hour-and-a-half since Ryan and Beau got here. Where the hell is Jamie? I don't have my phone on me, so I suppose he could've texted, but unless he was vomiting or got hit by a bus, there aren't many excuses for him not being here.

I take a brief break to grab a water from the bar, mostly to calm myself down.

"You nailed this. Glad I recommended you," Mark Abbott says, sliding up next to me. He orders a drink, then turns to me, his brow furrowing. "Are you okay?"

"Fine." I force a smile, but I doubt I'm doing a good job of it.

Mark looks around, then back at me. "Where's Jamie?"

I shrug. "Don't know." There's only an hour-and-a-half left in the event, and he's still not fucking here.

"But he's supposed to be here," Mark says, not asks.

"Yep. He was supposed to be here over an hour ago. I'm not sure where he is. Maybe something with baseball. I don't know how the game was tonight."

Mark slowly shakes his head. "That's no excuse for him not being here when he said he would be." He meets my eyes, then the bartender shows up with his drink, and he grabs it. He nudges me with his elbow before he walks away. "You're important too. Remember that."

Sighing, I glug the rest of my water, then get back to it. I have a job to do, and that continues, whether Jamie is here or not.

THE LAST HOUR of an event is always the most chaotic. People are leaving, the kitchen and bar are slowly shutting down, the hosts are tired, and I'm trying to make sure everything is ready for when the tear down crew arrives.

I walk out of the kitchen, and nearly trip over my own feet when I see Jamie sitting at the bar, drinking.

He's two hours later than he said he'd be here. Obviously, the game didn't run late.

Lifting my chin and standing up straight, I walk over to him. Halfway there, he sees me and stands up.

"Hey, baby," he says when I get to him. "Everything looks amazing."

With his words, I smell alcohol, and glance over at his drink. "Are you drinking?"

"Uh... yeah?"

"Oh, so the Metros newest pitcher and my boyfriend, who is underage, is drinking at an event I'm running after showing up two hours late. Amazing. Do you have any idea how that looks?"

"Mands, I'm sorry." He reaches for my hands, but I step away.

"Not here. Not now. I'm working."

"Right," he says quietly.

"Enjoy what's left of the event. We'll talk later."

I spin on my heel, remembering the moment from two years ago when I told him he couldn't crash an event to apologize. I thought we'd come so far since then, but as I walk away, I'm hit with the same ugly feeling of being second best—of not being anyone's first choice.

JAMIE WAITED for me after the event and ordered a car service to take us home, but I wasn't going to get into it in the car.

The second we're through the apartment door, though, he immediately starts apologizing.

"I'm sorry. I—"

"Where were you?"

He swallows hard. "Tonight's game was rough, so a couple of the guys offered to help me out."

"And it had to be *tonight*?"

"I played like shit tonight, and I wanted to work through some of it while it was fresh in my mind."

Baseball will always be his first love.

The sting of that moment hits me all over again. He prioritized me. He spent months proving he cared for me before we made things official, and since then, he's continued to do that... until things have gotten difficult with baseball.

Did I ever come first?

"I'm sorry you had a tough game, but that's no excuse for you not being there tonight. Not only was it an important cause, but it was deeply important to me. I go to every single game I can be at for you. I travel with the team. I work my schedule and my life around what you do, and the one thing—the one night—I ask for, and you couldn't show up for me. Do you have any idea how that makes me feel?"

"I do—"

"It's not just that I wanted to share it with you, it's that I wanted your support. I wanted my person to put me first, and you didn't. Your career is important, and I've known since we started doing this that it's not something to take lightly. I've accepted that I can't always be your priority, and I'm okay with that. But tonight, you chose baseball over me when you didn't have to. That hurts."

"I'm sorry." I know he is. I can see it on his face. But words don't mean much right now.

"I'm going to take a shower."

Finding the clothes I set out for myself earlier, I head for the bathroom and lock the door. He can use the guest bathroom if he needs to. I need peace. Space to think.

I take off my pretty black dress, and toe off my heels, then I stare at myself in the mirror. Tears prickle my eyes. I don't bother trying to blink them back.

Steam fills up the room as I turn the water on burn-my-skin-off hot.

Numbly, I climb inside and go through the motions. I'm halfway through washing my hair when the sobs hit. I remember the way he helped me shower when I was sick, how he took care of me. He chose me over baseball, and I'd never felt more wanted—and even though we hadn't said it yet, I'd never felt more loved.

I finish rinsing the conditioner out of my hair, then lean against the back wall of the shower and sink to the floor, giving into the body shaking sobs.

Is this what our future looks like? Me begging to be chosen again? My chest tightens at the thought. I'm trying to trust that Jamie wouldn't do that to me, but today he showed me what was more important to him. Maybe it was just once, but it did damage to my already fragile heart. The urge to put my walls up, be mean, and push him away is strong, but that's not what a healthy relationship is, so I let myself cry it out until I'm ready to face it all again, even though I'm hoping he'll already be in bed, so I can just go to sleep.

After getting dried off and dressed in comfy clothes, I walk back into the bedroom to find all the lights on, and Jamie sitting on the bed with two lap trays of sushi on the bed in front of him.

Tears well in my eyes again, and he walks over to me, pulling me into his arms. "I'm sorry. I'm so sorry, babe. We got done early with the game, and I planned to practice for forty-five minutes, then head to the event and be there when I said I would, but I accidentally left my phone in my cubby and lost track of time. Then there was traffic—I..." He runs a hand through his hair. "Fuck. I'm so sorry. I hate myself for missing it. I'm insanely proud of you, and I missed out on seeing the best of it because of a stupid decision on my part. I hate that I hurt you, when all I wanted to do was celebrate you. I know my words can't fix it, but I needed you to know." He kisses my forehead. "I love you, and I'm honored to be your partner. I'm sorry I didn't show you that tonight."

He steps back and cradles my face in his hands, looking into my eyes.

It's so frustrating that in moments like this I still crave his touch even though he's the one that hurt me. I can't tell him it's all okay when it isn't, but I don't want to live in my anger and hurt, either. So I lean against him again, holding him tightly.

He runs his fingers through my hair, and I look over at the bed.

"When did you get that?"

"I had it delivered before I left for the stadium."

That's the boy I know.

Sniffing, I lean back and look up at him. "Thank you."

"Got your favorite wine too."

He takes my hand and helps me onto the bed, then hands me the glass of wine.

Once we're both sitting, he clinks his glass against mine. "To you."

"Thank you."

"So, I probably don't have a right to ask, but... I'd love to hear about the event if you're willing to tell me."

I stare at him for a moment. An earnest, apologetic look shimmers in his eyes.

"Okay."

Though my heart is hurting, I believe he's sorry and truly wants to know about the event, so I get cozy with him, dive into the sushi, and tell him all about it.

IT'S one of those mornings where I don't want to open my eyes and let the daylight filter in. I'm still exhausted, even though I slept like the dead. Jamie and I stayed up late eating sushi and talking about the event, then I fell asleep in his arms.

The remnants of my hurt from last night are still there, especially as I reach for him and find nothing but the cold bed next to me.

No falling back to sleep now.

Slowly, I peel my eyes open and sit up. As usual, the first thing I do is reach for my phone, but my hand hits a piece of paper. Pulling it to me, I see it's a note from Jamie.

> *Go check your office. There's something you need to see there.*
> *X– Jamie*

I guess that means it's time to get up.

My legs ache as I swing them over the side of the bed. And then my feet howl in pain when they touch the floor. I'm going to be on a regiment of heat and ice today. No more heels for events. I know better, but I did it anyway.

I grab my silky floral robe and wrap it around me as I walk out the master bedroom door and down the hall to the spare room, which is also my office. It's long, but a little narrow, and feels too office-y for me. I love the one at our apartment in Ida because it's a little cocoon of creativity. It's warm and cozy and brings out the most creative parts of me.

Oh well. At least I have an office here. At school, I work out of a small bedroom in the lake house I share with the hive mind. I have a small desk there, but after a couple of weeks, it's usually overflowing. This is spacious, at least.

I look around, remembering that Jamie sent me in here. Then I notice a new photo frame on the wall. Only it's not a photo inside it. It's a newspaper clipping.

A newspaper clipping talking about the success of the event—and me.

I glance at the clock and see it's around nine. That means Jamie went and found a newspaper and framed this before I even woke up.

"You deserve to be celebrated." I spin at the sound of Jamie's emotion-drenched voice. "I'm sorry I failed at that last night. As usual, you are a mesmerizing force of nature, and I'm honored to be your partner." He crosses the room to me, a bag from my favorite local bakery in hand. "That is to remind you of your success and your passion. You have the ability to grow your business into something even more incredible than it is now, and I have no doubt you'll do it."

"Thank you," I whisper, gratitude sweeping through me. "What's in the bag?"

He gets that sheepish boyish grin. "Breakfast sandwiches and hash browns." I groan at that, and he sets the bag down on my desk and wraps his arms around me, burying his face in my neck. "I love you so fucking much. I'm sorry. I'm sorry."

I hold him close, curling my fingers in his hair. "I love you too, and I know." Sucking in a breath, I lean back and look up at him. "I forgive you."

He rests his forehead against mine, then pulls me tight to him again.

And most of me revels in it. But deep inside me, there's a painful pinch of something else. Discomfort. There's a tiny piece of me that feels a little uncomfortable about how vulnerable I was with him last night. I almost feel stupid about it, like I was somehow overreacting, even though I wasn't. And being vulnerable with him now is an entirely different situation. A part of me wants to stop myself from doing it, and a little piece of my heart shatters when I realize why. He broke my trust last night—at least part of it—and despite how apologetic he's been, being vulnerable with him now comes with fear. Fear that he won't be careful with my vulnerability, and he'll hurt me again.

Is this the way our relationship is going to go now? He's always been my safe place, and the thought of losing that absolutely crushes me.

So I hold him tighter, trying to push all those thoughts away, because I don't want to let one bad night form a fracture between us we can't recover from.

18

Every Broken Feeling

Jamie

I'M GOING *to fix my shit.*

That's my meditation. I have no idea if that's how meditation is supposed to work, but I'm trying to chill myself out before my game.

Amanda's not here today, and that sucks, but after I fucked up and missed most of the biggest event she's ever been responsible for, I have zero room to ask her for anything.

I'm still kicking my own ass about that, but I'm trying to let it go. All I can do is be better from here on out, so like with my game, that's exactly what I'm trying to do.

There's a knock on my hotel door, and I grunt as I push myself off the hotel room floor and go to answer it. Probably one of the guys trying to convince me to go get lunch with them. I appreciate the effort to draw out my introverted self, but I like the peace of some downtime before a game.

When I swing the door open, though, it's not one of the guys. At least not one of the guys I'm expecting.

"Aren't you gonna invite me in?" Aaron asks.

I laugh, trying to cover the emotion that bubbles inside me. "Hell yes. Get in here."

I step aside so he can come in, and the minute the door closes behind us, he gives me a big hug.

Fuck, I don't like the emotion that swells in me when he does that.

"What are you doing here?" I ask, getting control of myself.

"Philly isn't that bad of a drive, and I had a few days free. I thought I'd come down and see the game. Marc told me what room you were in so I could surprise you."

"I'm glad you're here."

His brows pull in. "Are you okay?"

I shove my hand through my hair. "It's been a rough few games for me."

"I noticed you had some losses, but I didn't think you pitched poorly. I'm sorry. I should've checked in with you more. Why didn't you reach out?"

I shrug even though I know the answer. It's not something I'm great at doing, and the more isolated I feel, the more used to it I become and that makes it harder.

He pins me with a look. "What's going on?"

I walk over and sit down on the edge of the bed.

"It's been harder settling in than I thought it would be. I mean, I knew there would be changes, but I stupidly thought I'd pick up where I left off in AAA. Maybe not pitching no-hitters or complete games, but I wouldn't be sucking. I'm in a funk, but I don't know why, and instead of throwing balls, all I'm doing is dropping them. I let Amanda down last week because I was too focused on baseball. It's all fucked up."

He sits down next to me. "You're being too hard on yourself. But I get it. When you're passionate about something, you don't want to fuck it up. Do you remember..." He laughs to himself. "Well, I'm sure you remember when I'm talking about because it was when you met Amanda."

"The Christmas party?"

"Mhm. Well, specifically, I'm thinking of the day after."

I cringe at that. The day I went and yelled at him for not

having his shit together—for not fighting for himself. I deserve to eat a slice of humble pie over that right now. I was almost eighteen and thought I knew every fucking thing.

"I remember."

"You were trying to get to me, and you said something like 'it doesn't matter anyway because you were never going to play pro.'"

"If you're going to tell me I was a jackass, I deserve it."

"No. I was going to say that you were right. It was different. I never had dreams of going pro, but what's the same across the board is the fear of losing the thing you love, the thing that grounds you. And I know that's where your head is right now."

"Yeah. Every game, I try to set it aside and just pitch, but the first hit I allow, that thought creeps in, and with every subsequent hit or run, it gets louder until it's eating away at me."

"I know telling you to let it go isn't going to help. The mental side of the game is complex. But mental health is sort of my thing."

"Of course it is, Mr. Guidance Counselor."

"Soon to be, but yeah. But also as a pitching coach. With any sport, it's a mental game. But overall, I think pitchers and goalies have the worst of that. We rest the weight of the game on our shoulders, even when it's a team sport."

"So, what's your sage advice?"

"Forget about the game. When you go out there tonight, don't go out like a major league pitcher. Go out like you're pitching for the guys and Miles is the one catching the ball. Forget the expectation and remember why you love it. Because skill helps you, but it's the passion for the game that takes you all the way. Forget about everything else and remember why you love the game."

"Sometimes I miss just getting out on the field and shooting the shit with you guys."

He laughs. "Well, give it fifteen years and we'll be there again. Playing in some old man baseball rec league." He smacks my shoulder. "But you've got a career to build first so we can all listen to you tell us about when you were a badass professional ball player. If you can't get out of your head for any other reason, do it for the future bragging rights."

I let out a sigh. This is exactly what I needed. What I've been missing.

The one thing I didn't plan for was how isolating being in the majors would feel. It's a reminder of how important it is to stay grounded in my current friendships, but also to work harder to develop friendships on the team. It might not come naturally to me, but it's going to be essential for my survival.

And hopefully holding on to Aaron's advice—and remembering why I love this game—will help me do that... and help me get out of this damn slump.

Amanda

IT'S funny how easily I've started thinking of Ida as home. Sure, it's right by Woods Junction, but when I think of home, I think of Ida. Our apartment. My best friends. Some of my favorite restaurants.

Right now, I'm sitting at Jimmy's Coffee House, waiting for the potential client I'm meeting to get here. She's the one who requested a meeting several weeks ago, but I had to get through the crazy of the last few weeks first.

Lauren, the owner of Jimmy's—named after her late father— sets my coffee on the table.

"Thanks, Lauren."

"No problem. I haven't seen you around as much. How have you been?"

Small towns. Sure, the city has more options for food and entertainment. There's so much more to explore. But there's nothing like half the people who come in here knowing my name and stopping to chat. That's why it's become home.

"I've been good. Busy. Really busy."

She laughs and looks around. "I know the feeling. And I think I heard my mom talking about some big event you did down in the city?"

My cheeks heat a little. "Yeah. It was a gala. Really cool to be a part of."

"Well, congratulations. How's Jamie doing?"

"Good," I sort of lie. "He's settling in with the Metros. Living his dream." I do everything I can to keep the wistfulness from my tone when I say it. Things have been fine in the last week since the gala. Nothing else has happened. But I haven't been able to shake the unsettling wrongness—the tiny crack that formed that night. Mostly because it felt like the culmination of weeks of him struggling and me trying to hold everything together. I don't think that is going to change any time soon.

The bell over the door goes off, and a woman walks in, looking around.

I wave to Lauren as she walks off, then catch the woman's eye. "Lisa?"

"Hi. Are you Amanda?"

"That's me. Have a seat."

"Thank you. My partner is running a few minutes late, but she'll be here soon." Lisa lets out a little sigh. "I was so happy when your website said you were an LGBTQ friendly business. One event planner I spoke to sounded wonderful until I mentioned I was marrying a woman. Then she said some horrible things and hung up the phone."

I hate people. Why anyone thinks they get a say in who someone else loves is beyond me. Who I love and who I sleep with doesn't hurt anyone else. Love is love, and fuck anyone who thinks otherwise.

"I'm so sorry. I'd also happily take her name so I can make sure I never accidentally recommend her to someone. For the record, I want you to know this is an absolute safe space. I'm bi, and I want all my clients to feel safe being exactly who they are.

You deserve your dream wedding, and I hope I can help give it to you."

She looks like she might cry for a second, but nods. "Thank you. I saw you did a big event for a trans foundation. That's amazing."

"I came in late, and a lot of the planning was done, but it was an honor to be a part of it. But enough about me. How long have you and your partner been together?"

"About a year-and-a-half. We got engaged a couple of months ago, and are hoping we can scrape together a wedding before the end of May next year. She's going into her last year of college, and wherever she ends up going for grad school is where we'll be moving, but since our families are here, we want to do it before we leave."

"I've planned weddings in less time."

Her face lights up, but I realize it's not because of what I said. She's looking out the window behind me. "Here she comes now."

She gets up to greet her fiancée, and I stand, smiling, ready to introduce myself, but when they step apart, my blood runs cold.

"Amanda, this is—"

"Maci," I breathe.

Maci's eyes fly wide.

Maci. My ex-girlfriend. My ex-girlfriend who broke up with me and cut me out because she supposedly wasn't into girls after all.

My stomach lurches, though I try to keep a calm expression on my face.

"Amanda," Maci says quietly.

"You two know each other?" Lisa asks.

I clear my throat and look at Lisa. "I'm so sorry. I won't be able to help you, but I'll email you a list of event planners I trust who you can reach out to." My eyes flit to Maci, then back to Lisa. "I wish you the best."

Then I push past the chairs in my way and hurry out the front door.

"Amanda! Amanda, wait!" Maci yells, running after me.

No. No.

This is my worst nightmare. I must be in hell, because that's the only place one should have to endure this kind of torture.

I keep walking, but she doesn't give up.

"Amanda, please." Maci grabs my arm, and I spin around, a mix of heartbreak and fury warring within me.

"What do you want? I'm sorry I can't plan your wedding, but it would be a conflict of interest for me, seeing as I can't stand you."

She glances back at the building. "I... understand that."

"Great. I'm so glad you understand. We're done then."

"No. Please. I need to explain."

"Explain what? Explain why you're marrying a woman when you told me you didn't actually like girls. That it was all an experiment. That *I* didn't mean anything to you."

Fuck the tears that well in my eyes.

She opens her mouth, but I'm out of control. "Did you ever love me? Or was it all a lie?"

Ugh. One run-in with Maci and I revert to that pathetic, desperate girl.

"I—"

I wave my hand. "No. Don't answer that. I'm not sure which answer would hurt worse. You either loved me and lied and said you didn't and made me feel crazy, or you led me on the whole time. I don't know what's more awful. You didn't need to follow me out here. I'm not your girl. Clearly, I never was. So go back to your fiancée. I hope you have a lovely life together."

Then I turn on my heel and walk away, my stomach churning and tears burning in my eyes.

She's with a woman. No matter what way you spin it, her being with me was never an experiment. She knew what she wanted. It just wasn't me.

It's never me.

Tears trickle down my face, and I don't realize where I am or where I'm going until I'm standing in front of the bakery Mackenzie's family owns, staring up at her window.

"Mands?"

I slowly turn, but it's not Mackie standing there. It's Hyla.

In less than a second, I'm engulfed in a hug. "What's wrong?"

"Everything."

"Come on. Let's go inside."

She leads me up the stairs that go to the two-story apartment above the bakery where Mackie lives.

"Hey, Hy, what's—Mands... what's going on?"

"She needs some love," Hyla whispers.

They whisk me off to Mackenzie's room, and I end up sitting on the floor between them. I don't know how they do it—stay friends despite the emotional turmoil of their past relationship.

"What happened?" Hyla asks, wrapping an arm around me.

Mackenzie does the same, resting her head against mine.

"Why am I not enough?" My voice shakes, and all I want to do is give in to the crushing ache in my chest.

"You're more than enough. Anyone who says otherwise can go fuck themselves," Mackie says.

Tears come hot and fast, and I don't bother trying to hold them back. I'm an emotional wreck. Might as well lean into it.

"Tell us what happened," Hyla says, gently running her fingers through my hair.

I bite my lip, a wave of self-loathing hitting me. I don't deserve her comforting me after how I treated her when she and Mackie were first dating. I compared her to my horrible ex, and didn't see the woman she was beneath it all. Hyla is the friend everyone needs. She shows up every time in any way she can. She's always the one to uplift everyone. It took less than a year to realize my mistake, but I will always regret it. After all that, now she's the one comforting me without a second thought.

She wraps her hand around mine and squeezes tightly. "We've got you. You're safe here."

"I'm sorry," I cry.

"Why?" Hyla asks.

"Because I was bitch to you when we first met, and you didn't deserve that. You always deserved all the love and support possible. I thought—I thought you were like her..."

"Like who?"

"Maci."

"Her ex," Mackie clarifies.

"But you're not. I'm sorry."

"You don't need to apologize to me again. You've done that enough. And since then, you've showed up for me over and over again—in all my worst moments. You've protected me and taken care of me, and our friendship has grown beautifully. You've been there for me through every horrible moment, just like I'm here for you. *We* are here for you. Tell us what happened."

So I do.

"You are not the problem," Hyla says when I've finished. "It was never about you."

"Then why was I the collateral damage?"

"Because some people aren't strong enough to take responsibility for their own feelings and actions, and they hurt other people in the process," Mackie says. "I know this has always been a trigger point for you, but it seemed like you'd moved on or healed a bit from it over the years."

"I thought I had," I admit, my throat thickening with emotion again. "I don't feel like the strongest version of myself right now."

"How have things been with you and Jamie?" Hyla asks, getting right to the heart of things as usual. I swear, because she's walked through the hardest times, she always seems to know exactly what someone else's struggles are. And she's always ready to jump in and help.

"Hard," I admit. With that, I explain everything else that's been happening lately. The multitude of little moments that have built into something bigger—something harder to face. Especially when I'm facing it alone. "I'm trying to keep it all together and support him, but I feel like I'm failing at every turn."

"If you're always supporting him, who's supporting you?" Mackie asks.

I turn and look at her, then Hyla. "You. All the girls."

"But you have to let us," Hyla whispers. "You've been struggling alone for weeks and haven't told us. We're all here for you, so please don't hide from us."

"You mean I have to ask for help?" I joke, but it falls flat.

"It's either that or we start showing up on your doorstep."

"Yep. We'll create a whole rotation so one of us is there all the time," Mackie says with her signature troublemaking smile.

"I feel weak," I whisper. "Usually I muscle through things with a good attitude. Not being able to makes me feel like I'm doing something wrong, like I'm not trying hard enough—or I'm not strong enough."

"You're not failing. Or weak. You are strong and badass and so fiercely loving and supportive. It's normal to struggle with change. I know you're used to being superwoman, but you don't have to be. Give yourself the same grace you'd give any of us," Hyla says.

Why is it so hard to have grace for yourself when you'd never be as hard on any of the people you love?

"Thank you." I blow out a shaky breath. "I've really missed you all."

"We've missed you too."

"I have another suggestion." Hyla bites her lip. "Don't take this the wrong way, but you should consider going to therapy. I've learned the hard way that thinking you can manage it on your own never leads to anything but unnecessary struggle."

"I've thought about it." More than once, if I'm honest. "But I've talked myself out of it or convinced myself I didn't need it because when things are good, I'm fine. It's only when I struggle that I think about it. Isn't that just how life goes?"

Hyla smiles and squeezes my hand again. "You don't go to

therapy to be able to handle the good days. You go to therapy to work through what you need to so you have the strength and resilience to get through the hard days."

"Well, when you put it like that…" I sigh. She's right. I know she is. In the past, I've been able to muscle through hard times with a good attitude because underneath it all, for the most part, I felt settled and calm. That's not true anymore. I'm in a constant state of inner turmoil, so when my outside world gets chaotic, I don't have a safe place. "Is it okay to admit I'm scared?"

"Of course. If therapy was easy, everyone would be doing it," Hyla says. "Or if society and our healthcare system acknowledged how important mental health is and didn't trivialize and demonize it. But that's a battle for another day." She bumps her knee against mine. "We all love you, and we're going to get you through this. Actually… I think this calls for an emergency girls' night." I open my mouth, but Hyla pins me with a look. "Do not argue with me on this. You need to be surrounded by love."

I laugh at that because I wasn't going to. "No arguments. I was just going to ask if we could do it at my apartment. I want to be home."

Jamie is so back and forth it's hard to rely on him as a safe space. I haven't been a safe place for myself. But my home is, and I need that right now too.

Jamie

HOLY SHIT.

I'm kicking ass tonight.

There have been some tough batters on this team, but I've only let a handful of hits through and one run in five innings. For once I might make it a full seven or eight innings.

What Aaron said this morning stuck with me—to remember why I love playing, and being out here today with the sun shining and a light breeze blowing has had me in my element. Like I might as well be back on the field at Ida High, playing with my best friends.

Especially when I whip around and pick off the runner trying to steal second. I smile to myself and turn back toward home plate.

Two outs. Two strikes. One ball.

I've got this.

WE DOMINATED THAT FUCKING GAME. I stayed in through the seventh and only let one more run through. We won 6-3. It's a high I've needed for a while, and a reminder that sometimes I'm way too hard on myself.

"Nice pitching," Aaron says as I walk out of the clubhouse.

"Isn't that Rae's line for you?"

He laughs. "I didn't even realize it when I said that."

"Well, keep your dirty thoughts to yourself."

"You're hilarious. So, what's up now? Want to grab some dinner?"

"Yes, but I have a thing. You're welcome to come, but it might not be super fun."

"What is it?"

"I'm meeting with the reporter who's doing a profile on me. Emily."

"How's that going?" Aaron asks, amused.

"Fine."

"That good, huh?"

"It is *fine*. I hate it though. I'm not good at opening up to random strangers, plus I feel like I always have to be a certain way or maintain a certain image. That extra focus on me has also had me more worried about my games. When I'm losing, I keep thinking I'll be even more of a laughingstock. That her profile piece will be all about the pitcher who completely choked during his first season in the majors."

Aaron stops and puts a hand on my shoulder. "Okay, I say this with love, but you're not that important. You're not choking. Every pitcher has good and bad games. And contrary to what you seem to believe, baseball is a team sport. Relax and let her see the guy who loves baseball and is living the dream of so many kids out there."

I stare at him for a minute. "You're annoying, but I've missed your wise prophetic shit."

He grins at me. "Everyone needs a Gandalf to guide them on their journey."

"Nevermind. I haven't missed you *at all*."

"I'M LOVING THIS DYNAMIC. I'm seeing a whole other side of Jamie tonight," Emily says to Aaron.

"This is the real him," Aaron says easily. It must be nice to be an extrovert. To feel confident and easily talk with people. "It takes time for him to open up."

Emily laughs. "For anything but baseball. If I get him going on baseball stats or trivia, he gets much more talkative."

"Hey, I'm right here."

"He likes to be the center of attention, he just doesn't want to admit it," Aaron stage whispers.

Emily stifles a laugh.

I do feel more at ease now though.

"Maybe we could do more of the interviews at home when Amanda is there. Aaron's right. I open up more easily when I'm with people I know well."

Emily nods. "I'm fine with that. I want you to be comfortable around me, Jamie, and not worry about this turning into some sort of negative piece." I frown. Am I that obvious? "It's been clear with your answers—especially after games you've lost—that you're worried about that. You don't need to be. This is a piece about you, and from everything I've seen, you have integrity and a drive to succeed. That is how I build my pieces—around who the athlete is and what pushes them forward. Anyone can look up stats. Not everyone can get an inside look at what makes professional athletes excel at what they do, but also be just like everyone else."

Something about that relaxes me a little. Maybe if my agent had explained it that way, I wouldn't have been so uncomfortable with this whole thing. Then again, expecting someone who lives and breathes business to easily articulate the artistic nuance of writing might be too much to ask.

"Thanks. I'll work on relaxing more for our interviews."

A waiter sets a steak in front of me and I sigh happily. This is the best I've felt in a long time. The only thing missing is Amanda. I can't wait to tell her about the game.

For the first time in weeks, I feel like I'm on the right track again.

Amanda

GIRLS' night was everything I needed and more.

I'd forgotten how lonely I used to feel before I met this crazy tribe. They changed me for the better, and being without them has been a struggle. I'm excited to go back to school simply because I'll be a little more grounded. Sure, I've been here throughout the summer. I've supported my friends and we've had girls' nights, but I've been spread so thin I haven't enjoyed most of them the way I needed to. And I hadn't let them in.

As much as I still suck at being vulnerable, that little breakdown with Hyla and Mackie today was necessary. All the girls have a way of making me feel safe, but Hyla and Mackie both excel at it. Hyla because she knows the difficulty of being vulnerable all too well, and Mackie because she knows me so well and she's a quiet, thoughtful listener. She's always paying attention but never pushes.

We came back to my place and the peace that washed over me the second I was inside was another boost. All the girls were here, and we got so much takeout from Marion's Café—the definition of food cooked with love—and watched the baseball game.

It was good to see Jamie get a win, even if it made me feel a little guilty I wasn't there. But I know how much I needed tonight. I have to hold on to the things that fulfill me, even if it means I'm not at every game.

I also need to take care of myself, as Hyla recommended. The girls left about an hour ago, and I've spent most of the time since researching therapists online. I knew finding one in person would be too chaotic with how much I'm going from place to place, so I went through multiple companies and profiles until I found one that sounded right for me, then I snagged the first available appointment, which is in a few days.

Now I'm waiting for Jamie to call. Rae told me earlier that Aaron had made the drive down to Philly for the game, and I'm glad. Jamie needs support from people other than me. His parents try to go when they can, but with three young kids, it's difficult.

I'm exhausted, but forcing myself to stay up so I can hear about the game... and tell Jamie about my day. He's not here to give me a hug—though I was craving that by the end of the night—but he knows how to reassure me and make me feel better, even from a distance. Hopefully, his meeting with Emily won't go too much longer.

Needing a distraction, I put on my favorite season of *Friends*, determined to stay awake.

It's twenty minutes later when Jamie finally calls.

"Hey, baby," I answer. "Great game today."

He makes a happy noise, and again a pang of guilt hits. I wish I was there with him. We haven't gotten to celebrate enough lately.

"Thank you. Aaron gave me some good advice, and I think it helped." He jumps in and tells me everything that happened from his point of view, and it's refreshing to hear that happiness in his voice. As strange as it sounds, it feels nice to miss him too. Everything has either been chaotic or desperate. We haven't had a chance to miss each other in a good way, and the coziness of how our relationship used to be wraps around me. How we used to talk half the night when I was at school. "It felt so good to finally get another win," he says as he finishes telling me about it.

"You deserve it. I watched the whole game with the girls. I might've screamed when you had the 1-2-3 inning in the third."

He chuckles. "Wish you could've been there. But I get why you weren't. How was your meeting today?" he asks with a yawn.

That coldness runs through me again when I remember it. "Ah, not great."

"I'm sorry, babe." He yawns again. "Hold on a sec." There's a rustling sound, then he comes back on. "Just needed to get more comfortable. So, what happened?"

"Well, the girl I spoke with was lovely. And it actually really sucks because I wanted to plan her wedding. She's my dream client. She was excited, had some great ideas, and really looked forward to working with me. Plus, it would've been my first queer wedding. But I just couldn't do it. Because... the girl she's marrying is"—I suck in a sharp breath as my voice breaks again—"Maci."

There's silence on the other end of the line.

"Jamie?"

I pull my phone from my ear to make sure the call is still connected, and it is.

"Jamie? Can you hear me?"

Then I hear a soft snore.

"Jamie!" I yell, but all I get in return is another snore.

And just like that, all the warm, fuzzy feelings slip away. I forced myself to stay up even though I was exhausted. I listened to him tell me all about the game, but he couldn't even stay awake for a few more minutes to hear about my day?

I need my boyfriend right now, and he can't be bothered to even try to be here for me. This is the worst day I've had in a long time, and... *fuck.*

That crushing feeling of being alone hits me all over again.

Part of me wants to hang up, but another part of me is just mad. Mad that once again, he couldn't put me first, even for a few minutes.

"Today sucked," I whisper into my phone. "And I really need you right now, and it pisses me off that you aren't showing up for me."

Tears stream down my cheeks as I continue talking, letting out every broken feeling as I tell him about what happened today, even though he won't hear a word of it.

19
Restless Heart

Amanda

THERAPY ISN'T AS scary as I thought it would be.

Granted, this is mostly a get to know each other session, but still. I'm not sure why I thought therapy would be a therapist judging me, but it hasn't been that way at all. It's very supportive. The only assignment she's given me is to do something for myself. Not for my business. Not for Jamie. For me. Something that fulfills me, not drains me.

Admitting that I didn't have a clue where to start with that was hard, but again, she was supportive, not judgmental.

She also offered to look into resources for partners of professional athletes, since it's possible what Jamie and I are going through is a common issue. I hadn't thought of that. I hadn't thought to look into it. But it makes sense. These kinds of growing pains can't be unique.

That makes me feel a little better, but not great, mostly because Jamie still doesn't know what happened last weekend. It's been six days, and I'm not exactly withholding the information, but I haven't made another attempt to tell him.

I tried the following morning, starting with mentioning therapy, but he got distracted by some guys on the team and had to go. I told him when I headed for the office this morning that I had my appointment, but he was still in bed and barely responded. I'm not going to seek him out and beg him to pay attention to me if he can't be bothered to listen.

I haven't mentioned any of this to my therapist yet. That's next week's problem. I don't want to scare her away after only one session.

When we finish up, I walk out of the spare room and into the kitchen, where Jamie is cooking at the stove.

"Morning," I say, trying to be my cheery self, but the weight of what's unsaid between us is crushing me.

He turns around and meets my eyes. "Hey. What were you doing in there? Potential client?"

Well, unless I want to straight up lie to him... here we go.

"No. I had a therapy appointment."

He turns off the burner and puts something on a plate, then walks over to the counter, eyes narrowed.

"I didn't know—when did you start doing therapy?"

"This was my first session," I say tightly.

Something like guilt crosses his face. "When did you—why—why didn't you tell me?"

"I did."

He leans back like I hit him, throwing his arms out. "What? I think I would've remembered that."

"You would've had to have been listening in the first place to remember it."

"What are you talking about? When did you tell me this?"

"The night you won your game. But wait, you fell asleep the second I started talking about my shitty day."

He looks pained for a second. "I called you back the next morning."

"And I said it then too, but you got distracted by your teammates and hung up."

"Why didn't you tell me when I got back from the trip?"

I stare at him for a moment, not sure exactly what the answer is. Am I holding back from him because I'm angry and want to punish him or because I was afraid he wouldn't listen again and I wouldn't be able to take it? Or because I'm trying to keep everything happy and calm for him?

Option D. All of the above.

"I don't... know. Does it matter? You know now, right? I assume since your mom is a therapist, you aren't one of those dumbass guys who thinks therapy is stupid and would never want his partner to go."

"Call those people what they are—abusers who don't want to be caught. No, I'm not upset you're going. If you're struggling in any way, I want you to take care of yourself." He comes around the counter to me and wraps his arms around me. "And if I'm being an asshole, I want to know so I can deal with it."

Like he dealt with not showing up for me at the event?

I feel like such a bitch when I think things like that, but those thoughts pop in from time to time. Unresolved anger? Probably. Something else to work on in therapy.

But I don't want to feel that way, so I hug him back.

"This summer has been crazy."

"It has. Which is why it's extra important to celebrate our anniversary on Monday. No game or practice that day. All I have to do is work out in the morning, then I'm yours for the day. We can explore the neighborhood if you want. Or I can use my newfound status to get a reservation somewhere fancy."

I can't help but scowl at that. I love that we have a whole day together, but I don't want fancy. I want real.

Pushing out of his arms, I look up into those stunning blue orbs that captivate every time.

"Not to be completely lame, but could we stay in? We've barely had any time together that isn't rushed or crunched. I want to enjoy us."

"Yeah. Of course. I'll find a great sushi place to order takeout from. I'm happy to spend all day locked in this apartment with you." Though we both grimace as we look around the room. "I promise we'll find somewhere better eventually. Until then—"

"We'll make the most of it," I say gently. He's trying.

While intention isn't everything, it matters, and I appreciate his intentions are to be together and enjoy each other because despite all the chaos of the last month-and-a-half, that's what our anniversary should be. A celebration of us and how far we've come.

Jamie

I'M DETERMINED to make today the best anniversary possible. It's only our second one, and last year was relaxed with a fun dinner at our favorite sushi place back home after a day spent at a nearby lake. Then we had a night full of talking and sex. Classic anniversary vibes.

But after how I let her down a couple of weeks ago and the disconnect between us because of the crazy schedules we've had, I want this to be extra special.

I was surprised when she said she wanted to stay in. Normally, she's all about going out and exploring. The introvert in me doesn't mind, and neither does my horny side that doesn't just want to keep her in the apartment, but in bed all day.

I hoped my workout would get some of the pent-up energy out of me, but it didn't. It's been too long since we've had anything but quickies, and I want to spend hours worshipping her.

That starts with non-sexual things, like breakfast in bed.

The one great thing about this neighborhood—though I'm sure it's true of almost any neighborhood in the city—is there's a little café and deli nearby that makes incredible breakfast sandwiches.

I got Amanda's favorite one. A western Florentine egg white

omelet on an onion bagel. With a side of hash browns. Because hash browns.

I swear Amanda sits up the second I walk through the bedroom door.

"What do I smell?"

"Your super fancy anniversary breakfast."

"Don't you mean *ours*?"

"Well, sort of. I'm having an egg white omelet with a side of hash browns. Not quite as fancy as your bagel sandwich."

"Gimme."

I laugh and sit down next to her with the tray. "You only want me for the food I bring you."

She looks at me sweetly. "It's a nice perk." Then she combs her fingers through my hair and presses her lips to mine in a raw, emotional kiss. "Happy anniversary, baseball boy."

I kiss her neck as she pulls away. "Happy anniversary, event queen. Or is it event queen of my heart? I don't know. That's your business thing, not a term of endearment."

She smiles softly as she pulls open the box with her food in it. "No. It's not. There's something you call me that I much prefer."

"Oh. What's that?"

She looks at me and drags her finger down my chest. "I love when you call me your girl. It makes me feel adored."

"My girl gets what she wants."

She bumps her elbow against mine, smiling happily as she digs into her breakfast sandwich. Sometimes I forget all she cares about are the simple things—like knowing she's loved—and I need to do a better job of showing her that.

"CAN I COME OUT NOW?" Amanda calls from the bedroom.

"One second!" I grab the last two boxes and chuck them in

the garbage, then run to the refrigerator and pull out the sushi. "Okay, more like a minute."

Her laugh bounces around the apartment.

I sent her for a nap and a bath an hour ago, thinking that would give me enough time to get this all together, but I'm cutting it close.

After breakfast, we ended up leaving the house and going for a walk—Amanda's idea—then we came back and watched a movie before making lunch. Amanda found a recipe for sheet pan nachos because she wanted to spoil me as much as I spoil her. They were delicious, and once the off-season hits and I have more time to cook, I'll be making them all the time.

Once I have all the sushi set out on a tray, I carry it to the living room and set it in place on the ottoman, then I walk toward the bedroom, switching off lights as I go.

When I get there, Amanda is breathtaking in a white silky slip dress that hugs every gorgeous curve of her voluptuous body.

"Fuck," I hiss as I take her in.

That wicked smile shines on her face. "You look good too."

At her request, I'm in dark blue athletic boxers and a tight black tee.

Then she grazes her hand over my semi before kissing my neck and looking down the hall.

"What surprises do you have up your sleeve?"

I loop my arm through hers, guiding her forward. "Come and see."

When we get to the living room, her breath catches as she stares up at the ceiling where I've hung about twenty strands of warm white twinkle lights, both regular and star shaped, creating a cozy, warm ambience that our apartment usually lacks.

"This is beautiful. Thank you."

I lead her around the couch to the floor, where I have blankets and pillows set up along with our sushi.

"I know we haven't quite figured out how to make this place a home, but I wanted this to be a warm, comforting space tonight."

"You pulled it off."

Grabbing the tray of sushi, I pull it closer, then pick up one of the pieces of spicy crab roll and hold it out to her. She nibbles at it before using her tongue to tug it into her mouth.

"The first time we ever hung out, you told me you were a slut for spicy crab sushi. Well, I'm a slut for watching you eat it."

She laughs at that. "Now I know why you get me sushi so much."

I press a kiss to her cheek. "Because it makes you happy, and I love seeing you happy."

She sets down the piece of sushi in her hand and tackles me, kissing me deeply.

I think our anniversary has been a success so far.

THE SUSHI IS GONE and we're a sweaty heap tangled under a blanket.

I was planning to give Amanda a massage, but we only made it five minutes before she found a hard muscle on me that needed a massage, and well, here we are.

Combing my fingers through her hair, I soak in the comfort of her body wrapped up with mine.

"Do you have any fantasies?"

Amanda and I have anything but a vanilla sex life. We love to explore and play, and while it hasn't happened as much recently, it's a part of us. We've never done any role play, and haven't gotten much into kinks—other than some mild breath play and spanking, but that's barely kinky. I'm open to exploring most things with her, but we've never really talked about specific fantasies.

"Like sexually?"

"Yes," I say with a laugh.

"Uh..." Her cheeks go bright red, and I poke her in the ribs.

"You do. Tell me."

"Okay. This is... like I don't need to act on it, but for me, the ultimate fantasy would be having a threesome where both a man and a woman were wholly focused on me." She covers her face with her hands.

"My little praise princess. Of course you want to be the object of desire." I kiss her neck. "And you should be."

Slowly, she peels her hands off her face and looks up at me.

Sweeping some hair away, I meet her eyes.

"You know, if you ever wanted something like that, we could find a way to do it."

Her eyebrows shoot up. "Really?"

"Yes. I mean, I'm not interested in a poly relationship because I could never share your heart, but for your pleasure and to embrace that piece of your sexuality... I'd do that."

She rests her hand on my cheek. "That's very sweet. In reality, though, I wouldn't want to be with anyone but you. That's like an in another life kind of fantasy... an I want to read about it in a book kind of fantasy."

"I'll buy you every one I can find."

"What's *your* fantasy?"

"I'm a simple man. My fantasy is always you on your knees, choking on my cock with your mascara smudged. Hm, and I guess I see you wearing heels too."

"We can make that happen."

She kisses my chest, and I curl my fingers through her hair.

"What's your fantasy for life overall?"

She's quiet for a moment, and when I look, I can see the emotion swimming in her eyes.

"This," she whispers. "You and me together. Fulfilling careers. Still close with our friends. Living our best lives. Happy."

I gently graze my lips over her forehead. "That's not a fantasy. It's our future."

She rolls toward me, wrapping herself tighter around me. "I hope so," she says, almost too softly to hear.

"It will be."

These last couple of months have been busy and chaotic, but I don't ever want her to doubt how beautiful our future will be, so I hold her close, running my fingers through her hair and whispering how much I love her in hopes that I can calm her restless heart.

20
Eyes Shut

Amanda

"HEY, AMANDA?"

A pretty girl with long, light brown hair smiles sheepishly at me.

"Hi. Paige?"

She sighs heavily and drops into the seat across from me at the little café tucked just inside a hospital.

"Thank you for this." She grabs the coffee cup in front of her and takes a sip. "It's rare I get out of the NICU these days, and when I do, it's never to do something for myself."

"How's your little one doing?"

"Getting stronger every day. Hopefully, we'll be home by the end of August." She sniffs, then waves her hand. "Anyway, what made you reach out?"

I'm not sure exactly why the event planner who planned most of the gala is the first friend I'm trying to make here, but there was something about the vibe of her work that made me feel like we'd hit it off. And when I look at the clearly exhausted woman across from me, I feel a certain kindred spirit with her. Our exhaustion comes from two different places, but both of us have prioritized ourselves last.

"First, I wanted to let you know you did a phenomenal job planning that gala. It was easy for me to walk in and pick up the pieces. I made sure your business cards were set out along with mine because you deserve as much—if not more—of the credit."

"Thank you."

"It's what you deserve." Because she needs to hear that. For very different reasons, this woman is holding her whole world together, and while I don't know anything about her partner, I'm certain she still needs to hear that she's worthy. "The main reason I reached out to you wasn't that, though. Honestly, I'm new around here, and I don't live here full time, so I don't have any friends." I clear my throat. "My therapist said to do something for myself because I don't do that enough, so this is me reaching out. Not asking for anything, but seeing if you need a friend too. Based on how you work, I thought we might get along as more than just business associates."

She swallows hard. "I'd really like that. I haven't been here long either. My husband and I lived in Savannah until about six months ago. We moved up here for his job, and while I don't regret it, my focus on rebuilding my business and then my pregnancy means I don't have any friends here—or much of a support system. My husband is great, but he works a lot."

"What does he do?"

"He's a lawyer. Mostly deals with business and contractual stuff. He was the one who recommended me for the gala. But, uh... how did you end up here?"

"My boyfriend got called up to the Metros."

"Oh. Wow."

"Yeah. It's been... busy. Lonely."

"I understand that feeling. Some of the wives from my husband's law firm have offered to bring dinner, but no one has met me where I am—literally. So, thank you."

"I'm happy to do it. I'll be back at college soon, but I'll probably be around on weekends, and I'm happy to buy you a coffee and just relax with you whether it's here—or hopefully at your house soon."

"God, I hope so. I'd love that."

"Good." I blow out a breath. "There was one other reason I reached out. It might not be at the front of your mind right now, but I thought maybe we could team up. Not business partners or anything, but be each other's backups or in case of emergency person for our businesses."

"That would be... amazing. I haven't had a lot of time to think about my business lately, but when I have, I've been worried."

"We can talk about all that later, but let me know if there's anything hanging over you still that I can help with. For now, let's get to know each other?"

"Sounds great."

I SPENT the subway ride home going over my calendar and to-do list.

I leave to go back to school in a week-and-a-half. Jamie is traveling for the four days before I leave. He'll be back the night before I leave. I was supposed to go with him—even though he won't be pitching—so we could have a little more time together, but now I'm not sure I can do it.

I need to go back to Ida before I head back to school and get a bunch of stuff from our apartment. I've got to make sure everything is set up for the cleaning person to come once a week and that building security will keep us updated on any issues. Then I really want to spend a little time with Jace and my brothers—even Josh. He annoys me, but he's still my brother and we always spend time together over the summer. I missed our family vacation this year. The only one I've ever missed other than the year I was horribly sick.

When Jamie took care of me.

My heart still hurts after everything that's happened in the last few weeks, though the last week has been better. I don't want to say it's because he hasn't pitched, but I think it might be part of it. It's been less stress. With the team being closer to playoffs, they're matching pitchers up against specific teams and players, which means Jamie is pitching for the first time tonight since his win.

I'm hoping having less stress and coming off a good game last time will have him in a good space for tonight.

I don't know how to talk to him about not going on his road trip with him. As much as I want to, I know it'll leave me too stressed, and when he's here, I want to be present with him. On the road, I'd have less time with him anyway, and traveling right before I have to drive five hours back to school sounds awful.

Guilt flashes through me, but I do my best to put it aside.

I still haven't told him about my run-in with Maci—other than the times I tried and he wasn't listening. I know I need to, but it's hard to want to when I was vulnerable—something he knows is hard for me—and he didn't show up the way I needed him to.

I'm trying to work through that on my own and let it go because I don't want to be bitter, but it's impossible not to notice the change in our relationship. Once the season is over, I'm hoping we can take some time together and work through it all, but until then, I'm trying to hold on and keep it all together.

My therapist was right, though. Doing something for me made a huge difference in my mental health, and the idea of having a friend here makes such a difference too.

"Hey, baby," Jamie calls as soon as I walk inside the apartment. "How was your coffee?"

I set my stuff down and walk into the kitchen. "It was good. I think I might've made a solid friend."

"Good."

"How was your morning?"

"Fine." He walks over and kisses me. "Did a little workout and relaxed. Actually, I did some yoga and meditation."

"Oh?"

"Trying to find some balance."

"That's good," I breathe.

"Anyway, I was just going to warm up some of that extra falafel for lunch. Want some?"

"Yes, please."

We walk over to the kitchen, and he goes to the fridge while I sit down on a stool. He sets a few containers on the counter, then pauses and looks at me.

"Oh, before I forget, Emily texted earlier to see if she could interview you either tonight or sometime in the next couple of days, since we'll be on the road trip after that."

Ah, shit. Well, I'm not going to lie to him, even if I didn't particularly want to discuss it now.

"Uh, yeah. That's fine, but... I'm not sure I'm going on the road trip."

His head snaps up. "What? Why? You're going back to school in less than two weeks. You're supposed to come."

"I know, but I was looking at the calendar today, and I have too much to do and I need to go back home before then too, and I think it would just be easier if I stayed. If you were pitching I'd go, but—"

"But spending time with me is too much to ask for?"

Oh, is he fucking kidding right now?

"Do you think I *want* to be away from you? Of course I don't."

"Then come. Figure out the rest later."

"There is no later! I already figured out the many things I have to do, and I'm trying to prevent myself from completely burning out by spreading out what I need to do instead of trying to squeeze it all in at the last second."

"Good to know where I fall on your priority list," he mutters, turning away from me.

Fuck. That.

I shove my stool back and march around the counter. "Did you just accuse me of not prioritizing you? You clearly haven't been paying attention for the last couple of months. I have been running myself ragged, doing everything I can for you. Taking care of you. Sacrificing myself, my health, my wellbeing *for you*. And you have the audacity to complain because I'm not going on a road trip you aren't even playing in? Don't you dare say that I haven't prioritized you when you've barely remembered I have needs outside of you and your career for the last two months."

"What the fuck does that mean?"

I stare at him, not blinking, not moving an inch. "Why did I decide to go to therapy?"

"What—because you needed to focus on your mental health."

"But what was the catalyst?"

"I don't know. You didn't tell me."

"I told you *twice*. But you weren't listening. For someone who claims to always see me, you've had your eyes shut a lot of the time lately."

He stares at me for a moment, anger giving way to something softer.

"Why did you start therapy?" His voice is hushed and uncertain.

"Because that queer wedding I was so excited to have the opportunity to plan was Maci's wedding."

His eyes go wide. "What? But she told you it was all an experiment—"

"Believe me, I know. And I reminded her of that after she chased me down the street. Then I spent the next hour crying with Hyla and Mackenzie, and I realized how deeply I've neglected myself. That I didn't have a safe space inside me because I was in a constant state of upheaval and turmoil. And when we talked that night, I let you tell me all about the win you worked so hard for, and when it was finally my turn, when I tried to be vulnerable with you and tell you about the worst day I'd had in a long time, you fell asleep. Then the next morning, I tried again, and you got distracted by your teammates and had to go. Do you know how that feels? To need your person so badly and have them completely tune you out?" My voice breaks. "I've spent the last two months sacrificing my mental and physical health for you, all the while understanding how essential baseball is. And you've done nothing but take advantage of that."

"I didn't realize—"

"That's not an excuse. It's part of the problem."

We stare at each other for a long moment.

"You should eat, so you're ready for your game later. I'm going to take a bath."

With that I push past him, grab my favorite wine from the fridge, and head for the bathroom because fuck it all. I'm doing another thing today that's only for me.

Jamie

I CAN'T GET out of my head.

This game has been a complete disaster. It's been raining on and off. Our hitters can't find the ball even when it's right in the center of their zone. And I've let hits and runs through in every inning.

Right now is the worst, though. We have two runners on base and two people have already scored. We're not just losing, we're being demolished, and I'm responsible for a good chunk of that.

I don't feel grounded in my body right now. A part of my mind is somewhere else. It's hearing Amanda's words over and over.

I knew I was fucking up, but I didn't realize it was that bad. Why the fuck didn't she talk to me sooner?

I roll my shoulders and try to shake it off. Usually when I feel like this, I'd look over at the family section of the stands, but today, I'd probably see Amanda glaring at me.

Fuck it.

Focusing on the plate and my catcher's glove, I wind up and throw. It's the perfect pitch... for the batter to wallop over the center field wall.

I'm not even surprised when Marc jogs out to the mound. Even though I'm coursing with rage—at so many things—I don't argue when he pulls me. My head's not in it, and I don't deserve to be out here.

I'M ALMOST surprised when I see Amanda waiting for me after the game. Hell, I'm a little surprised she came at all, seeing as she's been spread so thin lately. If I'm destroying her life so much, she could at least have the decency to tell me.

I'm holding on to the dream—the career—I've worked so hard for by a thread, and it hasn't left a lot of mental space for anything else, but we're still us, right?

I'm doing the best I can. Why is that not enough?

She's surprisingly calm when I walk over to her, but why wouldn't she be? She let everything out on me right before I had to pitch. It's no wonder I played like shit.

When I get to her, she looks at me like she wants to say something, but doesn't. I'm too pissed to say anything. Not here. Instead, we walk silently to the car, then climb in the back seat, enduring a painfully quiet forty-five-minute ride back to the apartment.

I hate how far the apartment is from the stadium. Who gives a fuck about how nice our little neighborhood is when it's so damn far away from where I have to spend a huge chunk of my time?

Amanda keeps glancing at me, but doesn't say anything. Of course not. Why would she talk to me when she can bottle it up and explode at the worst time?

When we get back to the apartment, I'm dangerously close to

throwing shit and having a tantrum. I'm too keyed up. Too pissed off.

I don't say a word to Amanda when we walk through the door. I just drop my shit and storm toward the bedroom.

"Jamie…" she calls, following me.

I clench and release my fists, the anger inside me boiling over.

"Why did you do that?" I yell when she walks through the bedroom door.

She jolts back. "Do what?"

"Why did you pick a fucking fight with me right before the game? I couldn't think—I couldn't focus. I threw one of the worst games of my life because of you!"

Amanda goes eerily still, then crosses the room, her icy gaze set on me.

"I did not pick a fight. We *had* a fight, and I held you accountable for how you've been treating me. Don't you dare blame me for what happened at that game. *I* am not responsible for your emotions. You're an adult. You need to learn how to manage those yourself. When something is hurting me and I have to run an event, I have to put it all aside and be in that space and in that moment. Maybe I can't let all of it go, but I have had to learn how to do what I need to do when I need to do it. Granted, I'm a woman, so we're trained to do that from a young age. Smile or someone will think I'm rude. Be friendly to everyone I meet or they'll think I'm a bitch. Control my temper or I'll hear a snide comment about how I must be on my period. I spend my life managing my fucking emotions, and I will not enable you to put your emotions on to me. They are your responsibility. Your mental health is your responsibility. You need to step up and learn how to handle those things yourself, or eventually, you're going to run out of people and things to blame, and you'll be left with nothing."

She storms past me toward the bathroom.

"I'm going to get ready for bed. Sulk if you need to. Work through your emotions. Figure your shit out, but do not talk to me like that again, and if you can't do that, then don't expect to sleep in this bedroom tonight."

She walks into the bathroom, slamming the door behind her. All I can do is stare at the dark wood and kick myself.

She's right.

She was right earlier, and she's right now.

My mental game has been shit most of the season, and that has nothing to do with her. She still shouldn't have waited to tell me how she was feeling until she exploded, but I didn't give her a lot of options.

For someone who claims to always see me, you've had your eyes shut a lot of the time lately.

The words ring in my ears, cutting deep as they were intended to.

Fuck.

How did we get here?

I stare at the door for a minute longer, then change into comfortable clothes and walk out of the bedroom.

I need to figure out my shit, but more importantly, I need to figure out how to start fixing things with my girl.

I BARELY SLEPT LAST NIGHT. I crawled into bed around three, but all I did for another hour was watch Amanda sleep.

The transition to the majors has been rough for me, but I didn't realize how deeply it was affecting Amanda—affecting us— because I wasn't paying attention.

I've always told her I see her, and I'm not sure how to fix how little I've *seen* her over the past couple of months. I know her well enough to know it can't just be words. It has to be action.

It's going to take time, and that's frustrating and stressful because we don't have a lot before she's back at school and I'll be lucky to see her a weekend or two each month.

But I can't fix anything if I don't start trying.

Slowly, I reach over and run my fingers through her long, silky hair, hoping when she realizes it's me touching her, she doesn't slap my hand away.

Amanda

THE GENTLE CARESS of fingers over my temple pulls me from sleep.

It takes me a moment to orient to what's happening—what happened.

Yesterday was not good. Two fights. Two messy, complicated yelling matches. Not really matches, I guess. I did most of the yelling.

I wanted last night to be better. I had my second meeting with my therapist yesterday after Jamie left for his game, and I told her all the ugly details. She was entirely unfazed, and gave me some helpful tips in addition to talking through some of my feelings with me. But the most important thing was the reminder that Jamie can't read my mind, and even though I was mad at him, keeping my feelings from him didn't serve a purpose—it hurt both of us more. It's okay for me to be angry, but I have to tell him I'm angry. Preferably when we're both in a space to listen calmly.

That wasn't last night. When he blamed me, pure rage flowed through me. After I yelled at him and had time alone to process, though, that wasn't what stuck with me. It was the anger in his eyes. He's never looked at me like that before.

Yet here he is now, gently stroking my hair to wake me up. I flash my eyes open and look at him. There's regret and pain in his eyes, but it's surrounded by tenderness. A tenderness that makes me want to burst into tears because I've been craving it.

"I'm sorry. I know those are just pretty words at this point, but they're where I need to start. I'm so sorry. Sorry I blamed you.

Sorry I hurt you. Sorry for all of it." He gently rests his large hand on my cheek. "Things aren't good right now, are they?"

Slowly, I shake my head. "Neither of us has done a great job of focusing on our relationship."

"You have," he whispers.

"No. I've prioritized you. I haven't prioritized us. I also haven't been talking to you, and I'm sorry for that too."

He closes his eyes for a moment. "I remember you telling me once that growing up, the squeaky wheel always got the grease, but you never learned to squeak loud enough. But the thing is, you should never have to squeak with me. I don't know how to fix this, but I think it has to start with talking—or you talking and me listening. Why didn't you talk to me sooner? Especially about what happened with Maci?"

I could say it was solely because I was angry, but I know that's not the truth.

"I was mad. But mostly... I was struggling, and I needed my person. I was vulnerable with you, and when you didn't take the time to listen to me, it made me feel unwanted." He opens his mouth to say something, but I wave my hand. "I don't need you to apologize again. I just need you to understand. You're my person. You're always the one I want to comfort me, and when I don't have that..." I trail off as tears spill from my eyes.

He wraps his arms around me and pulls me tight to him. It's what I've needed for too long. To be held. To know I'm safe. To know his mind isn't somewhere else. All of him is here with me.

"I'm sorry I didn't talk to you sooner. I was angry and afraid to open myself up again."

"I understand why you didn't. I'm sorry I blamed you for last night. I was angry and wanted someone to blame, but it's not you. It's never you."

"Do you understand why I said I can't go on the trip? It's not because I don't want to. I want to. If I could, I'd be with you all the time, but I can't maintain the other parts of my life if I do that, and I'm—"

"I understand," he whispers, voice shaking. His fingers curl into my hair as he holds me tighter. "It wasn't fair to get mad at you for that. Everything feels better with you, and that's why I wanted you there. I wasn't thinking about you." He buries his face in my neck. "I'm sorry for the pressure I put on you, but I can never apologize for the way I need you. Even when I'm doing it wrong, even when we're a mess, I need you."

His lips press into the skin of my neck, and I tilt my head, desperate for more. I've missed this. Us. The connection we have. It's always been a brilliant white flame burning between us, but it's dimmed recently.

He lifts his head, pulling back, but I tug him closer, grabbing his cheeks in my hands. "I need you too. I've needed you more than I can put into words. I need us. I love you."

"I love you too."

Frantically, I pull him to my lips. He slips his hand under my shirt as we both give in to the love flowing between us, what we've both neglected but need now more than ever.

He pulls back again and looks at me, awe in his eyes, like I'm the most beautiful thing he's ever seen. Like nothing else could ever hold his attention the way I do.

"You're perfect," he murmurs.

Then it's rough kisses and fumbling to get our clothes off.

My emotions are out of control, and I can't stop the tears that spring to my eyes.

"I love you," he rasps, the same emotion flowing out of him.

We haven't done the best job at communicating, but we can communicate like this. We can bask in our love and let it heal us.

His hot mouth slants over mine, and he wraps his hand around the side of my neck and he pushes inside me.

I cry out at the mix of pleasure and the achy pain still deep in my heart.

"I love you. I need you. You're everything."

Tears fall down my cheeks as I hold him close, bodies flush as we move together.

"I love you. I love you. Please don't let me go. Don't let me go," I cry.

"Never." He thrusts in harder. "You're mine. Forever."

Our emotions overtake us as we move together, our love working to fill some of the cracks in my aching heart.

I don't know where we go from here, but giving in to the intense, beautiful love between us can't be a bad place to start.

21
Desperate, Pathetic Girl

Amanda

"I'M GOING TO MISS YOU." Jamie's voice breaks as he stares down at me, my face cradled in his hands.

The last ten days went by too fast. After our fight, we've been closer and gentler with each other, but we didn't really get into the root of our problems. I don't regret how we handled things that night. We needed to reconnect both physically and emotionally. But now I'm leaving with things still off balance, and I'm worried all we did is slap a bandage over a gaping wound.

I keep telling myself it'll only be six to eight weeks until his season is over and we can be together again—hopefully fully heal things. I can survive eight weeks. I survived the last eight weeks. Somehow.

"I know," I whisper, looking into his shimmering blue eyes. "I'll miss you too. But we'll do what we always do. Talk every night. Text all day. Phone sex. And I'll be back down as soon as I can."

He nods and pulls me tight to him. "I love you."

"I love you too."

Tears line my eyes, and I hold him tighter. Saying goodbye is always the worst, especially when we won't see each other for a while.

"Okay." He steps back, wrapping his hands around mine. "Drive safe. Text me when you get there."

"I will. I know we'll talk plenty before then, but I still want to say it in person... good luck on Thursday."

"Thank you."

We stare at each other for a moment more, then he sweeps me into his arms, dipping me back in an all-consuming kiss. I want to sob at the passion and tenderness of it—the aching desire that makes me feel wanted and deeply loved. I want to hold on tight and never let go.

When we slowly unfurl, he wipes some tears off my cheeks and kisses my forehead.

I need to go, but I don't want to. Five hours alone in the car sounds horrible.

Jamie takes my hand and leads me around the car, then opens my door for me. "I don't want you driving when it's dark. You should get on the road." He clears his throat, trying to hide the emotion in his voice.

I nod and turn to get in, but he grabs me and presses me against the car door for one last fiery kiss. My skin prickles with want, and part of me wants to say screw it and leave tomorrow. But I need a couple of days to settle in before school starts. This is my last year. This time next year we won't be saying goodbye, and when the season ends next year, we'll be living together full time, no road trips to tear us apart. It'll just be us.

I can't wait.

This time when he lets me go, he helps me into the driver's seat, then leans down and kisses my cheek.

"Drive safe, baby. I love you."

I give him my brightest smile. "Love you too, baseball boy."

He smiles at that, then steps back and shuts my car door.

I look back as I'm pulling out of the parking spot, then I'm off for five lonely hours to Old Lake Town.

NOTHING LIKE A THERAPY session to cap off a day of travel and moving back into the lake house with my friends. It was originally supposed to be during my time back home while Jamie was traveling, but we had to reschedule. I figured I'd get it out of the way, but my therapist is on fire today and low-key making me regret it.

"Why didn't you talk more about the disconnect between you two while you were together?" my therapist asks.

She says it matter-of-factly. Like she's asking what the weather is.

But maybe that's how I should be looking at it. Like it doesn't have to be big and dramatic, but part of life. Part of normal discussions. Jamie and I should be talking about those things. But we didn't.

"Were you holding back because you were angry?" she prods when I don't answer.

"No." Ugh. *This* is why I can't make it matter-of-fact. Because of the ugly emotions that swell inside me when I think about it. "I wanted to enjoy things being happy for a few days because there's been so much chaos."

"And talking about the hard things would've ruined that?"

I bite my lip and force a deep breath. "I was afraid it would push him away, and then he would push me away."

All my feelings and fears about being unwanted or not chosen swirl around me.

"Amanda, have you ever heard of rejection sensitivity?"

"I've heard it mentioned in the past, but not much else."

"Well, there's a lot of nuance to it, and it's not an official diagnosis, but you seem to be rejection sensitive within your interpersonal relationships. You've mentioned feeling unwanted or not chosen or that you're afraid of those things. Do you feel that's the case?"

I swallow hard. "Yes. It's one of my biggest triggers."

She looks at me thoughtfully. "Often, those types of feelings are brought on by a traumatic event or repeated small traumatic events. Does anything in your life stand out to you?"

Fuck. I've never felt this called out in my life.

"It's—there are several different things I could point to. I was always the kid who had to ask for attention. It was never freely given. But there is one bigger thing too..." Then I explain about Maci. What she did. "I felt almost gaslit when she walked away and had her mother tell me never to come back. It was like she couldn't face the reality that we shared something and needed to make it one-sided—make me feel crazy for thinking she felt anything for me. It still eats away at me. Sometimes I think if I could just get closure, it would fix all my problems."

"Closure isn't a reality most of the time. Expecting anyone who we've had struggles with to tell us what we need to hear to move on is unlikely. And ultimately, the healing from it is still found within. What would knowing the truth of her feelings help?"

"I wouldn't feel crazy. I'd know it wasn't my fault."

"Her treating you poorly was not your fault. It's clear you had a relationship. You don't continuously partake in consensual intimacy with someone if there's no relationship of any sort. Whether or not she meant the words she said is irrelevant. Those words meant something to you, and you're allowed to feel hurt because she went back on them. Holding on to that desire to know *why* is only hurting you."

"Ouch."

She smiles softly. "What do you do with that *ouch* now?"

"Work through it?" I ask with a hopeful smile.

"Exactly. I'm here to help find tools that work for you to do exactly that. And knowing you struggle with rejection sensitivity means we can find coping skills to help with that too."

"Thank you," I say, even though I know I don't need to. This is her job, but this is the first time I've felt like I'm regaining some of my power and agency. Understanding myself better means I have a chance to heal more, and I want to do that.

Jamie

I'M NOT LOOKING FORWARD to tonight's game. Amanda has been gone for five days, and I've barely slept the entire time. I'm not sure why. Because she's not here? Or because things have been messy at best between us? Or just because I'm so exhausted, but I can't settle my mind?

This season has taken a toll on me in more ways than I could've imagined. I got on the scale this morning while I was brushing my teeth, and I was shocked to see I'd lost ten pounds.

I feel like the absolute worst version of myself, and I don't know how to climb out of the hole I'm in.

I have to try to get my head on straight before the game tonight, though.

Remember why it's fun. Why I love the game.

But that only goes so far. I'm too disengaged. If anything, I want to get on the mound this afternoon and completely tune out the world.

My last game was a disaster, and if there's one thing I have to do, it's tune that out. I hate the shift toward matching pitchers up with teams; it means either small gaps or massive gaps between pitching. It's been almost two weeks since I last pitched, but my next game after this is in two days.

Whatever. Maybe I need to lean in to how crappy I feel today and focus on getting my head straight for the next game.

When have I ever thought that before? *Who cares if it's a crappy game?* No. That's not me. I rise to the occasion. I figure out my shit. I overcome. I'm going to do that. It's time to get back on track.

I'M NOT BACK on track.

This game hasn't been an absolute shitshow like the last one, but I'm still struggling. I'm the definition of phoning it in right now, desperate to make it through this game without screwing anything up too badly, but I'm far from doing well.

We've gone back and forth between winning and losing all game, with several innings at a tied score. We're ahead now, in the top of the sixth, but I already walked one batter—and not on purpose.

Fuck, I'm a mess. As I wind up and throw the next pitch, I'm not sure where my mind goes, but not where it's supposed to because not only is my pitch way off, it catches the batter in the arm.

I put my head in my hands and grumble to myself as the catcher jogs up to the mound. He puts a hand on my shoulder. "Are you okay? You don't seem like you're here."

"I am. Sorry."

He gives me a sympathetic smile, then smacks my shoulder. "Get your head in the game. You've got this."

Then he's gone. Not the most useful conversation, but I haven't put the time into getting to know him like I should have. Yet another way I've failed.

What would Miles have told me? Somehow, he'd have read my mind and given me some sort of prophetic statement to get me through.

I look over at the family section of the stands, and the emptiness weighs on me.

I can't think about that right now.

Sucking in a deep breath, I get ready, then throw the first pitch to the next batter. Who hits a perfect double, allowing the guy on second to score and the guy I hit to get to third.

Fantastic.

Marc might as well pull me at this point, because I'm only going to keep making things worse.

"EXCELLENT GAME TONIGHT," our first baseman says derisively as he walks by me. Dude is an asshole on a good day, but he's not wrong tonight.

We won, but barely, and only because our reliever pulled it together. My game was shit.

"And you had so many shining moments tonight," Declan says. "Like when you fumbled what should've been a perfect double play."

"Ignore him," Ryan says to me. "We all have rough games. Keep your chin up. Let me know if you ever want to work on anything. I'm happy to help."

"Thanks."

Beau slaps me on the shoulder. "That's it. We're going out after this. You need alcohol and greasy food to cleanse the system."

"That's the opposite of *cleanse*," Declan says.

"Come on," Beau prods. "What do you say?"

"I've got to meet the reporter doing that profile piece tonight."

"Perfect. We'll come too. Get you some good food and make sure you're nice and relaxed before she gets there."

I stare at Beau and a few of the other guys, who are nodding.

Fuck it. Why not? I need to bond with the team.

"Let's do it."

Amanda

IT'S after six when I finally get home from my second day of classes. Whoever decided college should start mid-week is brilliant. It's best to ease us in so we don't quit after two days. If it wasn't my final year, I might want to.

I kept an eye on the score of Jamie's game throughout class, but it kept going back and forth. Once I've set all my crap down, I collapse on my bed and pull out my phone to check the final score. The Metros won, but the reliever got the save.

My stomach turns. What kind of space is that going to leave Jamie in tonight? He wasn't planning to call me for at least another hour, so I force myself off the bed to get some food, but when I do, a sick creeping sensation works its way through my stomach.

Maybe this isn't all worry about Jamie. I haven't felt good for the last two days. I'm fatigued despite sleeping, queasy—more like nauseous right now—and I don't have much appetite. Plus, I'm bloated. But that's probably because of my period.

My period?

I blink a few times, then grab my phone and look at the calendar, counting backward to when my last one started.

Five-and-a-half weeks ago.

Oh no.

No. No.

This—I... shit.

I knew I missed a few birth control pills here and there with all the back and forth and traveling, but not enough to... I can't be pregnant, can I?

What if I'm pregnant?

I grab my phone, but remember Jamie had the meeting after the game tonight. Instead of calling, I type out a quick text.

> Hey, uh, semi emergency… could you call me as soon as you get this?

I set my phone down, then get up and pace. But I'm still nauseous and end up right back on my bed. What would it mean if I'm pregnant? I'd be giving birth before the school year is finished. And in the midst of Jamie's season.

How would I manage a baby when I'm building my business and he's gone all the time?

My chest tightens. Grabbing my phone again, I start researching everything about the effectiveness of the pill I'm on and then spiral down a black hole of pregnancy symptoms and timelines.

After more than a half hour with no call back from Jamie, I call him. But after four rings, it goes to voicemail.

"Hey, it's me. Can you please call me back as soon as you get this? It's important. Love you. Bye."

Another half hour passes, and there's still no phone call.

> Jamie, please. I need you to call me.

Then I call again. Maybe he can't hear his phone. "Please call me back. I need to talk to you."

Panic sets in when more time passes with no phone calls or texts from him. Every text has been delivered, so I know he has service.

> Where are you?

> I need to talk to you.

> Please answer.

I call again, but nothing.

> Answer your phone!

I sink to the floor and call again, almost screaming when I get his voicemail again.

Dropping my phone on the floor next to me, I pull my knees up to my chest. This is my worst fear come to life.

There's a knock on the door as it swings open. "Hey, Mands. I'm supposed to grab you for a late dinner. There's a surprise... guest. What's wrong?"

Mackie kneels in front of me, wrapping her hands around my arms.

"Jamie—Jamie's not answering. It's been almost two hours, and he won't answer. He won't—"

"Take a deep breath," Mackie instructs.

But I shake my head. "I think I'm pregnant."

Her eyes go wide, but she doesn't miss a beat. She pulls her phone from her back pocket and types something out. Then a few moments later, my door opens wider and the girls stream in. Rae, Sarah, Chelsea... and Hyla.

"Surprise," she whispers as she sits down next to me and takes my hand.

"What happened?" Chelsea asks.

I don't know how to answer that. They know things have been tough, but this is the lowest I've felt.

"I might be pregnant. And I've spent almost two hours calling Jamie, but he hasn't answered."

"Do you want one of us to get you a pregnancy test?" Sarah asks.

"No. I want to wait until I can at least get him on the phone to take one," I sniff.

"Then we'll wait with you," Rae says.

And of course, they do so much more than that. They bring food upstairs. Mackie specifically brings me a buttered plain bagel, while Hyla tells us stories from her flight attendant life to distract us.

I keep calling Jamie, but no matter how many times I call or what I text, he doesn't answer.

My stomach is burning with fear as my chest clenches in pain.

When it's nearly four hours after his game, the panic sets in, and I can barely breathe.

Please answer. Please, please answer.

It goes to voicemail again, and I'm in full hysterics.

"Why isn't he answering?!" I am the perfectly broken picture of an ugly-crying train wreck as I throw my phone across the room. I swore I'd never be this girl. This pathetic mess of heartbreak. I'd never do it again. Then Jamie Henderson walked into my life, melted my walls, and made me believe I was worth something. Worth everything.

Mackenzie sweeps some hair from my face. "Maybe he had something with the team."

"No," I rasp. "The game was over hours ago. And even if he went out with the team, that's no excuse for him not answering."

I look around the room at my best friends. The women who chose me when I felt like I wasn't worth choosing. Mackenzie, Hyla, Rae, Sarah, and Chelsea. All five of them stopped what they were doing and surrounded me with love the second I needed them. Of course they're here. Ride or die. We always show up for each other.

But as much as I love them, they aren't the ones I need right now.

Everything is spiraling out of control, and it's supposed to be Jamie who's walking through this with me.

This can't be happening.

Not now. Not like this.

More tears stain my cheeks as my best friends move in closer, forming a circle of love around me.

"He promised he'd always show up when I needed him," I whisper, wrapping my arms around myself.

But that was before.

Before he achieved his dream. Before he was a major league baseball player.

He convinced me I was his dream too.

And maybe I was until he got what he really wanted.

Maybe I was an idiot to believe there was room for me and baseball in his life.

Maybe I was a desperate, pathetic girl for believing I meant *more* than the game he built his life around.

I know I'm desperate now because all I want to do is call him again. I want to believe I'm not in this alone.

"Oh, shit," Hyla mutters, blinking at her phone.

"What?" I ask, my chest tightening. Panic overtakes me. What if he was in a car accident? What if he's dead?

Oh God.

"Is he okay?" I cry.

"He's... okay."

Hyla glances at Chelsea, who looks at the screen and bites her lip.

"Just tell me!" I yell.

Slowly, Hyla crawls over to me, taking my hand as she flips her phone screen toward me.

My blood runs cold, and I'm hit with a new level of agony as my world crashes around me. Because staring back at me is a photo of Jamie—his face clearly visible—with his arm slung around some girl as they walk into our apartment building.

No. God fucking no. Not this.

"Do you want Aaron to call him?" Rae asks me.

Breathing is hard, let alone speaking right now.

Never in a million years did I ever think Jamie would cheat on me. It was hard to trust when we were first doing distance, but he showed me over and over that he only had eyes for me. The only thing I've felt I was in competition with was baseball. Am I that stupid?

I keep staring at the photo, not wanting to believe it.

I'm not sure I do. After that one instance having lunch with Mark, I know how things can get twisted. But who is he with, and why would they be going into our apartment? With his arm around her?

I've always given him my complete trust. But this...

I don't know what to believe. And when he's not answering me, what other option do I have to believe? Am I the most naive person on the planet to believe there must be another reason for this?

Aaron walks into the room and looks at everyone. "What's going on?" Rae must've asked him to come up here when I didn't respond.

She shoves her phone in Aaron's face. "Call him and figure out what's going on."

Aaron curses under his breath, and pulls his phone out, hovering by the door as he calls Jamie. I don't know if I want him to answer or not. But it doesn't matter.

"Jame, you need to answer your fucking phone and call your girlfriend back," Aaron growls at Jamie's voicemail. He pinches the bridge of his nose. "I swear to God, I'm going to kick his ass. Do you want me to drive down there?"

"It doesn't matter," I mutter. "It's done."

"We'll keep you updated. Let us know if you hear anything," Rae says.

Aaron nods and walks out of the room.

"It might not be true," Hyla says gently.

"It doesn't matter. He isn't answering. He isn't going to be here for me the way I need him to." I look around at my best friends. "Can someone get me a pregnancy test?"

Mackie immediately stands up. "On it."

She kisses the side of my head and walks out of the room.

The girls close the circle around me, wrapping me in a cocoon of love and support while I wait to find out my fate.

Jamie

A FAINT BUZZING tickles my brain.

What is life?

I roll my tongue around my mouth. Did I swallow a bunch of cotton balls last night?

What the fuck happened?

I remember the game. I remember Beau and a few of the guys from the team handing me shots.

The buzzing starts again, and it takes a second to realize it's not in my head.

I turn and reach for my bedside table, groaning in pain when I move my head.

I'm guessing this is what a monstrosity of a hangover feels like.

I shove the phone to my ear without looking at the screen.

"Hello?"

"He lives!" Aaron's voice is not playful. He sounds downright murderous. "Tell me you woke up alone this morning."

I grunt as I push myself up to sitting. "Of course I'm alone. Why the fuck wouldn't I be?"

He laughs bitterly. "Oh, you have no idea what kind of shit storm you're in, do you?"

"No. I just woke up."

"Who is she?"

"Who is who?"

"The girl you had your arm around as you walked into your building last night."

Confusion drenches me. "What—how—"

"So help me God, if you cheated on Amanda, I will help the girls string you up by your balls."

"Me too!" a voice calls from the background. Trevor. That tracks.

"I didn't cheat on her. I... Give me two seconds." My mind is fuzzy, and I'm still trying to make sense of what he's saying as I make my way out to the kitchen, fill a glass with water, and down it all. "Okay, I'm back."

"Get to the point a lot faster."

"What point?"

"Who was she? Where did she sleep? Why was your arm around her?"

"Relax. It was just the reporter who's doing a piece on me. My dumb ass got drunk last night before we were supposed to meet. She was pissed, but she took pity on me and made sure I got home. She went as far as my apartment door, then she left."

"Then why the fuck weren't you answering your phone last night?"

I squint for a second. Was I not answering? My phone... well, it's in my hand now. I pulled it out of my bag when I stumbled into the apartment because I needed to set my alarm—I glance at the clock—which didn't go off.

Sitting down at the counter, I take a few deep breaths. "It was in my bag. I didn't realize..." Everything finally slams together in my mind. "How did you know about the reporter helping me home?"

"You're all over the tabloids and gossip sites."

I stumble to my feet, horror slicing through me. "Amanda. Amanda?"

"Oh, she saw it. But that's not the worst of it. She needed to talk to you before any of that happened. She called you a billion times last night."

"Fuck!"

"That's more like it. Call her. Right. Now. And you better fall to your knees and apologize."

"Yeah. I'll talk to you later."

I hang up, and though I'm about to press Amanda's number, I pause to look through the literal hundreds of missed calls I have from her, the guys, my parents, my agent, and the Metros PR team.

I quickly open my browser and search my own name. What comes up is a grainy picture of me, arm around Emily as she helps me inside. No one can see her face, but even from behind she looks nothing like Amanda, and my face is completely visible.

I scramble to call Amanda as I realize how colossally I've screwed up.

"Are you alive?" Amanda's icy voice fills my ear.

"Yes. And I'm sorry. I'm so—"

"We need to talk. In person."

"Uh, can—"

"Meet me at our apartment in Ida at one."

What can I say to that besides yes?

"I'll be there."

"Good."

"Amanda—"

"We'll talk later."

Then she hangs up.

My head is pounding almost as loud as my heart as I drop my phone on the kitchen counter. Then I pick it right back up again and call for a car to take me to Ida, so I can spend the ride figuring out how badly I've messed up everything else.

I'M SITTING at the kitchen counter of our apartment back home. The one I surprised Amanda with three months ago. I'll never forget how happy she was. I thought this was going to be the place we started the next chapter of our lives. I've missed the comforting feeling of home it gives.

The door clicks open and I jump up, desperate to have my eyes on her.

She walks in, face ashen, and eyes as cold as ice.

"Hi," I say lamely.

"Hi. So, did you cheat on me?"

Just like that. I shouldn't expect anything else from her.

"No. I would never, ever cheat on you."

Her eyes shimmer with tears. "And I should believe you why?"

"Because I've shown you over and over again who I am. We've built years' worth of trust."

"The funny thing about trust is it takes a long time to build, but only seconds to destroy. You may have shown me who you are —or who you're supposed to be—but you showed the world something else with those photos."

"It was Emily. I was supposed to have an interview with her, but after the game some of the guys wanted to take me out, so we went to the restaurant where I was meeting her, and I might've let them get me rip-roaring drunk. I'm not proud of it. When Emily showed up, she was pissed at me for wasting her time—which is more than fair. She's a decent person, though, and helped get me home. She came into the building but never into our apartment. It was less than five minutes. I have the tapes from security—"

"I don't need the security tapes. Maybe it's stupid, but I never really believed you would cheat on me."

For the first time, I feel a bit of relief. Until she continues talking.

"The thing is, the rest of the world doesn't care what the truth is or what I believe. All they care is what a picture says, and that picture makes you look bad and me look stupid. Do you have any idea how many phone calls and texts I've gotten from my family asking about it? Do you have any idea how those articles ripped *me* apart? The person you're supposed to love and protect."

I avoided reading the articles, and I stupidly didn't think they would say anything about her.

"*With the way his girl looks, it's no wonder he had to cheat.* Let's see, then there were the people who decided that I must've been having an affair with Mark Abbott after all, and that's why you cheated on me. But I think the best one was *she's stupid if she thinks she can compete with the ball bunnies or the women in his social circles now. She's a one and he should have a ten.*"

I fucking hate people.

"I'm sorry—"

"For which part?" She steps up to me and shoves my shoulder.

"For getting drunk and being irresponsible, for making us tabloid fodder, or for ignoring my phone calls when I was breaking down and needed you the most."

"I wasn't ignoring you. My phone was in my bag—"

"I don't care!" she yells, tears cresting in her eyes. "Do you even want to know why I was calling you? Because it started hours before that fucking picture."

"Why?" I whisper, wanting nothing more than to grab her and hold her close, but I know that'll only get me slapped.

"While you were out getting drunk with your teammates, I realized I might be pregnant."

My stomach drops and my blood goes cold.

Pregnant?

How would we deal with that? Are we ready for a child right now? Where would we live?

"Are you panicking right now?" she asks, almost smug. "Is your life flashing before your eyes while you try to figure out what this would mean and how we'd manage it?"

"Uh... yeah."

"Well, that's how I felt last night, only you weren't standing mere feet from me. You weren't answering your phone at all. I stupidly wanted to wait to take a test while I was on the phone with you because I thought you'd want that. Because I needed you! But you weren't there. So after waiting and stressing for hours, I took one with the girls there to support me."

I swallow hard, staring, waiting for her to continue. "And?"

"Don't worry. It was a false alarm. You don't have to worry about the burden of having a child with me."

This time I can't stop myself. I grab her, trying to pull her close. "It wouldn't be a burden."

She shoves me off her and steps back, tears spilling down her cheeks. "How can you say that when you've made *me* feel like a burden for weeks? I haven't asked for much. I've supported you. I've gone on as many road trips as I could. I wasn't in the same town for longer than three days at a time most of the summer. I exhausted myself, ran myself ragged, and did everything for you, and all I have asked for all summer is for you to give me a shred of that in return! But when I needed you the most, you couldn't even pick up a goddamn phone. You couldn't do one simple thing for me."

She covers her mouth as if it'll keep me from seeing the sobs that rack her body.

Tears well in my eyes as I watch her, pure hatred rushing through me at how much pain I've caused her.

Slowly, I walk over to her and rest my hands on her arms, waiting to see if she'll shove me away again. She doesn't, but she takes half a step back, putting more distance between us.

"I'm sorry. I'm so fucking sorry. I know that's not enough—tell me what to say. Tell me how to fix it. Please."

"It's not my job to tell you how to fix this." She lets out a shaky breath. "I need space, Jamie."

"No. Please... we can—"

"Stop. I need you to hear me right now. This summer has been more difficult a transition than either of us were expecting, but over the last few weeks, I've realized something. You knew—generally, at least—what this life looked like, and you signed up for it. But I didn't. And now I need to take some time and figure out if this life is what I want. If I can manage it."

My heart plummets. My chest tightens. That sounds a lot more like a breakup than it does space.

"No. I—don't leave me. I... I'll quit. I'll quit baseball, but I don't want to lose you."

"This isn't a breakup or an ultimatum. If you ever make the choice to leave baseball, it can't be for me. Or all you'll do is resent me. And you've missed the point if you think I'd ever want you to give up on your dream." She gently rests her hand on my cheek. "All I've ever wanted is to mean as much as baseball, so sometimes you'd be willing to make me your first choice. And I thought I was, but..." She swallows down her tears. "A lot has happened. Now I need time and space to figure out what I need. You need to do the same. Let's take a couple of weeks, then we can talk and figure out... where we can go from here."

Tears fall down my cheeks as she steps back.

I grab her arm, not willing to let her go. I can't let her go.

"Please. Don't leave. I love you."

She stares at me for a long, painfully silent moment. "Do you love me? Or am I just a comfort blanket you're afraid to let go of?"

Shock burns through me that she could ever think that. "Amanda..."

Her lip trembles, but she steadies herself, then leans in and kisses me on the cheek. "We'll talk in a couple of weeks."

With a lingering look, she walks out the door.

I stare at the closed door until my eyes are blurry with tears, then I fall to my knees, sobbing.

I can handle losing a lot of things. My best game, my sense of normalcy, the daily support of my friends. I think I could even handle losing baseball. But losing Amanda?

There'd be no coming back from that.

She's my person. My best friend. The love of my life.

And I broke her. Now I have to face the consequences, and pray there's still a chance we can find our way back from this, even if the hope in my heart is cracking and fading away.

22
Fix Your Sh*t

Amanda

I DON'T KNOW why I'm at my parents' house. They're not home. I should've just gone back to school. I wanted somewhere that felt less lonely. But nothing helps with the loneliness in my heart.

Pushing the front door open, I'm surprisingly met with the smell of lemon and garlic.

"Hello?" I call.

A moment later, Pete appears. "Hey, little sis. Come on. Food's almost ready."

My brow furrows. "Food?"

Pete drags me to the kitchen where he and Josh are cooking.

"Shrimp scampi?" I ask.

"It's what you ordered every time we went out for dinner anywhere that wasn't sushi," Josh said. "We figured you'd need something comforting right now."

He walks over and pulls me into a hug. I'm so surprised and overwhelmed that I burst into tears.

"How did you... know?"

"We saw the headlines," Pete says. "Then Rae called and gave us a heads up on what was happening."

Of course she did.

"Shouldn't you both be at work?"

"Well, I work for Rae's dad, and he's understanding," Pete says.

"I just called out," Josh says with a shrug as he steps back.

"Thank you," I sniff.

Pete sighs. "Look, I know there was a time—a good chunk—where we didn't do the best job of taking care of you."

"Especially me," Josh says.

"But we're your brothers. We've got you."

I wipe at my eyes and nose, then sit down at the table.

"I'll take it."

Pete brings over plates and they both sit down.

After I've had a few bites, Josh asks, "So, what really happened?"

"He didn't cheat on me," I say quickly. Even in the midst of all this, I still want to protect him.

"We figured. We've known him almost as long as you, and he's never looked at you with anything but adoration."

That makes me choke up again.

But after another bite of pasta to strengthen myself, I tell them everything that happened this summer.

"So what happens now?" Pete asks when I'm finished explaining.

I shrug. "We take some time and figure out what we both want from our relationship. Then we can decide where it goes from there."

"We'll have your back, whatever you need," Josh says.

My face pulls into a grimace. "It's weird that you're being so nice to me."

He laughs. "Contrary to popular belief, I'm not an asshole."

Pete snorts at that, and Josh punches him in the arm.

"I'm not. Not totally. Yes, I can be a dick sometimes, but you're my sister. I love you."

"I love you too." I take another bite of pasta and shrimp, savoring the delicious garlicky flavor. "Can I ask you guys a question?"

They both meet my eyes.

"Sure," Pete says.

"Do you... do you think people can suddenly fall out of love?"

"I don't know the answer to that, but I know what you're asking me," Josh says. "And I can tell you I didn't fall out of love with Jace. As much as I wanted to be, I was never in love with her to begin with. So don't use that as an example."

"Looking around at the people in our lives, I believe that love can last," Pete says. "But it can also fade if you don't take care of it. You have to be willing to fight. Look at Mom and Dad."

I scrunch up my face. "What do you mean?"

"You're probably too little to remember, but they fought all the time when we were kids. It wasn't until I was a lot older that I asked Mom why that stopped. She said they started going to counseling and prioritizing their relationship again," Pete says.

"Wow."

"For what it's worth, I don't think the love between you and Jamie is fading, but it needs some TLC," Josh says.

"Look at you being wise," I tease, trying to cover the achiness in my voice.

"After all these years, I was due."

"Thank you both for being here for me. It means a lot."

"We're dumbasses like ninety-seven percent of the time, but we're here to help if we can," Pete says.

I go back to eating my pasta, something like relief settling in my chest. Nothing fixes heartache, but pasta and having the support from my family that I've wanted for so many years helps a little bit.

Jamie

EVERYTHING IS FUCKED.

My agent and the Metros PR team handled the photos of me, making it clear it was just a friend helping me home, and I issued an apology for underage drinking and promised to set a better example in the future.

I also had the pleasure of my dad going up one side of me and down the other while my mom reminded me that drinking only worsens mental health.

Yet here I am, staring at a glass of whiskey at ten in the morning.

How the fuck was it only yesterday that Amanda said she needed space and walked away from me? I have to play a game today, but how the hell do I do that when everything else is a mess?

I reach for the glass, but before I can pick it up, a hand swipes it from me. I have a full jump-scare moment wondering who the fuck is in my apartment and how they got in here, but then I look up and see Aaron.

I still don't know how he got in here, but at least he's not here to kill me.

Most likely.

"That's a bad idea," he says as he dumps the alcohol down the drain. "This cocky, pain-in-the-ass seventeen-year-old told me once that alcohol doesn't solve problems."

I grunt at that. "How did you get in here?"

"You have me on the approved list. I told them I was here to surprise you and they unlocked the door for me."

I rub my hand over my forehead, and he leans against the counter, staring at me.

"So, why are you drinking at ten in the morning?"

"Because everything is fucked."

"So why not fuck it up more?"

I shrug. Because everything feels worthless at this point.

Next thing I know, Aaron is standing in front of me, shaking me by the shoulders.

"You know, someone told me once that you can't just let life happen and give up. You have to fight. For baseball. For your girl. For yourself."

I remember the words so clearly. I didn't say them exactly like that because it was framed by Aaron's experience and how he'd been acting, but that was the sentiment. It was the morning after the Christmas party where I met Amanda. Aaron had been drinking at the party, and I remember thinking I never wanted to be the guy who used alcohol to drown my pain. Glancing at the glass in the sink, I realize how deeply I've failed and how unimpressed the younger version of me would be—hell, even the version of me from earlier this summer would hate who I've been lately.

"I wasn't in the mood to listen that morning, but your words still struck a chord, so let me remind you of the most important ones. Get your shit together, Jame. You're better than this."

He's right. Past me was right.

This is not who I am or who I want to be.

"Where do I go from here?"

He clamps his hand on my shoulder. "Start with the baseball stadium. Stop trying to fix everything at once and focus on one thing. Since you've got to pitch in six hours, I'd recommend that be baseball."

I let out a pathetic laugh. "Thanks for coming down here."

"We show up for each other. We always have. Plus, I wasn't going to miss a chance to call you on your shit."

This time my laugh is fuller. "I'm glad you're here. You staying for the game?"

"I wouldn't miss it."

I blow out a breath. I'm a mess, but I have to start somewhere if I'm going to clean it up. As much as I want to wave a magic wand and fix things with Amanda, there's work I need to do on myself before I'm ready to show up for her and be the man she deserves.

I KNOCK on Marc Demoda's door, ready to eat yet another slice of humble pie.

"Come in."

I walk in, expecting to be on the receiving end of a snarky comment or maybe a smack to the back of the head.

"Jamie. How are you?"

I stop wincing and look at him. He's standing next to his desk looking genuinely concerned.

"Honestly, not great. It's been a rough few days, but that's my own doing. I wanted to apologize to you personally for my behavior lately, both on and off the field. I didn't cheat on Amanda. I—just got drunk and acted like an idiot."

He... laughs. "Welcome to major league baseball. You've had your first scandal. It's a rite of passage."

"You're not mad?"

Again, he laughs. "You've never looked me up, have you? Let's just say I'm no stranger to bad press."

"So... I don't need to be worried?"

"Worried about what?"

"My place on the team. Being traded or sent back down to the minors?"

He squints at me in disbelief. "Wait. Have you been worried about that this whole time?"

"Uh, a little."

"Jamie, you're in your first year in the majors and we've won half the games you've played. You're not perfect, but we're not looking to get rid of you. You're a part of our talent and we want to build on that. Trust me, there's only one person on this team we'd like to get rid of, and it's not you. Is that why you've been struggling so much?"

"Not entirely. A lot of it is not measuring up to my own standards."

"Well, give yourself a break, because you're doing fine. AAA and the majors are two entirely different things. As much as you might want to, walking in here and rocking it your first season is unrealistic. Be patient. You'll get there, but you have to get out of your own way."

Shoving my hands in my pockets, I nod. "Yeah. Uh, to that end, is there any chance I can get in with the sports psychologist today or in the next few days?"

"I'll make it happen."

"Thank you."

He claps me on the shoulder, and I let out a long breath. Despite the fear and uncertainties about my relationship, I finally feel some peace about my game, like I'm moving in the right direction, and after months of feeling completely out of sorts, I'll take it.

THE AIR on the mound is clearer today. Or maybe that's my head.

Why does it take almost losing everything to realize how fucked up things are?

Is it just me?

Given how many times I've watched my friends do this exact shit, I know it's not. Probably that whole it's always darkest before the dawn thing.

Although for me it felt more like I was drowning, then I realized I was face down in a stream and all I had to do was stand up.

Not my proudest moment, but it's been a whole summer of that.

Breathing in the fresh air, I refocus. Now isn't the time for that.

Marc sent me right to the sports psychologist after I went to see him this morning. It was almost like he was waiting for me to say I needed it. I wouldn't put it past him. That's what good coaches do, right? See what their players need.

The psychologist said something that I've used as my focus all game.

Only focus on what I can control, especially in this moment. Combined with Aaron's reminder to focus on one thing at a time, I've been in a better space all game. Which must be how I made it to the top of the seventh inning for a change. I know this will be my last inning. Though we have a decent lead, I know we could still lose the game.

But I can't control that.

All I can control is how the ball leaves my hand and crosses the plate.

There's a runner on second and two outs.

One last batter is all it will take for me to finish my part of this game strong.

One thing at a time. One pitch at a time.

The first pitch is a strike. The second is fouled off. The third is a ball. The fourth is fouled off.

My catcher gives me the sign for the next pitch, but it's not the one I want to throw.

I can't control that.

All I can do is control how I throw it. So I lock in and focus.

The ball whizzes across the plate.

"Strike."

Pride fills my chest as the batter walks away.

I fucking did it. I closed out seven innings with our team on top.

Glancing over at the stands, I find Aaron, who nods at me while clapping.

A couple of my teammates smack me on the back as we head for the dugout.

That success was not an omen of good things to come. It was proof of what can happen when I get out of my own head. I'm still going to have bad games, but my goal from here will be to make this my normal—the default I can return to after the bad ones.

That's one thing down. Now I just have to figure out the rest of my life.

23

Boys Are Dumb

Amanda

TWO. Weeks.

That's how long it's been since I talked to Jamie.

I hate it.

Don't get me wrong, I've been doing a lot of thinking. A lot of focusing on myself. A lot of extra therapy.

Every few days, Jamie sends me a voice note. Never apologies, just telling me he's thinking of me, he loves me, and gives me a little snippet of what's going on in his life, what games he's won—even though I know because I've watched them all.

He's pitching better than ever, which sent me spiraling for a minute, wondering if he's better off without me. Until he sent me a voice note saying he wouldn't have turned his game around if it wasn't for me.

It seems like what happened two weeks ago was a wake-up call. Not that I was trying to force his hand, but walking out the way I did might've done that. He seems like he's doing better, and in some ways, I am too, but in others, I feel like a pile of trash.

I miss him. I want to be with him. He's pitching on Sunday, and I was debating going down to his game, but we haven't talked yet. And I don't want our first point of connection to be across the field.

Plus, Jace will be here soon to spend the weekend with me, which I'm excited about. We didn't see each other enough over the summer.

Rae is standing by her closet when I walk into the bedroom she and Aaron share.

She turns to me with a warm smile and soft eyes. "Hey. How are you doing?"

"I'm stressy, depressy—"

"And a little messy?"

I flop backward onto her bed. "More than a little."

She lies down next to me and takes my hand. "Been there. I know how much it sucks. But I also know what it's like on the other side, and I promise you it will get better. Even if it feels like you're living in the song *Down Bad* at the moment."

"Ugh, *The Tortured Poets Department* is so good." And fully my vibes right now.

She laughs at that. "At least Jace is coming to visit, right?"

I nod.

"Have you talked to him?"

"No. I think... I want to. But I'm not sure what to say. I made such a dramatic exit with all my talk about needing to decide whether I want the life that comes with dating a professional baseball player, but I don't care. I want him and that life comes along as a package deal."

"Maybe you should tell him that."

"It makes me feel stupid. Like I was overreacting."

Rae turns her head and stares at me until I turn and look at her.

"You were not overreacting. Everyone in this house will agree on that. He screwed up. You're allowed to have feelings about that and let them out—to hold him accountable. And if you've discovered that you don't care about the difficulties of life dating a professional baseball player, then you did what you said you were going to do and figured it out. Now you need to figure out what's really holding you back."

She kisses my cheek, then hops off the bed, getting back to organizing her closet.

She's right. Slowly, I push myself up. I need to organize too—not my closet, though. My life.

JACE HAS MADE it her mission to make sure I've been having fun and have been distracted since she got here Friday night, but as we sit on the dock looking out at the lake as the fog lifts off it on Sunday morning, Jace nudges her knee against mine and gives me a gentle smile.

"What are you thinking about?"

"What comes next. What to say to Jamie."

"Maybe you should figure out how you're feeling first."

I sniff over a laugh. "That's the tricky part, isn't it?"

"Can I tell you what I see?"

"We both know you're going to anyway." And I'd do the same for her.

"You're rightfully angry at how Jamie treated you and figuring out how to live the life of a professional baseball player's significant other is challenging for you. But those aren't the things that are holding you back from reaching out to him and working through this."

"I hate you," I mumble, pulling my knees up to my chest.

"Talk to me."

I rest my chin on my knees and stare out at the lake. "I'm scared. I'm scared that this disconnection and the moments he wasn't there for me mean he's not really in this. Or baseball will need to be his focus and he'll let me go." Tears trickle down my cheeks. "My therapist said she thinks I struggle with rejection sensitivity, and I agree with that. I have some coping skills to use, and I'm trying to, but it's really overwhelming, and the person I need reassurance from is who I pushed away. I don't know how to ask for that reassurance now."

"In a perfect world, what do you want to happen?" Jace asks.

"I want to be with him. I love him. That hasn't changed, but I need to know he loves me too. I don't want to have to question it, and that's all I've done lately. Then I get scared that pushing him away has driven a wedge between us, and maybe I shouldn't have done that."

"It's okay to take time and space to figure out what you want and need. You can love him and want to be with him, but still hold him accountable."

She's right. Those are all the same things the practical part of my brain has been saying, but my heart is afraid of being broken, and my rejection sensitivity is telling me to run.

Staring out at the lake, I take a few deep breaths and focus on one of the coping skills my therapist recommended, which is to challenge negative thoughts.

Jamie is still fighting for me. He wouldn't do that if he didn't care.

But even if he was going to reject me, I can't change that. I have to face it, and trust that I can navigate through it.

More importantly, though, I need to trust what we've built and not let my fears or my mental health get in the way. I told him to be responsible for his mental health, and I have to be responsible for mine.

I don't want this to be the end of us, so it's time to face my fears, stand up, and start fighting again.

Jamie

WEIRDLY, one good thing came out of my night getting drunk with some of my teammates—I'm more at ease with them now.

They didn't give me shit afterward; they were supportive and only teased me a little.

I've been working with the sports psychologist regularly, and that has helped me too. His most recent recommendation was to consider creating a pregame ritual for myself. He said it could help me get out of my head and focus on the game. Like walking into a new space and shutting the door behind me.

"Anyone have any ideas for a mantra or pregame ritual?" I ask as we get ready in the clubhouse.

"Have you never done any kind of pregame ritual?" Corey asks.

I shrug. "Most of the time, I was acting like an idiot with my friends. That was my pregame ritual."

Marc, who overheard me ask that and stopped to listen, says, "Well you're surrounded by idiots to do that with here."

"You want something to get you focused on the game, you should think about why you're here. The best moment of your life," Beau says.

The best moment of my life. There's a flash of Amanda in that gorgeous sundress on our first official date. Then there's a memory of dancing with her at Rae and Aaron's wedding—and how we laid in bed that night talking about what we'd want our wedding to look like. Another flash of Amanda, but this time it's her lying naked beneath me during a marathon sex session. Then a glimpse of her decked out in Knights gear for my first game with them.

"Whoa, where'd you go? That long of a memory?" Beau asks.

I laugh. "I—why would my best moment or moments help ground me in baseball?"

Beau's brow furrows. "Being drafted..."

My eyes go wide. *Oh.*

"Wait. Is that not your best memory?" Beau asks.

"I'm going to guess not," Ryan says, trying not to laugh.

"Life is more than the game," Marc says, smacking Beau on the shoulder as he walks away.

Conversation continues, but I turn back to my cubby. As I get ready, the best and most important moments with Amanda play through my mind like a greatest hits album.

Over the last two weeks, I've tried to find ways to show her I know I messed up and I want to move things in the right direction. Other than leaving her those voice notes, I haven't come up with much, but suddenly an entire plan unfolds in my mind. I've gotta be out of my head and focused on pitching soon, but until then, I grab my phone and start typing up ideas.

MY FOURTH WIN in a row feels good, even if I wish Amanda was here to see it. But I'm going to take care of that. I have a plan. Or the beginning of one. I'm going to need a lot of help, and maybe a miracle, but I'm determined to make this happen.

"Mom!" I call, waving as I get to where the group of friends and family are waiting for the players.

She grabs Penny's hand and comes over to hug me.

"Great game, honey."

"Thanks." I bend down and give Penny a hug, but when I let go, I'm on the receiving end of her sassiest glare.

"How come Amanda isn't here?"

As I stand up, I exchange a look with Mom, who knows the whole story.

"Wait," Penny says, eyes filling with tears. "Did you break up?"

"No. No, buddy. We didn't. We're just having a hard time right now."

"Why?"

"Because I did some things that hurt her feelings."

Penny's tear-stained eyes lift to me. "Did you kiss another girl?"

"No. I would never do that. But I wasn't showing Amanda that I cared about her the way I needed to."

She huffs and rolls her eyes. "Of course you weren't. Boys are dumb."

Mom stifles a laugh as I sigh.

"You're right. We are. I'm working on a plan to fix it. Want to help me?"

Her little face lights up. "Yes, please."

"Good. Because I'm going to need all the help I can get, and probably some advice too," I say as we walk out of the stadium together.

"You have to grovel," Penny says, like she did two years ago.

Fuck, I am done screwing up with Amanda. She deserves to have everything. All my love. All the happiness. Peace and comfort.

I'm going to give her all that and more. Penny's right, I need to grovel, and my way of doing that is showing Amanda how deeply I love her.

MY MOM and Penny are asleep in the spare room. She pulled Penny out of school so they could visit for a couple of days. Cal was jealous, but the kid can barely sit through an inning of baseball, let alone a whole game.

Now I'm staring at the notebook in front of me. Part of my plan is ambitious, but I'm hoping if I put it out into the universe, I'll get what I need. What *we* need.

When my phone goes off, I'm hoping it's one of the people I contacted following up, but I almost fall off the bed when I see it's a voice note from Amanda.

I'm slightly afraid, but also hopeful.

Turning the volume up, I press play, letting her beautiful voice fill the room.

"Hey." She pauses, and I can tell from her breathing that she's trying not to cry. *"I, um... I miss you. I guess I just wanted you to know I'm thinking of you. And you're really hot when you're all confident on the mound."* She sniffs, and I'm torn between heartbreak and relief. *"Um, I think we should talk soon. Even if it's just over the phone or text. Anyway, uh, I think that's all. I just wanted to... I don't know. Okay. Bye."*

I listen to it again and then one more time, reveling in the sound of her voice.

She reached out. She misses me. I still have a chance, and I'm not going to waste it.

I listen one more time, then send a text back.

> I miss you too. Thanks for the message. I've been wanting to talk too. Maybe we could start with texting throughout the week? And then... would you come to my game on Thursday? I'll send a car so you don't have to drive.

The little dots as she types are agonizing and last for what feels like hours before a text comes through.

MY GIRL

> Texting sounds good. As for the game... I don't know. I might have plans.

My heart sinks and frustration builds inside me. We need to fix this and she might have other plans?

But then I read the text again, and I remember what she said the first time I ever invited her to a game.

Too bad I have plans.

She teased me afterward that I didn't ask who those plans were with.

I pick my phone up again.

> Any chance those plans are with a certain Metros pitcher?

MY GIRL

Maybe.

> Think you can score me an invite?

MY GIRL

I'll do my best.

> Good. Well, have a good night, okay? Sleep well.

MY GIRL

Thanks. You too.

I set my phone aside and lay back, my mind racing almost as fast as my heart.

There's a lot to do before Thursday, but I'll skip sleeping if I have to, I don't care. This is my chance to make things right—to start, at least—and I'm not going to blow it.

By Friday morning, Amanda will be in my arms again, and she'll know with certainty that those arms will always be her safe place.

24
However You'll Have Me

Amanda

I SLIDE into my seat at the stadium shortly before the start of the game.

I had a couple of classes I didn't want to miss this morning, and Jamie said that was fine—that he'd rather talk to me after the game when his focus can be solely on me and we can spend the rest of the night together.

That might've made me swoon a little. It was a glimpse of the boy I love. The one who has always fought for me.

And him sending a car to pick me up also made a huge difference. Five hours where I could relax and get some work done and not worry about dozing off was a breath of fresh air.

It takes a lot of effort not to gaslight myself into thinking I overreacted. That I should've been more patient, when the truth is we might not be here now if I hadn't reacted how I did. I'm not naive enough to believe he's magically doing better because I said I needed space, but I'm hoping it was a trigger to help him see how bad things were.

I can admit that I didn't make that clear enough. I didn't talk along the way. I didn't try to find solutions. Either I tried to do everything for him or I blew up at him. My anger and hurt was warranted, but I could've handled it better.

From here, I want us both to handle it better.

He's not on the field yet, and it's killing me. I want to see him.

To entertain myself, I open my texts and scroll through our conversations this week. At first they were tentative. Then gentle. Then playful. Then flirtatious. We didn't talk on the phone at all. We both agreed we'd feel too compelled to try apologizing or talking through things, and we want to do that in person.

I smile as I read the last text he sent me.

BASEBALL BOYFRIEND

I hope you know you're mine for the night. Once I have you in my arms again, I'm not letting you go.

And ugh, swooning again.

I'm trying not to get ahead of myself. We need to talk. We can't go right back into flirting and pretending things are fine. I'm cautiously optimistic, even if I'm not looking forward to going back to that damn apartment. It doesn't feel like home, and it's hard to be centered when you don't feel comfortable in your surroundings.

The singer takes the field for the national anthem, and I stand with everyone else.

Finally, through the sea of people, I catch a glimpse of him, standing outside the dugout with his hat resting over his heart.

As I sit back down, I can't take my eyes off Jamie. I'm waiting for him to look this way—for the moment, his eyes land on me.

He says something to one of his teammates as he puts his hat back on, then he jogs out to the mound.

When he gets there, he turns his head and searches for me.

I know the moment he spots me, and even across a stadium and from under his ball cap, I can feel his blue eyes burning into me.

This is us.

Not the frustrated, closed-off, not communicating bullshit we did all summer. *This* is us. Two people who can feel our connection across a baseball field.

I'm not getting ahead of myself. We have a lot to work through.

Screw it. I'm totally ahead of myself, just like I'm head over heels for him, and I have been for years now.

SEEING the cool confidence I'm used to when Jamie is pitching was an added boost of excitement tonight. Some of our best sex has been after games where he killed it.

Tonight wasn't perfect, but it was much more in line with his typical pitching. Plus, they won the game. They've been on a hot streak leading to the playoffs, and there's a good chance they'll be either the first or second seed for their division, which puts their chances at making the playoffs high.

My stomach lurches as players stream out. It's been almost three weeks since we've seen each other, and more than a month since we saw each other in a happy place.

My body flushes when Jamie's heated gaze lands on me. He walks right to me and sweeps me into his arms, picking me up and spinning me around.

He sets me down and brushes his thumb over my cheek, looking into my eyes.

"I missed you."

I open my mouth to respond, but he steals my words as he slants his mouth over mine, swallowing the squeak of happiness I emit.

He doesn't linger—which is good because there are reporters watching—but it's enough to show me exactly how much he missed me.

"Ready to go?" he asks.

"Yes, please."

He takes my hand and leads me to the waiting car. Once we're inside, he pulls me against him, holding me tightly. I rest my head on his shoulder and bask in the easy comfort that I've missed.

He's quieter than I was expecting, his thumb rubbing up and down my arm as he holds me.

His breath hitches and his chest shakes, making me lift my head so I can look at him.

He pinches the bridge of his nose and sniffs.

"Sorry."

I move closer, my achy heart clawing to reach his.

"It's okay. I'm here. We're together."

He sniffs again, resting his head against mine and curling his fingers through my hair.

This isn't what I was expecting. Maybe stupidly, I was expecting an immediate show. An immediate apology and for him to try to show me everything will be okay.

But outside of the last couple of months, that's never been Jamie. When he sits in the quiet and recognizes the problem, he doesn't use words to fix it, he uses action.

This tiny, quiet moment shows me more than any words could how sorry he is.

We hold each other, emotion swirling around us, for a bit longer, until the car pulls to the stop.

Jamie takes a big breath and wipes his eyes. "We're here."

My brow furrows. As nice as it was to get lost in that moment, I didn't completely get lost. It hasn't been anywhere near the length of time it takes for us to get to our apartment.

"Where are we?"

He opens the door and takes my hand. "Trust me?"

The sincerity and hope in his eyes undoes me.

My heart pounds harder, the truth sounding in every beat.

"Yes."

I swear he breathes out a sigh of relief. "Come on."

We get out of the car in front of a three-story building in a smaller, relaxed neighborhood. It's more rustic than where our apartment is, but not run down.

"Seriously, where are we?" I ask again, but this time because I like it. It's somewhere I could come and explore before Jamie's games if it's that close.

"Let me show you."

He pulls out a key card that allows him inside the building, then gets out a regular key to unlock the next set of double doors.

He opens them, then leads me inside the warm, inviting space with old wood floors. There's a security guard at a small desk who nods to Jamie.

Maybe this is some kind of vacation rental thing?

There's also a little coffee station with a fancy coffee-espresso maker and a couple of tables with chairs.

Jamie pulls me past them to the elevator, across from which is a door with the number one on it.

We take the elevator up to the third floor and walk past a storage area to a door with the number three on it.

Jamie digs out yet another key, then opens the door, but before he lets me inside, he smiles and kisses my cheek.

I'm not sure what to expect when he pushes the door open. Low lighting, candles, and rose petals? A completely barren space with a blanket on the floor? A space that looks like a stock photo? But what I see is the last thing I was expecting.

I stop in my tracks and spin back to face him, seeing that hopeful hesitant look on his face again.

"What is this?"

"I might've stolen my own thunder since I already did this once this year... but this is ours. Our new apartment."

Tears flood my eyes, and I have to blink them all away as I spin around and take it all in again. Our furniture is here. My favorite pillows and blankets from our apartment back home. Some of them, at least.

"How did you—when did you—are we going to move all this stuff back and forth between here and back home?"

He laughs at that very specific thought. "No. Because these are all new things. Same couch and pillows and blankets that match as best they can. I tried to recreate our home in Ida back here because I want this to be our home too. You deserve a safe space, and I'm sorry I didn't give you that." He blows out a shaky breath. "But until I was here, I didn't realize how much I needed it too."

I throw my arms around him. "Thank you. This means... so much," I choke out.

He runs his fingers through my hair and hugs me tighter. "Do you want to see the rest of it?"

"Yes. Yes, please. Show me everything." *Tell me everything.*

Again, he takes my hand. The kitchen and living room are completely open to each other. There's no specific dining space, but there's room for a small table at the far end of the living room. The wood colors and rustic feel are similar to the ones at our apartment back home, but not manufactured to be that way—it's like they grew like this. Everything is seamless, homey, lived-in— in the best ways.

"There are a couple of downsides. There's only one full bath and the spare room is small, but I don't care. I'll pay to put our friends up at a good hotel when they visit."

"I don't care. This is perfect. My soul feels happy here."

"And you haven't seen the best part yet."

He opens the door to the spare room, and my eyes light up. Much like the one back home, it's like my own personal cozy nook. A little smaller, which actually makes me like it even more.

"Come here. There's something I want to show you."

I follow him inside and quickly notice the three bulletin boards hanging above the desk.

"Three?"

"You're always working on multiple things at once. Each thing should have its own space."

Any residual anger I was holding on to fades. *This* is the boy I fell in love with. Not because of the big things like an apartment, but because of tiny things like knowing I need multiple bulletin boards. The way he sees me.

I stop at the shelf on the other side of my desk where two photo frames and two bears sit—both new.

In one of the frames is a picture of me with my parents and my brothers at Disney World when I was around twelve. In the other is a picture of Jamie and me at Rae and Aaron's wedding. We're holding each other close, staring into each other's eyes as we dance. It was a candid moment the photographer caught, and it's the physical display of our love. In between the two frames are the bears. One is a cute little tan one with a white shirt on it that says "Ida, NY" with logos of a bunch of businesses on it. It's something they did for charity earlier this year. The other bear is bigger and is holding a plastic frame of me with the hive mind at the lake house after a water gun fight.

"So you'll always have the most important people close by, even when they're not right here."

I turn to him, already sniffling.

He watches me for a moment, like he can't believe I'm really standing here, then he smiles and picks up two small whiteboards and hands them to me.

"What are these for?"

"They're our communication boards. You were right that I wasn't seeing you, because I wasn't listening to you. There's a bigger one in the kitchen, and when we're in the same place, we can both write down any big feelings or struggles we're having throughout the day, and after dinner—or a game, whatever—we can sit down and talk about what we wrote. If we haven't already. And when we're apart, we'll each have one of these. We'll write what we're feeling or struggling with and show each other when we talk via video call. Accountability is important, and I wasn't being accountable to our relationship."

Fudge.

Tears stream down my cheeks. This is... exactly what I need. What we need.

"I'm not sure I was either. I was in fix-it mode. Trying to keep you happy."

He nods. "I shouldn't have put that on you. But also, I don't want you to take that on. Please, don't ever enable my bullshit to keep the peace. All it does is destroy *your* peace." His voice breaks. "I'm sorry I was complicit in that. You deserve so much better than what you got from me this summer, and I'll do everything I can now to make it better. To heal us."

I fight back a sob and collapse against his chest. "Thank you for this. I needed this. I needed you."

"I know you did. I'm so sorry. And to that end, um, if you want to, I'm open to going to counseling together to keep working through what happened and to figure out how to make our relationship stronger going forward."

I pull back and look up at his glassy eyes. "Really?"

"Yeah. I can't take full credit for that idea. My mom brought it up and talked about how fundamentally it changed her and my dad's relationship for the better and made them stronger. So many people see it as a last resort, but when you're going through hard things or big transitions, it's a way to stabilize and strengthen a relationship. That's what I want. For us to be rock solid."

"Me too. And yes. I think that's a good idea. But maybe after your season is done. We could find someone in Old Lake Town. If you're willing to come share a crappy full-size bed with me in a house with six of our best friends."

He laughs, then softly brushes his lips over mine. "I will go wherever you are. I don't care how tiny the bed is as long as my arms are around you." He cradles my face in his big hands, thumbs on the sides of my cheeks. "I am so deeply sorry for the ways I've hurt you. You've always asked me to prove things to you. To show you. But sometimes, I think you need to hear the words too. Because you didn't hear them enough from the people in your life before.

"I love you, and I wouldn't be who I am without you. I need you. I need you like I need air to breathe. Not because you make me comfortable. Not because you make me whole. It has nothing to do with me and everything to do with you. You're pure magic, Amanda. Being the one who stands by your side is the best position I've ever played. And you and me? That's the most important team I've ever been a part of. The only future I care about is the one with you in it. I could live a thousand lives, achieve a thousand dreams, but they'd all be empty without you. Baseball was my first love, but you're the love of my life. I can only live without one of those things. I need you, Mands. I love you. I'm sorry I haven't been the man you've deserved lately, but I'm working hard to fix that, and if you let me have this chance, I promise you I'll never stop."

I fully break down. Tears pouring out of my eyes, chest shaking, snot bubbles coming out of my nose. It's not sexy, but it's real. It's raw. It's as honest as the words he just said, and for once, I don't feel a need to question them. I don't need him to prove it. I know they're true because I feel them in my heart.

"I love you too. I'm sorry I didn't open up to you the way I should have. I was so afraid of being hurt—of losing you—"

"You will never lose me. I'm yours. Forever. You're mine. Got it?"

I nod, and he lifts me into his arms, capturing my lips in a bruising kiss.

I wrap my arms and legs around him, holding on tightly as he carries me out of the room.

"There's one room we haven't seen yet," he mutters against my lips.

My core heats, desire pouring through me and mixing with the intense emotions.

He carries me into our bedroom, and again, I'm hit with the overwhelming sense of home. He's taken a few of the wall hangings from our apartment back home and hung them up in here.

"What do you think?"

As he sets me down, I spin around and take it all in. There's a half-bath attached and a big window that looks out on the street.

"I'm just wondering how comfortable the mattress is."

He wraps his arms around me, hands firmly gripping my ass. "You want to find out?"

I sigh happily. "I want you. However you'll have me."

He stares at me for a moment, emotion flitting through his eyes, then his lips are on mine again, and it wouldn't matter where I am, I'm home. As long as I have his heart and he has mine, I always will be.

Jamie

FUCK, Amanda is stunning. She's beautiful, no matter how she looks or feels. But seeing her naked, splayed out on this brand-new bed, finally looking peaceful again—she's never been more gorgeous.

As much as I want to take her hard and fast, we've been apart too long, and I want to savor this. Part of showing her how much I care is giving her multiple incredible orgasms, right?

I'm so thankful she loved this apartment, but more thankful that she is who she is. That she's so deeply loving and forgiving. I'll spend every second of my life honoring that. She deserves nothing less. After tonight, I know we'll not only get back on track, but on a path to being even better than we were before.

For now, though, we both need the physical connection, and I'm in the mood to play, be a little rough, and make her scream.

Kneeling between her legs, I grab her thighs and haul her glistening pussy to my mouth.

She groans and fists the sheets. She's always liked it a little rough. I'll never forget the time she came just from how hard I fucked her mouth.

Ugh. I have to get control of myself or I'll be the one coming without a touch.

I lap at her clit with my tongue, not making any effort to go slow.

"Fuck, Jamie," she whines. I love when she whines my name.

She rolls her hips, crying out in desperation.

I keep going until her body starts to go slack, then I pull my mouth away.

She lets out a frustrated whimper.

"Are you edging me?"

I fight back a laugh at her exasperated expression, then kiss her nose while I slip two fingers inside her.

"So what if I am?"

She groans again, wiggling her hips as she tries to get some friction for her clit, but I don't let her have any.

"We've been apart three weeks. Isn't that enough edging?"

I softly kiss her lips. "You're so cute."

I move my fingers faster until she's writhing under my touch. Then I pull them out.

"I'm seriously going to cry," she complains.

I suck on her neck and play with her nipples as I reach my other hand to the bedside table and pull out one of the new toys I bought. It's a simple vibrator, but supposedly the perfect combination of gentle and powerful.

Laying behind her, I turn the vibrator on and tease her nipples with it, then lower it down to her clit.

Her fingers tangle in my hair as she rides the vibrator, and it's so sexy I almost let her come.

But not yet.

"Jamie, please," she groans when I pull the vibrator away.

"Please what, baby?"

"Let me come."

Tears form in the corners of her eyes, and that's exactly where I want her. I want it so explosive she can't talk or think or breathe.

Settling between her legs again, I stroke her clit with my fingers, then push them inside her again. With my other hand, I lower the vibrator over her clit.

"Oh, oh fuck."

She whines and whimpers, her head thrown back as she fists the sheets. She's shameless as she rides the vibrator and my hand.

All her muscles are tight, her toes digging into the sheets.

"Please," she chants. "Please, please, let me come. I'm a good girl. I'll be such a good girl. I'll scream your name. I'll—I'll—please! Oh my god."

She explodes like fireworks, body spasming and shaking as she screams my name. Her orgasm comes in long drawn-out waves, and her clit is so over-stimulated that every time she thinks she's done, another one hits.

She's crying when she's finally finished—tears of relief and happiness.

Tossing the vibrator to the side, I roll her onto her stomach, wrap my hand in her hair, and thrust into her as hard as I can.

"Yes," she grunts, face buried in the pillows.

I use her hair to yank her back. "What was that? You like being fucked like a dirty slut?"

"Yes. Harder. Please."

Slipping my other hand between her legs, I rub her swollen clit, and she whimpers again.

"You have another orgasm for me?"

"Yes. Please. I need it."

"Look at you using your manners."

She makes a nonsensical noise, and it spurs me on, working her clit as I fuck her into the mattress, hoping I can last long enough for her to come again.

When she cries out, I have to take a breath. She's close, but so am I.

"Are you going to come for me, baby?"

"Yes…"

Hold on. Just a little longer.

Pulling tighter on her hair, I thrust harder, and that sends her over the edge. Her hands clench the sheets as she milks my cock.

"Come with me," she moans. "Fill my pussy. Show me I'm yours."

"Fuck," I groan. My orgasm tears through me, ripping the breath from my lungs.

I collapse beside her on the bed, wrapping my arms around her from behind, but she rolls over and wraps her body around mine, grabbing my face and kissing me deeply with all the love that's been burning inside us with nowhere to go these last few weeks.

We hold each other tightly, lost in the depths of our love. Everything else slips away. There's only her and me. Nothing else. The rest of the world could be burning and I wouldn't know. She's all I need. All I care about.

I've made plenty of mistakes with her, and I know I'll make more, but I refuse to ever fail her so badly again.

I'll protect her heart and the love between us with everything I have for as long as she'll let me.

AMANDA'S STOMACH RUMBLES LOUDLY, and I laugh, pausing midway through braiding her hair.

"Is my girl hungry?"

"Mm maybe." She buries her face in my chest. "I don't want to get up."

After our first round of sex, we got lost kissing, then ate nachos in bed and had one more round of sex before falling asleep in total bliss.

"I hear there's a place a couple of blocks over with great breakfast sandwiches."

She perks up a little, then looks around the room.

"Wait. How did you find this place? And when? And how'd you move everything in here?"

Right. That.

While we've talked plenty about us, caught up on more of how we were both feeling—and struggling—over the summer, and what we missed over the last few weeks, that topic didn't come up.

"Honestly, I got really lucky. My original plan was to have a bunch of apartment listings to look through and maybe go see this weekend because this plan only started taking shape on Sunday."

"Sunday? Do you have some kind of time magic?"

I laugh at that. "No. But *we* have some good friends. I sent texts out to everyone I could think of to see if they had any connections or knew of anywhere that might be more our style. Mark Abbott was the first person to respond. It turns out his girlfriend Frannie's family owns this building and her sister lives in the apartment below us. I saw it on Monday afternoon right before the game and knew it was right. Then I called in every favor I could think of. Dani found similar or exact matches to the key things I wanted at places near here and made sure I could get them all here by today. Mark, some of his football friends, and a few of the guys from the Metros helped with moving stuff in and setting up. Then Dani made a trip down yesterday to help with all the details. I offered to pay her, but all she wanted was snack money so she could order as much food as possible at Mark's game last night."

"Wow," she breathes.

"What are you thinking?"

"How grateful I am. How much I missed this. Not being spoiled, but feeling... cherished. And having a home. That made the summer so much harder."

"I know this season is almost over, but I want to be prepared for next season. Plus, I was thinking we should come down here when the fall semester is over and spend a week enjoying the magic of Christmas in the city."

"I love the sound of that." She sits up suddenly, eyes drifting out the window. "I'm ready to go explore."

She bounces out of bed, a huge smile on her face, and it's such a contrast to our anniversary a month ago. She didn't want to go out because she was too overwhelmed and didn't like the area. Now she's in her element. So am I. We're both right where we're supposed to be.

We spent the summer barely surviving. Now it's time for us to thrive again.

I follow her into the bathroom, heart full and ready to live my best life with the girl who is more than any dream I ever could've imagined.

25
Unyielding Happiness

Amanda

"YOU'RE VIBRATING WITH EXCITEMENT," Rae says as I stare out at the field.

"Tonight decides whether they make it to the division series." I chew on my lower lip. It's not just excitement, it's unrelenting nerves.

Jamie was surprisingly calm going into tonight. But I've seen the difference in his mental health over the last couple of weeks. It's strange that we've been together for two years, but I'm still learning things about him. Like what happens when he truly gets stressed. He's too hard on himself. And when he feels like he needs to fix things and doesn't know how, he panics and tries to force it—which usually makes it worse.

Looking back now, I saw snippets of that before we started dating. After our first ill-fated kiss. He didn't know what to do, then he panicked and crashed my event because he was desperate to fix it.

Once he calms down and focuses on one thing at a time, it all comes together.

Understanding that now means I can support him better.

While Jamie was unsurprised about my rejection sensitivity,

he said understanding it—and the coping skills I have to use—can help him be a better partner too.

We're still planning to go to counseling in a few weeks when the season is done. I've already found someone in Old Lake Town that we'll be going to in November. I hope it'll give us the tools to strengthen our relationship, so we never have a repeat of this past summer.

"He's got this," Aaron says confidently. And that actually calms me down a bit because Aaron is great at reading pitchers in general, but especially Jamie.

Our little section—not the family area this time, but right on the first base line above the dugout—is filled with *our* family. Both actual and chosen. Rae, Aaron, Trevor, Chelsea, Mackenzie, Miles, Dani, and Jesse are all here along with my parents, Pete, Josh, and Jace, and, of course, Jamie's whole family. Calvin is bouncing like someone fed him crack, and Mila is already whining, but I don't care. The amount of love here is incredible.

The best part is knowing it's not just for him. It's for me too. I'm working on reframing things I see as rejection or perceived rejection, and I'm also working on noticing the small acts of acceptance and love that the people around me show. Some people—like the hive mind—are obvious with their affection. My family isn't, but that doesn't mean it's not there.

I'm learning a lot about myself and how to manage my mental health, and I'm grateful I'm doing it now. I've always wanted to be the best version of myself, and I'm proud of myself for putting in the work to do that, even when it's hard to look into the deepest, darkest pieces of myself.

Emily, the reporter who did the piece on Jamie, is also sitting in our section with her girlfriend, who is apparently a photographer. She snaps photos of everyone getting ready on the field.

Though the profile piece hasn't been published yet—they're waiting to see how far the Metros make it in the playoffs first—we got to read it, and it's a beautiful piece chronicling the ups and downs of the game, the highs and lows of the first season on a major league team, the importance of mental health, and the tenacity and grit it takes to make it in professional sports.

Reading it made me even more proud of Jamie—and how far we've both come in the last month.

We all stand for the anthem, then watch as some person I've never heard of comes out to throw the first pitch. I don't know you. I don't care who you are. I want to see my man.

As Jamie finally takes the field, I'm on my feet and screaming. When he gets to the mound, he looks for our section, then his eyes land on me and he winks.

That confident-cocky smirk dances on his lips, and no matter how this game ends, I'm going to be on my knees celebrating him tonight.

With a lingering look, he turns away, and I watch as he sets everything aside and channels all his energy into the game.

My heart is beating out of my chest with pride.

Then he throws the first pitch, which lands with a smack in his catcher's glove. I cheer louder than I need to, but I don't care. I'm a goner for this man, and I want the world to know it.

Jamie

I'M the starting pitcher for the last game of the Wild Card series. At one win a piece, this is the game that decides whether we move on to the divisional series.

And I'm the starting pitcher for the team I dreamed of playing with for years.

It was a rocky start, but I know I deserve to be here, and I will fight with everything inside me to play the best possible game of baseball.

I throw my second pitch, another strike, and smile to myself. Not out of cockiness, but out of comfort. This is where I'm supposed to be, and this is what I'm supposed to be doing. I'm proud of myself, and that's something I couldn't say a couple of months ago.

Third pitch. Another strike. There's nothing like starting a game with a 1-2-3 strikeout. I channel that energy and soak in the feeling of the breeze on my skin and the sense of control I have on the mound.

One batter down, two more to go.

THE WORST PART of being the starting pitcher is having to leave the game, especially when I'm pitching well.

Today's game has been tight, but we've held on to a lead all game.

The first game of the series, we won easily by a landslide. The second was back and forth and we lost in extra innings.

It's the top of the ninth now, and even though we're up by two runs, one inning can change that. Sure, we'd have a chance to come back, but to lose it now, when we're this close? I'm going insane, and I know the rest of the team is too.

"I don't know if I want to watch or look away," Ryan says.

"Same," I say, but my eyes are glued to the field.

When I'm out there pitching, I can breathe because at least I'm in control. Being out of control right now might give me a heart attack.

The batter fouls off the ball, and we all groan.

There's one out and one guy on base. I'm digging deep and trying to throw all my calming pitching energy to our closer. He's good, but I'm sure the stress is getting to him. He throws another ball, and this one is a strike.

We all breathe a collective sigh of relief. Two outs.

One more and we win.

The energy here is intense, but there's a camaraderie too.

We're in this together, win or lose. But fuck if we don't want the win.

My mind goes to the stands. I swear I can sense the intensity of Aaron watching from here. We're not playing together anymore, but it still feels like he's a part of this team too.

Amanda, I'm sure, is watching with bated breath, and looking hot as fuck in my jersey and a Metros ball cap.

The crack of a bat hitting the ball draws my focus back to the field.

"Come on," Corey says.

Dec scoops up the grounder and sends it to second as we all watch.

When we see the umpire's call, we all burst from the dugout.

Holy shit. The Metros are moving on to the division series.

The other team leaves the field as we all join together near the mound, celebrating.

Over my teammates' shoulders, I see Amanda in a crowd of a bunch of other family members waiting at the gate. When security finally lets them through, we all break apart, and I soak it all in as Amanda runs across the field to me and leaps into my arms.

"You did it!"

Her lips land hard on mine before I can respond, the forcefulness of it almost knocking me over.

Laughing, I set her down, cupping her cheek with my hand.

"Were you panicking watching the end of the game?"

She lets out an exasperated breath. "Of course I was. I wanted you to get the win. You deserve this moment."

I sweep her into my arms, holding her close as joy fills me. Not the high of the moment, but pure unyielding happiness at where I am right now.

Every step I made along the way was a play for my future. Not just standing here tonight, but standing here with Amanda in my arms. This is all part of the life we're building together, and I can't wait to see where it leads.

Epilogue
Winter Days
2 Years Later

Amanda

"LAST ONE. PERFECT," Hyla says, pulling the curling iron from my hair and stepping back.

My makeup is done. My hair is done. Now it's time to put on my wedding dress.

"Who's going to help me into this?" I ask with a laugh.

It looks tighter than it actually is on me, but getting everything settled just right is a challenge. It's my fault for choosing a strapless dress, but this one spoke to me.

After planning plenty of weddings, the last thing I wanted to wear was a traditional white dress. When I saw this luscious red velvet one, I knew immediately it had to be mine.

I'm in one of the spare bedrooms in Rae and Aaron's beautiful farmhouse, and surrounded by our closest friends and family, we'll be getting married downstairs in their living room.

Another thing I didn't want—a big wedding. Partly because of the press, but mostly because I want to celebrate the love Jamie and I share. That's all that matters to me. Quiet and simple is what we both crave when it comes to our relationship, especially during the off-season when we can slow down.

In a few days, it'll be five years since we met at a little

Christmas party in downtown Ida. Now we're out in the country, surrounded by beautiful rolling hills. Our dream house is being built just around the corner, and we've entered into one of the most peaceful stages in our life.

Jamie is doing well with the Metros, and we've settled into a good groove during the season. I split time between New York City and Ida, and only travel for select games where he'll be pitching—and usually not for the full road trip. Once I finished college, my business exploded. Near our hometowns, I'm typically planning weddings and occasional charity events. Down in the city, I'm often planning fundraisers and galas, though I've planned a couple of weddings too.

Jace, who is now not only my best friend, but my sister-in-law, comes over to help me with the dress, along with Mackenzie. The room is filled with the women I love, Rae, Sarah, Chelsea, Dani, and Hyla, plus one more addition to the girl gang—Amelia, Miles's wife. Our tribe has grown and blossomed since I first met the girls, and there are some tiny new additions either here or on the way.

My heart fills with joy as I glance at Sarah's round stomach, and then around the room at the women who have loved me to my very core and chosen me over and over again. It was sometimes hard to see the unconditional love in my life, but with them, it has always been vibrant.

As one of the last of the friend group to get married, I'm honored to have them all here with me, and grateful to have them supporting me every day.

"READY?" my dad asks as we stand in Rae and Aaron's kitchen, waiting for the music to start.

"So ready."

Today is five years in the making, and I can't wait to see my love, my best friend, my baseball boy waiting for me.

Oh, mental note, I need to change his contact info to *Baseball Husband*.

I love the sound of that.

The music starts, and I shift back to the moment at hand. I want to be present for every beautiful moment today.

When we round the staircase that runs between the kitchen and living room, Jamie's eyes immediately land on me.

He lets out a shuddery breath as he watches me. Aaron claps him on the shoulder, but Jamie doesn't take his eyes off me. Tears slip down his cheeks as he watches me walk to him, and when our eyes meet, I get teary too.

Five years of chaos, falling for each other, and beautiful, all-consuming love. I knew there was something special about him the day we met, but I had no idea it would lead us here. More than four years together, and I'm more in love with him than ever.

When I get to the front, I hand my bouquet to Jace, then turn to face Jamie. He wipes his own tears, then mine, and leans in to kiss my cheek.

"Hi," he whispers. "You are... mesmerizing."

"And you look hot as..." I bite my lip, and he smiles at me.

We wanted to keep this short and sweet. We wrote our vows to each other in notes we read last night. Today it'll just be the exchanging of rings and the promise to hold on to each other, fight for each other, and walk through this life together.

He takes my hands, his eyes shining with love for me, and the unending promise that we're always in this together. And really, that's all that matters.

THERE'S nothing like the feeling of swaying in my husband's arms to a love song.

My husband.

I love, love, love the sound of that.

His fingers trail through my hair as we dance to Andy Grammer's *I Am Yours*. A song that so completely sums up how we feel about each other.

"I love you," he murmurs in my ear. He's said it so many times today, like he simply can't hold back, and it makes me feel utterly adored.

"I love you too. What are you thinking about?"

His chest shakes with a laugh. "How I used to hate winter because it meant no baseball." He leans back, cupping my cheek as he studies my face. "Now I love it because it means I have months of you all to myself."

I press onto my toes and slant my mouth over his. The way I kiss him is practically indecent, but I don't care. He's mine. My strong, sweet, introverted, kind, quiet, deeply loving man.

"When you stormed my event that night to apologize to me, did you think this is where we'd end up?" I ask as I land back on flat feet. I'll put my heels on for him later when I take off everything else. Except maybe the underwear that says NY Metros Wife on them.

"Marriage was more than my eighteen-year-old mind could fully understand, but I knew I saw a future with you that was worth fighting for. You're worth everything."

I lean against him again, lost in our love. He sees me like no one else ever has, he loves me whether I'm put together like this or a full-on hot mess express. I never knew how loved I could feel until I loved him and let him love me in return.

"*We're* worth everything. Us and the future we're building together." After a beat, I ask, "What do you think will happen next?"

He presses his lips against my head. "I don't know, but as long as you're next to me, it'll be perfect. You've always been my wish, my dream, my everything, and you always will be. That's the only part of our future that matters to me."

Ugh. As usual, *swoon*.

But I love swooning over my baseball boy, the man who showed me what unconditional love could be—my husband.

Yeah, I can't wait to call him that *forever*.

The End

Find Jamie & Amanda's **bonus chapters**, learn more about **the hive mind's stories** (*the Friends Like This series*), the other **Ida Heartthrobs** (*The Forever Fight- Jesse & Dani*; *The Perfect Love-Trevor & Chelsea*), learn more about Bethany's books, grab bonus chapters and freebies, sign up for her newsletter, join her Facebook group (Bethany Monaco Smith's Book Besties), and more here:

A Note from Bethany

Thank you so much for reading Jamie & Amanda's love story! I hope you enjoyed all their angst, banter, swoony moments, and their sweet happily ever after. In case you missed it, you can grab their bonus chapters on my website.

I love writing baseball boys, but most of the ones in this book (the pro players at least) aren't mine! They belong to my author friend Jenni Bara, so if you want more from the Metros, be sure to check her out.

And if you want more from Ida, check out the rest of the Ida Heartthrobs series, the Friends Like This series, the Freaking Love series, and the Ida Romance series. If you want to know more about Mark Abbott, check out The Last Lie. And if you want to know about Amanda's fave local authors, check out The Last Love Story (Jade Jackson) and Always Mine (Zoey Holloway).

Thanks again for reading!
XO,
Bethany

Bethany's Books

Freaking Love series
First Love
Real Love
Forever Love

Friends Like This series
Friends Like This
Falling Like This
Broken Like This
Love Like This
Married Like This
(a Friends Like This bonus novella)
Together Like This
Heartbreak Like This
Family Like This
Future Like This
Nothing Like This
Trust Like This
Always Like This

Ida Heartthrobs series
The Forever Fight
The Perfect Love
The Future Play

Baker Girls series
The Last Lie
The Last Key
The Last Love Story
The Last Thing
The Last Person

Ida Romance series
Reckless for You
Faking It for the Holidays
Waiting for Your Heart
(free novella)
Everything for You
Running Back to You
Stealing Your Perfect Heart
(free short story)
Caught Up In Your Love

Lacy Creek series
Finally Yours
Always Mine
Only Ours
Complete Trilogy

Standalone
Fake It Till You Fall
(free novella)
Lost In My Heart
(free short story)

The Future Play Playlist

The Future Play Playlist is available on Spotify

- You're Not Special, Babe- Orla Gartland
- Everything Has Changed- Taylor Swift, Ed Sheeran
- Close To You- Gracie Abrams
- gold rush- Taylor Swift
- Let Her Go- Passenger
- Take My Breath Away- EZI
- Crash and Burn- Savage Garden
- Love Somebody Again- Forest Blakk
- So High School- Taylor Swift
- Feels Like- Gracie Abrams
- The Archer- Taylor Swift
- Falling Like The Stars- James Arthur
- Still into You- Julia Sheer
- Before You- Benson Boone
- Eyes That Ain't Yours- 2 Lane Summer
- Photograph- Ed Sheeran
- How Much Do You Love Me- Kelsea Ballerini
- I'm a Mess- Bebe Rexha
- Messy- Chase Rice
- Cosmic Love- Florence + The Machine
- Believe- Mumford & Sons
- You're Losing Me (From The Vault)- Taylor Swift
- Tell Me- Hunter Hayes
- coney island- Taylor Swift, The National
- The Prophecy- Taylor Swift

- Almost Everything- Wakey!Wakey!
- Still- Hunter Hayes
- Trying- Jordan Davis
- Hearts Don't Break Around- Here Ed Sheeran
- Never Let Me Go- Florence + The Machine
- Ride- Chase Rice, Macy Maloy
- Before I Loved You- Phillip Phillips
- I Am Yours- Andy Grammer

About the Author

Bethany Monaco Smith is a writer-mom. When she's not busy hanging with her boys, she's writing beautifully messy love stories.

She loves happily-ever-afters and cries at every emotional moment, whether reading, writing, or watching. When she's not mom-ing or writing, you can find her binge-reading on Kindle Unlimited, supporting fellow indie authors, and having sushi dates with her SIL. Bethany survives on coffee, rewatching the same TV shows over and over, and her KU subscription. She lives in the Southern Tier of NY with her husband and two sons.

For more about Bethany and what she's working on, follow along on Instagram or on her website, bethanymonacosmith.com. Stay in touch by joining Bethany's exclusive Facebook group, Bethany's Book Besties & signing up for her newsletter.

Acknowledgements

Special thanks to Jenni Bara for letting me have fun with the NY Metros

Cassie & Lacey, thank you for helping make this and every book possible.

To my betas, Shani, Ryann, Mel, and Stephanie thank you for reading and giving me all your thoughts.

To the reader team group chat, thank you for always being so wonderfully supportive.

The BOD squad for being a safe & supportive space.

And to all my readers for being here. You're the best!